Valhalla REVEALED

A NOVEL

ROBERT A. WRIGHT

Robert A. Wright

Published by CreateSpace

Author's Note
This book is a work of fiction. Names, characters, places, and incidents are either the product of the author's imagination or are used fictionally, and any resemblance to actual persons, living or dead, business establishments, events, or locales is entirely coincidental.

ISBN: 1494772442
ISBN 13: 9781494772444
Library of Congress Control Number: 2013923500
CreateSpace Independent Publishing Platform
North Charleston, South Carolina

Introduction and Acknowledgments

* * *

Valhalla Revealed is the second of my sequential novels that describes how two fictitious families face the adversities of the twentieth century. It covers the period 1945–1979, a rich historical era indeed. It follows my first novel, the prequel *Beyond Ultra*, which was set in the period 1915–1945.

As a family saga, this novel describes how its key protagonist confronts the trauma of wartime family losses and begins a decades-long quest to find his missing brother. Along the way, the book's two families face the crucial challenges of this era and help to shape history. They must cope with the leftover wreckage and secret activities of World War II, the emerging Cold War, the decolonization of Africa, and the emergence of globalism. Set in Spain, Africa, and the United States, among other locations, *Valhalla Revealed* accurately portrays the actual events of this era.

This novel also richly portrays some well-known political and other figures from this era, such as Spain's dictator Francisco Franco and Cuba's revolutionary Che Guevara. It also portrays lesser-known figures such as CIA Director Allen Dulles and Admiral Luis Carrero Blanco, who was Franco's key adviser until his assassination in 1973.

More important, *Valhalla Revealed* explores how key individuals behind the scenes, most of them unknown to the public, influence the key decisions and are the real policy makers and action figures. My main fictional protagonist in *Valhalla Revealed* is Paul Hoffman. He and his buddy, Jack Kurtz, and Paul's Spanish cousin, naval officer Alberto Ortega, are such individuals.

As an author of historical novels, I attach great importance to historical accuracy. Accordingly, I thoroughly researched *Vallhalla Revealed* and its predecessor. My research included the usual literary and Internet sources, but I also traveled to Spain in 2011 and 2013 to study key sites and meet with important officials who were knowledgeable about the events in my novel.

Along those lines, I am deeply indebted to Antonio de Oyarzabal of Madrid, Spain, and his charming wife, Beatrice. Sr. Oyarzabal served as a

Spanish diplomat for nearly four decades, and his last post was Spain's ambassador to the United States from 1996 to 2000. As a young diplomat in the sixties, he played a key role in the decolonization of Equatorial Guinea, formerly Spanish Guinea, a key setting in this novel. Antonio gave very freely of his time and insight and escorted me to many key locations in Madrid that served as a backdrop for the espionage and other events in this book, as well as for key events in Spain's recent history. He also graciously read the manuscript and provided critical insights and advice that allowed me to ensure historical accuracy.

I would like to thank Maria Jose Lopez de Heredia, from one of Spain's most prominent winemaking families. She generously provided me with considerable detail on the history of winemaking in Rioja, the setting for many scenes in this book. I have tried to capture this remarkable culture in the fabric of the plot as well as the setting.

I also thank the Puelles family of Bodega Puelles in Abalos, Rioja. They were our gracious hosts while we stayed in Abalos to research the settings for the fictional village of Alabos in this novel.

Naturally, I am grateful for the support I received from CreateSpace for helping me to publish this book.

Above all, I am grateful for the support and encouragement of my wife, Marcia, and numerous friends who read *Beyond Ultra* and are patiently waiting for this sequel.

Robert A. Wright
Bellingham, Washington
December 2013

The Best Years of Our Lives

* * *

World War II had ended the prior year. America stood supreme on the planet as the only major nation to not only survive intact but prosper as a result of the war. America was a huge net exporter of nearly anything imaginable and even exported a little oil, although that situation would quickly change.

Anxious to rid itself of wartime shortages and rationing, America began a consumption binge that was to fuel prosperity for the next quarter century. This was propelled by pent-up demand, technological innovation, and a generation educated under the GI Bill. America soon realized that it must continue to export to ensure prosperity and therefore must rebuild Europe to create markets. The result was the Marshall Plan, named after General George Marshall, America's wartime chief of staff and postwar secretary of state. This plan was spectacularly successful in restoring Europe's war-ravaged economies and even benefited most neutral countries. Only Spain, led by Francisco Franco and ostracized for its support of the German Nazi regime during the war, failed to benefit from America's aid.

In Eastern Europe the situation was grimmer. The victorious Stalinist Soviet Union quickly threw a cordon, christened the Iron Curtain by Winston Churchill in his famous 1946 speech, around the "liberated" countries of that region. Czechoslovakia was the last to fall in 1948. By then, the tension between the United States and the Soviet Union had created the Cold War. The United States would emerge victorious in the first battle of the Cold War, as it staged the Berlin Airlift to relieve a Soviet blockade. But the war would continue to escalate as the Soviets ended America's nuclear-weapons monopoly in 1949. The story of how the Soviets stole America's nuclear secrets is now well known, but perhaps there is more to that story than is commonly realized. The Cold War would eventually escalate with a real "hot war" in Korea in 1950.

There were also stirrings in the Third World as people in the European colonies became restive and began demanding their freedom and independence.

Robert A. Wright

Symbolically, on September 2, 1945, the day Japan formally surrendered, ending World War II, Ho Chi Minh proclaimed Vietnam's independence and launched an anticolonial war against their French masters. The nationalist stirrings quickly changed the world order as India, Pakistan, and Burma achieved independence from Great Britain in 1947 and 1948, and Indonesians won against their Dutch overseers, achieving independence in 1949.

The inevitable momentum continued as the Vietnamese beat the French in Indochina in 1954. Change then began sweeping through the African continent as rebellion and turmoil spread. The French, British, Belgian, Portuguese, and Spanish colonial masters resisted futilely, unable to stem the tide and unwilling to prepare their subjects for true independence. This later resulted in untold tragedy and misery as the Cold War found its way to Africa, and white supremacist regimes in South Africa and Rhodesia (Zimbabwe) chose to resist the inevitability of majority rule.

Millions had died and millions of families had suffered during the war. Two families in particular, the Ortegas of Spain and the Hoffmans of Germany, were caught in the middle of it, their agony beginning in the tragic Spanish Civil War. Yet it was the two world wars and a colonial venue that created the circumstances under which these two families would unite and prosper, determined to build their lives and dreams regardless of the circumstances in the world around them.

The two families' saga began years before with an obscure battle in German Cameroon in 1915. Karl Hoffman led his surrounded German comrades to safety in the adjacent neutral colony of Spanish Guinea, where he reunited with his childhood sweetheart, Pilar Ortega. They married, had three sons, and prospered after the war. In the thirties, however, tragedy stalked them as sons Hans and Ernst, sent to Germany to be educated, entered the German Wehrmacht, while youngest son Paul was sent to America in 1935 to avoid that fate and the looming civil war in Spain.

Paul Hoffman came of age in America, was educated at Columbia, and met his future wife, Liz Kurtz, there. He also met her brother, Jack Kurtz, an OSS officer, and Paul was soon involved in dangerous espionage activities in Spain. After the war, family losses weighed on him. Brother Ernst was dead, Hans was missing, their mother, Pilar, was tragically killed on the first day of war, and his father was isolated in Spanish Guinea. Yet Paul was determined to face this reality and lead his family into the future.

Paul Hoffman was not yet aware of how Hans came to be missing. The operation code named Valhalla by the Germans had swept up Hans, a U-boat captain, and his uncle, Walter Hoffman, into a web of intrigue. They had left Germany in the closing days of the war with a secret cargo. Neither Paul nor his friend Jack Kurtz could obtain any information about his missing relatives even as the OSS reviewed German records.

These events would continue to haunt Paul and his family as he rose to meet the postwar challenges and opportunities. Eventually, as with most mysteries, the pieces would come together, but in some unpredictable and totally unexpected ways.

The Principal Characters

The Spaniards

Karl Hoffman: born in Germany in 1892; served in German Army *Schutztruppe* in Africa in World War I; became Spanish citizen; manages family cocoa and coffee business in Spanish Guinea.

Pilar Ortega (deceased): Karl Hoffman's wife; born in Spain in 1896; mother of Paul, Ernst, and Hans; died on first day of World War II on liner *Athenia* after it was torpedoed by U-boat on which son Hans was first officer.

> Hans Hoffman (missing in action): born in Spain in 1917; German citizen; U-boat officer in World War II; conducted special operations under direction of his uncle, Walter; disappeared in April 1945.

> Ernst Hoffman (deceased): born in Spain in 1918; German citizen; German *Luftwaffe* pilot shot down in April 1945.

> Paul Hoffman: born in Spanish Guinea, Africa in 1921; Spanish citizen; served as an agent in the Office of Strategic Services (OSS) in Spain with brother-in-law, Jack Kurtz, during World War II; leads the Hoffman-Ortega business enterprises in America.

Ernesto Ortega: Pilar's brother and leader of family business interests in Spain.

Anna Ortega: Ernesto's wife.

> Alberto Ortega: born in 1915, Ernesto's first son; an influential officer in Spanish navy.

> Lucia Aznar Sedeno: Alberto Ortega's girlfriend; married in 1957.

Alfonso Ortega: Ernesto's son; leader of family real estate holdings in Spain.

Francisca Ortega: Alfonso's daughter; born in 1948.

Anita Ortega: Ernesto's daughter and the family wine maker; born in 1919.

Beatriz Ortega: Anita's daughter; born in 1948.

Beatriz Anita Ortega: Beatriz's daughter; born in 1975.

Isabel Ortega: Anita's daughter; born in 1960.

Antonio de Ortiz: Spanish diplomat.

Francisco Franco Bahamonde (historical figure): Spain's dictator from 1939 until his death in 1975.

Luis Carrero Blanco (historical figure): Spanish naval officer and Franco's closest associate and adviser until his assassination by Basque separatists in 1973.

The Americans

Liz Kurtz Hoffman: Paul Hoffman's wife and Barnard graduate; born 1922; met Paul at Columbia University in 1942.

Robert Hoffman: Paul and Liz's son; born in 1947.

Pilar Hoffman: Robert's twin sister

Jack Kurtz: Liz's brother; born in 1919; served as OSS officer in Spain in World War II.

Sharon McKenzie: Jack Kurtz's girlfriend.

Ramon Ortega: Paul Hoffman's great uncle; immigrated to America in 1890s; American citizen.

William Donovan (historical figure): World War I hero; partner in New York law firm; led the Office of Strategic Services (OSS), America's spy service in World War II.

Allen Dulles (historical figure): Led OSS efforts in Switzerland in World War II; partner in law firm Sullivan and Cromwell with his brother, John Foster Dulles; later led the Central Intelligence Agency (CIA) 1953–1961.

The Germans

Walter Hoffman (missing in action): Karl Hoffman's brother and admiral in the German navy; born 1890; disappeared in April 1945.

Kirsten Hoffman: Walter Hoffman's daughter; born in 1932.

Claus Hilgeman: German navy officer; worked for Admiral Walter Hoffman during World War II.

Heinrich Mueller (historical figure): notorious head of Hitler's Gestapo; disappeared in May 1945.

Otto Skorzeny (historical figure): German officer famous for rescuing Mussolini in 1943; escaped to Spain in 1950.

Franz Liesau (historical figure): German agent in Spain in World War II.

Erich Traub (historical figure): German scientist active in biological warfare experiments in World War II; brought to United States after war in Operation Paperclip.

Reinhard Gehlen (historical figure): German officer and spy in World War II; served CIA following war; later head of West German intelligence service, the BND.

The South Africans

Hendrik van den Bergh (historical figure): South African police official.

Balthazar Johannes Vorster (historical figure): South African; German sympathizer in World War II; apartheid advocate; served as prime minister 1966–1978.

Dieter Gerhardt (historical figure): South African naval officer.

Johann Hartman: German immigrant to Swapkomund, Southwest Africa.

Heinz Hartman: Johann's nephew.

The Portuguese

Alexandre Santos: Portuguese secret police (PIDE) agent; began career in 1941; assigned to colony of Angola in 1943.

Artur Ferreira: Portuguese PIDE agent leading foreign intelligence and counterintelligence; assigned to Lisbon.

The French

Henri Fortier: agent in France's foreign intelligence service, the SDECE (later the DGSE); assigned to African operations.

The Equatoguineans

Wekesa Ondo: Served with Karl Hoffman in World War I; manages the plantation workforce in Spanish Guinea for Karl.

>Felipe Mukasa Ondo: Wekesa's grandson; educated in Spain; manages business operations for Karl Hoffman on Spanish Guinea cocoa and coffee plantations.

Francisco Macias Nguema (historical figure): the brutal dictator of Equatorial Guinea 1968–1979; executed by his successor and nephew Teodoro Obiang Nguema.

The Russians

Vladimir Morozov: head of foreign intelligence and counterintelligence for the MGB (later KGB).

Yuri Sergei Kozlov Castillo: key MGB (later KGB) agent in South America and later Africa.

The Czechs

Alfred Koecher: Allen Dulles associate from World War II; worked for CIA.

Pavel Frolik: part of the "Gehlen Organization" of German spies on Eastern front in World War II.

Karl Frenzel: SS agent during World War II assigned to activities related to Operation Valhalla.

The Cubans

Ernesto Che Guevara (historical figure): Cuban revolutionary.

Jorge Sanchez: foreign intelligence operative in *Direccion General de Inteligencia* (DGI).

The Others

Margarita: Paul and Liz Hoffman's nanny.

Helga: Paul and Liz Hoffman's part-time housekeeper.

Spain and Its African Colonies: 1945–1976

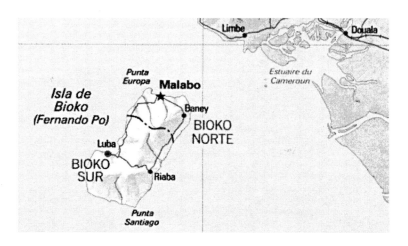

Fernando Poo, Spanish Guinea (Currently Bioko, Equatorial Guinea)
Capital Santa Isabel (Currently Malabo)

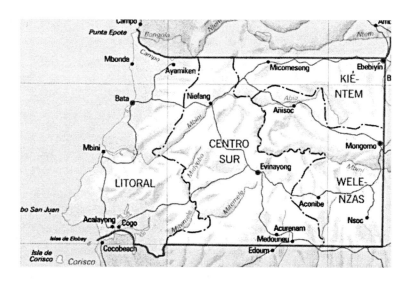

Rio Muni, Spanish Guinea (Currently Equatorial Guinea)

What sort of dream is that, Odin?

I dreamed I rose up before dawn
To clear up Val-hall for slain people
I aroused the Einheriar,
Bade them get up to strew the benches,
Clean the beer-cups,
The Valkyries to serve wine
For the arrival of a prince

-From the tenth-century Norse poem, *Eiriksmal* (Anonymous)

Part I

* * *

Turbulence

1946–1949

New York City.
January 1, 1946

* * *

Paul Hoffman stared at the winter scene in Central Park through the huge bay window in his uncle's Fifth Avenue penthouse. He closed his eyes, reliving last night's nightmare about his two brothers. He realized he should be happy with his present condition, but the circumstances of his oldest brother's disappearance gnawed at him.

Paul took another sip of the fine amontillado sherry from the Ortega family Bodega in Jerez, Spain. That caused him to think about his mother Pilar's tragic death on the first day of World War II, on the torpedoed liner Athenia as she and Paul's father Karl were trying to reach Paul in America. He quickly blotted that out as he tried to return to the present and celebrate the symbolism of the New Year.

Paul realized he had much to be thankful for as he assumed the mantle of leadership from his father for the Hoffman and Ortega families' enterprises in Spain, America, and Spanish Guinea in Africa. These included wine in Spain, cocoa and other commodities from Africa, and thriving export-import and shipping interests in America. The two families, originally joined in their bond by wine making, became increasingly wealthy over the years. Paul now pondered some bold moves in both America and Spain.

He was even more thankful for his recent marriage to Liz Kurtz, whom he had met at Columbia three years ago. Paul's best friend was her brother, Jack, an OSS officer during the war, also a Columbia graduate, and now a student at Harvard Law School. Paul's bond with Jack was ironclad, because they had both engaged in clandestine activity that helped keep Spain out of the war and deceived the Nazis on Allied invasion plans.

Paul was proud of what he did to aid America and Spain during the war, and he was proud to think of himself as a Spaniard living in a multinational world on four continents. He thought about the contrast between the conditions in Spanish Guinea, where he was born in 1921, and his current circumstances living in luxurious splendor in New York. He remembered playing in the cave with his brothers Hans and Ernst on their plantation in Rio Muni, the mainland portion of Spanish Guinea. He closed his eyes again as he thought of Hans, wondering where...

No, he thought. *I mustn't dwell on the past or on events over which I had no control and no prospect of changing today.* Paul looked at his watch, remembering that Liz and Uncle Ramon would soon be returning from the LaGuardia airport with Jack, who was scheduled to arrive on a flight from Boston. Paul was looking forward to seeing his good friend and finding out how he was weathering his first year of law school.

There it is again, the vision of Hans, Ernst, and Paul playing in the cave. Why can't I shake that image? What's so special about it? Paul thought again about how Hans and their uncle, *Vizeadmiral* Walter Hoffman, had mysteriously disappeared near the war's end. Jack found out that the Nazi SS and Gestapo had issued warrants for their arrest. Why? *Why can't I discover what happened?* Paul himself had survived two SS assassination attempts in the war, as a result of his work for the Office of Strategic Services, the OSS, in Spain. His own survival only made his frustration about his brother more real.

Paul snapped out of this nightmare as he heard to door to the penthouse open. They were here. *Finally I can forget this for a while and celebrate.*

The nightmare would return in ways that Paul could not then imagine.

2.

Asuncion, Paraguay.
January 1947

* * *

Franz Liesau Zacharias and Reinhard Gehlen rose from their chairs as former Gestapo Chief Heinrich Mueller entered the room and approached them.

"Welcome, gentlemen. It's a pleasure to see you both here finally." Mueller motioned for them to sit down. He then joined them as they sat on wicker chairs around a square glass table in a living room with panoramic windows on three sides. The room was part of a large isolated house several miles north of Asuncion, Paraguay's capital, on a hill overlooking the Paraguay River. As Mueller sat down, another man, dressed obviously as a servant, entered.

"Erich, if you are ready, please serve our guests coffee and other beverages."

The servant bowed toward Mueller without speaking and left the room. Mueller turned toward the other two men.

"So, Franz, did you have a good journey from Spain?"

Liesau Zacharias, a former SS operative with deep ties to the Spanish equivalent of the Gestapo, the *Brigada Politico Social*, the BPS, responded.

"Yes, Herr Mueller, it was a huge improvement in efficiency since my last trip to South America. I took an Iberia Airlines DC-4 and the total time en route from Madrid to Buenos Aires was only thirty-six hours, with stops in Villa Cisneros, Spanish Sahara, and Natal and Rio de Janiero in Brazil. We'll never need to take the long sea journey again, and I suspect we will use Iberia's service frequently."

"Yes, it's marvelous how air travel has advanced." Mueller then turned toward Gehlen. "I hope your journey from America went as well."

Reinhard Gehlen, former SS officer and the former head of German espionage against the Soviet Union, responded. "Yes, thank you, it went smoothly. Of course, the Americans think I'm in Buenos Aires. I can only remain here a few hours if my trip to Paraguay is to remain undetected."

"We understand. Perhaps you can enlighten us on your arrangements with the Americans, Gehlen," Mueller replied.

"We are quite fortunate. The Americans are desperate for intelligence information about the Soviets. In return for the use of our network behind Soviet lines, I have negotiated the release of hundreds of our former SS colleagues. The Americans know about our activities to obtain passage for our colleagues to Argentina. Like the Spanish and the Vatican, they are looking the other way."

"Yes, that is a stroke of good luck," Mueller replied, paused, and continued. "Perhaps soon I will be able to leave this godforsaken place myself and join the rest of our organization in Argentina."

Liesau replied with an alarmed tone. "Herr Mueller, that would not be wise; both Gehlen and I have been cleared of war crimes charges. You, on the other hand, are the most senior leader of the Reich who disappeared without a trace. As head of the Gestapo, were you to surface now, it would place our entire organization at risk. We all admire your bold and dangerous escape from Berlin in May 1945 and the four flights you took to get to Spain. But you must remain here in this safe house until more time has passed. You will still be able to control our organization from here and direct the reconstitution of the Reich."

Mueller scowled, but as he looked at Gehlen, he could see that he agreed with Liesau. He sighed, thought carefully, and finally replied. "Yes, I reluctantly agree with you. So thinking about our plans and organization, let's shift the discussion to the status of Operation Valhalla. Liesau, what were you able to determine regarding the location of the Valhalla cargo?"

Liesau looked quickly at Gehlen and then turned to Mueller to reply. "We cannot yet locate where the Valhalla cargo is located in Spanish Guinea or even ascertain positively that it arrived there."

As Mueller frowned, Liesau quickly continued. "We were never able to locate the precise storage location in Spanish Guinea. Our main agent there, Gerhard Hoepner, disappeared without a trace in late May 1945. He was the only one in direct contact with Walter Hoffman. Walter, the U-boat's captain, Hans Hoffman, and his father, Karl Hoffman, may be the only living individuals who know the storage location, assuming the U-boat actually arrived there."

"So, if I hear you correctly, we cannot be sure the U-boat delivered its cargo?" Mueller replied as he looked at each man.

After a long pause, Gehlen finally replied. "I was able to obtain some intelligence from my American friends, but only at risk that they might learn more about Valhalla. It seems that on April 22, 1945, an American naval group detected a Type 21 submarine while attacking and sinking a Type 9 in mid-Atlantic. The sonar trace, which was recorded, was later matched with the signature of a Type 21 that the Americans captured. I quietly dropped the matter lest they realize that a Type 21 had actually departed on a long-range mission. That Type 21 boat could only have been U-3696, since no other Type 21 reached the mid-Atlantic before the war ended. If the boat got that far, we may presume that it made it to Spanish Guinea and deposited its cargo."

As Gehlen concluded, the three men looked at each other.

Finally, Mueller replied. "So we may assume that Karl Hoffman may be the only available person who knows the location of the Valhalla cargo. Is that right, Liesau?" Mueller emphasized the name as he turned to the former SS agent.

Mueller watched Liesau squirm in his seat before replying. "I'm not sure, Herr Mueller. I left Spanish Guinea on May 4, 1945, on the last ship to leave the colony before our surrender. It is possible, indeed probable, that Karl Hoffman, his son, Hans, and brother, Walter, were responsible for Hoepner's disappearance."

"Yes, I see. I must also ask three additional questions. Where did U-3696 sail after departing Guinea? Does Karl Hoffman's son Paul also know about Valhalla, and what does his cousin, Alberto Ortega of the Spanish navy, know about it? I was disappointed to learn that we failed to eliminate these two potential traitors before the war ended. I am led to believe that these families, Hoffman and Ortega, have betrayed our cause. So what do we intend to do about this, gentlemen?" Mueller raised both of his hands to encompass the other two men as he concluded his summary.

After a long pause, Liesau answered. "It would be unwise for Gehlen to press his luck with the Americans in order to discover more intelligence from their files. I suggest that for now, we merely keep a watch on Paul Hoffman in America to see if he is privy to Valhalla. Meanwhile our friends in the BPS can keep tabs on Alberto Ortega in the Spanish navy and Karl Hoffman in Spanish Guinea. Perhaps we will surface something in this manner."

Liesau quickly added a thought. "Even this will be difficult. Alberto Ortega is well connected with Luis Carrero Blanco, Franco's top aide. In addition, Karl Hoffman is closely protected by the current governor in Spanish Guinea, even to the extent that it inhibits BPS surveillance. We also do not know where the U-3696 went after leaving Spanish Guinea. I would add that—"

Mueller abruptly cut him off. "I don't care what the limitations are. I would remind you gentlemen that our preparations for Valhalla were so secretive that only one set of documents was prepared for the mission, and those are presumably in the hands of Walter or Hans Hoffman or are located in some unknown location in Spanish Guinea. That means that we have no access to the codes that control tens of millions of Swiss francs and US dollars in the Valhalla Swiss bank accounts. Between the absence of those funds and the critical secrets in the Valhalla cargo, we are stymied in accomplishing Valhalla's mission. I am also worried that without these funds and the Valhalla secrets, we will be delayed in taking our plan to the next step with our developing organization in Argentina."

There was a long silence as the other two men absorbed Mueller's thoughts. The silence was nearly total as Mueller listened to the quiet swishing of the overhead fan. Liesau finally broke the silence.

"Herr Mueller, we will closely watch the Hoffman and Ortega families for further clues that will help us. Meanwhile, we must look beyond Argentina, which is a little hot for us right now. We are courting our friends in South Africa. That may be a better future base for us. Let's meet again in a few months to assess our progress."

"All right, Liesau, I accept your recommendations for now. But for you, the work is only beginning. You have done well in establishing bases for our operations in Spain and Argentina. I do note your concerns about our visibility in these two countries, and I approve your discreet overtures to our friends in South Africa. I want regular updates from you on that." Mueller than turned to Gehlen.

"Meanwhile, Gehlen, I think you should enhance your contacts with our American friends—and keep close tabs on Paul Hoffman. I can't believe he accomplished what he did in Spain with no assistance. Who else in America was working with him when he acted as a double agent for the OSS while ostensibly working for the SS?"

"He had the active assistance of Jack Kurtz, an OSS officer at the time, and the lead operative for OSS operations in Spain. Incidentally, Hoffman married Kurtz's sister Elizabeth, so we have an extended family here to deal with."

"Yes, Gehlen, I can see that. It seems that the Hoffman, Ortega, and Kurtz families have conspired, either intentionally or unintentionally, to thwart our mission to complete Operation Valhalla."

With that thought, and as the servant delivered coffee and other refreshments to the three men, Mueller stood up, walked slowly to the picture window overlooking the river, and stared out at the waning afternoon sun.

3.

Swakopmund. Southwest Africa.
June 1947

* * *

Johann Hartman sat quietly in the shade of the small outdoor café in this small town on the South Atlantic coast in the middle of the Namib Desert. He was waiting for his nephew, Heinz, to arrive after his meeting with some other recent German immigrants. The town was named Swakopmund because it sat at the mouth of the Swakop River. It was settled by German immigrants in the late nineteenth century, when the colony of German Southwest Africa was created. As Johann sat sipping his coffee, he thought about the place where he now lived as well as the events of the last two years.

During World War I, the colony was invaded by the adjacent Union of South Africa, which was allied with Great Britain in the war effort. Since then this huge, underpopulated territory was administered by South Africa as a mandate originally under League of Nations supervision. It was now under the auspices of the United Nations. The South African officials and a few UN administrators usually kept a low profile, mostly staying in the territory's capital, Windhoek, about 250 kilometers to the east.

The local German community was very tight-knit. When Johann, his nephew, and about forty-five other new German immigrants arrived in mid-1945, they were quickly and quietly integrated into the local community. The group arrived quietly by fishing boat in smaller groups over a period of several weeks. Their story was that they had emigrated from Germany through Portugal and adjacent Portuguese Angola. Nobody in the local community asked any further questions about their origin.

Johann was the de facto leader of the group. He personally knew many of the local community leaders, having befriended them during a 1926 port visit when he was an officer on the new German cruiser *Emden*'s first extended training cruise. He thought how lucky he was to have stayed in touch with the local community during his nineteen-year absence.

Johann's thoughts were interrupted as he saw Heinz approach, and he motioned for his nephew to join him at the table.

"So how did the meeting go?" Johann inquired as Heinz sat down.

"It went fine, Uncle. Everybody seems to be integrating into the community all right, but there just aren't enough jobs for everybody. None of our group wants charity from the community, and our initial funds are nearly exhausted. Have you thought about what we will do about that?"

"Yes; I'm hoping we will soon be able to get South African passports. I'm planning to travel to Windhoek in the near future to inquire about that. Once we have them, I plan to fly to Switzerland to access our accounts there."

"Are you planning to access our special accounts, Uncle?" Heinz did not need to elaborate.

His uncle looked around before replying. There were no other patrons outside. "No, that wouldn't be prudent right now. I will only access our family accounts. It was fortunate that your grandfather transferred our assets there early in the war. We can use our own money to support the group for now. We don't want any undesirable attention from interested parties in Germany—or elsewhere."

His nephew merely nodded, understanding the issue and in complete agreement.

4.

Greenwich Village, New York City,
July 1947

* * *

Paul Hoffman and his best friend and brother-in-law, Jack Kurtz, sat in their favorite Greenwich Village bar, the White Horse Tavern. They were celebrating Paul's entry into the world of fatherhood. Liz had just given birth, to twins no less, and Jack raised his beer mug to toast Paul, his sister, Liz, and newborn infants, Robert Karl and Pilar Susan. Pilar's birth had preceded her brother's by about ten minutes. The two newborns' names reflected their four grandparents.

"So, Dad, how does it feel?" Both men raised their mugs.

"It's nothing short of miraculous. It's like having a complete family in one fell swoop. I already cabled my father; I'm sure he'll be ecstatic. It'll be good for him to think outside of his little African empire and have a reason to come here to visit."

"Yeah, it's pretty amazing, I guess. To think of my little baby sister as a mom is something I'll have to adjust to."

"Well, 'Uncle' Jack, maybe it's your turn to join the party. Of course it might be helpful to find the woman of your dreams first!"

Both men laughed as Jack shook his head. "No way, old boy, I need to graduate from law school first. I've never worked so hard in my life. I'm looking forward to finishing so I can get on with life."

As he replied, Paul noticed Jack again discreetly watching a nondescript man sitting at the bar. Paul had noticed him several minutes ago. The man quickly averted his eyes from Jack's casual glances.

"I hear you, Jack. So you'll soon be a famous lawyer with a lucrative practice."

"Yeah, right. I can hardly wait."

Paul immediately sensed the shift in Jack's mood. "So was it something I said?"

"Nope, but pay attention to me. Do not, I repeat, do not look at the bar. We've been under observation for the last fifteen minutes or so."

Paul stared straight at Jack before replying, but he instantly recalled the unpleasant events of May 8, 1945, when he was almost murdered in his own apartment by a Spanish BPS agent turned by the SS, presumably for his involvement in covert activity in Spain. Paul's quick thinking, and a little luck, turned the tables on the intruder, and Paul killed him in self-defense.

"All right, Jack, do you recognize him?"

"No, but I was in the covert business long enough to know that this guy is watching us for a reason, and not because we're so entertaining."

"All I could think of was that BPS agent and—"

"Don't get carried away, Paul. This probably isn't that serious."

"Probably, huh? Well I've always wondered whether there would be repercussions, and whether the Nazis who got away to Spain and Argentina would hold a grudge."

Paul noticed out of the corner of his eye that the man at the bar got up and headed for the door.

"He's leaving now, Jack. You can get a good look at him as he leaves."

"Yeah, I'm watching. It looks like he tried to dress like the locals but he missed the mark."

"Yep, I agree. He's not enough of a bohemian." Paul paused and continued. "Shall we try and follow him?"

Jack shook his head before replying. "No, let's not. I'll do a little checking with my former colleagues. Maybe there's something going on that we should know about."

"Like what, for example?" Paul replied.

"It's hard to say really. It's just that there's a lot of turmoil going on right now in the international scene. You mentioned Nazis in Spain and Argentina. Heck, we've got them right here in the States—hundreds of them. We scooped them up under Operation Paperclip as the war was ending, because we needed their scientific and other expertise. I hear we even made deals with a lot of SS guys and didn't look too closely at their pedigree."

"So are we making a deal with the devil? And why is it necessary?" Paul replied.

"Well, Paul, it looks like our rivalry with Russia is heating up. If you've been following the news it looks like we smartened up and are finally re-creating a central intelligence agency like the OSS."

"So there you are, Jack, an opportunity for you to do it again."

"Nope, not me. I need to finish school and get to work. They'll need to find somebody else this time."

Bata, Rio Muni, Spanish Guinea, Africa,
August 1947

* * *

Karl Hoffman walked over to the table in the Bar Gloria outdoor café that he frequented when in Bata and sat down to wait for his long-time friend Wekesa to arrive. As Karl sat down, he watched another white man walk by the patio. Karl only got a glance at the man's face, but he sensed that he had seen him before. He quickly turned back to his table just as Wekesa arrived.

Wekesa was a Bantu, originally of the Fang tribe inhabiting Southern Cameroon, Spanish Guinea, and Gabon. He served with Karl in 1915 and 16 in Cameroon in the *Schutztruppe*, the German colonial army. The two of them were instrumental in helping the surrounded Germans escape into neutral Spanish Guinea. After the war, Karl brought him to Guinea to manage the labor force on the family's plantations. Wekesa had been with the family for more than twenty-five years. He and Karl were both fifty-five.

As Wekesa sat down, Karl was about to provide some family news but noticed that Wekesa seemed unusually tense.

"Wekesa, is something wrong? You seem distracted."

"Yes. The man who passed you has been asking many questions to our warehouse managers in the last few days."

"What kinds of questions?"

"He wanted to know what our warehouse capacity is, and what kinds of things are stored in them. He claims to be a merchant from Madrid who may want to export manufactured goods to Guinea. He says his name is Franz Liesau Zacharias."

Karl immediately recalled Liesau from several meetings in 1943, when he was tasked with obtaining gorillas and other primates in Rio Muni for medical research purposes in Germany. "Wekesa, we need to watch Liesau carefully to see if we can find out what he really wants."

"Of course. Do you think he is after—?"

"Yes, we may presume he is," Karl interrupted. "The key question is, what's he doing here now?"

"Yes, that would be important to know. Perhaps you can raise the issue with the governor or maybe even the BPS, since we have good relations with a few of the local BPS agents."

"I'll talk to the governor, Wekesa. Liesau was himself on the BPS payroll at one time, as well as the Nazi payroll. I'm not sure how much I can find out."

"Who are these?" Wekesa was looking down at the photos Karl had laid on the table.

Karl beamed. "Those two beautiful infants are my new grandchildren. They were born last month in New York. I just got these today."

"You must be very proud. I remember when my first grandchild was born more than fifteen years ago. It is quite an experience."

"You're right, Wekesa. It's also a sobering experience as a new generation enters this uncertain world. Come on; let's go get some dinner, and then we can head back to the plantation."

Washington. DC.
March 1948

* * *

William J. Donovan and Allen W. Dulles sat in the circular Round Robin bar off the main lobby of the Willard Hotel, nursing their scotches and quietly talking about the international situation. The bartender discreetly moved to the opposite side of the bar after replenishing their drinks. Donovan and Dulles were the only patrons on this blustery late winter afternoon. Donovan was the head of America's wartime spy service, the Office of Strategic Services. He was listening to Dulles, his chief spy in Switzerland during the war, as he described the chaos in the newly created Central Intelligence Agency, the CIA.

"It's really pathetic, Bill, watching this happen, especially after what you created during the war. It's like we didn't learn anything from the experience."

"So what about the new CIA director—does he know what he's doing?"

"Hillenkoetter is probably a fine admiral, but in this position he's like a deer in the headlights."

"It's all politics, Allen. He was picked for the job because he offends nobody. Meanwhile, we've got all kinds of crises developing."

"I'm worried about the European situation the most. Czechoslovakia was the last democracy to fall in Eastern Europe. The only thing keeping the Russians at bay right now is our atomic monopoly."

"I wonder how long that will last," Donovan replied.

"According to my sources it won't last long. We're starting to learn about their infiltration of the Manhattan project, but my inside friends also tell me about some strange doings in Germany."

"What's going on there?" Donovan queried.

"Our source on the ground told us that there was some kind of radiation accident east of Dresden and west of Breslau. The Poles now call it Wroclaw."

"So what are you telling me, Allen? Have the Russians set up some kind of nuclear reactor there?"

Before answering, Dulles downed the last of his scotch and raised his hand to the bartender to order another round. He looked around the famous bar, with its dark marble top, and admired its rich wood trim and paneling on the walls. He then turned back to Donovan. "It might not have been the Russians. The accident may have happened in 1945."

Donovan's eyebrow arched as he considered Dulles's reply. He too paused briefly as the bartender delivered their drinks.

"So the sources we had when the war ended might have been right. Maybe the Germans did get a reactor going."

"That's not all. We also got some tidbits that the Nazis somehow preserved their nuclear secrets and a whole lot of other stuff we never got our hands on. These fragmentary rumors indicate that it was all squirreled away somewhere safe from the Russians and other prying eyes."

"What about our sources behind the Iron Curtain? We have Gehlen, don't we? If he ran the SS spying operation against the Soviets, he might know something."

"Yeah, Gehlen is available, but I'm not sure I trust him fully. I'd rather check some of our existing intelligence sources and reports first."

"I recall one report I read just before I left OSS in late September '45, and it—"

Dulles interrupted. "I remember that one, too. It was one of our guys examining U-boat records after the war. He found they might have been trying to hide the construction and deployment of one of their advanced Type 21 boats. He hypothesized that it could have been hidden so it could provide a way to get some important information out of Germany. Gee, what was our guy's name? I can't—"

Donovan interrupted this time. "It was Kurtz, Jack Kurtz, and he was one of my best agents. He led the operation in Spain."

"Yeah, I remember him now. Where did he end up?"

"He'll graduate from Harvard Law this year. I've kept in touch, so maybe there will be a spot for him at my firm." Donovan was referring to Donovan, Leisure, Newton, and Irvine, the most powerful corporate law firm in New York City.

"Not so fast, Bill. We might want him at Sullivan and Cromwell." Dulles was a member of the other leading New York firm, where his brother John Foster was a partner.

Both men smiled. The scramble for top law-school talent was always competitive.

"Thinking of Spain again, and the general situation with the Soviets, we might need to find a way to reconcile with the Franco regime to shore up our position in Western Europe," Donovan said.

"Yeah, my sources in the agency say the air force is worried. If we ever have to use atomic weapons, we don't yet have a fully operational bomber that can reach the Soviet Union, unless it flies a one-way mission, or we can use bases in Western Europe. The French and Italians don't want us there, and the situation is almost as bad in Britain. We might need Spain for bomber bases," Dulles replied.

"I hope the guys at the CIA figure this out. We could use someone right now in Spain to help lay the groundwork for reconciliation. We probably need someone in Czechoslovakia and Germany to dog the other issues, too."

"You're right, Bill. I wonder if someone could work all three areas."

The men looked at each other until Dulles finally responded. "You're thinking what I'm thinking aren't you?"

"Of course. Kurtz would be perfect for this job."

"Well, it would be hard to send him in alone. I mean being an attorney as a cover would be fine, but he also needs to have a client doesn't he?"

"Yep, and I know one that would be perfect," Donovan responded.

"So who's the lucky cover guy?"

"Kurtz worked with a guy in Spain named Paul Hoffman. He's a Spaniard, actually, and Kurtz's brother-in-law. I attended the wedding. Their actions helped keep Franco out of the war. Hoffman was also one of our key guys in Operation Fortitude to deceive the Nazis on Overlord, regarding the location of the invasion site."

"So what's the plan?"

"I think when our young friend Jack graduates in June, we're going to invite him for a visit to see if he'll join the cause."

18

Greenwich Village, New York City.
July 1948

* * *

Paul and Jack were back at their favorite haunt, but this was no casual gathering. They hadn't seen each other in six months, and the two close friends were there to celebrate Jack's recent graduation from law school.

Unlike some of the times when they hung out here, this evening the place was packed. They stood together at the bar to begin the evening's celebration. Both men were handsome and tall, about six foot two, towering over many of the other patrons. Paul had sandy, full hair and was lean and wiry. Jack had an additional twenty pounds but was muscular and had a square face. His close-cropped hair was one shade lighter than Paul's. Like most men in their late twenties, they exuded confidence yet blended in with the exotic characters at this West Village dive. Its clientele typically included working-class longshoremen from the nearby docks on the Hudson and an eclectic mix of writers and other assorted bohemians.

"Jack, I have to hand it to you. I wasn't sure a guy who likes to party as much as you could actually graduate from law school."

"That's the truth, my friend. I'm sure glad law school is only three years and not four. I wouldn't have made it through another year. I'm also sick of leading the life of a monk and that, my good man, will change now for sure."

Both men laughed as they downed the rest of their beer. Jack raised his hand to the bartender for another round.

"Well, I don't blame you on that count, Jack, but what's your next move going to be…besides with the opposite sex?"

"That's a good question. I was going to start setting up a round of interviews. That's when Bill Donovan called. I'm meeting with him this week to talk about a job with his firm Donovan, Leisure, Newton, and Irvine."

"Damn, that's the top of the pack. I always knew you would go far and fast."

"That's a bunch of bullshit, Paul. Most of these top law-firm jobs are already sewn up early in the third year for most guys. I'm wondering what he wants."

"Well, I wasn't going to say it, but you did work for him during the war and that probably counts for a lot."

"Yeah, I suppose you're right, but I'm still wondering if there isn't some similar scheme up his sleeve now."

"Why would you think that? He left the OSS when the war ended, right?"

"I'm not sure you can ever leave the clandestine world, once you were in it as far as he was."

"I'm sure you're right. In any case that's not in your blood, is it?"

"I'm tempted to say absolutely not, but I'm still very curious to see exactly what he's got to say."

8.

Johannesburg, South Africa,
July 1948

* * *

Hendrik van den Bergh reached out his hand as Franz Liesau rose to greet him in an out-of-the-way corner of the lobby in the Sunnyside Park Hotel. Van den Bergh sensed his guest's shock, since at six foot five, the Afrikaner towered over Liesau. As usual he tried to put his guest at ease. "I welcome you to Johannesburg, Liesau. It's good to see you after what—it's been at least a couple of years now."

"Yes, that's about right, I guess. It's been far too long. I want to personally thank you for faithfully keeping your commitment to help us with immigration issues for our people."

"I'm glad I was able to help, Franz. By the way, how was your journey? How did you get here?"

"I came in from Lisbon on Pan American 150, a Lockheed Constellation, I believe. It was very comfortable. We stayed over in Dakar and the next day stopped at Accra and then Leopoldville on the way to Johannesburg."

"That's excellent. Well, to bring you up-to-date, my status has improved considerably since we last met. As you know, after several years I was finally released from government detention for my activities with the *Ossewabrandwag* during the war. Our efforts to keep South Africa out of the war against Germany did not succeed, but our fortunes changed last month with the national elections. Our movement now controls the national government, and change is happening rapidly. In my new position, I am charged with speeding up the process of absorbing refugees from Germany. In fact, I just assumed a position as police administrator for operations in Southwest Africa, which we administer under the UN mandate."

"Yes, that is exactly what I wanted to discuss with you," Liesau replied. "Since much has happened in the last two years, I wanted to ensure that we set up a regular process to coordinate our activities."

"Of course, that is our aim also. I hope to speed up the process of getting your people set up with identities in South Africa. Also, in looking at records relating to my new position, I've noticed that there was a large influx in German immigrants in Southwest Africa since 1945, particularly in Swakopmund."

"Where did they all come from, and how did they get there?" Liesau said.

"Some came by ship, some by land, and a small number appear to have arrived from Portuguese Angola in small boats."

"Do you know their identities and former positions in Germany?" Liesau replied.

"Not yet, but that is one of my first priorities when I arrive in Windhoek next week. I also plan to visit Swakopmund immediately." Van den Bergh was curious about his guest's interest in these particular Germans. "You seem very interested in the recent arrivals in Southwest Africa, Franz. Is there anyone in particular you are looking for?"

"Well, yes, I suppose. We thought there might be some former members of the German navy, the *Kriegsmarine*, who might have ended up there."

Van den Bergh noticed Liesau squirming in his seat and decided to move to another subject. "Well, I'll certainly look into this when I arrive in Swapkomund. Let's talk a little about funding, if you don't mind. Quite frankly, it continues to be expensive for us to accomplish all of this resettlement activity. I was hoping you could provide us with some details on how you will share these expenses."

"Of course, Hendrik, I'd be delighted to provide such detail. Why don't we talk about it over dinner?"

"That's a great idea. Let's go to the dining room here. The food is excellent."

Moving to the dining room, van den Bergh thought about the discomfort shown by Liesau when discussing former members of the German navy. He decided he would expand his investigation of the recent arrivals both before and after he visited Swapkomund.

9

New York City.
July 28, 1948

* * *

Jack Kurtz walked through the main door of the building housing William Donovan's law firm at 41 Broad Street, a half block from the New York Stock Exchange. He stopped to admire the impressive lobby with its ornate columns and murals of sailing ships on the upper walls.

He quickly went to the second floor and checked in with the firm's receptionist. As he was ushered into Dulles's plush private office, the secretary closed the door behind him. He was shocked to see an unexpected guest stand up and come over to greet him.

"Welcome, Jack. I presume you remember Allen Dulles?" Donovan greeted Jack.

"Of course I do, General." Jack shook hands with Donovan and then Dulles.

"I believe it was in September 1944, Mr. Dulles, when you made it back to the States for a few weeks after your isolation in Switzerland."

"Jack, you have a great memory. Please call me Allen," Dulles responded.

"Sit down, Jack. How about a scotch?" Donovan offered.

"It seems a little early, but sure, that would be fine. On the rocks please."

Donovan made their drinks as Jack watched the bespectacled, silver-haired Dulles light his pipe.

A slight smile evident, Dulles took a few puffs and began the conversation. "So a new Harvard Law graduate enters the world. I hear you just finished sitting for the bar exam."

"Yes, sir—I mean, Allen. But it will be a few months before I learn my results."

Donovan handed the drinks to Dulles and Jack and then raised his glass.

"Here's a toast to the new law graduate." The three men raised their glasses.

"Well, thank you. It's good to have all that behind me."

"Yes, and now's it time to think about your next big adventure," Dulles replied.

"Have you been following the headlines, Jack?" Donovan quickly added, pointing to the *New York Times* copy sitting on the coffee table in front of Jack.

Jack picked it up and read part of it aloud. "Truman asks curbs—"

Dulles interrupted. "No, read the left column."

"WEST COMPLETES REPLY TO MOSCOW; LONDON TENSE; BRITAIN HALTS RAF DEMOBILIZATION; SMITH FLIES TO BERLIN; US JETS ACTIVE AS SOVIET MOVES UP PLANES—"

"Yes, I think that captures it all," Donovan interrupted this time.

"Good old 'Beetle' to the rescue," Dulles added, referring to Lieutenant General Walter Bedell Smith, US ambassador to Moscow, and Eisenhower's chief of staff during the war.

"Yeah, and I hear he's already in the running to replace Hillenkoetter as CIA director," Donovan replied.

"Just what we need—another errand boy and hatchet man at the helm," Dulles said.

Jack was uncomfortable at the way the conversation started but decided to add his own take on things. "It seems to me that if the Berlin Airlift succeeds, the Russians will back down."

Donovan and Dulles looked at each other as Dulles nodded. He then turned to Jack to reply. "You might be right, Jack, but this is only round one in what's going to be a long war of attrition. I hope it stays cold but if the Russians call our bluff, it could go hot or even nuclear. That's why we need to get into their heads and get behind the scenes to influence allies—or former enemies, even. For that, we need a few experienced, discreet men."

Jack instantly caught the drift as he looked at Dulles, who again smiled as he puffed on his pipe, and then to Donovan as he got up to refresh their drinks. Jack replied as Donovan handed him a full glass of Johnnie Walker Black on the rocks.

"Why is it I'm getting the idea that I'm not here to talk about a job with a prestigious law firm?"

"Oh, you are here for that, Jack. That's what we want to talk to you about, among other elements of our offer," Dulles replied.

"Yes, that's part of the plan. That's why Allen's here today," Donovan added.

Jack decided to clarify things rapidly. "Then, gentlemen, would it be too much for me to ask what it is you're offering—and who's offering it?"

"You're right, Jack, let's come to the point," Dulles continued. "The international situation is serious, and it involves a lot of flash points. I'm talking Berlin, Germany, Czechoslovakia, and Spain. I—we—need someone like you on the ground there, wheeling and dealing quietly, to find out key information, meet with our contacts, and influence events. I know you weren't expecting this, so I apologize for that."

"I guess I should be flattered, but I'm already twenty-nine, and I want to start my life, to make my mark, to—"

"To make some money. Is that the next point?" Donovan interrupted.

Jack paused and sighed. "Sure, I'll be honest. Why wouldn't I want that? I mean look at both of you. You're established; you've made it." Jack swept his hand around the office.

"That's true, Jack. Allen and I have both done well, but we're not as well off as you think. We both made sacrifices before and during the war, and even now."

"I'm sorry, I didn't mean to imply that—"

"Don't worry, Jack, we understand your point. We've been there," Dulles replied.

The three men sat in silence for several moments.

Finally, Jack cleared the air. "I know the situation in Europe, and I know that America's living a pipe dream now." He paused. "So how can I...be of service? I hope you're not trying to make me a bureaucrat."

"Actually, that never crossed our minds, Jack. The thing is you may be able to have your wish, even as you support the cause. In fact, neither Allen nor I are in an official capacity right now, but Allen is serving as an emissary of sorts for his friends in the CIA. We actually want to hire you, both of us, but Allen's going to make the formal offer for Sullivan and Cromwell. This will provide you with a lucrative position as a first-year associate or 'junior,' as Allen's firm refers to them. Now the rest of this is completely secret, Jack, and I mean totally. Do you get my drift?"

"Absolutely; I know the score."

"All right, I'll let Allen take it from here. Allen?"

"Jack, there are actually three important assignments here. The main one, but not the first, is that we want you to use some back channels to lay the groundwork for a rapprochement with Spain. We need them as at least a de facto member of the Western alliance, because we need Spain for bomber bases for the Strategic Air Command, SAC. We know you had contacts there during the war with progressive elements in the Franco government, primarily in the navy."

"That's true. They're probably still there and just need a little encouragement," Jack replied.

"Right. That will take a while for you to address, but first there are two more urgent items. We heard from some of my sources that I had during the war—and from some other sources—that there was a nuclear accident in Germany just about where the current German, Polish, and Czech borders meet," Dulles explained.

"A nuclear accident; I didn't think the Russians were that far—"

Donovan cut him off. "We don't think it was the Russians. The accident happened in 1945, our sources say."

"Then the rumors I heard on my last OSS assignment in Germany in September 1945 might have been true; the Nazis may have had a working reactor."

"Exactly, and that brings us to the third element of the assignment," Dulles said. "There's a little work to be done here, and a lot in Germany, to finish up the job we should have done during Operation Paperclip. We tried to scoop up all the Nazi scientists and their secrets, but it turns out that we may not have gotten them all—the secrets, that is."

"I'm OK with that last part, Allen. I know where to pick up. But exactly how am I going to get into East Germany to find out about the nuclear event?"

"You'll get a thorough briefing later, but you're right. Poland and the Soviet part of Germany are locked up tighter than a drum. There may still be a window through Czechoslovakia for a few more months, before the new Communist government drops the curtain there. Your mission there has two elements: get some intelligence from contacts we have there, and then get as close as you can to the scene of the 'event' and get a measurement of the background radiation for us. You'll have a little device that accurately measures that radiation, yet it will look like a fountain pen."

The room was again silent as the three men pondered the import of what had been said.

Jack again broke the silence. "I understand. My only question is that I might be a poor operative because of my lack of recent activity. I will especially need cover for the activities in Czechoslovakia and Spain. What would a new lawyer be doing in those places?"

"Right on all counts, Jack. You will need a cover," Dulles replied, looking to Donovan to explain.

"Jack, as a new lawyer, you would be representing a Sullivan and Cromwell client with extensive business interests or business development needs in those two countries."

"So who might that be?" Jack replied.

"Oh, it's probably someone who exports commodities desired in Europe, like cocoa and coffee; someone with a thriving export-import business here in New York; and above all someone who represents a neutral country with a multicontinent business empire," Donovan concluded.

It took Jack only a split second to realize who that would be. "So I'm supposed to recruit Paul Hoffman for this effort?"

"Yes, he meets all those criteria perfectly, and the two of you worked together successfully in Spain during the war. Furthermore he's enthusiastic, and from what I've seen from your records, he knows how to handle himself," Donovan answered.

"Since you would be representing a bona fide business client on this operation, the cover story would be perfect in both Czechoslovakia and Spain," Dulles added.

"Why should I put him in harm's way? He's my friend, after all."

"Jack, I suspect you and Hoffman are motivated by the same factors right now. Especially in actions that would help Spain reenter the world," Donovan replied.

Jack thought for a minute and then decided. "All right, sign me up. But I don't speak for Paul."

"We understand," Dulles answered. "But time is critical on the Czech operation. We have to move fast."

"OK. I'll see Paul again next week. I'll probably have his answer right away."

"That's perfect, Jack. If Paul agrees, come see me immediately. I'll get you hired on to Sullivan and Cromwell, you'll get your first client on day two, you'll both be briefed on day three, and you'll fly to Prague on day four," Dulles said.

Donovan refilled their glasses.

10.

Madrid, Spain,
July 31, 1948

* * *

Reinhard Gehlen and Franz Liesau met at a small café in the sleepy Madrid neighborhood to discuss their investigation of Operation Valhalla, specifically the current location of the precious Valhalla cargo.

Liesau began. "I wasn't successful in my efforts last year to find out if the Valhalla cargo is in Spanish Guinea and if so, where it is stored. I believe my presence there was detected by Karl Hoffman and his employees. My usual contacts with the BPS haven't served me as well there as here in Spain. In my view, I should turn more effort toward Alberto Ortega. He was the official in the Spanish navy who knew about Valhalla. It's been hard to get close to him, as he has had a sea command since '45. Also, he is protected by Franco's aide, Luis Carrero. However, I found out that he is due for a shore command soon, so he will be more accessible. It will be interesting to track his movements to see if they will reveal any clues about Valhalla."

"Yes, that's the approach we should use with him. We can get back to Spanish Guinea when we have more information." Gehlen replied, paused, and continued. "Perhaps you could also tell me what's going on in South Africa, Franz."

"Of course. As you know, my trip there earlier this month was success-ful. We now have a functioning network there, thanks to van den Bergh. We have funneled 'expense' money to them to compensate them for the relocation efforts."

"That's excellent. Did you learn any more about the recent arrivals into Southwest Africa, especially Swapkomund?" Gehlen said.

"I'm still trying to follow up on what van den Bergh told me. It's difficult to get information about the place. It's physically isolated, and the community there is tight-knit and protective of each other. I really haven't found a source in Europe who might explain where the recent German immigrants came from."

Gehlen thought about that for a moment. As he looked at Liesau, he could see that they might be sharing the same thoughts. *So*, he thought, *it's time to talk about it.*

"Franz, do you think it's possible that Walter and Hans Hoffman are among the new immigrants?"

"You were obviously reading my mind, Gehlen. Yes, I suppose it's possible, but I would need to find a way to penetrate the community to learn more."

"That's correct, Franz, but we should leave that up to van den Bergh."

"All right, should I get back in touch with him?"

"Not yet. Give him some more time to do his own groundwork. Maybe you should pay him another visit in a few months, but for now just let it ride."

"Fine, I'll follow up then." Zacharias paused and then continued. "What have you found out about Paul Hoffman in the last few months?"

"Ever since my people began observing his movements last year, we know that he stays in contact with Jack Kurtz, the lead OSS operative in Spain during the war."

"So, are they now operatives for the CIA? Perhaps they hold the key to Valhalla and where the cargo is located," Liesau replied.

"I'm not so sure, Franz." Gehlen considered carefully before continuing. "Kurtz just graduated from law school, and I know he wasn't an operative while he was in school. I also know that Hoffman has not been active since the war ended. In addition, I think it's likely that neither of them knows the details about Valhalla, although Kurtz may know that it exists. We know that the Allies broke our codes during the war, so they may have known that an operation called Valhalla existed, but not the details. Only the Valhalla activation messages were broadcast, not any of the details. No, I believe that Karl Hoffman and Alberto Ortega are the only visible members of the three families who were privy to Valhalla, and they have maintained the secret."

Before Liesau could reply, Gehlen realized there was one more important piece of information he should share. "By the way, Franz, we soon may have Otto Skorzeny at our disposal. As you know, the Americans tried him for war crimes, but he was acquitted. They were holding him for further hearings in Germany relating to denazification, but I just found out this morning that he escaped from the detention camp four days ago."

"That's really good news. What do we need to do to help him now?"

"That's currently being arranged. We will eventually get him here to Spain. I suspect from my CIA contacts that the Americans probably looked the other way as he 'escaped,' since he wasn't really a war criminal, and I believe the Americans want to eventually use his services. So when he finally arrives here, we can get him involved in our Valhalla investigation."

11.

Swakopmund, Southwest Africa,
August 1948

* * *

Johann Hartman sat at his favorite café sipping coffee and considering his next steps to help his small community of recently arrived immigrants. Since arriving in 1945, their initial funds had been exhausted. Only a few of the forty-five men in the party had found jobs locally. Johann reluctantly agreed when several of them announced they planned to go to South Africa for jobs as soon as they obtained passports. His nephew, Heinz, talked about joining them, but Johann had persuaded him to remain in Swapkomund a little while longer. He was pleased at least that he, Heinz, and several others in the group had been approved for South African passports. Johann was thinking about his planned trip to Switzerland in the near future when a man carrying a briefcase approached his table.

"Excuse me, Herr Hartman, may I join you?" The tall man asked in fluent but accented German.

"May I ask your name?" Johan replied, recovering from his initial surprise.

"I am Hendrik van den Bergh, and I work for a police agency in South Africa."

Johann thought quickly, but realized he had little alternative but to be hospitable. "Yes, of course, please sit down." As van den Bergh sat, Hartman continued. "May I ask the nature of this visit?"

"You certainly may," van den Bergh answered as he opened his briefcase, retrieved some documents, and then continued. "I would like to present you and your nephew, Heinz, with your South African passports." Van den Bergh handed the two passports to Johann.

Johann looked at the two documents and then at van den Bergh. He realized he must continue to engage this stranger without appearing uncomfortable.

"Well, thank you, Herr van den Bergh. You must excuse my momentary surprise, but I find it highly unusual that you would personally deliver these documents. It is a long way from South Africa."

32

"It actually was no trouble. My duties involve oversight of immigration into this territory, and I routinely review such document issuances with our immigration people. When I realized I needed to come to Swapkomund, I decided to bring these with me. In addition, I have an additional forty-three passports for the rest of your crew."

Johann momentarily froze as he heard the word "crew" and then answered. "I'm not sure I understand."

"Well, my information indicates that you all came here as a group, that you came by sea, and you and your colleagues all seem to have a maritime or naval background. Naturally I thought that you all must have served together, probably on the same vessel."

Johann again froze. He was not sure how to reply. "Yes, we all served together," he finally replied in a noncommittal way.

"I see. Well, I also wanted to tell you that I have issued work permits for you and your men, and we will assist them in finding jobs throughout South Africa. I know it's difficult to find work here."

Johann tried to craft his reply without being either unduly grateful or antagonistic. "Why are you doing this?" That was all he could finally muster.

"It's very simple, Johann. A new regime assumed power in South Africa in May, and we are determined to secure a future for Caucasians in our country. Our population, however, is seventy-five percent black. Two things must therefore govern our actions. One is to craft a set of laws that will formally separate the races and guarantee hegemony for whites. The other is that we must increase the number of whites in our country, and immigration is the fastest way to do that. Hardworking individuals such as you and your fellow crew members fall into that category."

"That's extraordinarily generous, Herr van den Bergh." Johann paused and then decided he must continue with his thought. "What is it you ask from us in return?"

"Only that you demonstrate loyalty to your adopted country. We don't care where you came from or what you did, but we do expect you to serve in ways that will become apparent as time passes," van den Bergh replied, smiling.

Johann thought for an additional moment and finally crafted his response. "I think that you can count on us, Herr van den Bergh. Quite honestly there is little for us to go back to."

12.

Greenwich Village, New York City.
August 1948

* * *

Paul entered the San Remo bar at 189 Bleecker Street, quickly noticed Jack sitting in the corner at an isolated table, and walked over to join him. It was late afternoon and the place was nearly empty, ahead of the evening crowd on this sultry afternoon. As Paul sat down the bartender brought a round of beers to their table. Paul noticed that Jack had already downed one, or more.

"Hey, Jack, great idea to come here instead of the White Horse. We haven't been here in a long time."

Paul looked around, noticing the black-and-white tile floor and pressed-tin ceiling that gave the San Remo a certain charm, although it typically entertained a gloomier, more eccentric crowd than the White Horse.

"I thought it would be fun for a change," Jack replied, taking a slug of his beer.

"So I can't wait. Tell me how it went at Donovan's firm."

Paul leaned toward his friend, eager to hear his report.

"Well, Paul, it was much stranger than I ever would have guessed."

Paul sensed that what he was about to hear wasn't what he expected. "All right, I give up. What happened?"

"Well, first of all, Allen Dulles was there."

Paul instantly knew that Jack's visit must have been more than about receiving a job offer. "All right, now you really have my attention."

"That's good, Paul, because you need to listen carefully to what I'm going to tell you, since you could be part of the offer they made."

"I don't know how that's going to work. I don't have a law degree." Paul laughed.

"Dulles wants me to come to work for him."

"That's at Sullivan and Cromwell?" Paul replied.

"Sort of, but there's another firm involved."

Paul looked at Jack, quickly sensing his real meaning as he put all the elements together. "So, are Dulles and Donovan involved in another enterprise—in the CIA perhaps?"

"You catch on fast, Paul. Listen, I'll cut to the chase. They want me back for some work in Spain by way of Czechoslovakia and Germany—and we need your help."

"Go on, I'm listening," Paul replied.

"Well, I'm going to be a working attorney at Sullivan and Cromwell all right, and I need a client as a front. Let's say someone who is anxious to export cocoa and coffee to the Czechs and has hired Sullivan and Cromwell, that's me, to represent him in negotiations."

"I get that. So, I'm part of the offer as a front. You mentioned Spain, too, Jack. What's the deal there?"

"We need Spain back in the Western world. It's all about bomber bases and a lot of other issues to shore up our position against the Russians."

"I get all that, too. SAC needs bases for its medium range bombers that can't reach Russia from US bases. The big thing for me is ending Spain's isolation."

"That's where you and I could team up to work our previous contacts over there. I'm thinking about your cousin, Alberto, and others. The problem is the Czech part could be dangerous, but it's all tied up in the same cover scheme and—"

"Jack, forget about that. We've done this before together, and I trust you. I want to get involved in this if it's important for both Spain and America. Now give me details."

Jack covered the plan with Paul and then summarized the next steps. "We're going to have to leave right away. Our window to get into Czechoslovakia may end soon."

"I can be ready this week. I already have plans to travel to Spain next month on family business and to attend a family reunion."

"That's great; after we finish the Czech business, we need to spend a week or so in Germany, sniffing for some contacts there who might shed some light on Nazi nuclear efforts—and some other developments that they may have hidden. The timing will then be perfect to head to Spain, where we may be for a few weeks."

"My existing plans dovetail with that nicely, Jack. Liz was planning to travel with our kids to visit the Ortega clan in Alabos in Rioja. It'll be their first time in Spain."

"Will Alberto be there?"

"Yep, I heard he has leave from the navy."

"So it should all fall into place. Let's drink to success."

As the two men hoisted their beers, Paul eagerly anticipated getting to Spain and finding some way to influence events there. He also anticipated visiting Germany. Perhaps he could learn more about his missing brother Hans.

13.

Approaching Prague, Czechoslovakia,
August 1948

* * *

As Pan American flight 180, a Lockheed Model 049 Constellation, *Clipper Invincible*, registration N88855, approached Ruzyne Airport in the Czech capital, Paul and Jack went over their briefing one more time. They left London late that morning, and the flight had stopped in Brussels and Frankfurt. They were arriving on time at 7:20 p.m., and despite their fatigue, the adrenaline was kicking in as they contemplated their arrival in the newly Communist country.

"All right, Paul, this may be our last chance to talk about this without the risk of being monitored. So who's our contact in Prague, and what's his cover?"

"We're meeting Alfred Koecher for dinner at 10:00 tonight at a restaurant in the Old Town Square. He's one of Dulles's contacts from the war, and he's an agent whose cover is a lawyer representing several coffee and cocoa distributors in the country."

"Great; we're likely to be closely monitored in most places we go, so what's the main key word we'll be using to communicate in these places?"

"Whenever we or our contact want to discuss any aspect of our intelligence gathering about the nuclear incident up north, we'll use the word 'proposal' as much as possible, as if we were discussing our business proposal to them."

"That's right, Paul. Just remember that you're anxious to cut a deal with them to import coffee and cocoa into the country. Koecher's cover has him representing distributors in Prague, Liberec, and Karlovy Vary. Liberec is the closest significant town to the German border up north, and Karlovy Vary is nearly on the western border."

"I got it, Jack. I'm still wondering about our other main contacts here, Pavel Frolik up in Liberec and Karl Frenzel over in Karlovy Vary. Dulles couldn't vouch for them as well because of their connection with the Gehlen organization. They're not contacts he previously knew."

"Yeah, that came through loud and clear. Frenzel was a former SS type, just a low-level guy, but he claims to have knowledge of the nuclear incident, and he's trying to spill it all and ingratiate himself with the CIA so they'll get him out of here. His family was driven out of the former Sudetenland after the war, and he wants out now. Frolik's background is a little murkier, and his ancestry appears to be more Czech than German. In any case, Koecher will set it all up for us."

Paul nodded and then stared out the window on the left side as the Connie descended and banked to the left, turning on to the base leg of the approach. Paul gazed at the pastoral rolling hills and lush green vegetation accented by a mellow sun still pretty high in the sky at this latitude.

"It's gorgeous, isn't it?" Jack commented.

"Yeah, and I was imagining flying the Spartan over this country as a way for us to get around."

"Paul, you've owned that plane for what, about eight years now?" Jack replied.

"That's right. I've flown it about twelve hundred hours. I've got fifteen hundred hours total flying time and an instrument rating. I just got my multiengine rating in a Cessna T-50. We're flying so much now on business in the States, I'm probably going to get a twin soon, most likely a Beech 18."

"Wow, you sure are committed to flying yourself for business transportation. Could you fly this baby we're on now?"

"Sure, probably, in a pinch, but it wouldn't be pretty."

At that moment the Connie banked one last time as an announcement was made by the captain.

"*Ladies and gentlemen, we've turned onto our final approach to the Prague airport. Please ensure that your seatbelts are securely fastened and have your passports and visas readily available. The authorities will thoroughly scrutinize your documents and luggage after we land. Thank you for flying Pan American.*"

"Well, Paul, this is it. Let's hope our careful planning will pay off."

* * *

"Gentlemen, welcome to Prague. I've got our table over here. I hope sitting outside is all right on this fine evening?" Koecher reached out his hand to Jack and then Paul.

"Outside will be fine, thanks," Jack answered.

After shaking hands, Koecher led them to their outdoor table at the small café on the south side of the square, adjacent to the old town hall. The café was packed on this warm, late-summer evening just before sunset.

"I hadn't realized how beautiful your city is," Paul commented, staring up at both the green domes of the Church of St. Nicholas and then to the right at the Tyn Church with its spires.

"Yes, we are rather proud of it, and fortunately neither the Nazis nor the Allies bombed it, so it's all intact. Say, how would you like some great Czech beer and a few appetizers?"

"That would be outstanding," Jack replied.

Koecher quickly motioned for a waiter and ordered. As the waiter left, Koecher looked around the other tables casually and began. "Since hearing of your interest in providing my clients with cocoa and coffee, we have studied your proposal very carefully."

"I'm happy to hear that," Paul answered.

"Yes, and we are anxious to hear your response," Jack added.

"We can certainly get into details later when we meet with my clients here in Prague and later in Liberec and Karlovy Vary. For now I want to emphasize that there are aspects of your proposal that you may not have anticipated that my client in Liberec may wish to discuss. Also I have verified some of the issues my client in Karlovy Vary has previously raised, and they appear to be genuine."

"We're interested in resolving those issues quickly so that we can conclude our agreement," Jack said.

"Yes, I understand that. Considering all the factors in play, we need to conclude this arrangement as soon as possible," Koecher answered as the waiter brought the first round of beers in huge mugs.

"Gentlemen, here's to success. *Na zdravi!*"

The three men raised their mugs as Paul looked around this famous square and at the diners around them, wondering what obstacles they would face in the next few days.

14

Liberec, Czechoslovakia,
August 1948

* * *

"It's only three more kilometers to Liberec so I should reiterate what I know about Pavel Frolik," Alfred Koecher began as he noted the road sign, turned the corner in his elegant but dated 1936 Mercedes 260D Pullman Limousine, and continued. "His name was provided by the CIA contact, and they emphasized that he is not part of Allen Dulles's wartime network, but he is part of another network."

"Right, but Dulles said we have to rely on him," Jack replied, not telling Koecher any more about Reinhard Gehlen's agent.

"All right, so be it. I certainly don't know much about his background. Upon contacting him several days ago when I heard about your trip, he informed me that he has extensive contacts across the frontier in both East Germany and Poland."

"What does he know about our mission?" Paul asked.

"Only that we want to talk to him about general intelligence matters. I didn't tell him about our interest in a nuclear incident, and since he did not raise the issue, he may or may not know about it."

"So if he doesn't tell us about it, we could assume that he's hiding it from us. It would be unlikely that a competent agent and his network would be unaware of a nearby nuclear accident of some kind," Jack said.

"Yes, that's true, so we should not tip our hand on the issue. To get you as close to the border as possible after our initial meeting, I've told him that since this is your first trip to Czechoslovakia you wanted to do a little sightseeing after the meeting, both in town and to the northwest and northeast of Liberec, very close to the frontier," Koecher said.

"So what are the 'sights' I want to see?" Paul asked.

"Besides the town hall in Liberec, you will want to see the tomb of Frederick I in Frydlant, which is a small town to the northeast, and also the scenery on the road to Rumburk, which is to the northwest. We won't actually get to Rumburk, since the road cuts through East Germany and is closed."

Paul nodded as they entered Liberec. He thought about how he would activate the special pen he had brought to measure background radiation. He and Jack had discussed the procedure they created on the flight into Prague. Either of them could announce the need to "record" some historical or geographical point of interest at the intervals suggested by their CIA briefer before they left New York. Paul hoped that he could activate the device discreetly enough when he wrote down the "scenery and historical notes" on the steno pad he carried.

* * *

"Paul, you should jot this down."

"Absolutely, Jack. Liz will love it. She'll be jealous that I got to make this trip without her. She made me promise to make a written record of all the sights I saw so she could get a feel for the country."

Paul stood in front of the tomb of Frederick I at the Church of the Holy Cross in Frydlant, the last stop on their "tour," as he clicked the pen and began writing a few notes on his steno pad. Per the briefing they had in New York, he had activated the pen eighteen times to record "notes," and the background radiation level, at prearranged locations. As Paul finished writing and clicked the pen, he looked up to see Pavel Frolik staring at him.

"You seem unusually diligent in recording this sightseeing tour, Mr. Hoffman. I wouldn't expect a tourist, let alone a businessman, to have such an interest in Czech history and geography," Frolik stated skeptically.

"Oh, you don't know my wife, Pavel. I minored in history at the university, but she is absolutely fanatical about it. She couldn't come on this trip because we have one- year-old twins, but I promised I would take excellent notes for her."

"I see," Frolik replied simply.

"So, Paul and Jack, this will be the last stop. We need to return to Liberec to get our car and then head back to Prague. Frolik, we appreciate your indulgence on this extra bit of sightseeing," Koecher concluded as he turned to Frolik.

"Yes, of course, I was happy to oblige. I'm sorry I wasn't able to provide you much additional information on the activities of our Soviet friends in Germany," Frolik replied as he again stared at Paul. Paul noticed Frolik's stare but maintained his neutral facial expression.

* * *

Within an hour, Paul, Jack, and Alfred were driven back to Liberec by Frolik and departed for Prague. As they drove away, Frolik pondered their unusual visit and decided he needed to contact Reinhard Gehlen to report the strange interest of a Spanish businessman and his American lawyer in the cultural and historical sights of Northern Bohemia. He also decided that his controller in the Soviet Ministry for State Security, the MGB, would want to know about this curious behavior. The controller was ostensibly the "economic attaché" in the Russian embassy in Prague. Frolik, a former SS agent for Reinhard Gehlen's organization, was turned by the Russians late in the war. His controller had standing orders to Frolik to be alert for any unusual activity in this isolated town. Frolik had heard rumors about the highly restricted area north of the frontier in Germany but decided not to be too curious. After all, he thought, that's how I've survived these last few years—by recognizing who the new masters are.

15

Near Karlovy Vary, Czechoslovakia,
August 1948

* * *

Alfred Koecher walked swiftly back to his Mercedes after making a call to Karlovy Vary from the small inn. As soon as he began driving again, he updated Paul and Jack on what he had learned.

"We'll go directly to the safe house rather than the town."

"What's going on?" Paul replied.

"I'm not sure, but one of my men said there is some unusual police activity taking place in town. He'll try to find out more and then come join us at the safe house. Meanwhile another one of my men is bringing Karl Frenzel there so that we can interrogate him."

"I'm hoping this will be more of a confession than an interrogation," Jack said. "We need for him to come clean right away on his knowledge of SS activities relating to any nuclear incident. We don't have time to beat around the bush."

"I'm sure Frenzel is anxious to cooperate, and my own investigation of his background suggests he is legitimate," Koecher replied.

As the Mercedes rounded a corner, a clearing opened up to their left, and Paul quickly commented on the view it offered.

"Look, there's an airport."

"Yes, that's the Karlovy Vary aerodrome. It's mostly inactive now because airline service has ended," Koecher said.

Paul then recognized another familiar object as he saw a small aircraft painted yellow sitting next to a small hangar.

"There's a Cub, probably a J-3. Is there an aero club here?"

"Yes, but it was closed by the government earlier this year. There were only a couple of pilots who were members, and my team here says they have disappeared. Also, the government seized the club's assets and confiscated the fuel they had." He paused and then said, "The safe house is only two kilometers away."

Paul mulled this over during the remaining several minutes it took to reach the safe house, located on a dirt road off the main highway and hidden deep in a stand of trees.

* * *

Jack and Paul were introduced to Frenzel using aliases, rather than their real names. They had been talking about a half hour. Jack continued probing as Karl Frenzel was summarizing his involvement in special SS activities during the war's closing days.

"All right, Frenzel, so tell us again what your role was and what activities your team engaged in."

"We were under orders to gather up all information and data that had been accumulated at these special sites, destroy the remaining evidence, and... liquidate any witnesses or participants in that activity."

"So what were you doing in the area north of Liberec?" Jack replied.

"The site was over the border on the German side, just west of the current Polish border. There was a small nuclear reactor there operated under SS supervision. We seized their documents and records and ordered the technicians to remove the control rods from the reactor. We then executed the technicians and fled the area just ahead of the advancing Russian forces. It was May 6, 1945, and it was our last assignment in the operation."

"You keep talking about the 'operation.' What was the name of the operation you were involved in?" Jack inquired.

Frenzel looked at Koecher, who nodded his encouragement, and then turned back to Jack. "It was called 'Operation Valhalla,' and it was led by both the SS and the Gestapo."

Paul immediately looked at Jack and was about to say something, but Jack's facial expression told Paul that they would discuss it later. Paul recalled Jack had asked him in October 1944 to raise the issue of Operation Valhalla with Paul's cousin, Alberto, in Spanish navy intelligence, when Paul was assisting Jack with an OSS operation in Spain.

"So there were other aspects to Operation Valhalla. What was the main goal of the operation?" Jack continued.

"Our mission was to accumulate all scientific and technical information relating to atomic and biological weapons, and other important scientific information. We were then to transport it to a safe place."

"Where were all these materials taken?" Paul interjected.

"Early in April 1945, some other SS teams moved all the materials acquired to that point to Flensburg, Germany, on the Danish border."

"What happened to them after that?" Jack said.

"I don't know. They were supposedly to be moved to a secure location, but I wasn't privy to where that was."

"How was the material to be moved?" Paul asked.

"I don't know that either." Frenzel paused, but then continued. "There was a rumor among us that it was to be transported somewhere by submarine."

This hit Paul like a revelation, but he suppressed his surprise. Jack, however, pressed forward with the point. "So who in the *Kriegsmarine* was coordinating with the SS on this operation? I need their names."

"I don't know; I wasn't privy to that information. But I do have many other names, including the names of agents connected with Valhalla who were in Germany and Spain."

"So let's have them," Jack replied.

Frenzel shook his head. "I have already given you critical information and the means for you to verify it. Before I give you anything else, you need to tell me how you will get me over the border and to a place where I will be safe."

Paul watched as Jack looked first at Koecher, back to Frenzel, and then over to Paul. Paul shook his head, and then Jack turned back to Frenzel.

"All right, we'll continue this later."

At that moment Paul heard an automobile approaching. Koecher quickly walked to the window and looked out as he picked up a revolver from a table. As he identified the driver he placed the weapon back on the table.

"It's my other agent," Koecher announced as he went to open the door.

The man quickly entered and began speaking in an agitated voice. "The police have established roadblocks and beefed up the border guards. I just got off the phone with Prague before coming here. They have suspended airline service to the West, and Pan American has been ordered to close its offices. From what I could learn, the StB is looking for our two friends here." The man pointed to Paul and Jack.

"What's the StB?" Jack asked.

"They're State Security, or *Statni Bezpecnost*, the secret police."

"Great, so how tight is the noose right now?" Jack asked.

"It's not good," Koecher's agent pulled a map out of his pocket, laid it on the table nearby, and began pointing to locations as he spoke. "All the main roads are being patrolled, and the border is closed. I don't see any immediate way out. You might have to go into hiding until we figure this out."

Paul thought about it for only a moment before proposing the solution.

"That's not necessary. The two of us will take that airplane we saw at the airport, and we'll fly across the border."

"But there are no pilots available," Koecher's agent immediately replied.

"There is no aviation gas available either, and the plane probably has none in it," Koecher added.

"No problem. I'm a pilot, and that plane can burn car gasoline, which I assume we can get."

Both Koecher and his agent looked startled, but Koecher replied immediately.

"Yes, I have gasoline, but only a twenty-liter can. Will that be enough?"

Paul was looking casually at the map that Koecher's agent had laid out. After looking at the scale and doing some quick crude measurements, he responded. "The border looks to be about fifty kilometers from the airport. With twenty liters, we'll have about sixty minutes' endurance to make a thirty-minute flight."

"How will you explain our absence, since you've visibly been escorting us the last week?" Jack asked, turning to Koecher.

"My agent will go to the police and report his car was stolen. I will go to them separately and report that you are missing."

"Are you sure that will work?" Paul added.

"Yes, please don't worry."

Frenzel, having nervously watched this exchange, interjected. "What about me? I may be under suspicion also."

"You needn't worry, Frenzel. There is no reason they would suspect you," Koecher replied.

"When we return, we'll make sure our people find a way to get you out," Jack added.

"Are there any guards at the airport to worry about?" Paul inquired.

"They are only on the commercial side of the airport. They assume there is nobody qualified to fly the small airplane, and the StB and their Russian friends haven't got around to watching every street corner...yet."

"Then gentlemen, I suggest we get moving right away," Paul said.

* * *

Paul, Jack, Koecher and Koecher's local agent quickly drove the short distance to the airfield and carefully and quietly drove up behind the small hangar to where the Piper J-3 Cub was parked. Paul got out and began inspecting the aircraft.

"This airplane looks nearly new," Paul commented as he checked the oil dipstick on the small Continental Motors sixty-five-horsepower engine.

"Yes, it was acquired by the aero club late last year, and it has hardly flown," Koecher's agent replied.

Paul looked at the small wire protruding from the twelve-gallon nose fuel tank, noticing that it was nearly touching the fuel cap. He bounced the wire against the cap, watched it rebound only an inch or so, and turned to Jack.

"Yep, it's nearly empty. Bring that twenty-liter jerry can and the funnel over here and empty it into the tank while I check out the rest of the plane."

In a few minutes Paul's check was complete. He took a brief look around the other side of the hangar at the ramp on the north side before returning to the Cub.

"All right, Jack, hop in the front seat. I'm used to flying this model from the back." Paul pulled out his map. He turned to Koecher as his agent finished a discussion with him and then quickly departed in the car.

"I'm planning to fly west-southwest to keep the time to the border to a minimum and avoid flying into East Germany by accident. I plan to fly low, but do you know if they have radar, planes, or other antiaircraft defenses on the border?"

"Yes, flying southwest is advisable," Koecher replied. "There are no antiaircraft guns that we know of yet, and the nearest Czech base with fighter aircraft is in Pilsen. Also, my agent is heading over to cut the phone line from the security office on the other side of the airport to town. They don't have a radio, so that should buy you twenty minutes or so after you take off before the border guards can be alerted. I'm worried about your takeoff, however. It is a long taxi to the runway, and they will surely spot you before you can reach it and take off."

"I'm not using the runway. The ramp in front of this hangar is about two hundred meters wide, and that's all I need." Paul activated the fuel-primer handle several times and then walked to the front of the Cub. He began pulling the propeller through several times to complete the priming process.

"Are you winding the rubber band or something?" Jack cracked as Paul came around back to the cockpit, reached in, opened the throttle slightly, and reached over Jack's head to flip the ignition switch over three clicks.

"Sorry, Jack, this isn't quite like that Pan Am Connie we flew in on. The Cub has no electrical system for starting so I'm going to hand prop it, so listen up. Put your heels on those two little mushroom-like devices on the floor. Those are the brakes. Put your left hand on the throttle and hold it there."

Paul turned to Koecher. "Thank you for your help, Alfred. I'm still worried about the aftermath of us leaving you in the lurch here."

"Don't worry, Paul. I'll be safe."

Paul shook Koecher's hand and then went back to the front of the Cub. He grabbed the prop on the left side, gave it a swift pull, and as he stepped back his effort was rewarded. The engine caught immediately and idled smoothly. Paul quickly walked around and pulled himself into the rear cockpit, fastened his belt, did a few quick checks, and put his right hand on Jack's shoulder.

"Are you ready for this, partner?"

"You bet, ace. Let her rip!"

It was a warm day, and the engine needed no further warming up. Paul quickly taxied around the hangar to the east end of the ramp, pointed the Cub west, stood on the brakes, and ran the throttle to full. Releasing the brakes, the Cub lurched forward as Paul kept a tail-low attitude. After only three hundred feet the Cub lifted off at forty miles per hour.

Paul pushed forward on the stick to keep the nose down to maintain altitude at only about ten feet above the ground and to let the airplane build speed. At best, he knew it would top out at between eighty-five and ninety miles per hour. The Cub raced across the airfield as Paul glanced quickly to the right to see several soldiers or policemen coming out of a building. He shouted to Jack.

"Hang on! I'm going to wait until the last second to clear those trees so they can't get a clear shot."

"You're the boss!"

The Cub just barely cleared the trees as Paul pulled back on the stick and then just as quickly pushed it forward to dive behind the trees to an open field on the other side. This kept them from becoming a target.

* * *

After twenty five minutes Paul watched anxiously ahead as they flew west at treetop level and maximum speed. He also noticed that the wire fuel gauge in the nose tank was descending more rapidly than he planned. He didn't want to fly slower to save fuel, realizing that minutes counted.

Then, as he pulled up and over a rise, both he and Jack shouted at nearly the same time, but Jack beat him to the announcement. "Shit, it's a guard tower!"

The tower was on top of a ridge. Paul made a quick decision and shouted at Jack. "I'm heading right for it to minimize our profile and time in his sight. If they're looking the other way, they won't hear or see us until we're right on them!" Jack grabbed the top of the instrument panel as the tower quickly loomed in the windshield. Paul could see the two guards drinking coffee and looking west. Just as they approached the tower both guards whipped around as they finally heard the Cub. Paul noticed the panicked look on their faces as they dove for the floor just as Paul pulled up at the last second, flew over the tower, and then dove down the other side of the ridge into the valley below. The Cub's speed quickly increased. Paul turned to match the ravine's curvature as they turned to the southwest, and they were quickly out of sight of the tower.

Paul continued at treetop level and maximum speed for the next several minutes and then climbed slowly to get his bearings. He couldn't match the scene with his map and just continued west, slowly gaining altitude. After several more minutes Jack pointed to the wire fuel gauge.

"Hey buddy, it's bouncing off the bottom!" Jack shouted.

"Yeah, I see that. I'm trying to get as high as I can so we can spot something," Paul replied, noting the rough terrain below him. As they cleared another ridge, a deep valley appeared below with a large town in the center of it. Jack pointed toward it.

"Yeah, that's where I'm heading," Paul responded. Several minutes later they approached the valley center. They were now about two thousand feet above the ground as Paul looked for a landing spot.

"Hey, how much gas do you think is left?" Jack shouted.

He was promptly answered as the Cub's engine sputtered and then quit.

"Does that answer your question?" Paul said in the suddenly silent cockpit as he lowered the nose to the right glide angle for an engine failure.

"Now what?" Jack said in what Paul thought was a very calm voice.

Just then, as Paul turned left and then right to search for a landing site, he noticed it—a grass runway with several olive drab airplanes parked there. He headed for the airstrip, pointing out the runway to Jack.

"We're heading for that airfield."

Paul quickly assessed that he would make it and even be a little high. He set up an engine-out approach, turned twice to line up with the runway, and at the last moment put the Cub into a forward slip to spill off their excess altitude. He leveled out just above the grass runway, pulling the stick back in his gut as the Cub bled off speed and made a smooth touchdown about one-third of the way down the runway. It rolled to a stop in front of several US Army L-5 liaison aircraft.

They had been in the air forty-five minutes. The sign on the small shack behind the parked planes said "Bayreuth." Soldiers were running to the plane.

"Say, isn't this where the Wagner operas are played?" Jack said rather casually.

"Yeah, I think we might have found our own Valhalla."

16

Munich, Germany,
August 1948

* * *

Paul Hoffman gripped the letter tightly, closing his eyes to suppress the tears forming as he read the unsent letter from his deceased brother, Ernst. His brother had written the letter the evening before he was killed in his German jet fighter in April 1945, only a month before the war ended, and the letter was consequently not posted.

After a long moment, Paul opened his eyes and sighed deeply. He looked down again at his brother's last words to him: *"Although I do not know how this will end as I perform my final missions, I will always treasure the time we spent together with our shared passion for flying and the joys we had growing up."* Paul put the letter down and closed his eyes again as he relived the times that Ernst referred to.

He finally opened his eyes and looked at his packed bag in his hotel room and then his watch. Jack should be arriving any minute he thought, as he quickly recalled the events of the last few days.

After their harrowing flight and escape from Czechoslovakia, he and Jack quickly connected with American military authorities, who had orders to provide them all cooperation. They were taken to Munich, and today Paul was waiting for Jack to complete his last meeting. Paul was curious as to their next stop and hoped it would be to other locations in Germany where he might find more information regarding the whereabouts of his missing brother, Hans.

That thought caused Paul to pick up Ernst's letter and reread the other passage that had troubled him: *"Hans said he would try to write you, but he and Uncle Walter are involved in an important mission that they are planning. It is consuming all their energy. I can't say any more about it, and it is so crucial to Germany's future that I should not even say this much. However, to avoid the censors I will give this letter to a friend who is going to Switzerland in three days. She will post it there. By the time you receive it, I'm guessing the war will be over."* Paul put the letter back on the desk as he thought about its meaning.

When they had arrived in Munich, Paul set out to locate Ernst's *Luftwaffe* commander, and he found him there in Munich, where he and Ernst had last served. The officer provided Paul with the unsent letter as well as Ernst's personal effects. He was unstinting in his praise. He told Paul that Ernst had served heroically under his command, noting that it had followed a period when Ernst was on a special assignment flying a transport aircraft for his uncle, allowing him to be with Hans also.

Paul thought about these new pieces in the puzzle. *So Hans was working with their uncle, and for a time it appears that Ernst was also. What could the mission have involved? Was it related to the Operation Valhalla that Karl Frenzel spoke about in their meeting in Karlovy Vary? Were Hans and Walter Hoffman associated with the rumor of the U-boat mission that Frenzel had mentioned?*

Paul's consideration of these questions was interrupted as the door to the hotel room opened. Jack Kurtz entered and excitedly summed up what had transpired in his recent meetings.

"Well, the shit has hit the fan for sure. The Czechs have quietly hushed up any publicity regarding our aerial feat and are saying in their controlled press that the airplane had been stolen by 'criminal elements' rather than American spies. They didn't want to acknowledge that the other side could have gotten away with this. We offered to return the plane but the Czechs said that although it was state property it was a 'bourgeois tool' and they had no need for it. They obviously want to hush this up for some reason."

"Does their desire to hush it up have anything to do with Operation Valhalla?"

"I'm not sure, but we're going to Copenhagen next to follow up on that."

"Why are we going to Denmark?" Paul asked, disappointed that they wouldn't be staying in Germany, aborting his plan to look for clues about Hans.

"Bill Donovan wants us to meet Colonel Lunding, a Danish army intelligence officer, who was in the cell next to Admiral Canaris in the Flossenburg concentration camp. Canaris was the head of the German *Abwehr* and played both sides during the war. It caught up with him, and he was executed by the Nazis there on April 9, 1945. Donovan is still curious about his opposite number's last days."

"That's all we're going there for, just to talk about Canaris?"

"Actually it's a lot more than that. When Lunding heard that we were interested in U-boats, he mentioned he also had some information on a Type 21 boat that departed Denmark in early April 1945 on a special mission."

"That might allow us to confirm what Frenzel told us in Czechoslovakia," Paul replied, realizing that this might provide important information about Hans.

"You got that right. So let's get going. We're expected at the airport in two hours. A C-45 will fly us to Copenhagen."

17

The Citadel, Danish Army HQ, Copenhagen, Denmark.
September 1948

* * *

Jack Kurtz shifted the conversation after the initial discussion regarding Admiral Canaris was over. "So, Colonel Lunding, you told us you had some information regarding a Type 21 U-Boat operating out of Denmark in April 1945."

"Yes. It had been operating out of a cove on the west coast of Jutland in early April. Its presence was spotted by a Resistance unit when it entered the cove, and they began monitoring its activity."

"When did it finally depart the cove?"

"It was very early the morning of April 6. The team had observed the Germans loading boxes, canisters, and other cargo on the boat before it departed."

"How did you know it was a Type 21 submarine? Can you describe it?" Paul interjected.

"I can do better than that; the team took photographs in the early morning twilight just as it was leaving its mooring to depart. Please excuse me. I'll call my aide, and he can bring them to us." Lunding turned to pick up his phone as Paul squirmed in his seat, wondering if the photographs would show any of the crew. It seemed like forever, but within two minutes Lunding's aide entered his office with a thick file, walked over to the Colonel's desk, and quickly displayed its contents.

"Gentlemen, this is Major Pederson. He was leading the team on the morning of the U-boat's departure. One of his men on the other side of the cove was spotted by the Germans and was shot and killed as he tried to evade. His sacrifice allowed them to move in closer to take these pictures," Lunding explained as he displayed the photos. Paul and Jack leaned over the side of his desk to view them.

"I'm sorry to hear about your comrade," Paul said simply. The two Danes and Jack solemnly nodded in agreement.

Paul turned to the photos and quickly focused on the close-up of the men on the small bridge of the U-boat, and Jack scanned the other photographs.

Jack, who completed an analysis of Type 21 U-boats as part of his last OSS assignment, quickly reached his conclusion. "Yep, that's definitely a Type 21 boat. The small, low bridge and the streamlined hull are markers. I wonder if it was modified internally so it could carry all that cargo."

"We were wondering that ourselves. What mission could it have been on?" Lunding replied.

As Lunding and Jack continued that conversation thread, Paul merely stared for several minutes at the two hazy silhouettes on the bridge of the U-boat, trying to positively distinguish their identity.

"Paul, do you recognize them? Are they your uncle and brother?"

Paul snapped out of his trance in response to Jack's persistent questions. "Ah, I'm not sure. I guess they're just too fuzzy to tell. No, I can't identify them from these photos," Paul replied, as he finally looked at Jack, who did not reply but merely nodded and quickly looked back at the other items in Lunding's file.

As Jack continued his conversation with the Danes, Paul stared out the window, realizing he had told Jack a little white lie. Despite the fuzzy photos, Paul recognized the unmistakable signs. It was the jaunty position of the captain's cap and stance of the tall officer and the round face and darker features of the shorter officer. It was Hans Hoffman and his uncle, *Vizeadmiral* Walter Hoffman.

18.

Dzerzhinsky Square, Moscow, USSR.
September 1948

* * *

Colonel Vladimir Morozov looked up from the personnel dossier he was studying, smashed his cigarette in the ashtray, turned in his swivel chair, and stared out the small window of his office in the Lubyanka Building. He shook his head as he thought of what a perfect match Agent Yuri Kozlov was for the new assignment Morozov would give him.

As a key officer in the first main directorate of the Ministry of State Security, the MGB, Morozov had responsibility for certain intelligence and counterintelligence operations outside the Soviet Union. Morozov, born in 1900, had been in intelligence almost from the beginning of his career. He fought in the Red Army from 1918 to 1920 during the civil war following the revolution. In 1920 he joined the Cheka, the secret police force, and had been in the service since then as it evolved through the GPU, OGPU, NKVD, NKGB, and finally to his current position.

Almost from the beginning, Morozov gravitated to foreign operations. Through the years he kept a low profile, surviving various purges by offering unquestioned loyalty to his superiors. Ironically, by eschewing internal politics and personal ambition, Morozov now had wide discretionary authority to run foreign operations. He thought about that for a second and then turned back to his desk and pushed the intercom speakerphone button.

A male voice answered immediately. "Yes, Comrade Morozov?"

"When Comrade Kozlov arrives, please bring in a complete tea service, Vasiliy."

"Yes, Comrade Morozov."

Morozov turned back to his desk, lit another cigarette, and looked down again at the thick file. He noted to himself the agent's full name was Yuri Sergeivich Kozlov Castillo, a rather unusual name for an MGB agent, or any Russian, for that matter.

Morozov went through the whole file again, noting the key facts. Yuri's father was Sergey Kozlov, born 1890 in Murmansk, educated at the Lomonosov Moscow University from 1908 to 1912, specializing in foreign languages, especially Spanish, Portuguese, French, and English. A hero during the Russian Revolution, he joined the Cheka in 1921, the year after Morozov, who remembered him as a rising star.

Kozlov was tagged for foreign operations in 1923, sent to Venezuela, and ordered to burrow deep into the society to obtain a cover, before slowly establishing a chain of espionage agents throughout Latin America. He succeeded in this, forming a successful import-export business in Caracas. In 1925 he married Marta Castillo, who came from a prominent family and was secretly an ardent Communist. Yuri was born in 1926, and growing up he was called Sergio, a Hispanic version of Sergey.

Having successfully established an espionage network, the elder Kozlov was ordered back to Moscow for intensive debriefing in mid-1939 by way of England, Sweden, and Estonia. Kozlov brought his family. The cover story was that the family was going abroad to set up a European subsidiary in England, Scandinavia, and Poland.

Arriving in Leningrad on September 1, 1939, Kozlov's fate became attached to the new European war. Their cover story was changed, and forged telegrams were sent back to Caracas, stating that they had made a brief business stop in Warsaw and were on the run, trapped by the hostilities. They then disappeared.

After the Nazis attacked the Soviet Union in 1941, the elder Kozlov was killed at Stalingrad in 1942 while heroically leading his unit after other senior officers had been killed. For this he was posthumously awarded Hero of the Soviet Union. In 1943 his wife, Marta, and daughter, Anna, died during the siege of Leningrad.

Morozov shook his head, moved by the family sacrifices so typical of Russians during the war. His amazement was only enhanced as he plowed back into the file and focused on the details of Yuri Kozlov. In 1943, the seventeen-year-old joined the Red Army, intent on avenging the deaths of his parents and sister. He quickly distinguished himself in battle, especially during the final battle for Berlin in April 1945. Promoted several times in the field, he was awarded Hero of the Soviet Union—twice.

In late 1945, Yuri was sent to the prestigious Moscow State Institute for International Relations. Like his father, Yuri had a flair for languages. Raised bilingual in Russian and Spanish, he spoke both without an accent. He was also fluent in Portuguese and English, acquired while traveling with his father to Brazil and New York during frequent business trips throughout the Americas. Most important, he was extremely intelligent, ruthless yet discreet, observant, and unquestionably loyal to the state.

Selected to join the recently reorganized MGB in 1947 upon completing his studies, he immediately demonstrated both his competence and his loyalty. Early in 1948, his file came to Morozov's attention.

Morozov closed the file, smashed the latest cigarette in the ashtray, and leaned back in his chair, thinking about Yuri's new assignment. He had briefly met Yuri the previous month. After that, another officer had provided Yuri with a preliminary background briefing on the upcoming assignment and requested that Yuri conduct some research before meeting Morozov again. Morozov smiled at that thought, realizing this would be the first test of Kozlov's insights and ability to grasp the mission.

At that moment the intercom buzzer rang. Morozov pushed the speakerphone.

"What is it, Vasiliy?"

"Comrade Kozlov is here."

"Excellent. Bring him in."

In a few seconds the door opened, and Yuri Kozlov entered, followed by Morozov's aide with the tea service. Kozlov walked up to Morozov's desk, came to attention, and greeted his superior officer and new boss.

"Good afternoon, Comrade Morozov. I'm reporting as ordered."

"Excellent, Comrade Kozlov. Please sit down and be comfortable." Morozov motioned to Kozlov and then turned to his aide as he finished laying out the tea service. "That will be all, Vasiliy."

His aide bowed stiffly without saying anything and then quickly exited the office.

Morozov observed his subordinate for a moment, noting he was tall and handsome with dark hair and a few Latin features but clearly Caucasian, with blood of both Russian and Castilian origin. He sat there alert and expressionless, looking utterly relaxed yet expectant.

"May I offer you some tea, Yuri? I hope you don't mind the informal since we will be working closely together."

"Thank you, Comrade Morozov. I'll have plain tea, please, and Yuri is fine, sir."

Good boy, Morozov thought as he poured the tea. Informality can only work one way in the MGB. He also remembered the observations in Yuri's file. He drank his tea straight, did not smoke, and drank alcohol only moderately, but he was fond of and very knowledgeable about wine.

Morozov finished pouring the tea, sat down, faced his new employee, and got down to business. "So, Yuri, how would you summarize the key elements of this assignment?"

Morozov noted as Yuri carefully sipped the tea, obviously collecting his thoughts before replying. *Yuri is aware that this is a test*, Morozov thought.

"Comrade Morozov, this assignment will be challenging, but I understand the key elements, and I have a plan. First of all, my cover story is solid. When I arrive in Caracas, my associates and family will learn that my parents and sister were killed when the Germans bombed Warsaw. I survived but was dazed and somewhat amnesiac. A Polish family took me in, and I later ended up in a refugee camp for foreign neutrals after liberation. I was finally repatriated through Sweden, and my memory 'returned' this year. I will contact Caracas when I arrive in Stockholm to begin this assignment."

"Excellent. Please continue."

"Regarding my long-term assignment, it is clear that I need to reactivate and invigorate the network my father established in Latin America and expand it using his export-import business as a front. I also need to expand it to Spain and Portugal, since we have been deprived of good intelligence links in Iberia because of the fascist regimes there. I will use the trading leverage I will have as a Venezuelan with links to our domestic oil and agricultural sectors, since these commodities are in short supply in Iberia, and especially in Spain."

"That's an excellent analysis. What about the third element of your assignment?" Morozov prodded.

"I am to place special emphasis on discovering the origin, importance, and current status of the wartime Nazi scheme known as Operation Valhalla. In that regard, I am to find a way through my business front to engage the Hoffman and Ortega families in Spain, Africa, and New York.

Fortunately, my research in the last week has uncovered some new intelligence information about Valhalla, plus what we have learned from recent events in Czechoslovakia."

"Go on, please."

Morozov was now sitting on the edge of his chair, leaning toward Yuri.

"First of all, the Czech StB managed to extract some key information from both Alfred Koecher and Karl Frenzel before they expired."

"Yes, it is clear that our newfound Czech comrades need some tutoring in the art of interrogation, rather than the crude torture that they used on those two," Morozov replied, noting the casual way that Yuri referred to the two men as "expired."

"In any case, Frenzel was especially forthcoming about the details of Operation Valhalla, claiming he told us far more than he shared with the two Americans last month. It is clear that the Nazis took great pains to gather all of their nuclear and biological warfare programs' information for safekeeping somewhere outside Germany."

"Yes, but how did that take place, who accomplished it, and most important, where did they take that priceless information?" Morozov replied.

"This is where my research in the last week has provided some answers. Based on Frenzel's confession, I examined our records regarding the German U-boat construction facilities in Danzig. Despite the German efforts to erase all information, their penchant for record keeping, our wartime spies there, and interrogation of shipyard workers yielded a treasure of information."

"Please continue, Yuri."

"It turns out that an extra Type 21 U-boat, U-3696, was built for a special mission and outfitted to carry cargo by reducing the size of its fuel tanks. The mission was under the joint supervision of the SS and Admiral Walter Hoffman, a key official in German navy intelligence. The sub was commanded by his nephew Hans Hoffman. In late March or early April 1945 it sailed for Denmark, where it was to receive the special cargo of Operation Valhalla. We don't know the exact date it sailed from Denmark or where it was sailing to, but one of our operatives in the Danish Resistance told us that he ultimately reported to a Colonel Lunding. Lunding's team of partisans and operatives monitored the operations of the U-boat while it was in Denmark."

"So what are the other connections here among these players?" Morozov inquired.

"Our agent in Czechoslovakia, Pavel Frolik, informed us that two Americans, Paul Hoffman and Jack Kurtz, met with him by arrangement of former SS operative Reinhard Gehlen, who now works for the CIA. According to Frolik they appeared to be too curious about activities, sights, and events near the border with Germany and—"

"Do you think they know about the nuclear event?" Morozov interrupted.

"It would appear so. However, they clearly don't know the full extent of it. For example, when the Czechs interrogated Frenzel, he claimed that he did not reveal to the two Americans the extent of his technical knowledge of Valhalla secrets. The Americans may now know that the Nazis had a working reactor, but Frenzel said that the Germans made even more theoretical progress on advanced nuclear weapons designs, including concepts such as— forgive me, but this is a little outside my expertise—but I believe he referred to 'thermonuclear' and 'enhanced radiation' weapons. He claimed all of this information was contained in the Valhalla package as well as breathtaking advances in biological warfare and associated pathogens."

"Yes, I see. Well, the Americans will get a surprise in the atomic-weapons arena sooner than they imagined. Between our own penetration of their weapons program and what we learned from the German reactor, we are now very close to our own weapon. Clearly, however, we must accelerate efforts to clean up the reactor site in Germany. Fortunately, the German effort to sabotage the reactor as they retreated was thwarted by one of the technicians whom the SS had left for dead. He was able to reinsert the control rods to arrest the uncontained reaction. But tell me more about what you learned about their research involving the biological pathogens."

"Well, the Nazis may have discovered the perfect weapon of mass destruction. The pathogen has a very brief incubation period, and then it is rapidly contagious and fatal to virtually every subject who has been exposed and not vaccinated. It then becomes nonlethal and harmless. In the form of spores it can be spread easily by saboteurs who are vaccinated and immune. The pathogen was discovered and synthesized, and a vaccine developed with difficulty. It would take an enemy months or even years to discover its composition and prepare a vaccine. Of course, unless we can gain access to the Valhalla documents, we will be unable to replicate this pathogen either."

Morozov thought about that for a moment. "Yuri, please sum up for me the human side of this little mystery."

"Well, we have two key figures from the Nazi regime, Walter and Hans Hoffman, departing from Denmark in 1945 with the Valhalla cargo, destination unknown. We also have two American operatives, Paul Hoffman and Jack Kurtz, presumably sponsored by the CIA, extracting information from Koecher and Frenzel and then making a daring escape to Germany in a small aircraft. Paul and Hans Hoffman are brothers, so there must have been some family connections at work. Frolik was able to access information from another Gehlen operative in Germany, revealing that Hoffman and Kurtz then traveled to Copenhagen. I was able to find out from a source we have there that they met with Danish Colonel Lunding. We may therefore presume that they know almost as much as we do about Operation Valhalla, but they probably don't know the exact contents of that cargo—or where the U-boat transported it. The two Hoffmans on the U-boat, Paul Hoffman, Jack Kurtz, their CIA masters, and some former SS and other escaped Nazis may know about Valhalla. There may be other accomplices. Along these lines, I have several more facts from my investigation that will help me."

"Please continue, Yuri." Morozov leaned forward in his chair again.

"Through our interrogation of agents and others in the Danzig shipyard and my analysis of captured personnel documents provided from another Gehlen operative in Germany, there are two other key players. They were SS officers attached to assist Admiral Hoffman with Valhalla. Gerhard Hoepner was sent to the German embassy in Madrid and then to their consulate in Santa Isabel, Spanish Guinea. He arrived in December 1944 and disappeared on the mainland in Rio Muni in late May or early June 1945. Claus Hilgeman was sent to the embassy in Lisbon and was then detached to the consulate in Luanda, Angola. We may assume that there is a connection to Valhalla in one or both of these places in Africa."

"Yuri, your investigation and analysis are excellent. These will be strong leads as you begin your work. I caution you, however, to proceed slowly and deliberately to avoid suspicion. Your success depends on obtaining the confidence of your subjects—especially the Hoffman and Ortega families.

Henceforth you will assume the name Sergio Castillo. We do not expect instant or near-term results. Your father was hugely successful in establishing our network in the Americas, because he did it over a sixteen-year period. I know you'll be equally patient."

"Of course, Comrade Morozov. I will proceed deliberately to accomplish my mission. I'm hoping that the international situation and America's changing posture will not establish any roadblocks in this regard."

"Yes, I understand your concern, Yuri. However, if you're referring to the current Berlin crisis, it's merely an opening gambit in what is likely to be a long chess match with America. Comrade Stalin is merely testing the waters to establish America's resolve. It would appear that they are resolved to stay in Berlin, judging from their airlift."

"I see. And what of the B-29 bombers they have sent to England?"

"We don't know if they came with atomic bombs or not. We will not allow the crisis to deteriorate to the point where we would find out. There will be other fronts in which we or our surrogates will be able to advance." Morozov then picked up a file from his desk, opened it, and continued. "We will only be able to contact you sporadically and indirectly, Yuri. I want to make you aware of three agents who can assist you. Two are in New York, and one is in Europe. They were retasked several months ago to support you with actions that should be useful to your assignment, which are specified in this file. In order to protect their identity and your cover, we have arranged for their roles and actions to take place gradually and autonomously, so that you will not need to contact them or control their activities for the time being. Please take this file and memorize it. Return it to me before you leave. I will leave it to your discretion as to when and how you will interface with and then control them. For the sake of simplicity we have designated them Agents X and Y, and the one in Europe is Z. Be especially cautious in activating Agent Z. You will realize that you already know this agent when you read the file. This individual is well placed by good fortune, and there are no others in this location."

Morozov handed the file to Yuri.

"Yes, Comrade Morozov," Yuri replied simply as he took the file.

Morozov paused and continued as he looked straight at Yuri. "There is one last element of your assignment. Pavel Frolik now knows too much about this operation, and his connection to the Gehlen organization is risky. I want you to go to Prague before Stockholm and, how shall I say it, obtain a 'final' debriefing from him to ensure that he will never contact Gehlen anymore. Need I explain further?"

"No, Comrade Morozov. I understand fully what must be done, and I will attend to it personally. You may have confidence in me."

"Yes, Yuri, I have full confidence in you, and I know your mission will be successful—all elements of it."

Morozov smiled and sensed that his new agent would do whatever needed to be done—and be as ruthless as necessary.

19

Grenada. Spain.
September 1948

* * *

"Gehlen, you need to determine the extent of this compromise before we face Mueller in a few months. This situation could be catastrophic for us."

Before reacting to Franz Liesau Zacharias's statement, Reinhard Gehlen contemplated the latest turn of events and considered the impact on Operation Valhalla. They were standing in a remote corner of the Alhambra, the ancient Moorish fortress in Grenada. The two men had agreed to meet there, because they were anxious to avoid repeated meetings in Madrid and other places where they might be noticed.

Gehlen looked up at the architecture of the alcázar, or fort, the oldest part of the Alhambra. Its classic Moorish architecture amazed him, even from this remote corner of the fortress just inside its arch entrance. They were the only persons there.

"Did you hear me, Gehlen?" Liesau persisted.

"Yes, Franz, I heard you. You must forgive me, but I find this place fascinating. It's the boundary between two famous cultures. European culture prevailed here more than four hundred years ago, preventing Muslim dominance in Southern Europe. Perhaps we need to take the long view of our project and what it means to us."

"What do you mean?" Liesau responded, obviously perplexed.

"What I mean is that Valhalla is still safe from those who know of its existence. There are only a handful of Germans and one Spaniard who know the exact location where the Valhalla cargo is stored, and only a few of us who know about its exact contents. The fact that the Russians and the Americans now know that such a cargo was accumulated and transported out of Germany is irrelevant, unless they can find where it was shipped. They cannot determine that unless they know who to ask and where to find them. Both Walter and Hans Hoffman have disappeared, and nobody but our little organization is aware that Karl Hoffman is also privy to that information."

"Yes, I see, but Mueller will still want to know how *we* will become privy to that information."

"That's true. Herr Mueller will want to know that, and we will eventually need to find out. That means we must find Walter or Hans Hoffman, or otherwise obtain the information from Karl Hoffman."

"What about his son Paul and his accomplice, Jack Kurtz?" Liesau asked.

"I do not believe they know that the Valhalla cargo is stored in some secret location in Spanish Guinea. Otherwise they would have retrieved it by now, and we would know about their discovery."

"So if we cannot find Walter or Hans Hoffman, how can we pry the information out of Karl Hoffman?"

"Franz, I do not believe it is possible to 'pry' the information from him, since he is well protected and remote in Guinea, and we have already determined that our initial presence was detected there. They will recognize you and me as outsiders. No, I believe we must heighten our level of surveillance of his son Paul Hoffman, since I believe that he and possibly Jack Kurtz will persist in their search for Valhalla, because the young Hoffman is likely intent on finding his older brother."

"We could try to confront him," Liesau replied.

"Really, Franz, what would that accomplish? He has proven as resilient and wary as his father, and we would be prematurely revealing ourselves. But don't worry, there may come a time and a place for direct action. Meanwhile, we can heighten our surveillance of the younger Hoffman and his friend, Kurtz. My guess is they will be returning to Spain frequently as a result of an increased need for Spanish cooperation with the Americans. They will be easier to observe in Spain because we have a large network here."

"We are due to visit Mueller in Paraguay in January."

"Yes, I know, so we should put our surveillance plan in place so we will have some new information for Mueller."

20

Alabos, Rioja, Spain.
October 1948

* * *

Paul took in the sweeping view around him as the Hoffman and Ortega families, today joined by Jack Kurtz, had their first full reunion since 1939. The large group was sitting on the west patio of the Ortega hacienda on a beautiful, warm autumn afternoon. The patio commanded views of the Ebro River valley to the south and the Sierra de Cantabria Mountains to the north. The patio and veranda wrapped around the south and west sides of the hacienda, and just inside was a large living area and adjacent dining room, where the family spent most of their time and where they entertained. The hacienda was at the top of a hill about a kilometer east of Alabos and just west of the village of Samaniego.

Jack, and Paul's cousin Alberto Ortega, a Spanish naval officer, watched as many of the clan posed for a photograph capturing four generations of the three families. Seated in the middle was seventy-eight-year-old matriarch Maria Ortega, with her son Ernesto Ortega, his wife, Anna, and son-in-law, Karl Hoffman, standing at her side representing the next generation. Seated were her grandchildren, Alfonso and Anita, who were Ernesto's children and Alberto's siblings, as well as their spouses, Francisca and Enrique. Also seated in front of Karl were Paul and his wife, Liz Kurtz. Kirsten Hoffman, whose father, Walter, had disappeared at the end of the war stood next to Liz. Finally, Maria's great grandchildren, the fourth generation, were represented by infants Robert and Pilar Hoffman as well as Anita's newborn daughter, Beatriz.

After the photograph, Karl and Ernesto, as the reigning patriarchs, excused themselves to attend to some business. Paul sensed this was the moment to grab Jack and Alberto for a very important meeting. He excused himself from the photo group and walked over to the two men on the other side of the patio.

"Alberto, would you join Jack and me for a while in the study? There's something we want to discuss."

"Of course. We have time before dinner," Alberto answered. He and Jack rose, and Alberto led the three men to the private study.

The thirty-three-year-old Alberto was shorter than either Jack or Paul and was prematurely beginning to bald, but he was stocky and fit. He had just been relieved as the executive officer on the destroyer *Jose Luis Diez* and was about to assume a special assignment with his old protégé, Luis Carrero Blanco, Francisco Franco's chief aide.

Paul and Jack were counting on this relationship.

As the three men entered the study, Alberto opened the small refrigerator and brought out a bottle of amontillado from the Ortega bodega in Jerez in the south of Spain. He opened it and poured them each a glass.

"I only started chilling it twenty minutes ago, so it should be just the right temperature. Paul and Jack, here's a toast to our families. *Salud!*"

As the three men raised their glasses, Paul decided to begin slowly. Since Jack's Spanish was better than Alberto's English, he began in the former tongue.

"So, Alberto, will you miss sea duty, or are you looking forward to your new assignment?"

"The answer is yes to both questions. I will miss the *Diez.* Ironically, I was the gunnery officer on the *Canarias* during the civil war, and we severely damaged the *Diez* when it served on the Republican side. I now feel an obligation to the ship and its crew. However, Captain Carrero and I have a long-time relationship, and I'm looking forward to my new assignment."

"I'm sure it will be an important step in your career. Your new superior obviously trusts you," Jack said in his fluent and finest but slightly accented *castillano.*

"Yes, I'm flattered that he seeks my advice and sources of information on a wide range of issues."

Paul saw his chance. "Alberto, Jack and I believe that your influence with Captain Carrero can be very important to both Spain and America at this moment."

Alberto looked at Paul, then at Jack, smiled, and poured them all another glass.

"So, I see you two may be up to your old pastime again. I remember a similar discussion we had in 1945 about the activities you were both involved in then," Alberto replied, gently ribbing the seriousness of Paul's tone.

"In a sense, I suppose we are. It's a little different now, however. Jack's law firm, Sullivan and Cromwell, represents our interests in America, so Jack is now a trusted family confidant as well as my friend and past partner in wartime...activities. But now I'm raising a broader issue that extends way beyond our three families and the priorities of that conflict."

"Go on, I'm listening."

"America is now locked in the beginning of a struggle with the Soviet Union, as you can see from the events in Berlin. America will need allies in this struggle and, more specifically, forward bases for its SAC bombers. It may be a good time for Spain and America to look beyond past events and search for common ground. Our countries have common interests in this emerging struggle. Not only that, but Spain desperately needs economic assistance so we can finally recover from the civil war."

"I certainly agree with all that. I would remind you both, however, that it was America that withdrew its ambassador in 1945, has not reappointed one, and has refused to include us in the Marshall Plan."

Paul knew that Alberto was correct and decided to get right to the point. "Alberto, that's all changed now that a so-called Cold War has emerged between America and the Soviets. America needs forward bomber bases, and Spain is an ideal location for them. In exchange, America would provide economic and military aid and give us credibility again with the rest of Europe. We and America would then be joined in the common struggle."

Alberto smiled, looked at Jack, and turned back to Paul.

"The way you referred to Spain as 'us' and 'we' gives me comfort, my cousin. It shows you still consider yourself a Spaniard first, despite having lived in America for thirteen years. So how do you propose we initiate this alliance?"

"You could raise the issue with Captain Carrero and enlist his support. It would be up to him to convince Franco."

"Carrero has already had informal conversations with the Americans. In February he met secretly with their chief of naval operations, Admiral Forrest Sherman, and emphasized Spain's strategic location."

"If you could make this work, Alberto, some kind of signal from Spain might be in order," Jack added.

"What might that be?"

"Perhaps Spain could offer to turn over a few Nazis who escaped here at the end of the war and maybe some of the Nazi gold and loot that found its way here. This could be a trigger that would allow America to reappoint an ambassador, and then both sides could get to the real issues."

Alberto paused before replying, obviously mulling over how to make it work, Paul thought. "This could be a way to start this process as you suggest. Franco is sensitive on the issue of repatriation of alleged war criminals, but there are a few rotten eggs we could offer up. We need to know that this effort is a serious American proposal. I trust you both, but Captain Carrero is a cautious man and may need to be convinced. Paul, would you be willing to meet with him to explain this plan? Perhaps this would not include Jack, so we don't overwhelm him."

"I can do that, Alberto. I could meet him in Madrid before returning to the States," Paul eagerly replied.

"Don't worry about me. I understand this should be Spaniards only," Jack said.

"All right, I will set up a meeting in Madrid. Let's drink to the success of this effort." Alberto refilled all three glasses.

* * *

Later, Paul returned to the study, hoping to find another glass of sherry. His father had already beaten him to it and was sitting at the main desk reviewing some documents.

"Oh, I'm sorry to interrupt, Father. I came for the last of the amontillado."

"That's all right, my son, come on in. I was just finishing a review of a few things. There's still enough in that bottle for a glass each."

Karl got up to retrieve the bottle and emptied it into two glasses.

"*Salud.* It's been a fine reunion for the family." The two men raised their glasses.

"It certainly has. I'm glad we had some time to be together, Father," Paul said as he hoisted his glass. He was happy that he had been able to spend a full day with his father the previous week, before Liz and the other family members arrived. It was a joyful reunion, but some things had been left unsaid, and hanging over the two men and unknown to Karl was what Paul had learned in Czechoslovakia, Germany, and Denmark. Paul struggled with that as he looked for some small talk.

"It's really amazing how well Anita speaks English. I couldn't believe it when I first arrived."

"Yes, she's been working intensively with a tutor for the last year. She correctly says it's the international language of business and will be important to our future efforts to market wine in America. I believe Anita wants to travel there in the near future."

"Yes, so I understand." Paul paused. "Have you enjoyed being around Liz, Robert, and Pilar?"

"Oh yes! It has been such a joy for me to see them. Especially little Pilar, she reminds me of..." Karl could not finish the sentence, stung by the memory of his granddaughter's namesake, his deceased wife, Pilar Ortega, killed on the first day of World War II when the liner *Athenia* was torpedoed.

Paul was stunned by the thought also. It just connected with his innermost thoughts and finally caused him to blurt out the question he most wanted answered.

"Father, do you know where Hans is?"

Karl was clearly caught off guard by the question. He looked up at his youngest son with an anguished look.

"No, I don't know. I wish I did, but..." Karl answered truthfully but hesitantly, clearly aghast at the sudden reopening of an old wound.

"Have you at least seen him or heard from him since the war ended?" Paul quickly retorted, interrupting both his father's answer and his thoughts.

"Paul, I'm ... sorry. This is just so...so...."

Paul walked over to his father and put his hand gently on his shoulder to comfort him, realizing from his father's shock what must be going on.

"I'm sorry, Father; I didn't mean to reopen painful episodes." Paul also realized that he could not add to the grief by showing Ernst's last letter to his father. But he also realized that his father's emotional reply might be hiding some other truth. He decided to forgo pursuing that line of questioning and quickly moved to a new subject.

"On another matter, do you remember my suggestion about acquiring a Twin Beech to replace the Spartan?" Paul asked, hoping his father would take the bait.

"Yes, I've thought about it, and I agree with you. It will carry more cargo and passengers and has better range. Plus it has the safety of an extra engine for my missions over the ocean and the jungle."

"Fine, then my plan next year is to order two Twin Beech aircraft for our operations in America and Guinea. I may also order a Bonanza for travel in Spain."

The two men then excitedly talked about aviation matters. Paul realized that he would need to come back to the issue about Hans with his father—in the future.

21

Madrid, Spain.
October 1948

* * *

"Captain Carrero, I firmly believe that we need American aid to help restore our economy, rebuild our military, and provide credibility with the rest of Europe. We would also be taking a stand against Soviet Communism. I was asked informally by my American contacts to serve as an intermediary for this message, but I can assure you that my sympathies are with Spain's needs and our future."

As Paul finished his summary, he looked first to Alberto, sitting at the side of Luis Carrero's desk facing Paul and nodding in agreement, and then back at Carrero. As Paul studied the man, he realized that Carrero was also studying him, as the naval officer arched his bushy eyebrows and looked straight at Paul.

"Señor Hoffman, I agree with your rationale, and I understand your role as a messenger and trust you as a loyal Spaniard."

Paul breathed a sigh of relief as Carrero continued.

"Our only issue will be selling the idea within the government. Besides their proposed signal regarding handing over alleged Nazi war criminals, which is a sensitive issue with us, I will need to not only sway *El Caudillo* but also foreign minister Martin-Artajo. On the other hand, the rest of our military should be in agreement. Our military equipment is obsolete, and America might be our only avenue for modernization."

"Captain Carrero, I am willing to continue as an intermediary in this process for as long as it takes," Paul replied.

"I accept your offer, Señor Hoffman. You have already been of great service to Spain in this regard." Carrero paused before continuing. "I visited Guinea in February. The African colonies are under my direct responsibility. While in Guinea, I met your father. I was very impressed with what he has accomplished and with his attitude regarding economic development."

"Thank you, Captain, I'm sure he would be pleased to hear that," Paul replied.

"Yes, that is very commendable, and your father is also an advocate for improving the lives of the African population. Insofar as that improves health, education, transportation, and other productivity measures, I am in agreement. We cannot, however, tolerate any advocacy of political change or nonsense such as potential independence. While I was there with the Director General of African Colonies, we and the governor were presented with petitions from some native tribes denouncing the so-called excesses of colonialism. I'm afraid that this inappropriate behavior may have been inadvertently encouraged by both the governor and your father, who is clearly the leader of the planter community. I hope you understand that I am not criticizing your father but merely trying to provide…feedback on the government's position. I hope you will take my comments in this vein, Señor Hoffman."

Stunned by Carrero's comments, Paul quickly recovered. "Thank you for the feedback, Captain. I understand your concerns, and I'm sure my father will also. Both of us share the same beliefs about Spain's future needs, and I can assure you that we are both motivated solely by those issues."

"I knew you would be cooperative, Señor Hoffman, and thank you for coming today. I wish you a safe journey back to New York. Commander Ortega will be my conduit to you for future contact as we begin this rapprochement with the Americans."

Realizing that the meeting was over, Paul stood, nodded, and quickly exited Carrero's office.

* * *

"So, Alberto, do you think I was too harsh with your idealistic cousin?" Carrero sat back in his chair as he crossed his arms and looked over at his subordinate, moments after Paul Hoffman exited his office.

"No, Captain, I believe he was pleased with your frankness and happy that you accepted his advice regarding the Americans," Alberto replied, somewhat stunned himself by the blunt tone of Carrero's remarks.

"Well, I believe that this plan with the Americans will turn out well. I'm more concerned about developments in Guinea. There is excessive turmoil now about decolonization in Africa and other places. We intend to put a stop to it in Guinea," Carrero replied, as he picked up a file from his desk, handed it to Alberto, and continued. "Do you know this officer?"

Alberto opened the file, leafed through it, and handed it back to his boss. "Yes, I served under him on the *Canarias* during the civil war," Alberto said with a surprised tone.

"He is to be the new governor in Guinea. We are recalling the current governor. The new governor's appointment will be effective in February 1949. Alberto, how would you summarize this officer in terms of how you think he will govern?"

"He was a stern taskmaster on the cruiser, yet he always let you know where you stood. I imagine he will be equally firm as governor in Guinea."

"That is precisely how we expect him to govern. His mandate will be to increase economic output, emphasize loyalty to *El Caudillo* and Spain, and stamp out any independence movement. I'm hoping that your uncle will adapt to all of this and work with the new governor. I get the idea that he is very much his own man, but we need him to continue his innovative economic practices. However, we will not tolerate any manner of disloyalty or non-compliance with our policies. I hope you understand my reasoning on this, Alberto."

"Of course I do, sir, and I believe that Karl Hoffman will understand these changes and comply with them," Alberto said, wondering whether or not that was actually true.

"I hope so, Alberto. That brings me to your status. With all of this activity with the Americans, turmoil in Guinea, and my own span of responsibilities, I will need you on my staff for an extended period. I know you wanted to continue your sea duty for a while longer, so I have a twist to your new orders."

"Yes, sir?" Alberto said expectantly.

"I'm returning you to the *Diez* as its temporary commanding officer, since your recent promotion to commander will permit this billet. This will be good for your record, but your sea duty will be temporary. I'm sending the ship to Spanish Guinea on a 'show the flag' cruise. Your real purpose there, however, is threefold. I want you to find out all you can on conditions there. Second, I want you to meet your uncle and ensure that his attitude on the political changes is positive. Finally, I need for you to question him about the status of the materials brought there under Operation Valhalla. You must be discreet, and hopefully Karl Hoffman will reveal the exact storage location of these materials. It would not do for someone else to locate them or remove them and thereby expose our wartime collaboration with the Nazis on such a sensitive matter, especially as we seek rapprochement with America. Along those lines, I'm concerned that the Americans might renew their interest in Valhalla at any time, so we need to ensure continued security regarding our involvement. Do you have any questions on these orders, Alberto?"

"No, sir, and I will do my best to execute them," Alberto replied, wondering how the visit would be received by his uncle. More important, he now began to wonder what Paul Hoffman already knew, or had recently learned, about Operation Valhalla.

22

New York City.
November 1948

* * *

Paul was expectant about his imminent meeting with Allen Dulles, William Donovan, and Jack. As he was ushered into the offices of Sullivan and Cromwell at 48 Wall Street and then into Dulles's suite, he realized it would be his first meeting with Dulles. Paul did not really know Donovan well either, even though he was a guest at Paul's wedding to Liz Kurtz.

As Paul entered the suite, Dulles extended a hearty welcome. "Well, here's the other half of the dynamic duo," Dulles exclaimed as he walked over to Paul, lit pipe in his left hand. The two men shook hands as Dulles continued walking over to the coffee table where Donovan and Jack Kurtz stood.

"I assume you know these two," Dulles said, as he relit his pipe.

"Yes, it's good to see you again, General Donovan."

The two shook hands, and Paul then turned to Jack.

"Nice offices, Jack, it sure beats our most recent accommodations."

The other three men laughed.

Dulles continued his hospitality. "Sit down, Paul, and make yourself comfortable. We have a lot to talk about. May I offer you a scotch? Oh, and please call me Allen. It took long enough to get your partner to concede a little informality."

"All right, Allen. I'll have it neat please, with a little water on the side."

"You're a connoisseur. We'll have to make a note of that," Donovan commented.

Dulles and his guests sat down, and Donovan started the conversation. "Paul, you and Jack did some outstanding work in Europe, your little airborne adventure notwithstanding. Since you are now equally privy with Jack on certain matters, I feel it's only fair to share with you some of the repercussions from your mission. But first I must have your assurance that you will keep these matters completely confidential. No one, and I mean no one—in or outside your circle—must be privy to this information. Do you understand this requirement?"

"Of course, General. Jack and I both know the score."

"All right, Allen will brief you now based on the latest update he obtained from...certain sources."

"Your mission in Czechoslovakia was incredibly important. Your observations and the data from your 'little device' confirmed our other data sources. It's clear that there was a nuclear reactor incident of some kind, and we are virtually certain it was operated by the Nazis during the last part of the war. That means that the Soviets scored a huge technological leap forward. Some of us now believe that a Russian A-bomb is imminent."

"What about the information we obtained from Koecher and Frenzel regarding Operation Valhalla?" Paul inquired.

"Their information was critical to verifying the importance of Valhalla regarding not only Nazi nuclear advances, but their advances in other areas."

Dulles paused, shaking his head before continuing.

"Unfortunately, that information came at a heavy price. The Czech StB picked up both Koecher and Frenzel. They took them to the *Domecek*, the StB prison in Prague, and tortured them. They are both dead, and we can't be sure how much they revealed."

"I was afraid of that. I was worried that our escape left them in the lurch," Paul said. He was shocked at the consequences of their intelligence gathering.

"Welcome to the world of espionage. Sometimes a heavy price is the cost of obtaining invaluable intelligence," Donovan replied.

"What about Frolik? Paul and I both thought that he seemed a little fishy. Could he have betrayed the other two?" Jack asked.

"I have to admit that's possible, yet we also just learned that Frolik too has disappeared. We don't know if he was scooped up by the StB or not. We now have a complete lack of new information. Czechoslovakia is closed up tighter than a drum and another addition to the Iron Curtain," Dulles responded.

"So based on what we also learned in Denmark, what is the next step in our search for the Operation Valhalla secrets?" Paul persisted. As he posed this question, he was unsure about what answer he was seeking—or wanted to hear.

"Other than confirming our previous knowledge and suspicions, we really don't know a lot more than before. It's clear that a Type 21 U-boat departed Denmark on April 6, 1945, for some unknown destination, and that it likely contained the Valhalla cargo. We've already covered all the likely places in South America and the Far East where it could have gone, and we haven't come up with anything."

"What about Africa?" Jack asked.

Paul flinched, stung by Jack's guess and secretly harboring his own thoughts. He quickly suppressed them, deciding he needed to pursue his suspicions later—on his own.

"For now we will forgo pursuing that question. There are more urgent issues for us to address," Donovan replied.

"That's right, Bill. We need to keep the momentum going with Spain. You two also pulled off a big coup in that regard. Luis Carrero Blanco responded to your challenge by turning over a few SS operatives, as well as some of the Nazis' loot. Now we need to respond, but Truman's surprise election victory is a problem. He hates Franco and may not reappoint an ambassador right away," Dulles said.

Paul thought about that briefly and decided to offer a bold solution. "Why don't we see if we can release some funds owed to Spain that are currently held up by exchange controls on capital? For example, our cocoa and coffee imports to America are paid for in dollars. In the past, the Franco government required us to convert some of that to pesetas, so they would have dollars available for critical imports. Lately that's been on hold because of currency controls on Spain. Freeing those funds would allow the new administration to signal a change without doing something more visible and controversial, such as appointing a new ambassador."

"Wouldn't that affect your interests adversely? I'm speaking now as your lawyer and adviser," Dulles responded.

"Not really. The dollars convert into an enormous amount of pesetas since the Spanish currency is so devalued. But our family can use them to buy up cheap land throughout Spain for future vineyard development, and also for acquiring choice oceanfront property in the south," Paul said.

"Then your plan may work. It could be done administratively at the Treasury, and it will stay out of the news. It should also be acceptable to Truman," Donovan interjected.

"There are several other things we can do," Paul said. "I recently had a meeting at the Chase National Bank with David Rockefeller, no less. I brazened my way into an audience and made the business case for more investment in Spain, providing we can get the right political climate in place. He agreed in principle to negotiating a commercial loan to Spain in the near future for targeted economic development. Beyond the banking community, we also need to reach the right politicians in Congress, who can lean on the Truman administration to come around on Spain."

Paul watched the amazed look on the faces of the other three men, all obviously impressed with Paul's analysis and initiative.

Finally Dulles responded, "That's a real display of taking charge, Paul. I know David real well and can put in a good word for you. I'll also follow up with my friends on the Council on Foreign Relations. I believe there are some friendly senators I can also talk to."

"I can also talk to my contacts in the Department of Defense. They can help us with making the military case for a rapprochement," Donovan added.

"All right, we now have a plan, but it's only the first quid pro quo in what's likely going to be a change that will take several years to complete. That means that Jack and Paul will need to keep in contact with Carrero and others in Spain. Actually, at this point, it's mostly Paul's show, since Jack needs to earn his keep at Sullivan and Cromwell." Dulles smiled at Jack.

"Yes, boss, I get the idea," Jack replied, forcing a smile.

23.

Asuncion, Paraguay.
January 1949

* * *

"I am outraged by your lack of progress in solving this mystery about the Valhalla operation!" Heinrich Mueller fumed as he stared at Reinhard Gehlen. He marched over to the picture window and stared out at the Paraguay River.

Gehlen and Franz Liesau continued sitting at the coffee table in stony silence, waiting for Mueller to finish his harangue.

"Furthermore, we can't afford to be patient much longer, now that the Americans may have renewed their interest in this enterprise. I'm also worried about potential compromises associated with the disappearance of your agent Frolik in Czechoslovakia. Perhaps the Russians are now aware of Valhalla," Mueller concluded, turning to face his two guests.

"I would remind you, Mueller, that even if both assertions are true, neither the Americans nor the Russians can possibly know where the Valhalla cargo is located. Only Walter, Hans, Karl, and possibly Paul Hoffman and Alberto Ortega know the precise location," Gehlen asserted.

"That's exactly my point, Gehlen! The traitorous Hoffman family seems to be impervious to your efforts to penetrate their conspiracy. So what are you planning to do to remedy this glaring lapse? Maybe we should take direct action against them at once."

"That would not be advisable, Mueller. As you may recall, in late 1944 and 1945 three of our agents met a violent end trying direct action against Karl Hoffman and his son Paul. Gerhard Hoepner is missing and presumed dead in Spanish Guinea, and our agents in Madrid and New York also met an untimely end trying 'direct action' against Paul Hoffman."

Mueller sighed, slumped slightly, walked back over to the coffee table, and sat down. He looked intently first at Gehlen, who maintained a neutral expression, and then at Franz Liesau, who looked uncomfortable, squirming in his seat.

Mueller scowled at him, turned back to Gehlen, and continued in a less agitated voice. "All right, I understand your point, but I won't approve of putting off more drastic action indefinitely if you are unable to find another solution. So what is your plan?"

"We plan to heighten surveillance of Paul Hoffman and his accomplice, Jack Kurtz. Now that we know they were engaged by the CIA to reopen the Valhalla case, we can expect them to continue their pursuit of leads. There is an irony here, in that I firmly believe that Paul Hoffman is not explicitly aware of his father's involvement in the operation. However, if his recent experience in Czechoslovakia and Denmark gave him new insights, he might now have some suspicions. We expect he might travel to Spanish Guinea to seek the truth and perhaps confront his father."

"So how will we be able to learn of such actions and ultimately the location of the Valhalla cargo?" Mueller replied.

"It is difficult for outsiders to penetrate Spanish Guinea. The colony is directly controlled by Franco's key aide, Luis Carrero. Carrero has recently brought his former subordinate, Alberto Ortega, Paul Hoffman's cousin, back on his staff. So in addition to our surveillance of Paul Hoffman in New York, we will find a way to increase surveillance of Alberto Ortega in Spain. We have a well-developed network of agents in Spain, as opposed to none in Spanish Guinea. Also, in a few months we are hoping that Skorzeny will be available to take over the Spanish operation," Gehlen said.

"I see. What about the situation with our friends in South Africa?" Mueller replied, turning to face Franz Leisau.

"I have recently been in contact with them, but they haven't turned up any leads on any suspicious ex-U-boat crew members who might have been on U-3696, including Walter or Hans Hoffman. I will check with them again in a few months."

"Very well. For now I accept the strategy that the two of you outlined. I will expect results sometime in the next year—or I will then insist on a more direct approach."

24

Ortega-Hoffman hacienda, Santa Isabel, Spanish Guinea,
January 1949

* * *

"Alberto, I'm really pleased to see you here in Guinea. I believe it's been more than sixteen years since you were last here. I hope you've noticed some positive changes."

Karl finished pouring the two glasses of manzanilla at the liquor cabinet next to the west-facing picture window in their hillside hacienda several kilometers southwest of town. He walked over to his nephew, handed him a glass, and looked expectantly at him.

"Yes, it was in 1933, just before I returned to Spain to enter the navy and begin officer training. I must say that it seems very prosperous here, and I'm proud of the role our family has had in shaping Guinea's destiny," Alberto replied.

Karl sat down across from Alberto, his curiosity piqued by Alberto's sudden appearance. He wasted no time in finding out why. "So what brings you here, Alberto, and in your own ship, no less? Congratulations and *salud!*" Karl and Alberto raised their glasses.

"Thank you, Uncle, it's my first real command of a major vessel, and I'm pleased I was able to make this voyage. I'm now working for Captain Carrero again, so my command will be temporary. I'll be working on his staff as soon as I return. Besides the obvious 'show the flag' aspect of my ship's arrival, there are several more specific reasons for my visit."

Karl realized that Alberto didn't sail thousands of kilometers just to "show the flag" or make a family visit, yet he decided to let Alberto steer the conversation.

"So perhaps you could enlighten me," Karl replied simply as he noticed Alberto squirming slightly in his seat.

"To get right to the first issue, I am here to notify the governor that he is to be relieved. A new governor has already been appointed. You are the only other person here who will receive this information, and I ask that you keep it in confidence."

Karl's initial shock quickly faded, as he realized that this action was inevitable, given the native demonstrations that had taken place during Carrero's visit early in the year. "That's unfortunate. The governor has been very effective and has worked closely with me and other planters to ensure prosperity here." Karl paused before asking the inevitable follow-on question. "Who is the new governor?"

"He is another naval officer. I served under him during the civil war, and he is a firm and decisive, yet fair individual."

Alberto then told Karl all the personal details, paused, and continued. "Karl, you need to adapt to this new development. Captain Carrero wanted me to express his satisfaction in your economic initiative and your continued leadership in this role, but he also wanted me to convey his insistence that you not interfere in the politics of the colony. He is especially insistent that you not encourage, and in fact discourage, any movement among the native population that calls for independence. This comes straight from Franco. Spain will firmly resist any move in this direction. It would be unwise for you to disobey or flout this guidance and direction."

Alberto paused to let that sink in, but Karl responded immediately.

"Can't they see what is happening in the world? Britain granted independence to India and Pakistan. The Dutch are about to lose the East Indies, and the French are in a shooting war with the insurgent Viet Minh in Indochina. If we are honest about this trend, we can prepare the locals for eventual independence, while ensuring the integrity of our economic interests in Guinea."

"Franco, Carrero, and others don't see it this way, Karl. They believe Africa is different, and it will be decades or longer before the locals can govern themselves. Meanwhile they are in favor of improving health, education, and especially infrastructure, such as roads and airports, since they will enhance economic productivity. Despite the tough economic situation in Spain, money will be available for these purposes. You should embrace this opportunity and agree to disassociate yourself from local agitators. I'm here as an early warning, and I hope you will receive these suggestions in the spirit in which they are intended."

Karl seethed as he processed Alberto's remarks, yet he realized that this development was inevitable. He would somehow deal with it. "I will follow your advice, Alberto. Are there other aspects of your mission?"

"Yes, I am also to become as familiar as possible with other issues here. Captain Carrero has many duties, so he will begin relying on me to assist him with African colonial issues in Guinea, Morocco, Ifni, and Sahara. I will be working directly with the Director General of African Colonies, and this will also work in your favor as we move forward to promote economic development in Guinea."

Alberto paused.

Karl sensed there was another issue to discuss. "Is there another matter you have for me, Alberto?"

Karl knew what that matter must be. He noticed Alberto squirming in his seat again.

"Yes, Captain Carrero wanted me to determine if the...special cargo from Operation Valhalla is still secure...and where it is physically stored."

"I thought that might be your other concern. To sum up, the cargo is safely stored and hidden. It was delivered in late May 1945 by my brother and my son, as you know. Afterward, they sailed away in their submarine and disappeared. I have not heard from them since then."

"Then they have not returned for the cargo? Has anyone else come to inspect it?" Alberto's tone expressed urgency.

"No. At the time the cargo was delivered, we had some difficulty with one of the SS officers, Gerhard Hoepner, who turned out to be working for the Gestapo and the worst SS elements. We were lucky to catch him in the act and...he is no longer with us. He would have been the only other outsider to know the location of the cargo. About two years ago, we also detected the presence of Franz Liesau here in Guinea. He also worked for the SS and had BPS contacts. He seemed to be snooping around, but I can assure you he knows nothing, and he quickly departed."

"I remember Hoepner, Karl. I helped him and another officer, Claus Hilgeman, to enter Spain in late 1944. They stayed at the family's hunting lodge in Andorra. Did you know Hilgeman?"

"No. Where is he now?" Karl replied.

"I don't know. He traveled out of Spain to Portugal, but he had some undefined role in Valhalla."

The two were briefly silent as each pondered the significance of that remark.

Karl finally summed up the situation. "I can assure you, Alberto, that the cargo is safely hidden."

"You must tell me where it is, Karl. If anything were to happen to you, it would be my responsibility to..." Alberto's voice trailed off as he implied the obvious concern.

Karl stared at his nephew for a long period, got up and walked back to liquor cabinet, returned with the bottle of sherry, and poured them each a refill. He then returned to his seat and finally answered. "Do you remember your last visit here, when Paul took you to the special place in Rio Muni where he and his brothers played as children?"

"Why, yes. I remember it was a cave near the hacienda on the Rio Muni plantation, a few hundred meters away, just off the airstrip and—" Alberto stopped in midsentence, quickly realizing the purpose of Karl's question. "Are you telling me that the materials are stored in that cave?"

"Yes, and they are quite safe there. I would be quite happy, however, if you decided to remove them entirely. They are an unpleasant reminder of my missing brother and son."

Karl watched as Alberto pondered that remark briefly before he answered.

"Does Paul know about Valhalla and our connection to it?"

"Not that I'm aware of. In fact, I don't want him to know, because then he too would be reminded of his brother's disappearance."

Karl thought about the small circle of those who were privy to Valhalla and quickly added another question. "What about the new governor? Does he know about Valhalla?"

"No, he does not, and we must ensure that he does not find out. The fewer people who know about it, the better it is for us. It would be catastrophic for Spain if our role in Valhalla was exposed, since we are trying to repair relations with America and the other European countries."

A long silence followed as the two men absorbed the impact of their exchange of information.

Karl finally decided it was time to conclude. "Alberto, it seems we have reached an agreement about this. I will continue to protect the Valhalla cargo until you direct otherwise. Meanwhile, I will try to implement your advice regarding the new governor, as hard as that may be for me."

Alberto simply nodded in agreement, as both men realized that they must continue dealing with both the legacy of Operation Valhalla and the current political environment.

25

New York City.
February 1949

***

Paul grabbed two beers from the front-room bar in the White Horse Tavern and headed for the back room. He was looking forward to his first Friday night outing with Jack since their November debriefing with William Donovan and Allen Dulles.

The front bar was busy on this cold winter evening as Paul walked back, admiring the tin ceilings and hardwood floors of this Greenwich Village dive. The back room was quieter as Paul traipsed along its black-and-white tile floor, back to the isolated table next to the steam radiator and the ladies' restroom.

"Here we are, partner; rounds one and two are on me. Now I want to hear about your first few months at Sullivan and Cromwell."

"Boy, where do I start? Well, I learned right away that all 'juniors' have to learn how to write a two-page letter justifying the acquisition of a new client. It's important because all of us, including partners, are expected to do the same."

"So what are the key criteria for justifying a new client?"

"It boils down to one thing Paul—money. Needless to say, I'm positively shocked by this craven requirement."

Both men laughed and hoisted their beer mugs.

"Man, I hope our firm passes your test."

"Not to worry, Paul. My best friend's interests and those of his business are covered."

"So you haven't told me whether it was worth going to law school and studying hard. Do you enjoy the work?"

An unusual silence followed, as Jack pondered that remark. Paul noticed his friend's enthusiasm drain as a response to the question.

"Actually, Paul, I have to tell you that the work is just...plain fucking boring. I had more fun getting into serious trouble with you in Czechoslovakia than anything I've done in the last three months. But the work sure is financially rewarding. For once, it's my own money and not my dad's. I guess I should be grateful for—" Jack stopped abruptly.

Paul sensed Jack's regret over his selfishness, his father having died the previous year. Paul immediately picked up the slack. "That's all right, Jack. He was real proud of you and would be even more so if he knew what you did in Europe."

Jack looked up at Paul and smiled, but he didn't answer directly.

Paul continued with what was on his mind. "I've thought a lot about our little escapade and the value of the information we obtained. I've tried to weigh it against what happened to Koecher and Frenzel, not to mention the entire population of Czechoslovakia. I think I'm coming up short."

"You can't let it grate on you, Paul. You and I have gotten a glimpse of the hard, ugly facts of the Cold War, and it's probably going to get worse."

That triggered another subject with Paul. He hesitated but blurted it out anyway as he leaned toward Jack. "I think I'm being followed a lot. I can't put my finger on it exactly, but I'm sensing that I'm under observation at various places."

Jack looked at Paul and took a swig from his beer before responding. "You, too, huh? I think it's more than a feeling. I *know* I'm being followed, and I want to find out who it is. I know it happened to us once before here, but I wrote it off as a fluke. Now I'm sure it isn't."

"Do you think it has to do with our experience in Europe?"

"Sure it could, or it could be. . ."

Jack didn't finish his sentence as Paul noticed him looking toward the front bar room. Paul turned and noticed three women sitting at an end table. One was staring at Jack and smiling. She was pretty with long raven hair, a tight, revealing sweater, a midlength skirt, and long boots. Jack returned her smile and turned back to Paul.

"I'll talk to Allen about it. He knows more about this cloak-and-dagger stuff."

"Well, if you find out anything, let me know. I want to make sure it's nothing important."

Paul was thinking more about his wife, Liz, and their two small children than about himself. As he mulled that over, he noticed Jack's attention was again diverted toward the bar. Paul turned just in time to see the raven-haired woman approach their table and then walk past it to enter the ladies' room. Paul couldn't resist a comment. "I knew something must be distracting you. Women are the one thing I can count on to revive my best friend."

As the two men laughed, they drained the last of their beers. Paul got up to get two more. When he returned to the table, Jack was in an animated conversation with the raven-haired woman. As Paul approached the table, the woman turned to engage him also.

"Your friend and I were just discussing whether he was sitting next to the ladies' room for a reason," she asserted in a soft, sultry voice.

"That's his *modus operandi* all right. Hi, I'm Paul, and I see you've already met Jack. Would you like to join us?"

"Thanks, but I think I better go back to my friends this time. My name is Sharon, by the way. I'll see you both again later, maybe."

She smiled politely at Paul and then turned and stared briefly but intently at Jack before returning to her table.

"Whew, she knows just how to hit the right buttons," Jack exclaimed.

Paul sat down, and he and Jack began laughing. Paul decided that Jack could use some maneuvering room.

"Hey, I think I mentioned before that I need to leave early. I've got some paperwork that I need to finish tonight so that one of our ships can clear the port tomorrow for Spanish Guinea. Liz then promised me a late dinner at home."

Jack smiled knowingly. "Thanks, buddy, I owe you one."

"Good luck," Paul responded simply. He then stood, walked to the front door, and left, smiling at Sharon on the way out.

26

Santa Isabel, Fernando Po,
Spanish Guinea,
March 1949

* * *

"So, Señor Hoffman, I will conclude by saying that I will work with you on economic development issues. However, I insist that political issues are strictly my province, and you should endeavor to avoid any encouragement of dissidence among the native population."

As the new governor finished his lengthy harangue, Karl carefully considered his response, grateful that Alberto Ortega's visit two months ago had provided him time to find a way to coexist with the new administration. It was clear that he would not be on a first-name basis with this governor, as he had been with the last three incumbents.

"Yes, Governor, I understand your position, and I will comply with your policies. Along those lines, I want to support your strategy for economic development, and I have an important issue to discuss."

"Yes, please go on," the governor responded eagerly.

"As you know, for several years Iberia Airlines has provided local air service between Bata on the mainland and Santa Isabel. Yet we have no scheduled air service to Spain. Instead, we must rely on circuitous connections on foreign airlines, and it still takes three to four days to reach Spain. The technology is now available to provide nonstop or one-stop, one-day air service. Such service may initially require a subsidy, but it will be justified by improved air transportation between Guinea and the mother country. With your permission I would like to travel to Madrid and meet with Iberia Airlines, the air ministry, and the Director General for African Colonies to advocate for such air service."

"That is an excellent idea. It would be important for a key planter and a person knowledgeable about aviation, such as yourself, to make such a case, and I will support you. This is a perfect example of the kind of cooperation

I am seeking with you, Señor Hoffman. Please proceed with your plan and keep me informed."

Karl noticed the first hint of a smile on the governor's face and was satisfied that he might have the beginning of a rapport with the man. His hopes were quickly dashed after a moment of silence.

"Is there anything else, Señor Hoffman?"

"No, I don't believe so."

"Then we are finished. Please keep me informed." The governor gave Karl a dismissive look.

Karl stood and, realizing the meeting was over, turned and walked out of the governor's office in the Palacio de Gobierno. Depressed, he exited the building, turned left onto Calle Sacramento, and then right on Calle de 19 de Septiembre. He walked quickly past the British consulate and the Gothic cathedral on his left and turned right to enter the Plaza España. He approached the statue of Angel Barrera, the governor from 1910 to 1924, and stood there a moment, fondly remembering that governor's stewardship. It was Barrera who had helped Karl and his comrades escape encirclement by the Allies in 1916, during World War I, in what was then German Kamerun. Barrera had allowed the Germans to be interned in neutral Spanish Guinea. As a result, Karl was able to marry Pilar Ortega and, with Pilar's father, Pedro, start their cocoa, coffee, and lumber empire in Spanish Guinea. Karl sighed as he thought of Pilar and realized the loss he still felt by her tragic death ten years prior.

Karl quickly erased that thought, turned around, and walked through the plaza. He turned left on Avenida de General Mola, and walked swiftly as the road turned right. He entered La Rosaleda bar and went to the outside patio facing the bay. It was nearly siesta time, but Karl ordered a manzanilla, and a few minutes later, another one. He reminded himself that he must swallow his pride and take whatever actions were necessary to reach an accommodation with the new governor. The Ortega and Hoffman families' future hung in the balance.

Not only that, but Karl needed to find a way to prepare for what he saw as the inevitable end of the traditional colonial era. He didn't know how that would unfold, but he did know that it would require a visionary approach that he must somehow implement in spite of the current governor and his policy.

27

Wichita, Kansas,
October 1949

* * *

"Please come in and sit down, Mr. Hoffman. I would also like to introduce Mrs. Beech."

Walter Beech, the founder of Beech Aircraft, and his wife, Olive Ann, rose and walked over to Paul, shook his hand, and motioned him to sit down. Paul noticed their conservative dress and manners. Walter was attired in a double-breasted suit, and his wife was in a stylish long dress, heels, and perfect hairdo. Paul really hadn't expected to meet them, but guessed that his six-figure order for three aircraft had something to do with it.

"We're pleased we could meet you, Mr. Hoffman. Has everything been satisfactory so far?" Mrs. Beech inquired.

"Yes, perfectly. I took delivery of the first Beech 18 this morning. The second is to be delivered in February, and the B35 Bonanza will come in late April. I'm eagerly anticipating their delivery."

"Where will you base the aircraft, Mr. Hoffman?" Mr. Beech asked.

"The first Beech 18 will be based at Teterboro, since our world headquarters is in Manhattan. The second will be based in Spanish Guinea in Africa, and the Bonanza will be based in Spain."

"I see. Are you sure we can't assist you with the export process?" Mrs. Beech asked. Paul noticed that she seemed to be more concerned with the details of the purchase than her husband.

"Thank you, but our business revolves around world trade, and we can handle those issues. For now, we intend to keep all three aircraft registered in the United States."

"Excellent. We will look forward to the second and third deliveries. Please contact me personally if you have any issues, Mr. Hoffman." Olive Ann Beech handed Paul her card.

After leaving the office, Paul returned to his hotel to get plenty of rest before departing for New York in the morning. His checkout in the Beech 18 had been rather perfunctory, taking only about two hours. Paul was a good pilot, but having very little multiengine experience, he had obtained some instruction in another Beech 18 prior to departing New York. That turned out to be a wise move. He knew that his father would need similar familiarization with the Beech. Paul had recently obtained his flight instructor rating and decided he would personally check his father out in the aircraft, since Karl had even less multiengine time than Paul. Paul planned to ship both the second Beech 18 and the Bonanza to Spain on one of their freighters. Paul and Karl would then ferry the Beech 18 to Africa. That would be an exciting flight of several thousand miles, and Paul had already started planning the trip.

The Bonanza would be a welcome improvement for getting around Spain, which had great distances, poor roads, antiquated railways, and sparse air service. Paul would use it on his now-frequent trips there, but wondered how to best use it when he was not in the country. Perhaps his cousin Alfonso Ortega could learn to fly it. Alfonso's brother Alberto was in the Spanish navy, and he probably had neither the time and interest, nor the need to learn to fly.

Paul resolved to raise those issues when he was in Spain the following month. As he turned the car into the hotel parking lot, he thought about his planned stop prior to Spain. He reread the last letter he received in August 1944 from his brother Hans. In the letter, Hans mentioned a fellow officer, whom his uncle had assigned him to work with, and described a visit he had made to that officer's home in Koblenz, Germany. Paul first planned to conduct some business in Cologne and Bonn. He would then visit his cousin Kirsten Hoffman at the family estate in nearby Bernkastel. He hoped she might have some information about her missing father, Walter Hoffman. Finally, he would head over to nearby Koblenz.

Paul was hopeful that either Kirsten Hoffman or Claus Hilgeman had important information regarding his missing brother and uncle.

28

Koblenz, Germany.
October 1949

* * *

Paul walked down the side street of the famous old walled city at the conflu-
ence of the Rhine and Mosel Rivers. The Roman general Drusus had established an outpost here in 8 BC. As he strolled toward his destination several
blocks away, Paul recounted his brief visit with his seventeen-year-old cousin,
Kirsten Hoffman, his uncle Walter's only child.

Unlike her mother, Erica, and Hans's wife, Freya, Kirsten survived the
final bombing of Cologne by seeking refuge in the Dom, its famous cathedral.
Walter was unaware of her amazing escape, due to the breakdown in communications near the end of the war and the fact that Kirsten was mistakenly
reported as having died in the raid. Since the end of the war, she had lived at
her grandfather's estate and winery in nearby Bernkastel with the couple who
ran the estate for the family.

Paul was pleased to see Kirsten actively involved in vineyard and winery
operations, where she was determined to carry on the family tradition. Since
she would reach legal maturity the following year, Paul thought that the family
should transfer legal title for half of the estate from Walter, who was missing
and presumed dead, to his daughter. The other half of the estate was owned
by Paul's father, Karl. The two men had inherited the estate from their father,
Wilhelm von Hoffman, who was killed by the Russians on his West Prussian
manor in 1945 at age ninety-three. Paul made a mental note to ask Jack to take
care of the legal issues, since Sullivan and Cromwell had extensive German
clients before the war and could probably navigate the thicket of German law.

Paul also quickly reviewed the first couple of days after his arrival in
nearby Cologne and then Bonn, where he began reestablishing commercial
contacts. Many of the contacts had been dormant for ten years or more. He
realized this would be a slow process, since Germany was still largely destitute
from the war. The Marshall Plan was changing that, and Paul noticed a frenzy
of construction and rebuilding in both cities.

Finally arriving at the address on his brother's letter, Paul walked up to the door in the old wood house, paused, and then knocked. In a short time the door opened, and Paul faced a slightly older man with very gray hair.

The man silently stared at Paul for a long moment before addressing him. "Yes, what can I do for you?"

Paul grew up bilingual in Spanish and German, learning English later, from a tutor. "I'm here to see Claus Hilgeman. Would that be you by any chance?"

There was another longer pause as the man again stared at Paul with a suspicious stare. He finally answered. "No, I'm not Claus. Who are you?"

"I'm Paul Hoffman. A letter from my brother Hans suggested that this might be where Claus lives and—" Paul was cut off as it finally registered with the man in the door.

"You're Hans's brother! Yes, I recognize you from a photograph now. Please come in."

Paul walked into the sparsely furnished house, following his host, who had finally relaxed.

"I'm Dieter Hafner. I served with both your brother and Claus. May I offer you some wine? I have a Riesling from your family's estate in Bernkastel, a really excellent 1945 *Kabinett*. The harvest was small that year, but it's very good."

"Yes, that would be excellent."

Hafner poured the wine, and they sat down. Paul soon realized that Hafner must not have many guests. He provided Paul with a lengthy monologue with valuable information on the last year of the war. He finally wrapped it up with some concluding comments.

"So, Hans was attached to your uncle for some special mission in late 1944, and he was assisted by Claus. After the war, Claus decided he could not remain in this house, where his wife was killed during the bombing. I lost my wife also, as well as my house, so when Claus left, he let me live here."

"I'm sorry for your loss. I lost my mother and one brother during the war."

"Yes, I'm also aware of your loss. But you haven't mentioned Hans. Where is he?" Hafner replied.

"I don't know. He disappeared at the end of the war, which is why I want to talk to Claus, since he might know something. Can you tell me where Claus lives now, Herr Hafner?"

"Yes, of course. He moved to Lisbon, probably to be far away from the memories here. He is fluent in Portuguese and spent a lot of time there, so it's like a second home for him. I'll go write down his address and phone number and be right back."

Paul waited impatiently for Hafner to return. He realized this could be a real lead. When Hafner returned, Paul thanked him and said he needed to leave. Within twenty minutes, he was back at his hotel, exhausted from his conversation but eager to contact Claus Hilgeman. Paul would be going to Spain next, for both a family visit and to contact Alberto again regarding Paul's new role as an emissary. He was due to fly out of Lisbon in about two weeks, and he intended to arrive there earlier than planned. This would allow him to contact Hilgeman.

His head had barely hit the pillow when he was jolted by the ringing phone. "Yes, what is it?"

"Herr Hoffman, I have New York on the line, and it sounds urgent."

Paul instantly sat upright with fear coursing through his veins. "Put the call through now please!" he responded. Seconds later he heard the voice.

"Paul, are you there? It's Liz."

"Yes, I'm here, darling. Are you all right? Are the children all right?"

"Yes, of course we are, but I needed to contact you because of something horrible that happened in Spain."

"What is it?" Paul was now on the edge of the bed.

"I received a telegram and then managed to get a call through to Alabos. Anita's husband, Enrique, has been killed."

"What are you saying? What happened to him?"

"I don't have all the details, but he was in Barcelona with his brother and father at some demonstration about Catalonian autonomy. Two policemen—I think they were called civil guards—attacked his brother with a club. When Enrique came to his brother's defense, they shot him. He died later in the hospital."

"My God, I can't believe this! Is Anita all right? What about the rest of the family?"

"I guess it's only considered to involve Enrique's family. The Ortega family has not been implicated by the police. Aren't you scheduled to be in Spain soon?"

"Yes, I'll be there in three days." He paused, thinking quickly. "I'll bring Kirsten Hoffman with me. She and Anita are very close."

"Yes, that's a good idea, and I want to be there also to support Anita," Liz insisted.

"Of course, and bring the children with Margarita. That way you'll have time to spend with Anita. Don't worry about the expense. This is a crisis for the Ortega family, and you need to be there. I don't want you leaving the children, since Margarita is so new on the job."

Paul was referring to their new Venezuelan nanny. There was no one else with whom they could leave their two-year-old twins.

Paul quickly finished his conversation with Liz and thought about this turn of events. He was struck by the differences between his homeland and America. In a political rally in the States, you weren't likely to be murdered by the police. He quickly suppressed that thought. Compromises must be made, he told himself, and change usually comes only slowly. He thought that change was moving excruciatingly slow in Spain's case, and he knew this would be a hard issue for him to balance.

29

Alabos, Spain.
November 1949

* * *

"So, we will ship both the Twin Beech 18 and the Bonanza aircraft to Cadiz on one of our ships sometime around June next year. My father and I will ferry the 18 to Guinea, and the Bonanza will remain here in Spain for our local use. We can fly it when we are here, but it would be helpful if one of you could learn to fly, so we could get more use out of it. Alfonso? Ernesto? Are either of you willing to take that on?"

Paul was sitting in the large room just inside the west patio of the Ortega hacienda. He was with Ernesto Ortega, Ernesto's son, Alfonso, and daughter, Anita, and his own father, Karl. They had just finished a successful meeting to finalize the annual plan for developing their far-flung enterprises and economic interests.

Ernesto looked at Alfonso and then back to Paul before replying hesitantly. "I'm really not sure about that, Paul. It sounds a little too complicated for me."

"I don't have time to learn to fly. Why don't we hire a professional pilot?" Alfonso added, shaking his head.

The room became silent. Paul was surprised; he had expected Alfonso to take up the challenge. Before Paul could ponder his reply, he received an unexpected answer.

"I will learn to fly the Bonanza," Anita answered confidently.

That response elicited a dumbstruck look from her father as Ernesto struggled to come up with an answer.

Anita continued before he could reply. "I intend to use the airplane to visit potential vineyard sites all over Spain, as well as our existing properties in Jerez."

"Who will teach you to fly the airplane, Anita? That should be quite difficult here in Spain. I doubt if any women know how to fly," Alfonso interjected.

"That's not true. The first woman pilot in Spain was Maria Bernaldo de Quiros, and she got her license in 1928. Is it a macho thing for you, Alfonso?"

"That's not fair, Anita. I was only trying to be practical and—"

"Your mother will strongly object, Anita! She will not—" Ernesto said, cutting off Alfonso, only to have Anita cut him off.

"While I respect both of your views, I have already made up my mind. As we already agreed, Beatriz and I will be going to New York in late December, and I will be in America for several months to market our wines. I've spent much effort producing top quality, traditional wines, and the Lopez de Heredia family in Haro has generously offered me advice on improving our process. As a result, the '47 and '48 vintages are superb, and the '47 may be the vintage of the century. We produced an enormous quantity of reds at crianza, reserva, and gran reserva quality levels. It makes sense to explore the American market, as well as wine-making practices in California. While I am there, I will learn to fly, thereby avoiding the chance of wounding the masculine pride of Spain."

Neither Alfonso nor his father could come up with a reply to that, so Paul did. "I can arrange for you to get instruction at our airport in Teterboro, New Jersey. When we pick up the Bonanza in April, maybe we can fly it to California, and you can get some practical cross-country flying experience before we ship the plane to Spain."

Paul looked at Anita, her father, and then Karl, who glared at him as if to say that he should not be stepping into an Ortega family argument. Paul looked at Anita, who was smiling broadly at him. It was the first time Paul had seen her smile since his arrival.

Actually, Paul thought that Anita was holding up extraordinarily well only weeks after the funeral of her husband. Paul also noticed how fetchingly beautiful his thirty-year-old cousin was, with her long, curly dark hair, thin shapely figure, and expressive dark eyes. He quickly squelched that thought and any desire that it might have represented.

"Thank you, Paul. I greatly appreciate your support. I'm looking forward to staying with you and Liz and your children," Anita replied, staring intently at him.

There was then an awkward silence, but the meeting was quickly concluded as everyone got up to prepare for dinner. Paul later came back to the room, walked over to the huge bay window, and stared first at the lovely Ebro River valley to his left, and then the scenic mountains and hills to his right. It felt like he had been standing for several minutes when he felt a hand softly touching his left arm. Startled, he quickly turned, expecting to see Liz. But it was Anita.

"I really appreciate you standing up for me, Paul. I feel closer to you than my brother and father. Enrique's death has made me cynical about the ugly politics here, as well as our conservative culture. To be honest, he and I had become estranged in the last couple of years. It wasn't just his activism in Catalonian politics that alarmed me. He treated me in a very subservient way, as if my dreams and aspirations didn't matter. He was also jealous of my influence in family business matters. He made his opinions about a women's role quite clear."

She walked slowly over to the window and stared out at the tranquil rural setting.

Paul reached for the right words. "I'm sorry, Anita. I didn't know."

She looked back at him, smiled, and walked back over. "It's all right, Paul. You could not have known. In any case, my escape is to concentrate on our wine-making ventures. That determination, and your kindness, has restored my initiative."

Paul smiled weakly as he looked at Anita, unsure how to respond. "Then we'll make your upcoming trip to America a productive one. I'll see that you get a proper flying experience."

"Are there any women flight instructors you know? I sense that the macho thing might be a problem in the States also."

"It won't be as bad as in Spain, but there definitely is a gender issue. I do know that there are women instructors at Teterboro. I'll set something up when I return."

"Thank you again, Paul. This will mean a lot to me." Anita pulled closer to Paul, put her arms around him, and hugged him briefly. As she released him, he felt a powerful surge and tingling, which he quickly repressed as he pulled away. "Let's get ready to join everyone for dinner. I'll see you shortly after I find Liz and my children."

Anita nodded, staring at Paul with a deep admiring smile. Paul smiled back weakly, turned, and walked out of the room.

30.

Lisbon, Portugal,
November 1949

* * *

Paul sat quietly on the barstool in the small bar at the Hotel Aviz and stared at the languid nude in the painting behind the bar. He was hoping he would receive a return call from Claus Hilgeman. Paul had phoned him several times, but no one had answered. He finally went to the address Hafner had given him in Koblenz. Hilgeman was not at home, so Paul left him a note. It was two more days before his scheduled flight back to New York on Friday.

Paul looked again at the nude and then around him at the heavily carved furniture, chandeliers, and thick carpets of this luxurious hotel, a noted haven for allied sympathizers during the war. It had also housed the Duke and Duchess of Windsor and other famous guests. Paul sighed and then ordered another white port from the bartender.

He had just received his drink, when a bellhop came over and told him he had an incoming call. The bellhop led him to the phone in the lobby, handed it to Paul, and left.

"This is Paul Hoffman. Who is this?"

"This is Hilgeman. Are you alone?"

"Yes, I am."

"The Aviz is not a good place to meet. I want you to go to the Hotel Avenida Palace. It's at Rua 1 de Dezembro number 123. Just walk down the Avenida da Liberdade a few blocks, and it will be on the right. I'll meet you in the lobby bar. Do you understand?"

"I'll be there shortly," Paul answered and then hung up.

Paul quickly left the hotel and walked south down Lisbon's main boulevard, anxious to meet Hilgeman. The note he left Hilgeman stated only that he was Hans's brother.

Paul approached the ornate Avenida Palace. With its classic *belle epoque* exterior, the hotel, built in 1892, evoked a more lavish period. He entered the main lobby and walked to the back lobby. He noted the high walls, marble floor, stained-glass ceiling, and exquisite furnishings. He entered the lobby bar to the left, admiring the deep rich colors of the wood paneling. He sat down at the curved bar and ordered another white port. There was one other patron at the bar.

The bartender brought his drink. Paul took a sip, turned, and watched for any sign of Hilgeman, having no idea what he looked like.

"Excuse me, but are you Paul Hoffman?"

"Yes, that's me." Paul turned back to face the inquiring bartender.

"The hotel switchboard has a call from your New York office. You can take it out in the main lobby."

"Thank you." Paul walked to the main lobby, puzzled because only Hilgeman knew where he was. His suspicions were aroused, but Paul knew he must play the game. He was directed to the lobby phone by the desk clerk. He picked it up. "This is Paul Hoffman."

"Do you know you are being followed?"

"I thought that might be a problem," Paul answered, his suspicions confirmed.

"Listen carefully. Go back to the bar. Do not make eye contact with anyone. Order another drink and tell the bartender you are expecting another call from New York. Then ask where the men's room is. Go toward it, but when you pass the spiral staircase keep going and exit the hotel. Walk quickly several blocks west and then north several blocks. Then go east to cross Avenida da Liberdade and head north on the first parallel street. Go to the Hotel do Imperio at Rua Rodrigues Sampaio number 17. I'll meet you in the lobby bar. Do you understand?"

"Yes," Paul answered quickly, visualizing the route as Hilgeman hung up. He returned to the bar and then followed the instructions. He arrived at the Imperio about a half hour later. He was sure he was not followed, but he doubled back several times on his route out of caution.

Paul entered the lobby through the wrought iron doors, noting also the round window to the right, which also had a wrought iron exterior grille. Impressed by the understated elegance of the lobby, he entered the bar to the right and sat at a table rather than at the small bar. There were no other patrons. The bartender came over to take his drink order. While waiting for his drink, Paul admired the rich wood paneling and the wood parquet floors.

He was also struck by the beautifully etched murals higher up on the walls, surrounding the entire bar. Each mural depicted a colony in the still large Portuguese empire. Paul marveled at each scene, representing Cape Verde, Portuguese Guinea, Sao Tome, Angola, and Mozambique, all in or around Africa. The vista continued to Asia with Portuguese India, Macao, and Timor all represented. He realized that this empire dwarfed Spain's small remaining colonial holdings in Africa. Spanish Morocco, Ifni, Spanish Sahara, and Spanish Guinea were a fraction of Spain's former empire in the Americas and Asia. Paul wondered how much longer the colonial era would last.

He suddenly felt a presence and looked behind him. A stocky but fit-looking man with light-blond, close-cropped hair was staring at him. Paul stood and extended his hand to the stranger. "I'm Paul Hoffman. Hans is my brother."

"Yes, I recognize you from a photograph taken in 1939. I'm Claus," Hilgeman replied, extending his hand.

The two men sat down, sizing each other up. The bartender came over.

"I'll have a white port also," Hilgeman said, turning back toward Paul.

"So who was following me?" Paul inquired.

"It could be any number of interested parties, I suppose. Why are you in Lisbon, and why did you contact me?"

"I want to know where Hans is. You served with him and my uncle. You must have some information about them."

"It could be that they did not survive the war since—"

"Let's not pretend and maintain this facade, Herr Hilgeman. Let me state the facts that I have already confirmed independently. On April 6, 1945, Hans and my uncle sailed from Jutland in Denmark in a Type 21 submarine. They were carrying a secret cargo under Operation Valhalla. I also know that they were detected briefly in an encounter with American warships on April 22, but escaped to continue their journey into the South Atlantic. My sources indicate that the boat did not travel to either South America or Asia, so that leaves Africa. Assuming they could only head to neutral territory, it is logical that they were headed for Angola or Mozambique." Paul looked up and pointed to the two murals behind Hilgeman to emphasize his point and then added one more thought. "It's also possible they stopped in Spanish Guinea along the way."

There was a pause as the waiter delivered Hilgeman's drink.

"You seem well informed, Paul, and please call me Claus. By the way, who are you working for, the CIA, perhaps?"

"No, I'm not in the CIA, but I am unusually well connected in that regard. Will you now answer my question?"

"I actually don't know where Hans is."

"Why should I believe that?"

Hilgeman shifted uneasily in his seat and took a sip from his port. "I had a very limited role in the mission. I don't know where either Hans or his uncle ended up. However, the nature of Valhalla is such that there are many parties who want to find them if they're still alive."

"Yes, I'm aware of that. I have had my own encounters with ex-Nazis and the Russians. In May 1945, an SS operative tried to kill me, but I got lucky, and he is no longer with us. More recently—"

"More recently you escaped from Czechoslovakia and found out that the Russians are also aware of Valhalla."

"So you know about my little adventure?" Paul replied.

"Yes, I have an extensive network of contacts in both Spain and Portugal. I not only learn about such things, but also about what former SS operatives are doing and what is taking place behind the so-called Iron Curtain. You must know by now what a dangerous thing it is to pry too deep into Valhalla."

"I don't care about that, Claus. I am determined to find my brother. I'll be visiting my father in Spanish Guinea in a few months, and I intend to pursue this matter wherever it leads. So why don't you tell me what you know?"

Another pause, as Paul noted Hilgeman pondering his question.

"I suppose I can make some inquiries from others. When are you returning to New York?" Hilgeman finally replied.

"The day after tomorrow, Friday; I'm booked on Pan American 151, leaving at 3:00 p.m."

"All right; I will look into this. Tomorrow night meet me for dinner at 9:00 p.m. at a restaurant in the Bairro Alto. It's called Va-e-Volte, and it's on Rua de Noticias number 100." Hilgeman wrote it down on a slip of paper and handed it to Paul.

"I'll be there," Paul replied firmly.

"When you leave the Aviz tomorrow, don't use the elevator. Instead take the stairs and leave the hotel through the back door. From now on you need to be ultracautious and aware of your surroundings," Hilgeman responded.

* * *

The next evening, Paul quietly left the Aviz and walked south and then west up the hill to the bohemian section of Lisbon, the Bairro Alto. As he turned to walk down Rua Diario de Noticias, he noticed large crowds for a Thursday on this unseasonably warm November evening. As he walked down the narrow cobblestone streets, he could hear the melancholy and mournful *fado* music wafting from numerous restaurants and bars in the alleys of the neighborhood. He finally came to number 100, noted the blue ceramic tiled walls across the alley from the restaurant, and then sat down at one of the outdoor tables. Within minutes Hilgeman joined him. They ordered dinner and got down to business.

"Paul, I was being truthful about Hans. I don't know where he is, and it appears that he and his uncle have completely disappeared. I will warn you again that it would be extremely dangerous for either of them to surface now if they are alive. Besides former SS officials, both the Russians and the Americans are anxious to find out more about Valhalla. You must respect that danger and realize that it applies to you also."

"I'll accept that risk, Claus. I will keep searching until I find him."

"I realize that you will persist in your search, but I expect that you and your father will have to come to terms with what that might mean for Hans and your uncle, if you ever find them."

"Thank you, Claus. I will deal with that problem as it arises."

The next day, on the return flight to New York, Paul pondered the recent turn of events and anticipated his planned flight to Spanish Guinea the following year with his father. He was also convinced that Claus Hilgeman was not being completely truthful.

31

New York City.
December 31, 1949

* * *

Paul walked briskly down Fifth Avenue late in the afternoon of New Year's Eve, recalling recent events and prospects for the New Year. Tonight he would celebrate with Liz, Anita, Jack, and Jack's girlfriend, Sharon.

Anita Ortega had arrived in New York two weeks before Christmas, and she and Liz had become fast friends as they shopped together for the holiday. Their nanny, Margarita, added Anita's daughter Beatriz to her responsibilities, and with the three children, the household now seemed festive and chaotic.

Three months ago, Paul and Liz had moved into Ramon Ortega's Fifth Avenue penthouse overlooking Central Park. Ramon was the ailing eighty-year-old uncle of Paul's late mother, Pilar. He had established himself in America at the turn of the century and built a thriving export-import business. His wife died of influenza during the 1918 pandemic. He never remarried, and they had no children of their own. When Paul came to America in 1935 to attend Choate and later Columbia, Ramon embraced him as his own, since Paul's parents were then in Spanish Guinea. After graduating from Columbia in 1943, Paul joined Ramon full time in the export-import business and also managed the shipping interests for the two families. Paul's business acumen and management had greatly increased the success of these enterprises over the last six years. Now he was expanding his management team, since he could no longer manage the day-to-day activities alone. During the recent visit to Spain, Paul's formal role in the ownership and management of the Ortega-Hoffman American empire was acknowledged.

Ramon had a severe stroke several months prior and was now confined to a nursing home. Paul visited him every day when he was in town, knowing he wouldn't live much longer. Paul also knew that he would inherit all of Ramon's business interests, the Fifth Avenue penthouse, and an estate on Long Island. The latter two properties were free and clear of any mortgages. Paul knew he would miss his great uncle.

True to his word, Paul had arranged for Anita to begin flying lessons right after the New Year. She would start in a Piper J-3 Cub, progress to a Cessna 140, and continue until she had earned a private pilot certificate. When they picked up the new Beech Bonanza in April, Paul planned to help her transition to the new airplane, a considerable jump in performance and complexity from the Piper and the Cessna. Paul quickly tried to erase Anita from his mind for now and turn to more unpleasant subjects.

The Berlin Airlift had just been successfully concluded, giving America its first Cold War victory. However, the country was still trying to recover from two shocking events that tempered this victory.

Russia had unexpectedly exploded its first atomic bomb in September 1949. This was followed by equally grim news in October when the Communists completed taking over China from the corrupt nationalist government, which fled to the island of Formosa. The recriminations from both events were now being felt politically. The Truman administration was on the defensive in the face of strong public and congressional criticism of American policies.

Paul knew that this turn of events might affect reconciliation between Spain and the United States. When he returned to Spain in the spring, he would try to conclude the back-channel deal that he had been brokering between American banks and the Spanish government. This could be followed by America naming a new ambassador and beginning to negotiate some form of alliance and aid package. Through Alberto Ortega's connection with Luis Carrero Blanco, Paul had successfully brought the two sides together. He believed it was only a matter of time until a treaty could be negotiated.

While he was pleased with these developments, Paul was most intent on solving the mystery surrounding his missing brother. He hoped that one way or another, the New Year would provide him with some additional leads to unravel that mystery.

As Paul finally reached the penthouse, he also realized the dangers that lurked behind Operation Valhalla. He resolved to be cautious as the new year and the new decade began.

Part 2

* * *

Emergence

1950–1959

Take up the White Man's burden—
Ye dare not stoop to less—
Nor call too loud on Freedom
To cloke your weariness;
By all ye cry or whisper,
By all ye leave or do,
The silent, sullen peoples
Shall weigh your gods and you.

-Excerpt from "The White Man's Burden" by Rudyard Kipling, 1899

32

In the air over eastern Arizona.
February 1950

*   *   *

The night was totally black as the Twin Beech sliced through the perfectly smooth air as it progressed westbound. Only the twinkling stars shone overhead. It was the new moon, and there were absolutely no lights on the ground either.

Paul was happy to enjoy the pleasure of the moment and take his mind off both the upcoming business visits and several issues that had been nagging him. He adjusted the red cockpit lights even lower so he could enjoy the ethereal moment. He felt completely detached from the earth. There was no sense of movement at all. The autopilot maintained heading and altitude as Paul glanced at the airspeed indicator, steady at 162 miles per hour. The device was calibrated for sea level, so he had to correct for altitude and temperature to determine an accurate true airspeed. He noted his 10,500 foot altitude and the outside air temperature and then pulled a small circular calculator from his shirt pocket and shone a small flashlight on it. He turned the wheels on the calculator, a kind of slide rule. He matched all the numbers and noted the result: 190 miles per hour true airspeed, as it should be at the current engine long-range power setting.

He turned off the flashlight and looked out the windshield and then the side window. *Yes, that's my true speed through the air, but how strong is the head wind and what is the speed over the ground?* He would soon be able to find those answers also.

He was following the Green 4 airway between Albuquerque and Los Angeles. It was defined by a series of "radio ranges" on the ground, whose signals could be received on the Beech's low-frequency radio. He had passed over the El Morro range in western New Mexico about a half hour ago. When he arrived over the Winslow, Arizona range, he could take the time it took to fly between the two stations, compare it to the 131-mile distance between them, and calculate his actual speed over the ground.

Paul adjusted his earphones as he listened to the steady hum of the "beam" from the Winslow range ahead of him. If he drifted south of course, he would hear the letter A—or dot-dash in Morse code—and if he drifted north of course, he would hear the dash-dot of the letter N. The overlapping dots and dashes merged into a steady hum when he was on course, or "on the beam."

Paul turned his thoughts back to the upcoming meeting with his West Coast manager tomorrow in Los Angeles. This might be one of the last meetings that he would personally lead in the field offices. The family's business had become so complex that he now had several vice presidents reporting to him. Paul loved staying hands-on with the business, but the real purpose of his trip was to take delivery of the aircraft in Wichita. He wanted to "shake it down" before shipping it to Spain and then ferrying it to Africa.

His thoughts were interrupted as he noted a faint A signal in the headphone. He reached for the autopilot and adjusted his course north a few degrees to compensate. Turning his thoughts back to the issues nagging him, Paul recalled his meeting with Claus Hilgeman in November. The lack of progress in his search for Hans was frustrating. Paul decided to take additional action to resolve the mystery when he and his father ferried the Beech to Guinea from Spain.

The signal in his headset was now a steady hum again and was getting much louder. Paul turned the volume down and looked out the front windshield. He immediately noted the small patch of lights on the ground ahead. That must be Winslow.

Thinking back to the ferry flight to Africa, Paul planned to suggest that they follow-up with a flight to Portuguese Angola from Spanish Guinea. This would help promote trading relationships initially established by his father during the war. Paul's real reason for this trip was to investigate his hunch that Hans and his uncle may have stopped there in the submarine carrying the Valhalla cargo. It was logical. Claus Hilgeman was involved in the Valhalla mission and may have spent some time there. It was a neutral colony during the war. But where would they have taken and stored the cargo? How would he find clues that might confirm his suspicion? Would that lead him to Hans?

The signal in the headset became even louder, but then abruptly faded away as the Beech flew over the "cone of silence." A white light on the instrument panel illuminated, and a higher pitch tone filled the headset—the station location marker. Paul checked the time and reached for the autopilot, to turn the aircraft left to intercept the 243-degree outbound range course. He settled on a heading of 250 to compensate for the wind. He noted it took forty-six minutes to cover 131 miles from El Morro to Winslow. He used the circular computer to calculate the ground speed at 170 miles an hour, versus his true air speed of 190. The headwind was stronger than forecast. He then turned the radio volume ultralow.

He realized that he must also confront his father regarding what he knew about the disappearance of Hans and Walter. Paul knew his father was holding something back. What could it be? How could he approach his father on such a delicate subject—and what would the consequences be?

Paul looked ahead, noting the blinking light beacon ahead of him. It flashed four "dots." He picked up his flashlight, flicked it on, and looked at the aeronautical chart. Yes, it was the code for airway beacon number forty-four, defining the lighted airway to Los Angeles. It was an older, more primitive system than the radio, but at least he wouldn't need to continuously listen to the annoying audio signals of the radio range. No wonder most of the old-timers were deaf. On this clear night he noted with satisfaction that he could make out the coded light for the next airway light beacon beyond and could also see the one after that near Prescott. Visibility must be about 120 miles.

Paul looked back at the empty cabin in the Twin Beech. He had ordered this aircraft with an austere interior and without deicing boots since they would not be needed on a working aircraft in tropical Africa. The first Twin Beech he had picked up the previous October was lavishly equipped for executive transportation. It had a writing desk, a liquor cabinet, and a private full lavatory, as well as deicing boots and more advanced radio equipment for operation in American skies. He knew his company's operations now depended on the aircraft for getting sales teams to meet clients and for other company needs. He had hired a chief pilot to run the burgeoning flight operations and instructed him to look for a faster aircraft that would carry a bigger load. The chief pilot had located a converted bomber, a Douglas B-23 "Dragon," that would meet the requirement.

Even though he was following the lighted airway Paul tuned in the Prescott radio range, dialing the frequency to 347 kilocycles and listening to the Morse identifier, dot-dash-dash-dot dash-dot-dash-dot. *Yes, PC is correct.* He heard the soothing sound of the steady beam, confirming he was on course, and then turned the volume down.

Paul thought about the meeting he had scheduled in Las Vegas three days hence with US Senator Pat McCarran of Nevada. The meeting had been arranged by Allen Dulles. McCarran was very pro-Spain, believing it would provide a bulwark against Communism in Europe. Paul hoped to capitalize on these sentiments to promote US foreign aid to Spain and a further reconciliation between the two countries. Paul had successfully brokered a $25 million commercial loan from the Chase Bank to Spain the previous February, but he knew that larger sums were needed and only the US government could fill that gap.

Paul worried about the mounting evidence that both he and Jack were often being followed. Who would be doing that and for what reason? Paul needed to find out. He had a hunch about it. Could it be that it was related to Valhalla? What else did he need to find out to solve this?

He considered the precaution he had recently taken. He took some firearms training and now frequently carried a Berretta M1935 pistol. It was difficult for Paul, as a foreign national, to get the necessary permit in New York City, but Jack and Allen Dulles had pulled some strings for him.

Paul wondered if he would use the pistol if the need ever arose.

33

Luanda, Portuguese Angola,
March 1950

* * *

Alexandre Santos looked up at the wall clock in his small office in the center of the city. He was expecting Hendrik van den Bergh to arrive any minute. He reached for the pack of cigarettes on his desk, extracted one, and lit it. As he took a few puffs, he wondered what Hendrik might want. Perhaps a return of the favor he provided several months ago?

Hendrik had flown in the previous day on a South African military flight from Pretoria to Windhoek, in Southwest Africa, and then on to Luanda. The flight serviced South African government offices in Windhoek as well as the consulate in Luanda. Van den Bergh was a periodic visitor to Luanda, since he and Santos had similar duties and periodically coordinated their activities.

Santos was the head of the Policia Internacional e de Defesa do Estado, or PIDE, in Angola. He had joined the secret police and intelligence agency in 1941 in Portugal, when it was known as PVDE. He quickly rose in rank and gravitated to foreign intelligence work. In 1944, he was involved in a special mission that brought him to Angola. He fell in love with the colony and elected to stay on, since he had no family ties in the mother country. An only child, his father was a diplomat who served in Germany during the thirties. Santos became fluent in German while there as a teenager. His parents were both killed in a freak car accident in Germany in 1939, and Santos returned to Portugal after finishing his schooling in Berlin.

Santos quickly rose to the head of PIDE operations in Angola. He married a local black woman in 1945, and they now had two small children. Unlike most other European African colonies, intermarriage was accepted in the Portuguese colonies, and the mixed-race children were automatically considered Portuguese nationals.

The intercom buzzer rang and Santos answered. "Yes, what is it?"

"Hendrik van den Bergh is here," a man's voice replied.

"Fine, send him in please."

Santos smashed his cigarette in the ashtray, rose, and walked around his desk as the office door opened. He walked over to greet his guest in their common language, German. "Welcome, Hendrik, it's good to see you again."

"Likewise, Alexandre. It's something I always look forward to."

As the two men shook hands, Santos looked up at the six-foot-seven van den Bergh. Santos was only five foot ten and pencil thin, with jet-black hair and a thin dark mustache. He had just turned thirty; his visitor was five years older.

"Please come and take a seat." Santos led his guest to a round table on the other side of the room. Van den Bergh sat down as Santos walked over to the adjacent liquor cabinet.

"May I offer you a glass of tawny port?"

"Yes, that would be fine, Alexandre."

Santos poured two glasses, returned to the table, sat down across from his guest, and raised his glass. "*Prost!*"

"*Prost* to you, my friend," Hendrik replied, raising his own glass.

Santos thought he should get old business out of the way first. "Hendrik, I want to thank you for returning the two agitators to us. They had been crossing the border with Southwest Africa with impunity for months, and you put a stop to it by rounding them up. I'm personally grateful to you, since I must keep a lid on dissent and prevent any disruptions by so-called independence movements."

"It was no trouble, Alexandre. Our two governments have a common interest in this regard, and we don't want these kinds of individuals either."

"I believe this will be an ongoing problem for us. Since the end of the war, these native movements seem to be cropping up everywhere in Africa."

"Yes, but we can control it," Hendrik replied.

Santos watched as van den Bergh downed the last of the port, looked casually out the window, and then turned back to Santos, clearing his throat.

So now I will find out what he wants, Santos thought.

"I was wondering if you could provide me with some important information, Alexandre."

"I will if I am able, of course."

"There are two individuals, former German nationals, who arrived in Swakopmund in June 1945. I have reason to believe that they arrived there by way of Angola, and that perhaps you may have been aware of the circumstances of their arrival. My information indicates that they arrived by submarine."

As van den Bergh paused for effect, Santos was dumbstruck by the request. Yet he maintained his composure as he finally replied. "Do you have more specific information on their identity?"

"Yes; their names are Johann and Heinz Hartman, but these are only aliases. They are actually *Kriegsmarine* Vice Admiral Walter Hoffman and his nephew, Hans Hoffman. I know this for certain, because interested third parties provided me with photographs of them. They are unquestionably the same individuals masquerading as the Hartmans."

"I see," Santos replied simply. It was now he who looked out the window as he quickly contemplated a better response. *What else does he know? How much should I tell him?* This only took a few seconds as Santos turned back to his visitor. "May I ask the nature of your interest in these two officers? Are you pursuing them for some offense they committed?"

"No, I'm not. On the contrary, we find them to be worthy immigrants who share common values with us. There are, however, third parties from abroad who are pursuing them for alleged crimes against the Nazi regime during the war. These third parties have provided me with their photographs and other details and asked for our help in locating them. To be more specific, the submarine in which they escaped contained critical items of inestimable value to Germany—or any other power that discovers them. The Hoffmans are in danger if they are discovered, so I am anxious to see that such an event never happens."

Santos considered this information and finally responded, "So you believe that their arrival in Swakopmund was through Angola, and that I have information on these events?"

"Precisely. In fact, we know that another *Kriegsmarine* officer, Claus Hilgeman, was involved in their disappearance, and that he was posted in both Lisbon and Luanda to facilitate the operation."

That clinched it, Santos thought. *He's telling me everything he knows to make any denial awkward—and also to give me a reason to collaborate. Well, I must therefore oblige him—up to a point.* "Your information is accurate, Hendrik. They did arrive here by submarine in June 1945. Based on prior arrangements between the SS and PIDE, I was directed to assist them in their transit to Southwest

Africa. They scuttled the sub, and I then provided them assistance in reaching Southwest Africa. From there, Walter Hoffman's associates from Southwest Africa, whom he met decades ago, took them to Swakopmund."

"That corroborates my information. What about the cargo the submarine was carrying?"

"It had no cargo, just the crew and their personal effects. I know this for a fact, because I was on the boat that took the crew off, and no cargo was unloaded. I saw the inside of the submarine briefly before they scuttled it, and there was no evidence of cargo," Santos replied.

"Where else had the submarine stopped after departing from Europe?"

"I really don't know, Hendrik. This operation was very compartmentalized. My only role was to assist them in their transit to Swakopmund."

"I see. Well, I can report that the 'third parties' interested in this operation are very persistent, and I fear that they pose a danger to both Hoffmans."

As van den Bergh paused again, Santos could see his guest struggling with how to proceed. Santos decided he must continue his cooperative approach. "I want to help you protect the Hoffmans, Hendrik, but I'm not sure what your expectations are. What do you think will happen next to change the situation—and how can I be of assistance?"

"Well, I expect that Walter Hoffman may soon join his nephew and other crew members in South Africa. I also anticipate that he may need to travel to attend to personal and other matters, which will increase the danger of his being discovered and exposed. It would be helpful if you could facilitate such travel. It may be easier for him to travel to Portugal en route to other locations in Europe where his business matters are. You and your organization would be very helpful to us in such matters."

"I agree that such assistance is required, and we will provide travel, limited protection, visas, and other necessary services to ensure that Hoffman can go safely to Europe and return without being detected."

"Thank you, Alexandre. Your offer is generous, and you correctly see the implications if Hoffman or his nephew were to be discovered. I will notify you when Hoffman decides he needs to make such a journey. Since he now has a South African passport with his alias, I may find a way to give him some minor contract position with our government that involves trade issues requiring travel. That would authorize him to travel on the military air shuttle we have established between Pretoria and Luanda. I recently changed the flight's itinerary so that it will stop at Swapkomund after leaving Windhoek before continuing to Luanda. From here there are air connections to Lisbon."

Santos was curious why van den Bergh was so interested in making it easier for Walter Hoffman to leave Africa. Could it be that van den Bergh is expecting to access the Valhalla operation in some way?

His question was answered as van den Bergh continued. "You know, Alexandre, Hoffman's involvement in that operation could be beneficial to both of us and to our countries. I also believe that our continued cooperation in this matter may lead to future collaboration between us as other issues surface." Van den Bergh rose as he spoke, indicating the end of the meeting.

Santos also rose to see his guest out. "I'll look forward to that, Hendrik. It was good of you to come. I'll see you out."

"Thank you, Alexandre, that won't be necessary. It was good of you to see me. I'll be in touch."

They shook hands, and van den Bergh quickly exited the office. Santos stood there for a minute and pondered the implications of van den Bergh's visit.

Clearly Santos and Claus Hilgeman would have a lot to talk about during Hilgeman's next visit to Luanda, scheduled for May.

Santos and Hilgeman were old friends, dating back to the late thirties. Santos's parents had been diplomats stationed in Berlin, and Hilgeman was assigned as a military liaison to the Portuguese embassy. Hilgeman came to Santos's assistance after his parents' tragic death. They had been close friends ever since. Hilgeman had enlisted Santos's assistance with Operation Valhalla in 1944, resulting in Santos's transfer to Luanda. Santos was familiar with Valhalla—more than he admitted to van den Bergh.

It would be in Portugal's interest to cooperate with the new apartheid regime in South Africa. But there were certain aspects of Valhalla that Santos knew he would never share with the South Africans.

There are several wild cards in this game, Santos thought. *What are Walter Hoffman's real intentions? Who are these "third parties" pursuing the Valhalla secrets? What will their next move be?* Besides the exiled Nazis that Santos believed were involved, did the "third parties" also include the Americans—or other countries?

Santos pondered these questions as he poured himself another glass of tawny. Yes, he and Claus would have a lot to talk about in two months.

34

Segovia, Spain.
April 1950

* * *

"Otto, I still don't understand why you provided van den Bergh with information on Walter and Hans Hoffman, not to mention Valhalla. Doesn't this compromise the entire operation?" As he finished speaking, Franz Liesau pointed his finger at his dinner partner, as if to accuse him of betrayal of their cause.

Former SS *Obersturmbannfuhrer* Otto Skorzeny did not immediately reply. Instead he finished chewing the latest morsel of the acorn-fed roast suckling pig, raised his wine glass for another sip, and then carefully wiped his face with his napkin. He then turned his head right to look out the window of the Meson de Candido restaurant to admire the ancient Roman aqueduct. The sunlight shone on the left side of his face, accentuating his old dueling scar.

Skorzeny was a famous SS officer during the war. He was most noted for his famous mountaintop rescue of Mussolini using a light aircraft. Recently escaped from American captivity, he was now a leader in the worldwide community of SS exiles.

Without turning back to face Liesau he finally replied. "Aren't you impressed with the aqueduct, Franz? It's a reminder of the engineering prowess and durability of the Roman Empire. That empire lasted hundreds of years, as opposed to the twelve years of the Third Reich."

"You sound like Gehlen. He is always talking about historical antecedents that he relates to our situation."

"Gehlen is right to make such comparisons, Franz, but he is sometimes too involved in the current political situation to make a decisive move. I understand this. The new reality is the confrontation between America and the Soviets. Gehlen is trying to increase his influence with the Americans, so he can eventually reconstitute a semblance of our movement back in Germany. He hopes to use America's fear of the Soviets as his means to do so. You and I, however, conduct our dirty business down in the trenches."

"That may be true, but I still don't understand why you gave van den Bergh so much information," Liesau replied, still perplexed by Skorzeny's action.

Skorzeny sighed, shook his head, looked briefly back at the aqueduct, and finally turned to respond. "Try to understand the logic, Franz. If van den Bergh is truly out to collaborate with us, the photographs and other specific information I provided will allow him to easily and quickly locate Walter and Hans Hoffman. If he does so and then does not then promptly notify us—and I suspect he won't—then we will know he is protecting Hoffman and his nephew. I did not provide him with details on the Valhalla cargo, the money in our Swiss accounts, or any other information about the importance of Valhalla. So he has no reason to force Hoffman to do anything, unless Hoffman himself decides that the South Africans are his new benefactors. In any case, we are no worse off than before. My actions could possibly force Hoffman to come out in the open or make some other mistake."

"If that is true, Otto, then we will be no closer to finding Hoffman or discovering some other avenue for locating the Valhalla secrets."

"Not necessarily; we have other individuals we can pursue for that information. This would include Hilgeman, Walter Hoffman's daughter in Germany, and Alberto Ortega in the Spanish navy. If all else fails, we can try once more to closely watch Karl Hoffman in Spanish Guinea, even though he is the hardest to access."

"What about Paul Hoffman and his friend Kurtz in America?" Liesau said.

"I suspect that they have incomplete information on Valhalla and no information on Walter Hoffman's location. We, on the other hand, know that the Valhalla cargo was delivered to Spanish Guinea. We also know that the U-boat did not proceed to South America after leaving Spanish Guinea. Considering the range of the U-boat at that point, they could only have gone to some other place in Africa. Only we know all this for certain, except perhaps Claus Hilgeman. That's why I have already planned steps to get closer to Hilgeman. This knowledge gives us an enormous advantage over the others."

"All right, Otto. I now understand your approach. So shouldn't we be redoubling our efforts to close in on Valhalla?"

"We must be patient, Franz. It isn't just Valhalla that matters. It is merely one tool, although its secrets will be a critical bargaining chip that we can use with other countries. Gehlen and I have formed a new organization, head-quartered in Madrid, which will follow up on our ODESSA organization. ODESSA's goal was to facilitate the escape of our comrades to safe havens in Spain, South America, and Africa. The new organization will be known as 'the Spider,' *die Spinne*, because we will be attempting to create a web of influence throughout the world. I plan to visit Egypt and other countries in the Arab world. I will market our skills to help them emerge from colonialism and con-front the new state of Israel. These countries are rich in oil, and the West will need them in their confrontation with the Soviets. America may one day re-gret siding with the Zionists in the establishment of Israel, but unfortunately the Jewish lobby in America is very powerful."

"What about Mueller? He is expecting results on Valhalla soon."

"That's correct, Franz. Mueller may be the biggest problem of all for us. He is unpredictable and does not understand that rash action will be risky, especially if his surviving the war is discovered. I'm afraid of what he might do and thereby put us all at risk. Also, we must protect our relationship with the Paraguayan government. They have helped us enormously, but they do not want attention from America regarding their assistance in sheltering SS and Gestapo officers. We are currently courting a rising Paraguayan officer, General Alfredo Stroessner, and he has indicated that future cooperation will be contingent on us controlling Mueller and his impulses."

"So what will we do about that?"

"Let's take this a step at a time. We should, however, not be afraid to confront Mueller about this."

Skorzeny looked out again at the aqueduct and then returned to his suck-ling pig. He had specific actions in mind regarding Mueller, should they be-come necessary.

35

El Pardo Palace, Madrid, Spain.
April 1950

* * *

Luis Carrero Blanco was ushered in and walked over to the desk where his boss, Francisco Franco Bahamonde, was seated. Franco lived and often worked in the palace, but it was unusual for the Spanish dictator to work or hold meetings on weekends.

"You wanted to see me, Your Excellency?"

"Yes, Luis. Thank you for coming on short notice on a weekend. Please sit down."

Carrero took the chair on the opposite side of the table, curious about what Franco wanted of him on a Sunday afternoon. He sat patiently as he watched Franco sift through some papers, obviously looking for a particular document, which he finally located.

He studied it for a moment and finally looked up at his protégé. "Luis, we have known each other and worked together for how long now, about nine or ten years?"

"That's correct, Excellency."

"In all that time, you have faithfully served me and offered advice when I requested it. Today I will be seeking such advice, and I want you to provide your honest assessment, regardless of whether it may be contrary to what others advise. Will you do that?"

"Of course I will, sir. That's my duty," Carerro replied, his curiosity now definitely stirred.

"I have received information from our regular surveillance sources and certain other contacts about a well-known family in Spain. Actually it is two families, Ortega and Hoffman, who were united by marriage. My sources are urging me to authorize an investigation of their activities during the civil war and world war and their current activities abroad, especially regarding a Paul Hoffman, who resides in America, and his father, Karl Hoffman, who resides in Guinea. Our sources seem to be concerned about their loyalty to Spain and their knowledge of certain wartime secrets. Does any of this make sense to you?"

Carrero was aghast at Franco's revelation. *Who could be questioning their loyalty and for what reason?* Yet he replied immediately and without hesitation. "Your Excellency, I can assure you that both Paul and Karl Hoffman are loyal Spaniards. In fact, the younger Hoffman has been hugely influential with America, and his actions have secured millions of dollars in loans from them. He has also laid the groundwork for a formal rapprochement with the American government that will likely lead to further military and economic aid. His father has been active in the economic development in Guinea. He also developed the recommendations that the governor in Guinea provided you in 1940, before your meeting with Hitler. I might add that he had two other sons who fought for us in the civil war. One was a pilot in the Condor Legion. He later died in the world war."

Carrero noted the surprised look on Franco's face. "In addition, sir, the Ortega side of the family is also unquestionably loyal. In fact, one of them, Alberto Ortega, is a key member of my staff. He was also a decorated naval officer during the civil war."

Franco nodded, looked down again at the document in front of him, and then asked another question. "The information I have indicates the Ortega family was somehow involved in a Catalonian separatist incident. Is that true?"

"No, sir. The youngest Ortega sibling, the daughter, Anita, was married to a Catalonian who was killed during that event. A subsequent investigation cleared the Ortega family of any involvement."

Franco nodded, looked again at the document on his desk, put it aside, and looked back up at Carrero. "Thank you, Luis. It seems that the information I had on these two families is slanted and obviously incorrect."

Franco paused, sighing as he looked out the window, before turning back to Carrero and continuing. "You know, Luis, this is a typical problem I face. I am always buffeted by the various factions trying to pull us in different directions. People think I avoid making decisions. I am also vilified abroad because of the stances I take on behalf of Spain. The reality is that I must try to steer a middle course that is loyal to our movement, yet in some way reaches out to the Western world in their battle with Communism. I admire Hoffman and his son, because they seem to understand this. Thank you for your advice, Luis, and do what you can to encourage their continued activities in this direction."

"Of course, sir; I will ensure that their activities continue." Carrero stood following the signal from Franco that the meeting was over.

On the way back to his residence Carrero pondered the significance of the "other contacts" that Franco referred to. *Perhaps Alberto Ortega can shed some light on that. It might be time to accelerate the developing reconciliation with America.* Spain desperately needed foreign assistance to get its economy moving again. Carrero remembered that Alberto had urged him to establish contact with an individual, a Catholic priest named Father Josemaria Escriva. The priest had formed a Catholic lay organization in 1928 named Opus Dei. The organization had just received sanction from the Vatican. Escriva and others in Opus Dei had joined forces with some younger economic technocrats, and they were beginning to urge modernization of the Spanish economy as a means of lifting people out of poverty.

Franco and the regime's political arm, the *Falange*, on the other hand, were following a practice known as *autarky*, or "self-sufficiency." These policies limited imports, foreign investment, and economic development. The disagreement on economic policies had been simmering for a while, but it was now beginning to emerge as a controversial subject. Carrero realized that he had no choice other than to immerse himself in it in order to protect not only Franco, but the country itself.

Yes, he thought, I will need to tell Alberto to work even more closely with his cousin and uncle on these matters.

36

Taos, New Mexico,
April 1950

* * *

"Maintain airspeed at seventy-five, Anita, and carry a little power into the flare," Paul urged, as Anita continued to fly a near-perfect approach to the relatively short dirt airstrip south of town. Anita completed the approach with a perfect landing that consumed less than half of the twenty-nine-hundred-foot runway.

"This airplane is much easier to fly than the Cessna 140, but I see what you mean about it being 'slippery' if you don't pay attention to speed control," Anita commented as she taxied back to the parking area at the east end of the airstrip.

Within minutes they secured the airplane, walked over to a nearby pay phone, and called the Taos Inn. The inn promptly sent an employee to pick them up, since there wasn't even a cab in town. They were shortly installed in their two rooms in this small, sleepy, out-of-the-way Southwest town that was noted as a haven for the literary and artistic community. Paul's dual mission was to allow Anita to see a good part of America while simultaneously gaining practical operating experience in the Bonanza on typical long cross-country trips. Anita's added objective was to meet with wine makers in California, in order to gain insights into wine-making practices and styles.

Paul reflected on their westward flight, as he changed and freshened up before cocktails and dinner. They had accepted delivery of the Bonanza the previous day at the Beech Aircraft plant in Wichita. Paul was checked out in the airplane yesterday afternoon, and Anita had her turn this morning. The factory pilot commented favorably on Anita's piloting skills. They weren't able to depart until midday, and Paul selected Taos as an overnight stop, since he had been there previously. He was intrigued by the town and its bohemian character, as well as the surrounding beautiful, stark terrain.

He soon met Anita in the well-known Adobe Bar, where they both ordered Manhattans. Anita was clearly primed by her initial experience in the Bonanza and her introduction to the American Southwest.

Anita gushed as she compared New Mexico to her native land. "This land is incredibly beautiful. The arid landscape reminds me of La Mancha, while the mountainous terrain is like parts of Andalucía or Navarra."

"I know. I never tire of flying over Western America, especially in such a capable airplane."

"Yes, I can see how the Bonanza will be important to us in Spain. The ability to cover 750 kilometers in three hours will be invaluable to our operations."

Paul smiled as he looked at Anita, and she smiled back at him. He then glanced at the other patrons in the already crowded bar on this last Friday evening of the month. He turned back to Anita. "I'm always amazed by the ironies of our history. Spain ruled this land two hundred years ago, but that era is long over. Yet I was born in one of Spain's last remaining colonies. I believe that our time in Africa will soon be up, along with all the other European powers. When the British left India, it presaged the end of the colonial era. I'd guess that within a decade it will all be over. We need to start planning how that will affect our businesses and families."

"I agree with you, Paul, but our fathers will have difficulties with that reality."

"I suppose so."

It then hit him how beautiful Anita was tonight. She was wearing a long black dress, with long sleeves that were sheer, and the dress had a modestly plunging neckline. It fit perfectly on her slim but shapely body, complementing her curly raven hair and dark brown eyes. This was contrasted by red, but not gaudy, lipstick and a beautiful silver necklace and pendant with matching earrings. With minimal other makeup, her face was radiant and the softness of her skin easy to contemplate.

"Did you hear me, Paul?"

"I'm sorry?" Anita's query snapped him out of his trance. "What did you say, Anita?"

"I was wondering how we can strengthen our businesses in America and Spain, knowing that the fate of the operations in Guinea is unpredictable."

"That's the heart of what we have to do. We'll need to gradually start convincing our fathers to begin such transition planning. Hopefully, Alfonso can help us with this."

"Yes, he will agree with us, but I'm afraid my brother is even more aggressive about the future. He envisions a major increase in tourism in Spain in the future. He wants us to develop the seacoast land we acquired in southern Andalucia. I hope that doesn't conflict with my dream to modernize our wine-making facilities and develop different styles of wine."

She paused and then blurted out a completely different thought. "Do you miss Liz and the children?"

Taken slightly aback by the shift in conversation, Paul blurted out his own answer. "Yes, of course. Every day that I'm out of town I miss them. Yet travel is part of what I must do, and I try not to dwell on my loneliness on the road."

"I feel the same way. I miss Beatriz so much, but I know I must persevere in my efforts if I am to succeed, and that this will result in occasional separations. After Enrique was killed, I was at first bitter, but I recovered from that, thanks to you." Anita smiled and unconsciously placed her hand on Paul's as he held his drink on the table.

"I think it's time for dinner," Paul announced, slowly withdrawing his hand as Anita raised hers from his.

They resumed their business deliberations over dinner. About two hours later, Paul announced the end of the evening's discussion. "We should get some sleep now, Anita. It will be an early and long day tomorrow. Our Los Angeles office staff is planning a party for us tomorrow night. On Tuesday, we'll head to northern California and Napa for your meetings with the wine makers."

"Yes, it's time," Anita said simply. As she rose, Paul rose quickly and pulled her chair out. Then he placed her shawl carefully on her shoulders.

She spoke softly as she smiled. "Thank you, Paul."

They walked out of the Doc Martin's restaurant, turned left in the Adobe Bar, walked past the reception desk and through the corridor to the back entrance and then out to the small plaza, around which were a block of rustic guest rooms. It was totally silent outside, and the night air was clear and calm. The moon was three days short of full and directly overhead, bathing the plaza in diffused light. The sweet smell of burning piñon from the room fireplaces filled the air. They walked slowly together to their adjacent rooms, each absorbed in their thoughts.

They finally reached the door to Anita's room. She turned to face Paul and slowly moved closer to him. Anita was five inches shorter than Paul, and she looked up at his face as she moved even closer. The moonlight accentuated her facial features and beauty.

"Thank you for this complete immersion in America, Paul." She raised her right hand and reached over to gently touch Paul's left arm.

Without thinking Paul reciprocated as he raised his right arm to touch his cousin's shoulder. Anita moved closer again. Paul instantly felt a powerful urge to hug her, but she beat him to it, pulling ever closer and reaching her arms around his neck.

Paul froze. He was torn between conflicting and powerful urges—a powerful physical attraction versus abiding respect, the excitement of time and place versus ancient taboos, and enormous desire versus incipient guilt.

She sensed this and gently pulled him closer as their faces nearly touched. He hesitantly leaned in to her as she kissed him, gently at first, and then sensually. He started to accept, closing his eyes, nearly ready to bow to his intense desire for her at this frozen moment in time.

He pulled back abruptly. He was anxious to send a message of restraint, rather than one of repulsion.

"I'm sorry Anita. I shouldn't have—"

"No, Paul, I am sorry. I didn't mean to..."

They looked awkwardly at each other. Paul saw the tears forming but then stopping, as Anita regained her composure and finished her thought.

"It's just that the night is so beautiful, and I feel so close to you. After Enrique died I was all alone until you...you rescued me from despair."

This time Paul took the initiative, bringing her back close to him, putting his arms around her, pressing her head to his shoulder, and comforting her.

"I understand what you went through, Anita. I too feel caught up in this moment. It's difficult under such conditions to restrain one's feelings," he whispered in her ear.

She accepted his embrace for several long minutes. She finally slowly pulled away and moved toward the door of her room.

"I hope you will forgive me for this, Paul," she said, as she opened the door and looked toward him.

"There is nothing to forgive, Anita," he replied. He smiled and finally backed away several steps to his door. He turned back again to her after unlocking his room door.

"Sleep well, Anita. Tomorrow we'll both revel in the joy of blue sky and unending horizons."

"I will, but this will always be a memorable night for us, I suspect. Good night, Paul." She stepped inside the door and closed it.

Paul looked briefly up at the moon, soaking up its soothing radiance, as his pulse returned to normal. He sighed and finally walked into his own room and closed the door—on both the evening and its powerful emotions.

37.

Swakopmund, Southwest Africa,
May 1950

* * *

"I want to be as frank with you as I can, Johann. I know your true identity as well as your nephew's. I know that you, your nephew, and your crew members arrived here by submarine. More important, I know the extent to which former senior officials of the Third Reich are trying to find you and the secrets of Operation Valhalla. They will stop at nothing in their pursuit of you, and I'm afraid without further protection and cooperation you and your nephew will be in extreme danger. So Vice Admiral Walter Hoffman, will you be frank with me and help us collaborate to prevent such events from happening?"

Hendrik van den Bergh concluded his summary. He planned this late afternoon meeting in the remote corner of a local restaurant and confronted his subject after lunch and some small talk. His summary was meant to be blunt.

Walter was dumbfounded. *How has he found out these details? What else does he know? What shall I tell him? What steps should I take?*

He instantly concluded that cooperation was his only option. "You are correct in your details, Hendrik. I am indeed Walter Hoffman. You have graciously aided me, my nephew, and the others without asking for anything specific in return, other than our loyalty. Well, you have it. To confirm that loyalty and perhaps expand the manner in which we cooperate, I will soon need to conduct some important travel. The results of that travel will become apparent on my return. Will you be able to assist me with arrangements? I have a passport, thanks to you, but I will need visas and travel arrangements."

"Yes, of course I can assist, Walter. Where will you need to travel?"

"I will need to start in Lisbon. I'd rather not say where else for now."

"Very well, I will make arrangements through my contacts in the PIDE in Luanda. We can get you as far as there, and my Portuguese friends will help from that point."

So, Walter thought. *That must be his information source.* At least he knew that the Portuguese did not have specific knowledge of where the Valhalla cargo was stored, what it contained, or any knowledge of the money in Switzerland. "All right, Hendrik. I will need to make an interim visit to Luanda to make arrangements. I expect the European travel will occur in several months."

"Excellent, Walter. Let's continue our partnership. We will also do our utmost to protect your identity and location from outside parties. I hope you realize that it might be too risky to let you and your nephew travel together."

"Yes, I agree. I want to ensure his anonymity now that he is in South Africa."

"I'll make the travel arrangements for your initial Luanda trip, Walter, and let you know." Hendrik rose, signifying the end of the meeting, and Walter quickly rose also. The two men shook hands and van den Bergh quickly departed.

Walter pondered what had just happened. He realized the game had now changed, and there would be more at stake. He formulated a plan in his mind and quickly decided on the actions he would take. He planned some drastic steps, which he knew he would have to execute carefully.

He also knew that his plan would be very risky.

38.

Luanda, Portuguese Angola, Africa.
May 1950

* * *

The three men sat around the table in Santos's office discussing the arrangements that he had made. Santos summarized them as they concluded their discussion.

"The tickets will be obtained from our national airline, TAP, and you'll be on flight 522. You'll leave Luanda at 6:00 a.m. on a Monday and travel through Libreville, Accra, Robertsfield, Dakar, Villa Cisneros, Casablanca, and finally Lisbon. You'll overnight at Accra and Dakar, and finally arrive in Lisbon at 8:00 p.m. Wednesday evening. I'm sorry this will take three days, but TAP is still using a short-range DC-3 on this route, because larger equipment is not yet available."

"That's all right, Alexandre. I understand the logistical difficulties, and I'm happy that it's not a three-week sea voyage," Walter replied.

Claus Hilgeman then took over the description of the itinerary. "From Lisbon you'll be booked on Iberia Airlines through Madrid, Barcelona, and on to Geneva. You'll leave at 1:45 p.m. Thursday on Iberia flight 72 and connect through Madrid on flight 42 to Barcelona, where you'll overnight. You'll take flight 46 the next day, arriving at Geneva at 5:00 p.m."

"So it will take five days to reach Geneva," Walter said with a sigh.

"Yes, and the return trip will be pretty much the same," Claus responded.

"You will have a Portuguese visa for business use and a Spanish visa for transit only. Claus is making your arrangements for Geneva and Switzerland," Alexandre added.

"All right, that should conclude our business for today. You must be tired, Walter, so let's head for the hotel. The South African military flight returns to Swapkomund early tomorrow," Claus said.

The three men quickly concluded their meeting, and Walter and Claus left Santos's office. After they were clear of the building and walking toward their hotel, Walter queried his longtime associate. "Will I really be returning the same way?"

132

"No, but I had to tell Santos something. I trust him implicitly, but he does not have total control over your security en route. Alexandre is one side of the PIDE, but there are also more sinister elements that may be collaborating with the network of ex-SS members."

"So what's my actual return itinerary?"

Both men paused as Claus retrieved a document from his briefcase and began reading the itinerary to Walter.

"Since you're arriving in Geneva late on a Friday, you'll need to lie low and out of sight all weekend. The Swiss are efficient, so I'm assuming you will get all of your banking done the following Monday. On Tuesday you'll begin the return journey on Air France through Paris and then on to Douala in Cameroon through Algiers and Kano in Nigeria. It's an overnight flight to Douala. The next day you'll take Iberia flight 203 to Santa Isabel, where it arrives at 4:00 p.m. I'm assuming you will want to meet your brother on the mainland rather than the island, so the next morning you will take the 9:00 a.m. flight on Iberia 202, which will arrive at Bata on the mainland at 10:30. You'll be South African businessman Johann Hartman with an appointment to see Karl Hoffman. He will pick you up at the airport. I'm assuming it will be quite a shock to him. You must be firm with him about your agenda, even though serious emotions may arise from your reunion."

"I can assure you that we will get over the emotions rapidly. His main interest will be Hans. I will be unable to help him locate him in South Africa, although I will deliver a letter that Hans wrote urging his father not to try and find him. He will cite the dangers involved to all of us if Karl tries to do that."

"We will see about that, but those are not my main worries," Claus replied.

"What are those?" Walter replied expectantly.

"I'm concerned about your alias. Your wartime photographs are widely available within the SS community and I assume the Spanish BPS also. We need to disguise you in some way. I'd like for you to let your hair grow longer, grow a mustache, and start wearing eyeglasses. You should also plan to dress down during your travel, but not so far down that you would compromise your alias as a business traveler. With all due respect, you need to look ordinary—not Prussian."

"All right, I will comply and will remain out of sight when I'm not in transit. What about the arrangements for the freighter?"

"There is a regular steamer that stops at the Portuguese colonies and occasionally at either Santa Isabel or Bata if there is cargo there. It will arrive in Bata several days after you. You should have the Valhalla items prepared and ready for shipment and labeled as 'books and documents,' so that they will be inconspicuous. After leaving Bata, the freighter will stop briefly in Sao Tome and Luanda. You should remain in your cabin during these stops. The freighter will then continue to Cape Town, where you will be able to reclaim the cargo. You'll need to make arrangements with van den Bergh, so you can transfer custody to him and explain what he is getting."

Claus paused and sighed. The two men stared at each other for a moment before Claus continued. "Tell me again, why are you doing this? It seems risky to expose ourselves and give access to Valhalla to the South Africans. I will follow your direction, but this will increase the outrage of the SS and their assorted acolytes. They will not ever stop trying to find you, Hans, and perhaps other members of your family."

"I am aware of the risks, Claus, but I have concluded that we're already the targets of a manhunt. I want to ensure that Valhalla will be available to the parties who are most compatible with us. Right now that only includes the South Africans. We also owe van den Bergh and your friend Santos our gratitude. I intend to put the Valhalla funds to good use to secure our future and reward them for their protection."

"All right, but you must exercise extreme caution on this mission."

"I agree, Claus. Will you accompany me on the entire round trip?"

"I had only planned to follow you as far as Lisbon. I didn't want to risk having us travel together and even be on the same flight through Spain. There are too many ex-SS members there."

"All right. Why not fly to Paris and join me there for the return flight south?"

Claus hesitated briefly, obviously considering all the elements. "All right, I will do that."

"Fine, then it's settled. Let's go get some dinner."

As the two men resumed walking to their hotel, Walter Hoffman mulled over their careful planning. Surely they had thought of everything. He realized that the wild card in this would be his brother's reaction to their reunion—and Walter's plan to remove some of the Valhalla cargo.

39

New York City.
July 1950

* * *

Paul watched as Allen Dulles lit his pipe and took a few puffs, his typical smile absent. Paul had been summoned to Dulles's Sullivan and Cromwell office in Manhattan on this last Friday of July to join Dulles and his junior associate, Jack Kurtz, to discuss some "important matters." The matters soon became evident.

"Well it's certainly a new ball game now that hostilities have started in Korea. Just look at these headlines in today's paper: 'US LINE YIELDS IN KOREA, DRAFT CALL INCREASED TO 100,000; SOVIET TO RETURN TO UN COUNCIL.' This is only the beginning. My guess is that there will be hell to pay over why we didn't see this coming."

Jack jumped in. "Will it cause a shakeup at the CIA?"

"Yes, and I'm sure Hillenkoetter will be out soon. It's anyone's guess who will be next in the barrel."

"Wouldn't you or General Donovan be a candidate for CIA director?" Paul responded, with an innocent tone in his voice. He knew it would probably stimulate the conversation. Out of the corner of his eye he saw Jack smile.

"Well, thank you, Paul, but I don't think that's in the cards in a Democratic Truman administration. However, they have blown the dust off the report I submitted in '48 about how the agency is organized. It set off a firestorm when some senators reread the thing. It looks like they might bring me on as a consultant in the fall for a few months to offer some updated advice on how to reorganize the place."

Dulles noted the surprised look on Jack's face. "I'm sorry, Jack. I was going to tell you soon."

Dulles looked at Jack and then Paul.

"Look, the reason I asked you to come by, Paul, is related to all this. You've done great laying the groundwork for reconciliation between Spain and America. Your meeting with Senator McCarran was crucial in garnering political support, and you've been successful in getting commercial loans for Spain. We now have to accelerate the government-to-government part. I'm convinced that Truman will finally appoint a new ambassador in a few months, but it will then take many more months for him to arrive in Spain and get official discussions going. In the interim, Paul, you need to keep things moving by continuing your role as an unofficial conduit with links to both countries. You've been successful in gaining Luis Carrero's trust, and you need to keep at it."

"I'm certainly intending to do that, Allen. It would be helpful if I could offer something to Carrero on my next visit that shows we're serious."

"You're right on that, Paul, so here's what you can offer. This information is secret, but I've been authorized by the air force to 'leak' it to you. Early next year, the air force will begin making temporary bomber deployments to Morocco as a result of an agreement with France. Of course, Spain has the protectorate of Spanish Morocco in the northern zone. Carrero will probably look good to Franco if he reveals this information to him before it is announced, and this will also increase your credibility. You should let him know that America is anxious to start the dialogue with Spain on defense cooperation. That might cause him to think about military cooperation, such as bases."

"I can do that as early as next month, when I'll be in Spain."

"Good, we can coordinate on other matters that you can discuss with Carrero. I'll make sure I get that to you early next week."

"Fine. Now if you wouldn't mind, I liked to change the subject to a business matter affecting the family, since you are our family's law firm. I'd like to find out the status of my cousin Kirsten's inheritance of her father's estate. I know you've already been working this issue."

Paul nodded toward Jack to acknowledge the advance work he had already done.

"Thank you for reminding me, Paul. The good news is that it's already done. Since Walter Hoffman disappeared on April 4, 1945, the five-year period specified by German law expired this last April. A ninety-day petition period has just been completed. Since Kirsten just had her eighteenth birthday, the estate can be transferred to her immediately. Your father, of course, owns the other half of the estate."

"That's fabulous news. Kirsten will be pleased. Of course, that means she also has access to the family bank accounts in Switzerland, doesn't it?"

"In theory, yes, but without access to the codes authorizing withdrawals from those accounts, she is out of luck. I'm sorry, but your father and his brother were pretty compartmentalized with regard to your grandfather's estate."

"Yes, it's no secret that they were not exactly close during the years of the Nazi regime," Paul replied, realizing there was much more to the story.

The meeting soon concluded. Later, on the way to meet Jack in the Village for their usual Friday night celebration, Paul pondered the inevitable concern nagging him. He now needed to find Walter Hoffman, since he not only held the key to where Hans was but also access to millions of Swiss francs.

40

Cadiz. Spain.
August 1950

* * *

"You must let me have access to that airplane! I own it, and I intend to taxi it over to the other side of the ramp to fuel it."

"That's impossible. You are a woman and cannot possibly be the pilot or be authorized to move it."

Anita seethed as the civil guard, expressing a mixture of contempt and authority, stared at her. Frustrated after fifteen minutes of fruitless discussion with the *civil*, she realized that holding her ground would accomplish nothing. She turned around and walked briskly away, intent on finding Paul.

She and Paul had tried very hard to maintain normal family relationships after their plane trip across America in the Bonanza. Yet an unspoken tension still simmered after their evening in Taos more than three months ago.

The Bonanza and the second Twin Beech had been shipped to Spain on a family freighter, reassembled, and readied at the Cadiz airport. Paul had already flown the Twin Beech to Madrid and left it at Barajas Airport. He returned to Cadiz so he could accompany Anita in the Bonanza on the flight to Madrid, in order to give her some experience operating in Spain. The plan was for Anita to then fly the Bonanza to Logroño in Rioja, the nearest airport to the family's properties there. Paul would meanwhile join his father, who was already in Spain, to ferry the Twin Beech to Spanish Guinea.

Anita finally located Paul in the customs office.

"So the Bonanza is refueled already?"

"No, it is not. You will have to take some drastic action if I am ever to operate it in Spain."

"What do you mean?" he replied, instantly tensing up.

"I need some different credentials than just my American pilot certificate. When we get to Madrid, you will need to get me a validated Spanish pilot certificate and some sort of document, from Franco himself if necessary, that says I am a pilot and am authorized to operate the Bonanza anywhere in Spain."

"That doesn't seem necessary, Anita. I mean—"

"Listen to me, Paul! We are in Spain now, not America, and it is still 1950. It might as well be the Dark Ages if you are a woman. We will be in Madrid tomorrow. Promise me you will get these authorizations for me. I don't care who you have to see. I've come too far to turn back on this now."

Paul noticed Anita's intense look, could not argue with her logic, and recognized that she was correct, as well as determined. "All right, I'll do it. I'm not sure how, but like anywhere, I suppose it's who you know that carries the day. Promise me one thing, however."

"What's that?"

"When you get the documents and have to use them, try to have mercy on whoever dares to question you first." Paul mustered a fake look of seriousness. Anita initially looked aghast, but then quickly realized that Paul was gently ribbing her for her direct personality. They both immediately broke out laughing.

"Paul, you are amazing. You know me so well, and anticipate my feelings even before I do myself." She reflexively came closer and reached her arms around him. Instantly, she must have realized what that might do to both of them and she pulled back.

"I'm sorry; I didn't mean—"

"Anita, please, it's all right. We needed something to break the tension between us. We have nothing to be ashamed of. Let's get the Bonanza refueled and get going. The day after tomorrow, my father and I have appointments with Luis Carrero, the air ministry, and Iberia Airlines. Sometime during these meetings I will find a way to take care of your documents."

Paul softly touched Anita's arm. Her immediate smile and admiring gaze reminded Paul that deeper feelings still existed between them.

41

Madrid. Spain.
September 1950

* * *

"How are the discussions progressing with Iberia Airlines and the air ministry?" Luis Carrero inquired of his guest, as the three men continued their wide-ranging meeting.

"They are progressing well, sir. My father has agreed to serve as a consultant to Iberia on the introduction of direct air service to Guinea. In conjunction with that, we agreed to stop at Tetuan in the protectorate, at Sidi Ifni, and Villa Cisneros in Sahara, in order that we may observe the status of airport and airway facilities in our African territories and thereby make recommendations to both Iberia and the air ministry."

"Excellent. This will be very valuable in terms of ensuring that future air service meets our economic development needs," Carrero replied. He turned to Alberto Ortega.

"Alberto, please follow up with your cousin after their trip to Guinea, and assist him any way you can in expediting their report to the air ministry and Iberia."

"Yes, sir," Alberto looked expectantly at Paul to remind him that one issue still remained.

Paul took the hint. "There is also the matter of future American intentions toward us. Along those lines, I am authorized to tell you that the American and French governments have reached agreement regarding the use of air bases in Morocco by the Americans. The basing agreement specifies that activity will begin there shortly after the New Year. This is an indicator that the Americans realize the strategic importance of this area, including Spain. They are anxious to discuss defense cooperation with us."

"I see. This is a positive development, and it is a sign that we will have a lot to discuss with the Americans, once the diplomatic and political hurdles we discussed earlier are resolved. Thank you for that valuable information, and also for your continued successful interventions with America on Spain's behalf," Carrero concluded as he looked at his watch.

Alberto started to lean forward in his chair as if to rise when Paul interjected.

"There is one more matter, sir, which I would like to raise with you."

"Yes, go ahead," Carrero replied, looking first at Paul and then at Alberto.

"We experienced some difficulties with some civil guards in Cadiz when we imported our two aircraft there the other day. They questioned the qualifications of the other pilot, even though that pilot had a valid pilot certificate and other paperwork. I would like to secure authorizations for the pilot from a higher level to ensure that future such incidents are avoided."

"Well, surely his pilot certificate should be adequate proof of his qualifications. I'm not sure I understand."

"Actually, the pilot is a woman, sir. It's Anita Ortega, Alberto's sister and my cousin. She will be using the aircraft to visit our wine-making properties throughout Spain, and she is hoping to avoid any confrontation with authorities." Actually, Paul knew that Anita was unlikely to avoid any confrontation when her interests were under attack.

Carrero looked at Paul, smiled, and then looked to Alberto.

"Very well. Alberto, let's prepare an appropriate authorization from the highest possible level in the government, so that our young aviatrix can proceed about her wine making and other business without any undue bureaucratic obstacles."

"Yes, sir," Alberto replied, with a stunned look on his face.

After the meeting concluded, Paul and Alberto left the building at 5 Paseo de la Castellana. It was the former Palacio Alcala-Galiano and now the Dirreccion de Marruecos y Plazas y Provincias Africanas. Luis Carrero directly ruled over Spain's African holdings from this building. When they reached the street, Paul turned to look back at the building, admiring the inlaid Moorish arches and other subtle features surrounding the second floor windows in a square building that otherwise had only modest architectural features. He turned to Alberto.

"He appears happy with the progress we are making with America. He seems to take a direct interest in any activity that promotes development in the colonies."

"Yes, he is exceptionally pleased and is happy with what you have done. It's interesting, however, that he was so indulgent regarding the incident you and Anita had. He is a very conservative man in a very conservative country with conservative views on the roles of women. I'm amazed that he so readily granted your request."

"I am also, but let's follow up right away so Anita will have her papers when she is ready to depart for Rioja in a few days."

"All right, Paul. Let's head across the street to meet your father. He'll be expecting us at the Embassy."

Alberto was referring to the Embassy Tea Room at 12 Paseo de la Castellana, across the street from the government building they just left. The Embassy was a noted place for the elite of Madrid to socialize. It was also a meeting place for considerable clandestine activity, as Alberto, Paul, and Karl all knew. They had no reason to suspect that anyone had reason to observe them today.

Paul and Alberto quickly crossed the street and entered through the Embassy's discreet side entrance. They quickly joined Karl in the main bar area on the first floor. Paul noted the marble and tile floors as he approached the bar. The three men were prepared to discuss business, but the subject quickly changed.

"Have we completed all of our work with Iberia and the air ministry, Father?"

"Yes, I'm happy to report. We can therefore leave for Africa in a day or two. I'll be glad to escape the prying eyes that are following me."

"What are you saying?" Paul asked, after recovering from the surprise.

"Yes, who is following you?" Alberto added.

"At first I thought I was imagining it, and then I thought I was overly paranoid, but I know for sure that I'm being professionally followed. They do it in pairs, changing the individuals occasionally so it's inconspicuous. It's hard to get a description of them because of their manner and dress."

Paul sighed. How much should he tell his father and Alberto? In fact, what did Alberto know about this?

"It's an unfortunate fact that Madrid has always been like that. It's a neutral city where many interests have a need to spy on one another," Alberto replied, as if reading Paul's body language.

"Yes, well with all the ex-Nazis, the BPS, and who knows what other organizations, I'm glad to be leaving soon," Karl said with disgust.

"It's not quite that dramatic, Karl," Alberto responded.

"Never mind; let's go to the Palace Hotel. There's a more discreet bar there off the main lobby, and we will have an easier time talking," Paul suggested.

As both Alberto and Karl nodded, the three men rose and quickly exited the bar. On the walk over to the Palace, Paul realized that he was not the only one experiencing the threat of surveillance. *Who could it be and what do they want?*

Paul decided that he and his father had to have an important talk when they reached Africa.

42

Logroño, Spain.
September 1950

* * *

"You must wait until my superior officer comes to talk to you. My associate will summon him immediately. I must detain you until he arrives to determine why a woman is flying this airplane."

The civil guard was firm but not condescending as his partner hurried toward the airport security office with Anita's pilot certificate and photo identification to inform their superior that a small private plane with a woman pilot had just landed on his turf.

"All right, I will wait. I will also take some documents from the plane, if you don't mind, so your superior will be able to review them when he arrives," Anita replied.

The young civil nodded and Anita quickly retrieved the documents from the Bonanza. She had anticipated this and was primed for confrontation if it became necessary.

She didn't have to wait long. She soon saw the other civil returning from the office, led by his superior officer. As the man came closer, she noted he was about the same height as her. She also saw that he had a repulsive grin, and he strutted while alternately looking at Anita and her identification photograph.

Anita was not shocked when she also noted the bulge in the man's groin. *So the stage is set*, she thought.

The man finally reached Anita. He continued leering at her for several long seconds as she waited for him to make his move.

"So, we have an unusual situation. My men observed you land and taxi in. I see from these American documents that you are a licensed pilot, but only in the United States."

"I'm sorry, Captain, but that's not quite true. I'm flying a US-registered aircraft. With a US pilot certificate that entitles me to fly in Spain, since our country is a signatory to the Chicago agreement of 1944, which permits reciprocal flying privileges in any International Civil Aviation Organization member state for a situation such as mine."

The civil officer changed his tone, as his smile changed to a smirk and then a frown. "We will see about that. Perhaps we can retreat to my office, where we can have a private discussion of the matter," he replied as his smirk returned.

"Not until you read these two documents, Captain," Anita replied. She handed two official documents to the officer, as his two subordinates looked on with apprehension.

Anita watched as the officer read the documents. His smirk gradually disappeared. She knew that now was the time. "As you can see, Captain, the first document is a letter from the air minister with his official seal. It authorizes me to operate this aircraft anywhere in Spain. My validated Spanish pilot license is attached. More important, you will note that the second document is an official authorization from the secretary to the president, Luis Carrero Blanco, which confirms that letter."

Anita paused until she saw from the horrified expression on the officer's face that he must have reached the final signature on that document. *It's time for the coup de grace* she thought. "Finally, I direct your attention to the countersignature and seal at the bottom of that document. It is none other than that of *El Caudillo*, His Excellency Francisco Franco Bahamonde."

By this time Anita could see the quiver that the officer was desperately trying to stifle. He finally looked up at her with a panic-stricken face as he started sweating profusely. She stepped back and deliberately glared at the man, sweeping her gaze up and down his body. She paused briefly at his groin noting with satisfaction that the man's ego was not the only thing that she had deflated.

"I am...so sorry Señora Ortega. If only I had known, then—"

"That's enough. You have already wasted enough of my time. I will not pursue this with Madrid if you order your men to assist me with my baggage and cargo and then let them help me take the airplane to our hangar."

"Yes, of course." The man barked orders at his two subordinates, who had been standing there listening and observing as their boss cowered before Anita. They quickly began unloading the Bonanza.

"Is there anything else?" the officer finally said with a higher pitch to his voice.

"I have only some advice, Captain. I know that you communicate with your superiors and other civil guard offices. I advise you to inform them about me, my airplane, my authorizations, and my need to travel unrestricted throughout Spain unmolested. In fact, I think you should do that immediately. Now."

"Yes. Yes, of course. I will do that…now," the man finally uttered as he bowed stiffly, turned, and quickly strode back toward his office.

In a short while, the Bonanza was safely in its hangar. Anita turned to the two uniformed men and noted their panicked look as she approached the first man and addressed him. "What is your name?"

"I am Corporal Sanchez," he stuttered.

"No, what is your given name?"

"My name is Pablo."

She turned to the other man. "And you?"

"I'm Alfredo."

"Very well, Pablo and Alfredo, please listen. I know you were only doing your duty today, and I appreciate that. In fact, I want you to consider doing me a favor."

Anita pulled a pouch from her bag.

Pablo merely stared at her for several seconds. Alfredo finally responded. "What is it you want of us?"

"I will be using this airplane a lot, but it will also be here at the airport for long periods. I know you are both busy with your official duties, but I was wondering if, in your spare time, you could both check the airplane periodically to make sure it is secure. Also, please notify me if some stranger inquires about me or the airplane. I know this service will take some of your time, so I want to compensate you for that."

Anita opened the pouch and pulled out four one-thousand-peseta notes and two calling cards. She gave two notes and a calling card to each man. She paused as the two men stared at the money, their eyes bulging out of their sockets. Anita guessed that two thousand pesetas was probably two or three months' pay for them. She continued her instructions.

"Please remember that I am doing this as a business proposition. If the arrangement is satisfactory, and I am pleased, then I may renew our relationship next year. Please also remember to contact me if an outsider inquires about me or the airplane. My phone and address are on the cards. Do you both accept this proposal?"

After a short delay, both men nodded enthusiastically. Anita then shook each man's hand, and they quickly left the hangar, speechless, their mouths agape. Anita watched them for a while as they walked across the ramp. She knew what she had done entailed some risk. She also knew that neither man was likely to report her for bribery, since they had accepted the money in each other's presence.

Anita finally sighed and turned to face the Bonanza. She stared quietly at it for several minutes as the tense events of the previous hour receded. Looking at the Bonanza caused her to remember that night in Taos. *Where is he now?* she thought. He and Karl were probably somewhere over northern Africa in the Twin Beech.

She closed her eyes and whispered to herself. "Please forgive me, Paul... but...I love you."

43.

Villa Cisneros, Spanish Sahara, Africa.
September 1950

* * *

Paul stared out the window of the Parador Hotel dining room and marveled at the whitewashed colonial buildings with their fortlike features, the Moorish architecture and parapets, the sun-drenched blue skies, and then the Atlantic Ocean beyond. It was similar to the scene in Tetuan, in the Moroccan protectorate, but without all the people or the bustle. The Sahara colony was more than half the size of Spain, yet it had fewer than seventy-five thousand people in its 116,000 square miles of mostly trackless desert.

Paul turned to see his father approaching. *I must keep it casual at first*, Paul told himself. He knew his father would rebel when pressed for information about Hans.

Karl sat down wearily and looked at his son, finally offering a weak smile. "Well, both the colonial officials and the airline staff were pleased with our visit. This dusty town and its airport are important only as a refueling and overnight stop on the way to South America, but we will need it as long as only the DC-4 is available for that air service. Iberia is seeking to buy Lockheed Constellations for the over-ocean routes. When they are finally able to afford that, we might finally get the DC-4s as hand-me-downs for same day air service to Guinea."

"When will that be?"

"Probably not for another two to four years. But in the meantime, I'm glad we will be leaving this wasteland tomorrow," Karl said as he looked out the window, as Paul had, taking in the view.

"You must admit that the starkness of the setting has a certain quality about it. It's like watching a scene out of *Beau Geste*," Paul offered.

"What's *Beau Geste*?"

Paul looked puzzled but then realized that his father's isolation in Spanish Guinea had deprived him of certain cultural elements. "It's a 1939 movie based on a book and starring Gary Cooper. It's about three French Foreign Legionnaires who are isolated in a desert outpost much like this one."

"Ah yes, Gary Cooper. I saw him in *Sergeant York* in Santa Isabel in 1942. That was only a year after it was released in America, so you shouldn't think we are culturally isolated in Guinea," his father replied, obviously reading Paul's mind.

"He won the best-actor award for that movie. He was nominated again two years later, but he wasn't selected for his role in *For Whom the Bell Tolls.* Did you see that, Father?" Paul instantly regretted that question.

Karl looked at him, at first with a frown, and then an indulgent smile. "So, I concede the point that Hemingway is banned in Spain. But I have read the book. You and I both know that it is slanted toward the republic in honor of Hemingway's politics. I'm no defender of the Franco regime, as you well know, but the republicans were equally guilty of atrocities. Even more important, they were incompetent administrators. They bungled the only chance for Spain to be a functioning democracy for a generation or two. We can largely thank Stalin's influence for all that. In a way, we should thank Franco for bringing stability to the country and confronting the Communists before it became fashionable in America."

"Yes, I agree. It is time to cooperate more with America in an alliance against Communism, and also to seek America's help in getting the economy going again. It might be the only way we can make progress toward a more open and just society."

"I see the influence you have had, my son. I'm proud of what you have done, but I would be cautious about the American alliance."

"In what way should I be cautious?"

"By granting the Americans bases in Spain, we are likely to become a nuclear target in the event of another world war. Although that risk is small, we should exact a heavy price from America for our cooperation."

"I think that's the general idea, and I will indeed be cautious as to how I proceed. Would you like to hear a summary of our remaining itinerary?"

"Yes; what does it look like?"

"We've already traveled 1360 miles since leaving Madrid, and we have about 2670 to go. Tomorrow we'll stop in Bissau, Portuguese Guinea, on our way to Monrovia, Liberia. We should get there in one day if the weather cooperates. The following day the plan is to stop in Accra, in the Gold Coast, on our way to Santa Isabel, hopefully arriving that evening if the weather cooperates again."

"I'm trying to visualize those distances in kilometers."

"Don't bother. Both the charts and the aircraft instruments are calibrated in English miles."

"Ah, yes. It's just as well, since four thousand miles is such a large number, and it would be even more so in kilometers."

Now is the time for me to talk about Hans, Paul thought.

"I hope you still agree to make the trip to Angola and South Africa in the Beech while I am here, so we can better coordinate with current and potential customers and with our export-import agents."

"That's still a good idea, since I haven't been to either place recently, and the aircraft is ideal for the task. Are you sure you will have the time?"

"Yes, I will." Paul mentally crossed his fingers. "Actually, the main reason I want to go is to look for Hans."

His father blinked in surprise and was momentarily speechless before replying. "What do you mean?"

"Father, I know that Hans and Uncle Walter departed Denmark in a U-boat in April 1945 with a special cargo. I also know that they made it at least to the South Atlantic. Hans would have insisted on stopping in Guinea before proceeding to their ultimate destination. Is that true? Do you know where he is? I'm sorry to surprise you with this, but I will not rest until I locate him."

Paul watched his father's look change from surprise, to agony, to resignation, and finally to determination as he recovered and finally replied.

"It's no surprise. I knew you would ask me this. To answer your questions, Hans and Walter did stop in Guinea on their way to wherever their final destination was. I know nothing about their 'special cargo,' only that they both told me that it would be dangerous for us to try to find them because of the nature of the cargo."

"I am aware of the danger. Didn't they give you any clue where they were going?"

"No, they said nothing."

"Thanks to my American connection, I was able to determine that they did not go to South America or Asia, so I'm certain they are somewhere in Africa. Both Angola and South Africa are likely places where they may have gone."

"Hans and Walter said we must not—"

"That doesn't matter anymore. It is apparent that we may be in danger anyway, as ex-Nazis and perhaps others try to locate that submarine and what it carried. Don't you want to find Hans? Don't you know he must still carry the guilt from the war, by the knowledge that Mother died on the Athenia, and that he was on the U-boat that sank it?"

Those last words must have stung. Paul watched his father close his eyes, grimace, and try unsuccessfully to suppress tears. Paul thought about getting up to comfort him but decided to wait.

Finally, Karl opened his eyes, sighed deeply, and responded. "I also want to find Hans. I tried unsuccessfully to relieve him of his guilt. I want to find him and release him from that horrible force." He paused. Then he said, "All right, we will try to find some evidence of his location, but I am not optimistic."

"That's all right. We must at least try."

Both men looked out of the window toward the setting sun. Each nursed his own memories of their missing family member and wondered if they would someday be reunited.

44

Cape Town, South Africa,
October 1950

* * *

Paul and Karl were mostly quiet at dinner in their hotel. Their stops in Angola and South Africa had been successful in a commercial sense. Both men, however, were depressed at the lack of success in their search for Hans and Walter. They could find no clues whatsoever of their missing relatives from officials, records, newspapers, or other sources. Tomorrow they would fly to Johannesburg, where Karl had agreed to drop Paul so he could catch a Pan Am flight home to New York. Paul had been gone nearly two months, and it was urgent that he return. Besides that, he missed Liz and the twins.

Karl poured the rest of their dinner wine and summed up the travel arrangements. "So you will head back to America. I feel comfortable with the Beech. I plan to stop in both North and South Rhodesia on the way back to Guinea in order to explore commercial possibilities in the British colonies."

"Yes, that's a good idea," Paul responded pensively.

"I'm sure that Liz, Robert, and Pilar can hardly wait to see you."

"Yes, they've probably been lonely. Last winter and spring were especially enjoyable for us, because Anita and Beatriz were visiting. Anita's stay was very rewarding for our wine-making operations, and she enjoyed America enormously. I'm also happy that we resolved her issues around operating the Bonanza in Spain. She plans to use the airplane a lot and I wanted to make sure she would be able to do so safely."

Paul waited for his father to respond, but Karl only managed a frown.

"Is there something wrong?" Paul asked.

"I don't know." He paused. "I've noticed that over the last three weeks you have talked a lot more about Anita than about your wife and children."

Paul was caught off guard. "It's just that I respect her determination after Enrique was killed. She could have withdrawn into a shell, but she didn't. She got beyond her grief to accomplish some courageous things."

"All right, that's all true. I just wondered whether your admiration went beyond just respect and was actually something more."

"What are you saying? She's my cousin and…she's family. Are you suggesting that I'm hiding something?"

"I'm only suggesting that other members of the Ortega family—and Liz—may have noticed your closeness with her, that's all."

The two men were silent for several minutes. Paul finally broke the ice. "I thank you for your…concern. I can assure you that Anita and I have the greatest respect for each other and would do nothing that would shame our families."

"All right, my son, I didn't mean to raise such an awkward issue, but I just wanted to caution you that misperception can be an important concern in such matters."

"I understand," Paul replied simply, uncomfortable and anxious to move on.

"I'd like to revisit the results of our inquiries. Have you noticed that in several instances officials in both Angola and South Africa have been hostile to our inquiries, almost like they were trying to cover something up or keep certain information from us?"

"Yes, I noticed that also. It could just be that we are foreigners intruding on their turf and that created the resentment."

"Perhaps they know something about Hans or Walter that they don't want to share with us, or perhaps they fear how a third party would react to their disclosing such information."

"I wouldn't read too much into it, Paul. In any case, we must admit that our search was disappointing and has reached a dead end."

Paul looked at his father and wondered why he was not as motivated to continue the search for his firstborn son.

"Just so you know, I will never consider it a dead end, and I intend to keep pursuing the truth, wherever it leads."

Paul noticed the noncommittal response and body language his father displayed as he failed to respond to Paul's challenge. *What else does he know that he's not sharing?*

Father and son sat there uncomfortably as they finished their dinner.

Paul had reached another decision. He must confront Claus Hilgeman again.

45

Near Coimbra, Portugal.
November 1950

* * *

Paul knocked quietly on the door of the room in the remote wing of the Palace Hotel in the Bussaco Forest in central Portugal, north of the old university town of Coimbra. He hoped it was the right room. Within seconds he had his answer.

Before letting Paul in, Claus Hilgeman leaned forward to look up and down the hall. He closed the door behind him and locked it after Paul entered.

Paul wanted to cut through the mystery right away. "This seems to be an extraordinary and remote place for us to meet. Why do we need so much stealth and secrecy?"

"Did you follow my instructions? How did you get here?"

"I did as you suggested. You wanted me to avoid Lisbon and somehow pick up an alias. I only took Pan Am 151 out of Johannesburg as far as Accra. I registered under a false name and took TAP to Villa Cisneros in Spanish Sahara. From there I made connections on Iberia Airlines to Madrid. My cousin met me there with our Bonanza aircraft. I told her I needed to make some business flights within Spain. I flew her to Vallodolid, where she could spend a couple of days inspecting some vineyards. I then flew to the small airport in Coimbra, without a flight plan and without checking in with Portuguese immigration when I arrived. My manager from our office in Porto had arranged to leave a car at the Coimbra Airport. I then drove here."

"Good, then it's likely they lost track of you, and they don't know we're here."

"Who is the 'they' you're referring to?"

"Paul, I don't expect you to understand all of intricacies of the situation, but I know that they are following both of us."

"Answer my question, damn it! Who is following us?" Paul raised his voice, feeling frustrated and in the dark.

"I'm sorry. It's a long story, but basically it's a web of former Nazi officials. I think Otto Skorzeny is the head of it. Not only that, but I'm now sure that other powers may be involved, independent of the ex-Nazi ring."

"Isn't Skorzeny the guy who rescued Mussolini? Also, what other powers are you referring to?"

"Let's talk about it over dinner. I believe our precautions were thorough and that neither of us was followed. We can find an isolated table in the dining room. There are very few people staying here now, and we should have privacy. By the way, you must try the local wine. I've already sampled some." Claus pointed to the nearly empty bottle on the table.

"Is that why we came here—for the wine?"

"No, we came here because this hotel is out of the way and far from the prying eyes of PIDE, Skorzeny, and any others who may be tailing us."

"All right, we can talk over dinner," Paul replied reluctantly.

"Make a reservation at nine. I'll meet you in the large bar and lounge area next to the dining room at eight. We can start our discussion over a drink. Stay in your room until then, so you minimize any contact with the hotel staff. Just to be on the safe side, don't make any outside calls."

"I'll see you then," Paul replied as Claus let him out.

* * *

Paul looked at his watch. It was 7:45 exactly. He sat in the rather large bar area where he was the only patron. He had left his room early, and was now sipping his rather crisp Chip Dry White Port from Taylor Fladgate. He admired the blue-tile murals on the walls depicting famous battles and scenes from Portuguese literature. *One of those might be the Battle of Bussaco,* he thought. It occurred in September 1810, when the Duke of Wellington led an Anglo-Portuguese force to defeat Napoleon's French army during the Peninsular War. That saved Portugal, although the monarchy only lasted another century and was deposed in 1910. This hotel was built as a palace for the royal family, on the site of the old convent where Wellington allegedly spent the night after winning his battle.

Paul shook his head as he reveled in the history of this place. He gazed at the huge alabaster marble fireplace with another mural above it, depicting a minstrel with a guitar. He also noted the six large windows with their gothic arches.

"May I bring you another Chip Dry Port, sir?" The waiter asked in reasonable Spanish, as he interrupted Paul's reverie.

"Yes, that will be fine." Paul looked at his watch as the waiter left. It was 8:10. Claus was running a little late. Paul thought that perhaps he had fallen asleep after drinking the wine, remembering the near-empty bottle in the room.

Paul looked up again at the murals. He admired one depicting three weary travelers with their heads drooped on horseback. *The means of transportation have sure improved since then.* He finished off the first glass of white port and daydreamed for a few more minutes.

He checked the time: 8:20. Claus was not the type to be this late.

Paul rose and headed out. He would take the outside shortcut that he found earlier through the rear courtyard to the remote hotel wing where Claus's room was located. He donned his leather gloves as he went outside into the chill November air. He reentered the hotel in the other wing and slowly walked to Claus's room. It was quiet; it seemed that no one else was staying in this wing.

As he approached Claus's room, he began to hear noises. He quickened his pace.

As he came closer, he heard a man's deep voice, abrupt and insistent. Paul slowed down, anxious not to reveal his presence. He was soon close enough to hear the other man's words.

"You will tell me what you know now, or I will end it for you rather unpleasantly!"

Paul's reaction was instantaneous. The adrenaline kicked in. *I wish I had my Beretta.* He quickly but silently moved toward the open door to the room. He saw the empty bottle of wine outside the room. He scooped it up and walked the last few paces.

He saw a heavyset man kneeling down, with his back toward Paul. The man looked like he was holding a knife to Claus's throat. He must have surprised Claus.

Paul's instincts took control. He lunged at the man, the wine bottle over his head.

The man turned when he heard Paul, but the split second it took Paul to swing the bottle down on his head was not enough for the intruder to rise and turn his knife on Paul.

The bottle smashed into the man's forehead. He keeled over backward. Amazingly, the bottle did not break.

Paul didn't delay. He raised the bottle again with both hands and brought it down on the man's head with all the force he could muster. The bottle shattered, and Paul heard a distinctive crack. The man's skull fractured.

Paul almost fell, but he caught himself on the bedpost next to where Claus was lying. His left hand hurt like hell.

Paul had no time to feel fear. It all happened in just a few seconds. He leaned over the fallen man and cautiously felt for a pulse. There was none.

With the threat gone, he wheeled around and knelt next to Claus, who was breathing heavily and lying on his back. Paul saw that he was bleeding profusely from a stomach wound. Paul grabbed a pillow from the bed, ripped the case off it, and placed it carefully on the wound to try to stop the bleeding. Claus immediately pulled Paul's hand away, as if to keep it from getting bloody.

"No...it's too late for...that," he said, struggling to get the words out.

"I'll go for help!"

Again Claus restrained him. "No...you must leave this place...or you'll be in serious trouble." Claus grimaced as he struggled for air. "I know you want...to find your...brother." He grabbed Paul's jacket.

Paul could see from the rapid increase in Hilgeman's breathing that he was nearly finished.

"Where is he?" Paul reached around Claus's head to raise it slightly.

"Go to...Luanda...see Santos...Alexandre Santos...PIDE...chief..."

At that point Claus relaxed his grip on Paul's jacket, closed his eyes, and gave one final breath. His head fell limp in Paul's uninjured right hand.

Paul gently put Claus's head down on the floor. He stood and looked down at the two dead men. This time it was his brain rather than his body that raced into action. *All right, think fast. Get back to the bar and act normal.*

He looked at the gloves, still on his hands. Good, no fingerprints. *I better not leave early or leave without checking out. Just close the door and walk away. Get out early in the morning, as planned.*

Paul quietly left the room, closed the door, and quickly walked back to the bar. He did not see a soul or detect that anyone had seen or heard what happened.

He returned to his seat and noticed his empty glass was still there. He looked at his watch. It was 8:55. He finally noticed that his rapid pulse and breathing had nearly returned to normal. He breathed deeply several times and closed his eyes. Maybe when he opened them, he would realize it was all a dream.

"Excuse me, sir. I'm sorry I forgot about you."

Paul's eyes opened with a start. "You forgot?"

"Yes, sir. I was called by the kitchen to assist with a room-service order, and I forgot about your drink. Here it is, and both glasses are with our compliments."

"Thank you. I'll take it to the restaurant for dinner. I want to eat right away. I am checking out early in the morning, and I need to get some sleep."

"Of course. Please follow me to the dining room." The waiter placed the port glass back on his tray. Paul followed him to the restaurant.

Remember, just act normal until you can get out of the hotel, get to the Bonanza in the morning, and take off. Anita will be waiting in Vallodolid.

As he sat down to the dinner table, he took off his gloves. His left hand was swollen. He must ask for some ice later.

As the waiter came over to take his order, Paul mentally repeated Claus's last words: *Luanda, Alexandre Santos, PIDE.*

46

Paris, France.
November 1950

* * *

Walter Hoffman looked worriedly around him in the airport terminal building. Claus Hilgeman had missed the rendezvous, and Walter's flight would be called soon.

He wondered what could be wrong. He quickly decided he must continue according to plan. He needed to rapidly return to the safety of his South African benefactors.

His activities in Geneva had come off without a hitch. He had all the proper documentation and codes to access the millions of Swiss francs in the Valhalla numbered accounts. He transferred them to a new numbered account in his own name, emptying the Valhalla account except for a token minimum balance. He then arranged to transfer the entire amount to a bank account he had established in Cape Town. The transfer would be complete by the time he got there.

He also checked his own private account, established with his father's assistance before the war. There were also millions of francs in that numbered account, but Walter decided to leave those alone for now, even though he had the codes with him.

His only regret was that the rigid Swiss banker insisted he must comply with the withdrawal instructions for the Valhalla account. He brusquely told Walter that, in accordance with the instructionsthat established the account, a record of the withdrawal would be sent to an address in Asuncion, Paraguay, stating that the money had been withdrawn by a South African passport holder named Johann Hartman, and the proceeds transferred to another numbered Swiss account. The banker assured Walter that whoever was at that address in Paraguay would be unable to touch the money now. The whole Swiss banking industry depended on such anonymity, and Walter knew the banker was being truthful.

Walter reviewed in his mind what he hoped would be a quick although painful visit to Spanish Guinea in three days. His brother would press him for information about Hans, but Walter would be unyielding on that matter. He knew he needed to focus on the very specific items from the Valhalla cargo that he intended to retrieve and later present to Hendrik van den Bergh in Cape Town. He hoped that the items in the cave on his brother's Rio Muni plantation were undisturbed. He, Hans, and the U-boat crew had carefully arranged and stored the items. In addition, Walter had a copy of the Valhalla cargo catalogue and inventory with him. It used a specific numbering system for each item. The boxes in the cave were all labeled clearly. It should be easy to find and retrieve the items he needed.

Walter knew that he had now crossed a very dangerous line. By accessing the Valhalla funds and part of the cargo he was betraying those remaining but very dangerous elements of the Nazi regime who would be outraged by what he had done. *It doesn't matter,* he thought, *since they already consider Hans and me as traitors, but they will accelerate their efforts to find us. That's why Karl can't be privy to where we are. It's also why we need to stay under the protective shield of van den Bergh in South Africa and Santos in Angola.*

In any case, Walter would be glad to get out of Europe, since all it represented was bitter memories. He thought of his wife, Erica, and daughter, Kirsten, killed in the last bombing raid on Cologne in March 1945 along with Hans's wife, Freya. His brother had suffered losses also. His wife, Pilar, was killed on the first day of the war, and his son, Ernst, was shot down in his Luftwaffe jet fighter in April 1945. *Yes, there is nothing here for either of us anymore.*

When he heard his flight being called, Walter rose and walked toward the gate with his bag. He was confident that he was doing the right thing, severing any remaining thoughts of their old lives and embracing their new reality and new masters in South Africa.

47

Lisbon, Portugal.
November 1950

* * *

Artur Ferreira looked at his subordinate, as the man stuttered while summarizing the results of his investigation of the two deaths in Bussaco earlier in the month. *Why am I plagued with such imbeciles?* He needed to speed things up while he waited for the man's underling, Inspector Coelho, to arrive. Coelho was much smarter than his boss, who had somehow risen to be a branch manager in the investigations section.

Ferreira had been with PIDE and its predecessor agency since 1933, when Salazar became the dictator. He was now responsible for special investigations and counterespionage operations in both the mother country and the colonies. Through those years, he had gradually tried to increase the professionalism in the division he ran, but the man standing before him was an exception to such progress.

"Stop babbling and try to summarize again what happened," Ferreria commanded.

"The two men appeared to have killed each other, sir. We questioned all the staff and guests. None of them heard or saw anything or appeared to have any motive for these deaths."

"Are you sure you questioned all the guests?"

"Well, no, three of them checked out before we and the local police were notified of the deaths. They included an Englishman, a Swede, and a Spaniard. We intercepted the Englishman and Swede at the Lisbon airport. After questioning them we are confident they had no involvement, and we let them board their flights."

"What about the Spaniard?" Ferreira replied, noticing that his branch manager appeared increasingly nervous.

"We could not locate him. He checked out early the morning after the deaths. There is no record of him with immigration or from any of our sources. But there is one perhaps unrelated event that happened nearby."

Robert A. Wright

The man paused as he searched nervously for a document in his case file. "Well, what is it?"

"A police officer in nearby Coimbra noticed an airplane depart from the small airport there very early on the morning following the deaths. There is very little activity at the airfield. That plus the airplane's unusual features prompted the officer to alert us later that day."

"What was so unusual about the aircraft?" Ferreira responded with increasing impatience.

"Its back end was different from most aircraft."

"Can't you be more specific, you idiot? You're supposed to be an investigator. What was different?" Ferreira was raising his voice now.

The other man looked terrified. "It looked like...like this!" The man put his two hands together in the shape of a V and raised them high in the air before continuing.

"The airplane was headed west, away from the officer, so he got a good look at its rear end, but he could not see the registration markings, and he had no camera." He blurted out the rest. "I thought it might be heading west across the ocean, perhaps to America."

"You're a moron! A small plane like that doesn't have enough fuel to cross the ocean. Sit down."

The man immediately complied. Ferreira's intercom buzzer rang. He picked up his phone. "What is it?"

"Inspector Coelho has arrived," a female voice said.

"Good. Send him in."

In a few seconds someone knocked on the door, and Inspector Coelho entered. He didn't waste any time as he approached Ferreira's desk, ignoring his supervisor seated next to where he stood.

"I have some new information, sir."

"Go ahead," Ferreira replied.

"I started with the *Aeronautica Militar* intelligence section. With the police officer's report from Coimbra and a copy of *Jane's All the World's Aircraft*, we were able to determine that the aircraft was likely an American-built Beechcraft Bonanza. I checked with our civil aviation authorities, and there are no such aircraft of this type registered in Portugal. I then contacted our opposite numbers in Madrid. They have one such aircraft located in Spain. It has an

American registration and is registered to an American company owned by a Spanish family. The aircraft is likely to be piloted by either Paul Hoffman, who lives in New York, or his cousin, Anita Ortega, who lives in northern Spain. It seems the Spanish BPS has quite a file on them, but they were reluctant to discuss it. I reminded them that we needed to continue our historic policy of exchanging information. They finally relented and offered that these two individuals, especially Hoffman, have a personal relationship with Luis Carrero Blanco."

"I see. So what conclusions and hypothesis have you formed?"

"We do not know positively that the aircraft spotted in Coimbra belonged to this family. Nor do we have any forensic evidence from the deaths that implicate them. We have been unable to locate the missing hotel guest who allegedly was a Spaniard. We do have a poor-quality physical description of the guest who is missing. We could try to match that with a description of Paul Hoffman, but even if they matched or came close, his special relationship with Spain's leadership cannot be ignored. Accordingly, I recommend no further action on that front. However, I believe you are aware of the special status of the dead guest who was registered in that room. We know, of course, that he was Claus Hilgeman, formerly of the German navy, rather than the alias he used to register in the hotel. From our discussions with the BPS, it appears that there may be some connection with the Hoffman family."

Coelho gave Ferreira time to make a further connection.

"I understand the issue concerning Hilgeman. Thank you for the synopsis. That will be all."

"Yes, sir." Coelho quickly left the office.

The branch chief also started to rise, but Ferreira said, "Sit down, please."

The man meekly obeyed and said nothing.

"I have good news. You are being promoted and assigned to the records branch. It's effective immediately, so get your desk cleaned out right away. Do you understand?"

The man stood, his face expressing a mixture of surprise and confusion. "Yes, sir. I'll move right away!" he replied and then quickly exited the office.

Ferreira sighed. Promoting someone and assigning them to obscure or meaningless activity was a time-honored but inefficient way of weeding out the incompetent in a large bureaucracy. The arcane civil service rules made it difficult to fire incompetent employees. He needed to unleash the young rising star, Coelho, however, and making him the new investigations branch chief was the way to move things forward.

He thought that Coelho's synopsis was spot-on, as was his sensitivity to the issues surrounding Claus Hilgeman. If only the division's other employees were so perceptive. *I have twenty-eight employees in my division, and only six are worth a shit. Well, this is the Portugal of Salazar, the Estado Novo. If I can't cut their balls off, maybe I can at least terrorize them. I can threaten to ship their useless carcasses to Sao Tome, Goa, Macao, or worse yet, Timor.*

Ferreira sighed again. He knew his fantasy had limits, although that was not so when the PIDE conducted interrogations. Waterboarding, sleep deprivation, and other methods were routinely used to gain confessions. Eventually, prisoners told jailers what they wanted to hear. Ferreira shook his head. *Civilized nations don't use these methods.*

Ferreira ended his mental soliloquy and turned his attention back to the Bussaco murders. He knew he must take one other action immediately to close the loop on this.

Tomorrow, he would send a coded cable to Santos in Luanda.

48

Over the North Atlantic Ocean.
November 1950

* * *

Paul sipped his wine after the stewardess replenished it, following the sumptuous in-flight meal. Despite the first class service, he couldn't relax on this flight. He was recounting the horror of Hilgeman's death and his own close encounter with the intruder on that recent night in Bussaco.

Paul looked out the window of the Pan American Boeing Stratocruiser and stared at the two massive starboard Pratt and Whitney engines of 3,500 horsepower. This Boeing model was used to provide the airline's most luxurious service across the North Atlantic. Today he was on Pan Am 101. It had departed London on schedule at 7:00 p.m. and was due to arrive in New York the next morning at 8:10 a.m.

After leaving Portugal in the Bonanza, Paul picked up Anita in Vallodolid in Spain. She had flown Paul to Toulouse, France, where he picked up Air France flights to Paris and then London. He deliberately avoided his usual route on Pan Am through Lisbon in order to preclude any possibility of detention or even arrest by Portuguese authorities. He wasn't sure they could trace him to the scene of the killings in Bussaco, but he wasn't taking any chances.

Paul had been gone nearly three months and longed to return to New York and his family. There were also pressing business matters to attend to, even though Paul now had a reliable management team in place. He knew that these priorities now came first, even though he was chafing at the bit to get to Alexandre Santos in Luanda, Angola.

Paul could not visualize the connection between his missing brother Hans and Santos, but Hilgeman's last words made it clear that a connection existed. It might take several months before Paul could engineer a time and purpose to travel to Angola, yet he knew he would obsess until he could make it happen.

In addition to family and business matters, Paul also had to maintain the momentum on improving American and Spanish relations through back channels. He had established these with bankers, US senators, and military officials who William Donovan and Allen Dulles had introduced him to earlier. He was hopeful that when an American ambassador to Spain was finally appointed, he would be able let the official bilateral channels between the two countries take over.

After he finished his wine and dessert, he decided it was time for a proper after-dinner drink such as a sherry, port, brandy, or cognac. He left his seat and headed for the spiral stairwell to the downstairs lounge, hoping that some time spent there would relieve the monotony of the sixteen-hour transatlantic journey.

49

Bata. Rio Muni. Spanish Guinea.
November 1950

* * *

Karl Hoffman looked at his watch again. It was 9:00 a.m., and the flight from Santa Isabel was due in ninety minutes. He was curious about his visitor, but the cable from Johann Hartman said only that he would be arriving to discuss cocoa imports to South Africa.

Karl was waiting in the Iberia Airlines office in Bata. He wanted to meet the airline station chief in hopes that he could provide more information on the passenger. Karl knew almost all the important businessmen and government officials in Guinea, and today he hoped his personal relationship with the station manager would yield some new information before Karl went to the Bata airport to meet Hartman. Karl had earlier provided the station manager with Hartman's information, hoping that his itinerary could be traced back to his point of origin.

As Karl waited he stared at the bench seat on the opposite wall of the Iberia office. Above the bench were two travel posters. Above one of them was a portrait of Franco in full-dress uniform. Karl shook his head. Franco had not only won the civil war eleven years ago, but he was still firmly in control in Spain despite continued economic deprivation and foreign isolation. *At least things are better here in Guinea*, Karl thought.

The station manager appeared from his office, and Karl rose to greet him. The manager was carrying a single sheet of paper. He stopped, looked at the paper, and then looked back at Karl to summarize what he had learned.

"Good morning, Karl. It seems your visitor started his trip in South Africa, all right. My station manager in Douala was able to secure some information from his Air France colleagues there. Hartman arrived there from Paris and then flew to Santa Isabel, where he spent last night. Before Paris, it seems that his itinerary included Geneva and Lisbon. He appears to be traveling alone. That's all I could get for now."

"Thank you. That will be helpful to me. Is the inbound flight on time?"

"Yes, and it appears that Hartman is the only passenger."

Karl quickly excused himself for the short drive out to the airport north of town. He watched as the twin-engine DeHaviland DH-89 Rapide landed and taxied in. The peculiar-looking biplane was dated, yet it had been providing local air service within Spanish Guinea for several years. Karl looked at the odd-looking aircraft and shook his head. He hoped that more modern aircraft, such as the Douglas DC-3, would soon be available to replace the ancient Rapide. More important, he was anxious to work with Iberia Airlines to introduce direct service from Spain using the airline's Douglas DC-4s.

The Rapide's engines stopped. The station staff quickly brought a small stool to the plane's cabin door. Within a few seconds, the single passenger deplaned. From a distance, Karl noticed the man was of medium height and had a small mustache, eyeglasses, and dark hair. As the sun shone on the man's receding hairline, Karl could see he was perspiring in the late morning heat and tropical humidity. Karl squinted at the man as he began walking toward the terminal and Karl.

As he approached Karl, the man remained expressionless. Karl finally saw his face clearly. He gasped.

"Hello, Karl. It's been five years, hasn't it?"

Karl was momentarily speechless, but he finally recovered from his shock. "My God, Walter, you're alive! Where is Hans?"

Karl moved forward to embrace his brother, but Walter had other ideas.

"Don't get too cozy, Karl. It's better if we appear to be strangers. I knew you would think first of Hans rather than me, but we can discuss this later in the privacy of your hacienda on your plantation. Shall we go?"

"Of course, Walter…of course we will. Let's go to my car. We can be there in less than two hours."

Karl helped his brother retrieve his luggage and then led him to the car. *There is at least one matter that will shock my brother when he learns of it,* he thought.

Their conversation was mostly awkward on the drive. Karl wanted to wait until a more suitable time to have what was likely to be an even more awkward confrontation.

The two brothers reached the Hoffman plantation and hacienda east of the town of Niefang ninety minutes later. The town was located in north-central Rio Muni, the mainland portion of Spanish Guinea, and sat astride the

Benito River, or Mbini River as it was known by the Fang tribe that predominated on the mainland. The name of the town means "limit of the Fang," to indicate the traditional western range of the Fang inhabitants in the colony.

The plantation's hacienda was about five miles, or eight kilometers, east of Niefang at the top of a prominent elevation of perhaps nine hundred meters, or about three thousand feet above sea level. These last miles were off the paved road, and the track led to the hacienda, an adjacent airstrip, and numerous other buildings supporting plantation activities. Karl led his brother to the guest quarters, and a short time later they were standing in the west-facing living area. From here, on the western edge of the high elevation, they could see the distant Benito River and the jungle beyond.

Karl poured them both a glass of fino sherry and handed one to his brother. Karl could wait no longer. "So, Walter, we have chatted about the plantation, I have learned you are in good health, and I presume I will soon learn why you are here. But you must tell me now about Hans. Where is he? Is he in good health? I must know!" Karl clenched his fist to his chest to emphasize the passion in his desire for his missing eldest son.

"To answer your question, the last time I saw him—about four months ago—he was fine. I do not know where he is currently living. He has begun a new life, and he and I agreed we would not constrain each other. The reasons for our disappearance and continued isolation have not changed. It would be dangerous for both of us, for you, and perhaps Paul and his family in America if we were to surface. You must understand that. In any case, there is nothing for either of us in our former world in Germany."

Karl realized he could not hide the truth about Germany from his brother. "You are wrong about that, Walter." He paused and then said, "Your daughter, Kirsten, is alive."

There was a complete silence as Walter tried to digest that news. His facial expression changed from shock, to confusion, and then finally to anger. "Do not play such games with me, Karl! That can't possibly be! She died with Erica and Freya in March 1945."

"That's not true. Erica left her in the Dom, the cathedral in Cologne, when she and Freya went to help Freya's mother. They were killed in that last bombing raid, but Kirsten survived, and she is alive and well in Bernkastel."

"Don't lie to me, Karl, because it's not—"

"I'm not lying!" He lowered his voice. "I'll show you."

Karl walked over to the shelf above the liquor cabinet. In the middle of the shelf were photographs of Paul, Liz, and their two children. To the right was a picture of Karl's late wife, Pilar, and also Anita Ortega. Karl retrieved the framed photo that was to the left of the others and walked back to Walter.

"Here, Walter, is a picture of your daughter taken on her eighteenth birthday early this year. Look at it…she's beautiful." He gently handed the photo to his brother.

Walter stared at the photo for nearly a minute, suppressed a tear by closing his eyes, and then finally sighed deeply before opening them and staring again at the photo. He finally looked back up. "She is all right then?"

"Yes, of course, and we visit her often and so does Anita. Their common interest in wine making is their bond. Kirsten helped make the '49 vintage a great success. You will be amazed when…"

Karl looked at his brother and realized he must tell him another truth. "But you can't see her, because you're dead."

Walter looked at Karl quizzically. Karl continued. "When you had been missing for five years, under German law you were presumed dead. Your half of our father's estate passed to Kirsten. That would include your money in Switzerland, but of course Kirsten does not have the codes to access that numbered account."

Karl waited for his brother to react. Walter looked at the picture, nodded his head a couple of times, and looked back at Karl as his face showed resolve. "You're quite correct. Walter Hoffman is dead. I am Johann Hartman. I will give you the codes to that Swiss account, and I am counting on you, Karl, to see that the money gets transferred to Kirsten. You can claim that you retrieved some family records and discovered the codes. It's the only solution. When I have finished my business here, I will again disappear, and you will never tell Kirsten of my survival."

The two men stared at each other for about a minute. Karl finally asked the other important question. "Why did you come here, Walter?"

"I came to retrieve some of the materials from the cave."

"What will you do with them?"

"That is really not your concern, Karl. My loyalties are now bound to a new reality, and I must serve those who took us in and protected us. So I ask you to help me transport them back to Bata. A ship will call there in several days, and I will depart with that material."

"Why don't you take it all? It is like a curse to me now, since it resulted in the loss of my son."

"I can't take it all with me. It is too much to digest and explain, and I prefer to do this quietly. Will you help me?"

Walter looked at his brother as Karl thought intensely and carefully about his choices. He finished the last of his sherry, put the glass down, and looked back at his brother.

"I will help you, if only to start the process of ridding me of that cursed cargo you brought here. I only ask one thing in return."

"What's that?"

"Will you at least deliver a letter to Hans for me?"

There was again a long pause before Walter sighed and nodded his head.

"Of course I will. I just hope you don't say anything that will wound him as a result of his disappearance."

"On the contrary, my brother, I only want to share some words that offer the possibility of healing, not retribution."

50

New York City.
December 25, 1950

* * *

Paul stared blankly out the broad picture window of their Fifth Avenue penthouse on this late afternoon of Christmas Day. The panorama of Central Park, with the Metropolitan Museum of Art to the far right, was always an impressive sight, but Paul was not taking in the view. All he could feel was the pall of death that seemed to hang over his world, overpowering the holiday.

Within a week of his return in November, his great uncle Ramon Ortega had finally passed away, bequeathing his entire enormous estate to Paul. Only a week and a half later Liz's mother died, following Liz's father by two years. The Kurtz family fortune was substantial, although small in comparison to the Hoffman-Ortega enterprises. Liz and Jack Kurtz would inherit it.

The death of family elders was not a public event, of course, but the increasing slaughter in Korea was. After a brilliant victory at Inchon in September, General Douglas MacArthur's arrogant discounting of potential Chinese Communist intervention resulted in a stunning American defeat at Chosin Reservoir with huge casualties. The war was now settling into a stalemate as the UN forces were evacuated from the port of Hungnam.

Of course, the death of Claus Hilgeman in Portugal still haunted Paul. He could not shake the fact that he had now killed two men. Killing the assassin in 1945 was clearly self-defense, but Paul was having a harder time regarding killing the stranger who had assaulted Claus. *Could there have been another option?*

Even the political climate reeked of death and conflict. The "Red Scare" was in full swing following Senator Joseph McCarthy's speech in February denouncing the State Department and others whom he deemed Communist sympathizers.

Most hurtful of all, however, was Liz's miscarriage and emergency surgery two weeks ago. She became pregnant as soon as Paul returned from Europe, but it ended only a month later. Liz was fully recovered and had been home a week, but the searing pain of its aftermath and other events of the year stung as Paul closed his eyes and relived them.

His thoughts were interrupted by a soft hand on his arm. "What were you thinking?" Liz Hoffman whispered.

Paul came out of his thoughts abruptly and turned to his wife. She was looking up at his face and smiling weakly, as if to test his mood.

He looked at his wife and instantly took in her beauty and warmth. She was a year younger than Paul and, although twenty-eight, she looked younger, with a perfect complexion, deep-blue eyes, modestly long auburn hair, and a very shapely figure. She was wearing a long dress and high heels, in the current fashion, as well as pearl earrings and matching necklace. She was already dressed to the nines in anticipation of their guests. Tonight, that would be Jack Kurtz and his girlfriend Sharon McKenzie.

"What was I thinking?" he finally replied.

"Yes, I think that's a fair question. I can see, however, that you weren't admiring the view."

She is so good at reading my mood. "That's a fair question, but I'm wondering if the answer will spoil our holiday dinner."

"So go ahead and try me," she said.

"Without getting too maudlin, I was thinking about losing the baby and my family's history."

"That requires an explanation," Liz said.

"I know. Well, as a result of your surgery, you can't have any more children. The same thing happened to my mother when I was born. My grandmother in Germany died giving birth to my father." He sighed. "I was just wondering if there was some curse on our family. I know it's superstitious, but it kind of gnaws at me. Maybe it's just because of Ramon and your mother."

Paul had not told Liz about the events in Portugal.

Liz looked at Paul pensively before answering. "I can sympathize with your feelings. I know there seems to be a general gloom in the air because of our family losses and...national and world events. But I prefer to be thankful for our two wonderful children, our successful life together, our good friends and family members, and our future."

He looked at her and his mood immediately changed. "That's amazing; you said just the right thing to snap me out of it." He broke into a broad grin, his deeper thoughts temporarily suppressed.

"Now that's more like it. By the way, since we have another hour before Jack and Sharon arrive, there was something I wanted your advice on."

"After you cheered me up, it would be my pleasure."

"Well, you know I've always talked about a journalism career. I've heard of a couple of opportunities to freelance for a few publications that could lead to something even bigger. The great thing about it is that I could do all my writing at home. If I needed to do any interviews I could work into that as the children reach school age in a couple of years. I could do the interviews and other research while they're in school. With both Margarita and Helga, I don't have any need to be here when the children aren't home."

Liz allowed Paul time to absorb that. Paul could think of no reason to disagree. Margarita was the children's full-time nanny, and Helga was their recently hired housekeeper.

"So, how about it? Does that sound all right?"

Paul came closer to Liz and put his arms around her before replying. "I think it's a fabulous idea. You have so much talent. What kinds of subjects will you write about?"

"Well, you know me. Fashion, style, and things like that don't interest me. I want to write about politics."

"All right, my future muckraker, I think we should drink to that. Let's have a glass of manzanilla!"

"That's a deal," she replied as Paul released her from their embrace.

He walked over to the liquor cabinet to pour the sherry from the family's bodega in Jerez, Spain. Paul wondered about what kinds of political issues Liz would write about. Regardless of the issues, he knew Liz would be a persistent and provocative author.

51

New York City.
December 29, 1950

* * *

Paul walked briskly up to Allen Dulles's town house at 239 East Sixty-First Street, just as Jack Kurtz walked up from the other direction.

Paul popped the question first. "Hi, Jack. So what's the big deal?" he asked. Dulles had called both of them the day before and asked them to come by at the end of the day.

"I don't have a clue. He said nothing at the office, but I was out most of this afternoon. I think I may have missed a big announcement to the staff. I sure hope this is important. You and I had a date!" Jack laughed.

Indeed, Paul and Jack had planned one of their increasingly rare after-work visits to the Village for a few drinks.

"Don't worry, we'll still get there. Liz gave me an evening pass—for a few hours, at least. So let's find out what's up. Go ahead and ring the buzzer."

Paul was pointing to the door, but Jack's hand was already in motion.

Within seconds, the door opened, and Dulles stood there, pipe in mouth, with a slight smile evident. He took the pipe out of his mouth and greeted his guests. "Well, you two are certainly prompt. Come on in."

Paul and Jack entered. Dulles closed the door behind them. "Let's go into my study and have a drink to toast the upcoming New Year. I suspect the two of you are headed out somewhere tonight, so I won't hold you long, but I have some important information for you."

As Dulles began leading them to his study, Paul and Jack looked at each other quizzically and then followed Dulles.

"I assume you boys want the usual," Dulles said as he entered the study with Paul and Jack behind. At the liquor cabinet, he reached for the bottle of Johnnie Walker Black. Dulles poured their drinks. They toasted the approaching New Year, and Dulles led them to the sitting area.

He didn't waste any time getting to the point. "You both know I've been mostly gone in the last few months, consulting for the CIA. Well, I'm headed back down to Washington on Tuesday. Beetle Smith asked me just before Christmas to be deputy director for plans at the agency. I accepted. All hell has broken loose in the world. Frankly, I couldn't refuse."

"That's great, Allen! You're the right man for the job now," Jack replied enthusiastically.

Paul noticed a wistful look on Jack's face, as if he might be envious of his boss's good fortune to be in the thick of the action again.

"I'll second that, Allen. It's important for the agency to have you inside again."

"Thank you both. I'm glad I was able to tell you personally. How about a refill on those drinks? I have some more items for you."

All three men downed what was left in their glasses, and then they walked over to the liquor cabinet. Dulles began talking as he poured.

"Paul, the work you've done with Spain has been incredible. Your groundwork has broken the ice. As you know, it was announced two days ago that Stanton Griffis will be nominated to be the first US ambassador to Spain in five years, and he'll probably assume his post in February. The recent sixty-three-million-dollar loan from the US government was preceded by the commercial loans you brokered. That's got things moving in Spain. You'll still be needed as an intermediary, I'm sure, but my role in that is ended. I hope you have good luck working with the State Department," Dulles concluded as he took a huge swig from his drink and then reached again for his pipe.

"Thanks again, Allen. I'll stay involved. It will take a while for the official machinery to pick up the slack."

"That's great. I hope you'll both stay in touch. It's not too far to DC, so I expect to see you there occasionally."

"We'll make it a point, boss," Jack responded without much enthusiasm.

"I won't hold you up," Dulles said, as he puffed on his pipe.

With that clue, Paul and Jack downed their refills and soon exited the house to grab a cab to the White Horse Tavern.

On the cab ride to the Village, Paul decided to ask Jack how he felt about Dulles's revelations.

"You almost looked disappointed about the news," Paul said quietly.

"I'm happy for him, but I guess I'm a little envious. He's headed to the center of the action, and I'm still here in a boring, albeit lucrative, law job."

"Don't worry, Jack. Somehow I feel you and I will get back in the action."

Paul wondered how that might actually happen, but he thought it might ultimately involve Operation Valhalla.

52

Estoril, Portugal,
January 1951

* * *

Otto Skorzeny and Franz Liesau met in the lobby bar at the Hotel Palacio following their meeting with Artur Ferreira of the PIDE in nearby Lisbon. On this cool and windy day, they were the only patrons in the bar of this famous hotel in the well-known resort town.

During the war, Estoril was a haven for spies, refugees, deposed royalty, and the wealthy. The Palacio was a hotbed for spies, yet Skorzeny felt comfortable meeting here while he was under the protection of the PIDE. He also liked the cozy bar.

"Franz, don't you think this bar has classic decor? The white-and-blue checkerboard marble floor, more marble on the bar, the lushly upholstered chairs, and the history of who has entertained here all give it a special ambience, I think."

"With the crisis we are facing, Otto, you should be thinking more about a solution, rather than engaging in your usual soliloquy about the arts, history, cuisine or whatever else strikes your fancy."

Skorzeny merely shook his head, glanced with disgust at Liesau, sighed, and then continued. "Don't worry, Franz, I am suitably alarmed by what Mueller has done. That thug he sent to Bussaco to accost Hilgeman met a deserved end. Unfortunately, Hilgeman is also dead. That leaves us nowhere for the moment. More important, I'm afraid of what Mueller will do next."

"It's clear that Mueller was outraged by the depletion of the Valhalla funds in the Swiss account. I'm not surprised that he ordered this action."

"Neither am I, but I did notice how neatly the two protagonists seemed to have killed each other simultaneously."

"It seems unlikely that they would have killed each other like that, Otto."

"Didn't you listen to Ferreira? There was likely a third party involved, and my guess is it was Paul Hoffman. We know he met Hilgeman in Lisbon the previous year. He was undoubtedly trying to get Hilgeman to reveal more about Valhalla, so that his quest for his missing brother would be served. He probably stumbled upon them while they were fighting. My guess is that Hoffman gave Mueller's thug the coup de grace."

"Do you think Hilgeman revealed anything to Hoffman before he died?"

"I don't know. What I do know is that very soon we will have to confront Mueller on his risky strategy of confrontation."

"What do you mean, 'confront him'?"

"Please leave that up to me, Franz."

"What do we do in the meantime about Valhalla?"

"I have sent an agent to South Africa under a false identity to try to discreetly investigate possibilities that might lead us to either Walter or Hans Hoffman. In a few months, we'll see what he turns up."

53

New York City.
February 1951

* * *

Sergio Castillo took another sip of the Bodega Ortega Tempranillo Reserva 1947. He swished it around in his mouth and, as he sensed the flavors and texture, he raised the glass to examine the wine's color. *The soft tannins and vanilla are amazing.* He placed the glass back on the table and stared at the bottle for a few seconds. *Yes, I must be patient, but someday I will meet the wine maker and tell her how pleased I was with this vintage.* Castillo sighed as he realized that patience in this case could mean several years.

He was dining alone at Delmonico's at 56 Beaver Street in downtown Manhattan. He had found it difficult to find the Ortega wines, especially the Reserva, at ordinary restaurants and stores. He was pleased to have found the Reserva from the superb '47 vintage, only recently released after the requisite three years' aging, at this restaurant. The Gran Reserva from that vintage would require two more years before it appeared.

Castillo considered this exercise an important part of his research, rather than a fine-dining experience, which it certainly was also. He looked around him at the other diners on this Friday evening. He knew they represented the cream of the crop in this center of world finance and capitalism. He wondered if any of them had ever dined in Moscow, where the experience would be somewhat different.

The dining and other research was only a secondary part of Castillo's purpose on this trip. It had also included stops at the nearby New York Cocoa Exchange and other locations so that he could acquire the necessary background prior to meeting face-to-face with Paul Hoffman. Castillo had been hugely successful in rebuilding the business in Venezuela that his father had created almost three decades previously. Some of the other business he had in New York related to export-import matters pertaining to that enterprise. He would need for it to achieve a little more success before he presented his proposal to Hoffman, and that would require at least a couple more years.

But even that was not the main purpose on this trip.

Castillo had followed the strict and exact protocol that Vladimir Morozov provided to him to contact Agents X and Y in New York. Castillo had successfully contacted each agent separately. He debriefed and retasked them in accordance with his plan. That had gone off without a hitch, and he was able to assess each agent's capabilities, loyalties, and discretion. He was satisfied with both of them.

The next move he took was risky. He met again with them, but this time it was jointly. He gave them specific orders that required them to collaborate and coordinate their activities with each other, and to accept Castillo as their controller. Previously they had been functioning autonomously, according to their original tasking. Morozov had not approved such an action, but he had not prohibited it either.

Castillo knew that his long-term success depended upon patient and painstaking individual steps that created a real-world front for the espionage network he was rapidly establishing throughout Latin America and here in New York. It was much riskier to be an operative now in the United States than it had been. Castillo noted the huge public pressure building under the Red Scare tactics being used in the US Congress and the FBI. Castillo found it curious that America ended up compromising some of the very freedoms they were trying to protect by allowing the FBI to function much like the MGB in creating elements of a police state. He had never been able to understand the chaotic conditions in the Western democracies. He was amused by the apparent hypocrisy practiced by American law enforcement as they turned the country inside out looking for Soviet agents, real and imagined.

Yes, perhaps it is poetic justice that America's potential downfall could come as they subvert their own democratic system. The waiter delivered his filet mignon just as Sergio Castillo, aka Soviet MGB Agent Yuri Sergeivich Kozlov Castillo, completed that thought. Tonight he would dine as well as the capitalist elite and plutocrats around him, in contrast to his normally ascetic lifestyle. Tomorrow he would continue patiently implementing his long-term plan.

54.

Cape Town, South Africa.
March 1951

* * *

"What have you learned about the information in the material that Hartman provided to us?"

This was the first question that Hendrik van den Bergh posed to Balthazar Johannes (B. J.) Vorster, after they were served tea at the quiet restaurant where they had agreed to meet.

"Our scientists and technicians were amazed. From the documents you brought, they selected the process for coal gasification and used the catalysts and other elements in the process to improve efficiency by an astounding amount in the tests that they conducted. They were stunned by the progress the Nazis had made. This is hugely important for our country, since we are increasingly being isolated for our apartheid policies. We have little petroleum, but we do have coal, so the strategic aspects of this are enormous."

Vorster was leaning forward as he concluded, and he could barely contain his enthusiasm. Van den Bergh feared he might fall over forward as he spoke. He was a heavyset but not obese man with bushy eyebrows and premature balding, although he was only thirty-five, a year younger than Van den Bergh.

"That's incredibly good news. Has anything else been discovered?"

"Hendrik, they are only beginning the process of analyzing the material. They were curious about all of the medical research, however, especially the experiments regarding organ transplants. It seems the Nazis experimented with humans as well as lower primates." Vorster's posture relaxed, as if to indicate the loss of some enthusiasm.

"I see," van den Bergh answered uncomfortably.

"We will continue our analysis, but you must tell me, Hendrik, if you think Hartman can gain access to other similar material. Where did all this come from?"

"I believe that it came in the submarine that Hartman—or in his previous life Admiral Walter Hoffman—sailed in with his nephew Hans Hoffman."

"Where did they deposit the rest of it?"

"I don't know yet." Van den Bergh looked briefly out to sea in this coastal restaurant and then back to Vorster. "I do know that it was not deposited in Southwest Africa. We have made a thorough search and investigation of all potential locations where it could be hidden."

"What about Angola or the other Portuguese colonies?" Vorster responded.

"I don't think that's likely either, although I'm certain that Santos and the PIDE had an important role in facilitating the U-boat's landing at the border between Angola and Southwest Africa. I was able to trace Hartman's travels on the outbound and return trip, on which he delivered the material to us. He arrived in Douala, Cameroon, from France, and then he flew to Spanish Guinea. He boarded the steamship there that took him to Cape Town, with stops at Sao Tome and Angola."

"Did he bring the material from France or pick it up in the Portuguese colonies?" Vorster replied, arching his eyebrows in curiosity.

"Neither. The material was too bulky, and it was too risky to bring it on a plane. I also believe Santos when he says he doesn't know where the rest of the material is, because of the way this Operation Valhalla was compartmentalized," van den Bergh concluded.

"So that leaves Spanish Guinea?" Vorster asked.

"Exactly, and I'm sure that our ex-Nazi friends know this, too."

"Then why haven't they gone and retrieved the rest of the material?"

"I believe that they know it is stored there, because it was part of their original plan for getting the material out of Germany. Unfortunately for them, it may be that only the two Hoffmans whom we have embraced—or I should say Hartmans, to recognize their new identity—know precisely where in Spanish Guinea the material is stored."

"Hendrik, we must ensure that these two are well protected from their former colleagues. I know you and I both spent time in detention camps during the war for our support of the *Ossewabrandwag* and the Nazis, but times are different now. We must distance ourselves from them. Our implementation of apartheid will cause us enough trouble in the world without also associating ourselves with a defunct Nazi Germany."

"I agree. In addition to the secrets he provided, Hartman was extraordinarily generous in compensating us financially for the costs we have incurred with resettlement of his crew. In fact, he insisted on compensating us personally, and I suspect Santos in Angola also, for the risks we took. He obviously has gained access to millions in hard currency that was reserved by the Germans for Valhalla."

"That's true, Hendrik, and it's also a good reason why we must keep this completely under a secrecy embargo forever. We should keep working with Hartman to see if he will be forthcoming with even more secret material—and funds."

"I will follow that approach, but I don't want to pressure him since he, his nephew, and his crew have shown extraordinary loyalty to us. It may take several years or longer for this to play out," Van den Bergh summarized.

"The timing you suggest is accurate, Hendrik. I will soon become more involved in political matters, and I expect to join the government. I want you to be my key operative in overseeing security and other issues related not only to Valhalla, but larger national issues and problems. We can rise together in the new South Africa. Perhaps this Operation Valhalla and its precious cargo will be a component of our success."

"I would be happy to see that happen," van den Bergh replied simply.

"Tell me, if you had to speculate on what other secrets are in this material, what would it be?"

"Based on the effort they put into it and how much they apparently still want it, I would guess that it could include key information on weapons of mass destruction."

"Such as?"

"My guess is atomic and biological warfare weapons."

Vorster merely nodded as the two men turned to stare out at the sea where the Atlantic and Indian Oceans met, each absorbed with their own thoughts about what that meant.

55

New York City.
April 11, 1951

* * *

Paul stared at the headline in the *New York Times*: TRUMAN RELIEVES M'ARTHUR OF ALL HIS POSTS, FINDS HIM UNABLE TO BACK US-UN POLICIES. He did a double take as he read it again and took another bite of his sandwich as he ate an early lunch at his desk. Paul had figured that might be in the cards, but he was still amazed that Truman had the guts to fire an American icon, even one who was guilty of gross insubordination.

He was still shaking his head when the intercom buzzed.

"Yes, what is it, June?" he responded to his secretary.

"I have your nanny, Margarita, on the line, and it sounds urgent!"

"Put her through."

It took a few seconds, and then Paul heard her heavy breathing.

"Hello, Margarita, what's wrong?"

"I'm sorry, Mr. Hoffman, but the children are gone!"

Paul leaped out of his chair. "What do mean they're gone? Where? Who? Where is my wife?"

"Your wife went to interview someone for an article. I stepped out to go to the local pharmacy to get some aspirin, and Helga said she would watch the children for a few minutes while I was gone. You said such temporary absences were OK so—"

"Never mind that now. Where would Helga have taken the children? You know she's not authorized to take them out of the apartment."

"I am not sure. She has never taken them out alone because of your restriction, only with me or your wife and—"

"Where do you usually go on your walks? Tell me now!" Paul commanded, trying to stay in control. He noticed that Margarita was tense and concerned but not frantic.

"Helga always liked it when we walked around the lake in Central Park across from the New York Historical Society, because the north end of it is so peaceful. We watch for wildlife so—"

"Yes, yes, anywhere else?"

"No, Helga does not know her way around Manhattan very well and stays close to the apartment."

"All right, listen carefully, Margarita. Keep trying to reach my wife through the magazine's office. Then try calling Jack Kurtz at his law office. Tell him what's going on. Tell him to meet me at the north end of the lake in Central Park. Do you understand me?"

"Yes, I do."

"Then do it now!" Paul said and hung up.

He ran for his coat, hanging on the rack in the corner, and went to grab the door knob but caught himself. He raced back to his desk, opened the drawer, and retrieved his Beretta M1935. He quickly checked the magazine and stuffed the pistol in his coat pocket. He then ran for the door. *I won't be caught without a weapon again.*

He blew through the door and turned hard right to face his surprised secretary. "Listen carefully, June. I want you to do two things. Call the police and tell them I think my children have been kidnapped. Tell them I'm going to the north end of the lake in Central Park. Then call Jack Kurtz at his law office, and tell him to meet me there also. This is an emergency! Do you understand me?" Paul thought that a backup call for Jack would be good in case Margarita forgot.

"Yes, of course, Mr. Hoffman, right away!" She immediately picked up the phone.

Paul raced out of the office suite, crossed the hall, and slammed the elevator button. *I hope this hunch is right.*

It was only a short cab ride. Paul hoped the police would be there ahead of him. As the cab stopped across from the Historical Society building, Paul threw a ten-dollar bill at the surprised cabbie, leaped out of the car, raced north up the sidewalk on Central Park West, and then turned into the park near the north end of the lake. There were no police in sight anywhere.

Paul kept up his brisk run and followed the perimeter path around the north end of the lake. *If they're not here, what will I do?*

He kept up the pace, his heart pounding. When he rounded a corner, he approached the bridge crossing the easterly arm of the lake.

He saw them. There was a man with his back to him. Facing him he saw Margarita, Helga and—*My God, it's Sharon McKenzie!*

Margarita was protecting the twins with her body. Sharon was holding Helga on the ground while looking up and shouting at the man, who was wearing a trench coat and a hat.

Paul started running to them. He caught himself, stopped, pulled out the Beretta, and flicked off the safety. He started running again, gun in hand.

When he was about twenty yards away he stopped, raised the pistol with both hands, and shouted at the man.

"Stop and turn around now!"

The man had already grabbed Sharon and slapped her once. He turned around to the right in surprise, spotted Paul, and started to reach into his left coat pocket with his right hand, releasing Sharon and letting her fall to the ground.

I will only get one chance at this, Paul thought.

The man retrieved the gun. He started to crouch. Paul anticipated this and had already pointed the Beretta lower.

He fired. The crack immediately scattered a flock of birds nearby.

The man turned to fire. Paul's first round had missed.

Paul fired again, and a third time. One round struck the man's right arm. He dropped his weapon. The other round grazed the man's forehead. Helga was screaming.

The man had gone down. Paul ran toward him.

Kneeling, the man reached again for his gun with his uninjured left arm.

Paul again raised the Beretta, took careful aim, and started firing. He was only twenty feet away by then.

He fired five more times. As the eighth and final round fired, the slide opened, the magazine empty.

The last four shots were superfluous. The fourth round had penetrated the man's right eye, gone through the brain, and out the other side of his skull. He was on the sidewalk.

Paul walked slowly over to the body, saw the huge hole in his right eyeball socket, and turned to Sharon. She was a little stunned from the assailant's last blow.

"I'm all right, Paul. The children…"

Paul ran the few paces to the children. Margarita was standing in front still protecting them. Behind her, little three-and-a-half-year-old Robert was standing in front of his twin sister, Pilar, who was crying in fear.

Paul ran over, hugged his son, and then reached for Pilar, scooping her up into his arms.

"Paul, what's going on?" Jack's voice was a surprise. Paul turned while still trying to console Pilar, who was sobbing and wrapping her arms around him.

From every direction Paul could hear sirens.

"Jesus, Jack, this guy was trying to kidnap my children."

"When Margarita and I got here, Helga was turning the kids over to him," Sharon said quietly. Her lip was bleeding. Jack came over, took out a handkerchief, and started wiping the blood off while putting his other arm around her.

Helga was on the ground whimpering. Paul looked at her coldly, walked over to Margarita and handed Pilar to her, and then walked over to Helga, crouching down to stare her in the face.

"Why did you do this? Who was he? Who do you work for? Tell me NOW!" Without thinking Paul dropped the empty Beretta, reached over with his right hand, and slapped Helga hard in the face.

She screamed. "I can't tell you, they'll kill me!"

"Who'll kill you? Tell me their names!" Paul, filled with rage, was raising his hand to strike her again.

"That's enough, Paul! We'll find out later," Jack said, grabbing Paul's arm.

I must get control of myself and my emotions.

"*Everybody just stop right there and don't move!*" The cop's booming voice was matched by his raised pistol. Other cops were converging on them now from every direction.

"Paul, listen carefully! I'll handle this. All right, do you hear me?" Jack grabbed his arm.

Paul looked at Jack, momentarily speechless. "Sure, talk to them," he finally replied as they were surrounded by police.

56.

Asuncion, Paraguay.
April 1951

* * *

"Well, hello, Skorzeny. This is quite a surprise. I'm glad to see you again, and I'm happy to see you escaped from the Americans. Come in and sit down. We'll have some refreshments and talk about old times."

Heinrich Mueller started to walk over from the panoramic picture window to greet his unexpected and unannounced guest.

"I'm not here to talk, Mueller."

Skorzeny was wearing a loose sport jacket with a noticeable bulge in the left side.

Mueller stopped walking and looked at Skorzeny, his glance askance and confused. "You're not here to...visit? Who let you in?"

"I let myself in. I know your housekeeper and your aide both have the day off."

"Then you must have something serious to talk about in private, Skorzeny," Mueller replied with increasing alarm in his voice.

"What you did to Hilgeman in Portugal was unacceptable. What you and your thugs tried to do by attempting to kidnap two American children of someone we need to subtly monitor is not only unacceptable, but it is a threat to our movement."

"Now you listen to me, Skorzeny! As head of the Gestapo I could—"

"You could what, Mueller? Your authority is nonexistent here, and your leadership in any capacity is no longer reliable...or desirable."

"Listen to me, we can talk this through. I'm willing to—"

Mueller's plaintive plea was interrupted as Skorzeny smoothly and rapidly drew his pistol with silencer from under his sport coat with his gloved hands and pointed it at Mueller.

"You can't do this to me! I was only trying to—"

Mueller did not finish his sentence. The first of Skorzeny's three quick shots found its mark in his chest. He fell forward onto the glass coffee table, which cracked under his weight and split in two pieces. He was dead before the fall was completed.

Skorzeny slowly and calmly walked over to the body. He reached down into Mueller's trousers, found a wallet, and retrieved the currency it contained. He then threw the wallet down on the body.

Yes, Skorzeny thought, *the police investigators will not look too closely at the evidence. They will merely conclude that Mueller was killed by a common burglar.* Skorzeny would ransack a few drawers and closets before he left to make it look like a robbery. Mueller was using an alias, so he would likely be buried in an untraceable grave.

Nobody would try to delve deeper into this crime, especially since before he came here, Skorzeny had greased the skids with, and the palms of, General Alfredo Stroessner, the up and coming Paraguayan army officer.

Nobody in the public would ever know about Heinrich Mueller's dramatic escape from Nazi Germany and then from Norway to Spain in May 1945. One of the worst butchers of the Hitler regime would remain missing and unaccounted for.

57

Washington, DC.
April 1951

* * *

"All right, Jack, I'm anxious to hear the postmortem. How did it all go down?"

Paul finished his question, downed the rest of his old fashioned, and raised his hand to the bartender for another one. He had flown down to Washington at Jack's request. They were now recapping the events of the last two weeks at the Town and Country Bar in the Mayflower Hotel on Connecticut Avenue, where they were both staying. Paul had just arrived by taxi from National Airport, where he had parked his airplane. Jack had arrived the day before.

"Jesus, what a mess. The CIA and the FBI are in a big pissing contest over it all. By the way, the G-men noted your 'uncooperative' behavior during their interviews."

Jack raised his hand for another round also. "That's because they remind me of the two FBI goons who tried to shake me down in 1943 and get me to be an agent for them against Spain. They also threatened me with deportation, even though everything was legal and proper, and I fired in self-defense, according to the police report."

"In a way, Paul, you're just a pawn in the power struggle that's been going on between the FBI and the CIA since the war. By the way, Allen went out on a limb to vouch for you."

"I'm sorry about that. I don't want him to fall on his sword for me."

"Don't worry, both Allen and his boss, good old CIA Director Beetle Smith, hate that bastard Hoover with a passion. You'll be amazed at how that ended."

"Don't hold out on me, Jack."

His friend looked around before answering, but there was nobody nearby on this weekday late afternoon. "Well, Beetle went to Truman, no less. Beetle told him that Hoover was interfering in an international CIA operation that was critical to national security, as I would say your efforts in Spain have been. Truman hauled Hoover's ass in there, with Beetle and Allen present, and told him to back off. Truman has a real set of balls, Paul, and I bet he'd like to fire two prima donnas for insubordination in the same month."

"How does he get away with that?"

"That's easy. Both Truman and Beetle are squeaky clean boy scouts, and Hoover has absolutely no dirt on them. What's even more frustrating for Hoover is that he knows there's dirt on Allen somewhere, but it's all buried in wartime events in Switzerland."

"So what about the investigation of Helga and the guy I shot?" That question stung Paul as soon as he said it. He had now killed three men—and abused Helga when she was lying on the ground.

"They identified the thug as an SS operative left over from the war. The FBI must have beaten the shit out of Helga, because she sang like a canary. She had met the head SS guy that she and the thug worked for, and she told the Feds where to find him. Apparently he reported to a key figure 'somewhere in South America,' according to Helga."

"So did they round him up?"

"No such luck; they went to his hiding place but before they could arrest him, he did himself in."

"What happened? Did the FBI bungle it?"

"Not really. The SS guy did what any self-respecting Nazi animal would do when cornered. He bit into his cyanide capsule as the Feds were beating his door down. He was dead within seconds."

"So that's the end of it?"

"It gets better, Paul. He turned out to be a dumb chief thug. In his apartment there were all kinds of records on the remaining SS and Nazi operatives in the States. Not only that, but Allen really leaned on Gehlen to cough up everything he had on any remnants of the Third Reich in America. They've all been rounded up within the last week. The network in America is now wiped out."

"Will they all get public trials?"

"That's not likely. Hoover wants to hush this up, since Commies and so-called traitors are his big thing. You can bet, though, that he will find a way to get even with Allen."

"That's all good news, Jack, except about Allen. I'm sure sick of checking my back side all the time."

"I hear you. By the way, how's Liz taking it?"

"She was apoplectic at first. I think she's calmed down now, but she's still worried about the children and their memories of it."

"They'll do all right, I'm sure." Jack replied.

"I hope so." Paul collected his thoughts and tried to put the pieces together. "You know, it's clear to me that this kind of desperate action wasn't due to some wartime grudge about what I did for the OSS in Spain, or even my role in Operation Fortitude to deceive the Germans about the Normandy invasion."

"Yeah, I agree."

"So I'm sure it was about Valhalla. They must have thought that I know where the cargo is located or where Walter and Hans are, and they were going to kidnap my children to force me to tell them what I know."

"That's pretty dramatic, Paul, but I guess it's possible."

"It makes me wonder who else might try to get to me in the future. We know that the Russians must have knowledge of Valhalla and an inkling of my role in it, as a result of our little Czech adventure in '48."

Jack was silent for a moment, obviously processing that assertion. "I suppose that's possible, too, but you can't get paranoid over it. We still don't know the significance of Valhalla, and what it was really all about. Besides, I doubt the Russians would stoop to kidnapping or some other dumb move."

Paul just nodded, but there was one more matter gnawing at him. "You know, Jack, it seems incredible that Margarita got there so fast, but even more amazing that she reached Sharon and that she was able to get there before me. By the way, I asked Margarita why she didn't call you. She said she did, but you weren't in the office."

"That's not true. I was there all afternoon. Your secretary reached me there. That's why I was able to get to Central Park almost as fast."

"I guess it was just the heat of battle. I didn't even think she knew Sharon that well—or knew how to reach her so rapidly."

"Yeah, that is a little curious isn't it?"

The two men were silent for several seconds.

"So what's next, or did I fly down here just to have a couple of drinks?"

"No. I thought it would be prudent to have you say hello to Allen and thank him. You should also meet a few of his guys at the agency just to make sure you have a few friends in the future, in case I'm not handy. Finally, as your attorney I recommend that I introduce you to a couple of people at the State and Defense departments. You should have some contacts for future back-channel efforts with Spain. But that's tomorrow. Let's go over to Georgetown for a few more drinks and a nice dinner."

"All right, you're on. Lead the way."

58

Near Tarifa. Spain.
June 25, 1951

* * *

Otto Skorzeny stared out across the narrow Strait of Gibraltar toward the hills of Spanish Morocco in Africa. From this roadside viewpoint at the southern-most tip of Europe, it was easy to appreciate the importance of geography, at a place where two continents and two seas met.

Skorzeny looked again at his watch and when he looked up the car was finally pulling in. Reinhard Gehlen stepped out and walked briskly over to Skorzeny. The two men stood there momentarily and stared at each other. They did not shake hands. There were no other bystanders at the roadside pullover.

"You're late, Gehlen."

"Yes, Skorzeny, I am. I'm actually lucky to be here at all. I have to take extraordinary measures to conceal my travels. The last thing I want is the Americans to know that I'm associated with *die Spinne.*"

"I understand that. Nevertheless, I had important information to share, but three days ago that all changed, although I only found out about the changed circumstances this morning."

"You're going to have to explain that, Otto."

"I had hoped to provide you with some breakthrough on Valhalla. An agent that I sent to South Africa sent me a coded message. He had determined that the two Hoffman traitors had made their way there by way of Southwest Africa. He stated the rest of the story was complicated and required an expla-nation in person."

"That sounds like a breakthrough."

"It would have been, except that my agent is now dead."

There was a long pause.

"What happened?"

"He was on board Pan Am Flight 151 on June 22 when it crashed in Liberia."

"Was the crash accidental, or...?"

"I have no reason to believe it was due to sabotage or some similar act. The problem is that all the work he accomplished over many months is now gone. We're back where we started. The two Hoffmans must be under the protection of the South African government. That means that our hope for collaborating with their government is dead."

Gehlen nodded. He walked over to the edge of the parking lot and stared at Morocco for a minute before turning and walking back to Skorzeny. "Otto, we must ease off on our search for Valhalla. Our relationship with the Americans is too important. After what Mueller did, it could have been a catastrophe. As it was, I had to turn over to the Americans everything I had on the remnants of our wartime network in America. Some of those assets we could have used, but now they're gone. We must concentrate on rebuilding an intelligence organization in West Germany that will serve the American Cold War efforts. That's the best way to confront the Soviets for now. In addition, the imminent American rapprochement with the Franco regime in Spain will cause him to tighten the noose on us locally. We must not abuse our welcome. Remember that the main reason he gave us refuge was because of what Germany did for Spain in the civil war, not in any way to revive the National Socialist movement."

"I understand all of that, but what about the Soviet interest in Valhalla? We know they have knowledge of it, and they may be actively trying to locate the cargo."

"Otto, we don't know that for certain, but they will face the same obstacles that we do without access to the Hoffman family."

"Maybe they are already penetrating the inner circle of Hoffman, Ortega, and Kurtz principals."

"I doubt that, Otto. In any case, we will certainly try to detect such activity. Meanwhile, there are other useful efforts that we can pursue. Tell me more about your efforts in Egypt to encourage their military to overthrow the monarchy."

59

In the air over French West Africa.
May 1952

* * *

Karl Hoffman savored the oloroso dulce sherry as the Douglas DC-4 slipped through the smooth night air in the African skies somewhere over northern Niger. It was the last course of the fine seven-course meal, and Karl was proud that the Ortega sherry was part of the menu. He thought that the full meal service wasn't practical in the middle of the night, but the airline was exploring all options before passenger service began.

Karl was on one of the final "proving runs" that Iberia Airlines was conducting for its inaugural direct flights to Spanish Guinea, scheduled to start in October. The flight had departed Valencia, Spain just after 10:00 p.m. and was scheduled to arrive in Bata just before 2:00 p.m. the following day, with a refueling stop at Lagos, Nigeria. Karl looked at his watch. It was now 4:00 a.m. Karl was the only occupant in the front of the passenger cabin. He got up and looked back. The cabin was lit dimly and there were about a dozen other passengers, mostly airline and government employees, all of whom seemed to be asleep. The two stewards were at the back of the plane, probably enjoying a smoke.

Karl was on this flight in his consulting role with the airline. He thought about that for a moment. *Well, it's time to consult with the cockpit crew.* Karl turned and made his way the short distance to the flight deck. He knew all the crew members, since he had flown with them several times on similar trips. The cockpit door was open, so he entered.

He came almost immediately to the navigator station, but he held back in the darkness as he saw the navigator come down from the astrodome. He had probably just completed some starshots, so he would be busy for a while. Karl watched inquisitively over the next few minutes, fascinated by the practice of the oldest form of navigation, still relevant in the age of aviation, because Africa had so few aviation radio aids.

Karl finally approached the desk as he saw the navigator complete his calculations. "How are we doing?"

"Hello, Karl. We're doing very well; on course with an unusually strong tail wind. I think we can make Bata nonstop with reserves."

"That's great news," Karl replied, moving closer to the desk to look at the navigator's plot.

"I just shot four stars, Polaris, Betelgeuse, Arcturus, and Dubhe. Normally, I only do three to get a good position. I'm looking at how it goes, since as we approach the equator the sky becomes quite different," the man said enthusiastically.

"Thanks for the update. Let's see what the others are doing," Karl replied.

He continued to make his way forward. The next two crew members were the engineer and radio operator, both bent over some paperwork and lost in their own world.

Karl continued forward a few paces. Both the captain and the first officer were staring into space, occasionally looking at the instruments or out the window. Karl was sensitive about disturbing them. The cockpit red lighting was very dim and, compared to the navigator, there was almost a complete lack of activity that could destroy the ethereal beauty of the night.

The captain turned, as he must have sensed Karl's presence. "So, have you been visiting the hardest-working crew member back there?"

"Yes, he just completed a starshot and informs me we have a great tail-wind and can probably make Bata nonstop."

"That we will do this one time perhaps, but it is a rare opportunity due to the prevailing winds. That's our fate in the primitive African skies. We are at the mercy of wind, sand, and stars, just as St. Exupery wrote."

"Yes, Captain, and he put his time in at Cape Juby in Spanish Sahara and wrote eloquently about it. Do you think he anticipated then the progress that would be made in only twenty-five years?"

"I'm sure he knew, but he was rather detached from the real world sometimes. Perhaps that's an author's fate."

"I'll not disturb you further, Captain. I'll take a nap now, so I can be awake as we approach Bata."

"Please come back up later and ride the jump seat for our arrival."

"I will."

Karl returned to his seat. Within a few minutes he was asleep.

* * *

He later awoke with a start as the sun poured through the window. He looked at his watch: 10:00 a.m. He had slept a long time. He decided to go up again to the cockpit, but first he went to the forward lavatory and spent a few minutes shaving and freshening up.

As he reached the cockpit, he stared out the left window and noted the huge mountain to the left. He looked out and slightly to the right of the aircraft's nose, and he could barely make out another peak in the distance, shrouded in mist. He walked up to the front of the cockpit where the captain and the first officer were also admiring the view.

"That must be Mount Cameroon to the left and Pico de Basile on Fernando Poo to the right."

"Excellent, Karl. We'll be landing in Bata in about an hour. The steward is bringing up a light lunch, and I'll have him bring yours also. Go ahead and take the jump seat."

"So, can we routinely do this nonstop?" Karl replied as he took the seat.

"I'm afraid not, at least in the DC-4. Someday we will get the Constellation and then it will be an easy nonstop flight, and in pressurized comfort, too."

"And beyond that perhaps we will have jet powered transports? The British just started operating the Comet from London to Johannesburg."

"That's quite an accomplishment, Karl, but we will have to see how it works out operationally. Iberia's biggest priority now is negotiating rights to serve America direct with the Constellations that we just ordered."

"Yes, both my son and I are involved in that effort."

"Your son has been quite successful in America, I hear."

"Yes, but he is a Spaniard first. Right now he's dedicated to improving bilateral relations between the two countries." Karl thought about that statement for a minute. *Yes, Paul has been successful in an increasingly multinational world that gets smaller by the day as the airplane and improved communications progress inexorably. How will that affect events on this continent—and in the world?*

60.

Bernkastel, Germany.
September 1952

* * *

"You seem to have everything under control in the vineyards, Kirsten. How have things been going otherwise?"

"Very well, I think. As you can tell, the '49 vintage was superb, and the yields quite high. Everybody in the valley says it's the best vintage since 1921. I'm hoping it will help establish our prominence again and maybe allow us to export a significant amount to America."

"Don't worry about that. I'll see to it personally that this vintage gets recognized in the States. You and I, after all, are partners in this enterprise. I have to manage this for my father since he is in Europe so infrequently," Paul responded with enthusiasm as he took another sip of the Hoffman Riesling Kabinett Halbtroken 1949.

"I'm really happy that you come by occasionally, Paul. Anita also visits even more frequently, and she has been very helpful with advice on the wine making. When your father is able to come here, he is also supportive."

Paul admired his twenty-year-old cousin for her guts and maturity. She was taking charge of a complicated business at a tender young age. He reminded himself that he had done the same thing at about the same age. He also thought that she was blossoming into a beautiful young woman, but he put that thought aside. She would probably have a beau soon enough, and it was none of his business to give her any advice in that arena.

She poured him another glass of Riesling. "Paul, I have a sensitive matter I want to tell you about."

"Yes, what is it?" Paul replied, alarmed by the tone in her voice.

"For some reason, in the last couple of years, there have been a few occasions when I thought I was under observation."

"What exactly do you mean?" Now Paul was really alarmed.

"It was nothing overt, or even something I could pin down and point to someone who was watching me. It might just be my intuition. I even hesitate to raise the issue."

"That's all right, Kirsten. It's good to trust your intuition. Can you associate it with any individual, event, or place, like when you are in the village?"

"No, it might just be a stray glance or some other gesture that seems to be more than casual, but it is always from different individuals who are complete strangers."

"Could it just be some male admirers that you caught in the act?"

"No, they were mostly much older, and some of them were women."

Paul mulled this over. Could it be a false alarm? Or could it be——? "Have you mentioned this to Eric and Hannah?"

"Yes, but they assured me that it was my imagination."

Eric and Hannah Diehl had managed the vineyard and the estate for many years, starting even before his grandfather General Wilhelm von Hoffman's service on the German army general staff during World War I. The Diehls were now in their seventies and in no position to protect Kirsten if the need arose.

Paul quickly crafted a plan. "As I said, Kirsten, it's better to be safe and trust your instincts. I think it would be important for you to have a general manager around who could look after the business and security matters while you concentrate on the wine making. Would you be willing to accept that idea?"

"Of course, if you think it's really necessary. I'd rather devote my attention to the vines and the wine making anyway."

"All right, I'll arrange it through our law firm. Even though it's in New York, they have extensive contacts in Germany going back many years. Money is no longer an issue since we were finally able to access your father's accounts in Switzerland."

Kirsten simply nodded.

Paul racked his brain trying to reconcile who might be monitoring Kirsten. The Nazi movement had been thoroughly eradicated in Germany and, most recently, in the States, as a result of the altercation in Central Park.

Who else could it be?

61

Luanda, Angola,
October 1952

* * *

"Have you attended to all the immigration and aircraft servicing issues, Felipe?" Paul inquired.

"Yes, all the documentation is complete, and the aircraft has been serviced for our return trip the day after tomorrow. I also reconfirmed our hotel reservation downtown and have arranged for a car."

"Good work. By the way, your flying skills are excellent, especially in an airplane as quirky as the Twin Beech."

"Thank you. Your father has been generous with his time instructing me in the Beech, and I have also been able to fly in the aero club in Santa Isabel. I'll complete the other administrative details and be right back so we can depart for the hotel."

Paul nodded and watched as Felipe Mukasa Ondo smiled and then turned to walk away. Paul noted that Felipe had piercing brown eyes and a handsome, sculpted face, and like many Bantus of the Fang tribe, he was tall. As was common in the native population of Spanish Guinea, Felipe was given a Spanish first name, followed by his given name in the Fang language.

Felipe was important to Paul's father because he was Wekesa's grandson. Wekesa had been at Karl Hoffman's side in Spanish Guinea since they served together in the *schutztruppe* in World War I. Felipe's father, Wekesa's firstborn son, had been killed in a plantation accident in 1935 the year after Felipe was born. Wekesa had raised him since then, and Karl had watched over his education. As a result, he had qualified as an *emancipado*, a native of Spanish Guinea who is entitled to most of the rights of Spanish citizenship. Most importantly, Karl had taken the steps needed for Felipe to obtain a college education in Spain, and he would be one of the few native inhabitants to do so. He was scheduled to leave for Spain in a little over two weeks.

After leaving Germany, Paul flew to Bata on the usual circuitous airline routing, but that was about to change. The inaugural Iberia Airlines direct flight from Spain to Guinea would begin in three days, and Paul's father would be on it. Paul timed his arrival in Bata so that he could fly the Beech to Angola while his father was in Spain, knowing his father would have frowned on the idea of the Angola flight.

He may have a point, Paul thought. *How will I find Santos tomorrow? How will I approach him if I find him? Am I taking a risk? After all, I may be a wanted man in Portugal, as a result of Claus Hilgeman's death. Well, tomorrow will tell.*

The next morning he woke up early. He had formulated a plan before retiring last night, and it was a simple one. He would ask the hotel staff where the PIDE office was, go there directly, and ask for Santos.

He and Felipe had breakfast, and Paul told him to meet him for dinner at the hotel. Paul hoped that wasn't wishful thinking. Felipe would visit their Luanda business agent while Paul was occupied with his main focus.

The hotel manager was a little unnerved at Paul's request for the PIDE office address. Paul assured him that he wanted to meet an acquaintance there, and the man reluctantly gave him the address. By 11:00 a.m., Paul had reached the PIDE office. He took a long breath and entered. He walked up to the man sitting at the front desk.

"Can I help you?" the uniformed man said in an annoyed voice.

"Yes, I am here to see Alexandre Santos, please," Paul replied in choppy Portuguese.

The man stared at Paul for a long time before replying. "Why do you want to see him?"

"Please tell him I have a message from Claus Hilgeman."

The other man's eyebrows rose slightly, but he finally stood. "Wait here," he said and then turned and walked into the adjacent office.

I hope this is a good idea because it might be too late to change my mind.

Paul stood there for several minutes. He looked around the room and took in the view of the austere office furniture, the portrait of Salazar above the receptionist desk, and the slow-moving overhead ceiling fan. The office reeked of cigarette smoke.

The office door finally opened. The uniformed man motioned Paul to enter. Paul complied. He entered and approached a man sitting behind a desk. The uniformed man left the office and closed the door behind him.

The two men stared at each other for a minute.

It's time to break the ice. "Good morning. I'm Paul Hoffman. My Portuguese is poor. Do you speak Spanish, English, or German?"

"I understand you have a message for me from Claus Hilgeman," Alexandre Santos said in German.

"Yes, but unfortunately they were his dying words, and your name was on his last breath," Paul replied in German.

Santos looked at Paul and frowned. "I'm not surprised. We were best friends." He paused and then said, "Did you kill him?"

"No, but I killed the thug who fatally injured him. It was too late to save Claus. I stumbled upon their struggle when I came to find him, because he was late for dinner."

"That makes sense. Of course, I know the other details of the case. You covered your tracks well, but not perfectly. Your airplane was spotted by a police officer when you departed the next morning. He could not positively identify it as you and your plane, but since you have the only Beech Bonanza registered in Iberia, we were able to infer your involvement." He raised an eyebrow. "You took a big chance coming here."

"I know, but I must find my brother, Hans, and I know that Claus tried to serve him and my uncle to his dying breath. I presume that he used his last words to guide me to you for a reason."

Santos leaned back in his chair, looked out the window and back at Paul, and then leaned forward again. "Well, you needn't worry. I am loyal to my late friend and those he tried to protect, including you. I must warn you, however, that it is becoming increasingly difficult to contact your uncle, and it is impossible to contact your brother as a result of…recent events. They needed to maintain a very low profile before, but now they must be invisible because they are hunted men."

"They're in South Africa, aren't they?"

"I don't know where they are now. You should give up your search. You will not be able to find your brother. If you could, it means that others could find him easier, and that means he would be dead."

Paul looked at Santos. Those words stung because they were so coldly logical—and accurate. He sighed. "I won't disagree with your assessment, but I will never give up my search."

"I understand. In similar circumstances I would do the same, but I am an only child. Claus was the closest thing to a brother that I ever had."

"I'm sorry for your loss."

Santos nodded his acknowledgement. "Sit down for a few minutes, my friend, and we can share some port and perhaps chat about a few things before you have to depart our beautiful country."

Paul nodded and smiled. *Perhaps I can maintain contact in the future with this unusual policeman.*

62

Bata, Spanish Guinea,
October 1952

***

"So I assume you had an interesting flight to Angola. What did you find out, or was this another fool's errand?"

Paul was caught off guard by the directness of his father's question. They stood on the airport ramp following the ceremony for the arrival of the inaugural scheduled flight from Spain.

"You certainly found out about it fast."

"I need to make a trip to Lagos, Nigeria, in a couple of days to settle some plantation labor issues. The hangar maintenance crew cabled me two days ago and said they would have the plane serviced as soon as it returned from Luanda."

"Well, to answer your question, the trip was not a fool's errand, even though I do not yet know where my brother is."

"I know better than to dissuade you from further efforts, but I hope you will accept whatever you find, even if it's bad news."

"Thank you for the advice. By the way, how was your flight?"

"Excellent, since it was so many years in the planning."

"Well, it's good to know that things are changing for the better in Africa."

"Do you really think they are, Paul?"

"What do you mean?"

"Did you hear about the new Mau Mau uprising in Kenya?"

"Yes, but I thought the British had it under control."

"They may or may not have it under control, but it isn't even the first such event. Nor will it be the last. The winds of change are blowing in Africa, and the cry for the end of colonialism and independence will grow louder. Just look at the recent past. Libya became independent in 1951; a coup overthrew the puppet British monarchy in Egypt a few months ago. It's only a matter of time until this spreads across the continent."

"Yes, but economic conditions are improving. Just look at what's happening here in Guinea. My contacts in the New York Cocoa Exchange predict that cocoa and other commodity prices will explode as world economies improve."

"It won't matter, unless these benefits reach the native populations. Cocoa and coffee are cash crops whose demand and prices are controlled by the Western world. None of the colonies in Africa have sustainable balanced economies. More important, we're not training or preparing the local populations for self-government and independence."

"What about Felipe? He could be the future for Guinea," Paul said.

"Yes, but we need more like him. The governor and those back in Spain will not permit enough like him to be educated. They think they can manipulate the population with a few slavish stooges as figureheads for a token local government."

"So what does the future portend here?"

"I really don't know, Paul. I really don't." Karl glanced at his son. "In any case, can you stay a few more days?"

"I wish I could, but I'm taking your advice and trying to spend more time in New York with Liz and the children. The new airline service is fabulous, but there is initially only one round trip every two weeks, so I'm booked on tomorrow's return flight to Spain. I hope you'll understand. Perhaps you will come to New York soon to visit us there."

"Someday perhaps, or maybe you can bring your family here to visit and show them your roots. I hope you'll understand that I also consider the people here to be my family."

Paul was stunned. He never expected his father to be so frank about his feelings, yet he was reassured. It meant his father understood where the focus of his life truly was.

63.

New York City.
December 1952

* * *

"Well, you're just a day overdue. At least you're not a day late and a dollar short, as the old saying goes."

"Very funny, Jack, but the crew had to shut down an engine on the Stratocruiser out of London, and we got stuck overnight in Shannon, Ireland, while Pan American fetched another one. By the way, where's Liz?"

The two men had just met in the baggage area and were waiting for Paul's luggage to be retrieved, so they could leave Idlewild Airport for the short trip to Manhattan.

"Since your revised arrival day created a little schedule problem, she sent me. Was everything all right in Germany?"

"Yes, thanks to you, and to Sullivan and Cromwell's excellent legwork, Kirsten now has a very capable business manager and surreptitious security overseer. I'm glad I made a quick trip to meet him and synchronize him with our business interests. I'm also glad to be back. I assume that not much has happened here since I left."

"Actually, more than you might have thought."

"What's going on?"

"Ike's election has propelled Allen into the spotlight. He's the frontrunner for the CIA director in the new administration."

"Well, that's a big deal."

"You bet. There's also a rumor that lots of things could change in an Eisenhower presidency, but nobody seems to have a clue about what he really thinks."

"That could be because he's a general and not a politician."

"Don't fool yourself, Paul. Ike is a politician, all right. He kept a wartime coalition in one piece in the face of a lot of prima donnas. I think he can hold his own when the chips are down."

"That's what I've heard. What about all the hysteria about a 'Red under every bed'? Has that all died down?"

"No, it hasn't. The Rosenbergs are still sitting on death row, so everybody is waiting to see whether Ike will commute their sentence, or at least Ethel's, to life imprisonment. McCarthy is still out for his pound of flesh."

"Regardless of that, Jack, the serious issues of the Cold War still need to be addressed."

"You're still one of the key players in all that, Paul. In fact, one of the reasons I'm glad I met you is to convey a request from the State Department for your 'advisory' opinions on the next steps in Spain."

"I was afraid of that. It means I have to go to Washington again. The bureaucrats in State pretty well disgust me. They seem to be no more effective than bureaucrats everywhere else."

"You were expecting otherwise, Paul?"

"I suppose not. I'm hoping that the final deal with Spain can be sealed next year. I've been spending too much time in Europe and Africa lately. I need to pay attention to business and my family here in the States."

"I hear you," Jack replied. "By the way, is there anything new on…your brother?"

Paul sighed. "No, but I'll keep trying."

"Maybe you're trying too hard. Maybe you should back off a little and just keep your eyes and ears open. Some breakthrough might be in the cards in the future."

"Maybe you're right, Jack…maybe you're right."

64.

Office of the CIA director, Washington, DC.
April 1953

***

Jack stood at the open door of his former boss's new office with a mixture of awe and curiosity. He had no idea why Allen Dulles had summoned him on such short notice—but he knew it wasn't to exchange pleasantries.

"Well, come on in, I won't bite."

Jack approached the silver-haired man, who motioned him to sit down. Dulles was puffing furiously on his pipe, but the characteristic half smile was absent.

"I'm sorry to ask you here on such short notice, but it couldn't afford to wait."

"That's all right, sir, I mean, Allen. I was only looking at some boring legal files this week anyway." Jack's lame attempt at humor fell flat.

"Listen, Jack. Some people think that Stalin's death last month could completely change US-Soviet relations. However, nobody knows who's really in charge. I stuck my neck out and predicted Malenkov would be the interim leader, rather than that old Bolshevik Molotov. I was lucky on that one, but the real power shift is yet to come. Did you hear the president's speech on the chances for peace?"

"Yes, and it sounded like an appeal to the Russians to tone down the arms race."

"We keep getting conflicting signals, Jack. Meanwhile, the hidden work in the field goes on. We desperately need a few good men in the field who can help influence events as well as keep their eyes and ears open."

Oh boy, here it comes.

"Jack, the reason I asked you here is that I need you on my team. I need someone with experience whom I can trust to do what needs to be done out in the real world. Don't worry, I'm not trying to recruit you into the Washington bureaucracy. You'd be out where the real action is, out where the game is played."

"What exactly would my position be?" Jack responded cautiously.

"As the director, I have a lot of flexibility. We have a limited ability to make midlevel hires. As a result of your OSS experience and law degree, I can bring you in on a GS-14 direct appointment as a field officer and assign you immediately to a field team. You wouldn't have to go through any of the career-ladder and civil-service bullshit. The pay is better that way, but it's not what you're used to, I'm afraid."

"That's all right, Allen. You said the magic words: I won't be a bureaucrat. I'm not worried about the money anyway. What you're telling me sounds urgent, and I know the score with the world situation. The Cold War still rages on, and that won't change."

"That's right. More important, the battlefields of the future are going to be on the periphery and won't involve confrontation between American and Russian militaries, as long as our nuclear deterrent strategy works. The Korean War is about to wind down, and we'll have other things to worry about, like Indochina."

"So what will I do?"

"Do you know Kermit Roosevelt?"

"Sure, everybody in the OSS knows Kim, grandson of Teddy Roosevelt and special-operations guru. He's considered too flamboyant by some, but I'd serve with him in a heartbeat."

"That's good, because you will be, in about two weeks."

"Where and what is it?"

"You're going to be developing the plan for the event."

"Again, respectfully, Allen, where and what is it?"

"It's going to be in Iran, and its code name is Operation Ajax. Its purpose is to shore up the Shah and get rid of the left-leaning Prime Minister Mossadegh."

"All right, I get the drift. I've been following world events enough to know the general situation."

"That's great, Jack. I know you'll be successful. Welcome back to the game."

As Jack stood and shook hands with the espionage legend, he could only wonder: *Where will all this lead?*

65.

New York City.
October 1953

* * *

"Well, look who's here." Jack greeted Paul in the baggage area at about eight in the morning on Friday.

"You picked me up a few months ago, so I thought I'd return the favor. How was the flight from Istanbul?"

"It was actually several flights. I was in a Douglas DC-6 from Istanbul to Frankfurt to London and then a Boeing Stratocruiser to here. It's a long flight, for sure."

"How long are you in New York?"

"I have a meeting this afternoon downtown, and then I thought I'd stay here for the weekend and head back to DC on Sunday."

"Sharon's sure looking forward to your visit."

"Yeah, I bet; me too." Both men smiled.

"What are you going to do about your relationship with her?"

"I don't know. I'm in Washington now, except for business travel. Sharon won't move down there. I don't know why. She's just a 'Girl Friday' for a bunch of small firms in Manhattan. She says she likes her independence, and that's that," Jack replied, frowning.

"Maybe it's for the best if you're going to be on the road a lot. Remember the saying 'absence makes the heart grow fonder'?"

"Very funny, Paul, but I guess if you and Liz have made it work with all your travel, then I shouldn't complain."

"That's true," Paul replied. *Should I ask him?* "So how'd it go in Iran? It sounds like it's peaceful there now."

Jack turned abruptly to his friend and scowled. "What are you talking about?" Jack replied brusquely.

"Jesus, don't bite my head off. It's been all over the papers. It looks like your efforts were successful and—"

"Listen, Paul, we're good friends, but don't ask me about my work again!"

212

There was a cold silence for a full minute.

"I'm sorry, Jack. I didn't mean to pry. We're always kept it close and confidential between us. I guess things have changed."

Jack sighed and then grabbed his luggage as it appeared.

"Look, I'm sorry, Paul. I guess I'm just tired from the flight. I haven't even asked you how things have been going in Spain. What's the latest?"

"Well, America and Spain sealed the deal last month with the Pact of Madrid. I was there for the ceremony. It was a cooperative defense and economic agreement, rather than a treaty, because the administration wasn't sure it could get Senate ratification. It's still a big deal. It looks like I can get off the treadmill for a while and concentrate even more on the home front, with the business and my family."

"That's really good news, Paul. It means that Spain is an ally now in the Cold War, even if it's not a formal alliance. What will happen next?"

"The good news is that the aid and economic package starts right away. That will keep the economy progressing."

"What about the military aid?" Jack replied.

"That'll kick in slowly. It's also needed because Spain's military equipment is so antiquated. I expect that you'll start to see SAC bombers from America slowly begin to temporarily base out of the three air force bases that the Spanish government agreed to operate jointly with SAC."

"That's great news also. What else will happen?"

"I'm looking forward to direct air service between New York and Madrid to start sometime next year. That'll make my life easier for sure, Jack."

"Well, I guess the world is changing."

"It sure is." Paul paused before continuing. "Now that we have your bags, we can get you into town, where Sharon will meet you. After you've gotten 're-acquainted,' maybe we can meet later and head to the Village for a few drinks. It's Friday, and I'm already thirsty."

66

New York City.
October 1954

* * *

"You have no right to lecture me about Guatemala, Jack! The CIA most certainly has blood on its hands and you might have been part of it," Liz Kurtz said. She could barely contain her anger as she stood her ground in front of her brother in her penthouse as their argument continued.

"Your problem, Liz, is that you don't know the threat we face in Central Anerica," Jack replied defensively.

"What threat is that? That the citizens of Guatemala might want self-determination and be safe from the plundering of the United Fruit Company?"

"This isn't getting us anywhere! I'm leaving before I lose control of myself," Jack replied as he turned and walked quickly to the door, just as it opened and Paul entered.

"See if you can talk some sense into your wife!" He quickly brushed by Paul and stormed out the door, slamming it hard behind him.

A momentary silence ensued as Paul looked from the door to Liz. He could hear her heavy breathing from across the room and walked over to embrace her. He held her for a long moment and felt her shaking. He finally pulled away and looked directly at Liz's face, noticing a tear forming.

"Are you all right? What was that argument about?

"I'll explain. Please read this article first," Liz replied, handing the open magazine to Paul.

Paul took a few minutes to skim the article and then looked back up at Liz, who had regained her composure.

"So what do you think?"

"I think it's well written and…provocative," Paul answered. He looked at Liz, whose facial expression revealed her hope for his approval for her article.

"Well, at least you're being constructive. That's more than I can say for Jack."

"Oh no, did you let him read it?"

"Yes, and he just about went out of his mind lecturing me on the Communist menace and the threat the Arbenz government posed."

Liz was referring to the June 1954 coup in which the elected president of Guatemala was overthrown because conservative interests, including US corporations, felt threatened by reforms pushed by President Arbenz. The CIA was rumored to be heavily involved in the coup. Liz had written the article on the coup for a national publication.

"You apparently did your homework. The most provocative assertions relate to the influence of US corporations and the premise that there was no Soviet conspiracy involved."

"That's right, Paul. Arbenz was no threat to America. By failing to back legitimate reform governments, we're actually setting the stage for later Soviet involvement that will stir up more violent revolutionary struggles."

"I'd have to say I agree with you. It reminds me of what my father is also preaching in Africa. I guess Jack doesn't agree."

"It's more than that. Sharon told me he travelled to Managua, Nicaragua, just before the coup took place. He had to have been personally involved."

"How did Sharon know that?"

"She says she saw an airline itinerary before Jack left."

"Doesn't that smack of snooping around? I know she's his girlfriend, but maybe she's getting a little too curious."

"Come on, Paul, there are lots of signs that Jack was involved not only in Guatemala but also in Iran last year. It's almost like it's a game to him."

"That's what Allen Dulles calls it: the great game. They take it very seriously and, after all, that's Jack's job right now."

"Then I can only wonder what comes next."

"Well, Liz, I hate to feed the fire, but when he was here last week he let it slip that he would be flying to Saigon soon."

"Oh, God, I thought the Geneva accords in July ended that war. What could the United States possibly be doing there?"

"I doubt we'll find out soon. The CIA probably feels it needs to be gathering intelligence anywhere a new power vacuum emerges."

"We just got out of one inconclusive war in Asia last year. I suppose Indochina will be the next crusade."

"Let's not jump to conclusions, Liz. The president made a conscious decision not to intervene directly to rescue the French."

"Yes, but we poured in millions, or maybe billions, in aid, and in the end all we were doing was backing a colonial power against an indigenous uprising."

"You sound like my father, but some people believe otherwise. They think the Russians or Chinese are involved."

"Not if we stay out of it. Ho Chi Minh and the Vietnamese hate China. They've fought lots of wars against China in the past."

Paul held judgment on that last comment. These issues were debated among government insiders, but the average American knew little about world history, geography, and politics. Paul always thought that was a grave weakness of American democracy, since the general population was unable to make an informed assessment of the many crises in the world.

So I guess that means that Jack, the CIA, and the government will have a free hand to decide the right course of action behind closed doors. Maybe Liz is right.

67

Hoffman Hacienda, Fernando Poo, Spanish Guinea.
October 1955

* * *

Karl Hoffman looked westward briefly through the broad picture window at the expanse of plantation lands and the ocean that lay about twelve kilometers away. From this elevated perch on the side of the nearly ten-thousand-foot Pico de Basile, Karl could see a good part of their agricultural empire. It was sunny, with billowing cumulous clouds, and the rainy season was just ending, so the visibility was very good. Karl nodded in satisfaction, reached for the two glasses of Ortega amontillado he had just refilled, turned, and took them over to where he and his son had been sitting.

"So what is your conclusion about the future price of cocoa?" Karl resumed the conversation as he handed the glass of sherry to Paul.

"Father, everybody I've talked with, including the New York Cocoa Exchange and the equivalent people in London, believe it will continue to increase rapidly."

"Did they guess for what period of time?"

"Years, but I guess they can't predict how long. Cocoa is a commodity, just like the coffee we grow, and right now the demand is soaring as the economies in Europe and America continue to expand. Meanwhile, new production hasn't kept up, so the supply is restricted, and we grow the world's best cocoa. Like all commodities or speculative properties, however, the bubble could burst without warning."

"That's what I'm afraid of, Paul."

"We could take advantage of it by increasing production. How much more land capacity do we have?"

"We have a little unused land here on the island and some on the mainland, but we're nearly at the limit. I guess I'll go ahead and plant on all available remaining land. In the final analysis, I'm worried less about speculative economic swings than about the political situation."

"What troubles you the most?" Paul asked.

"If you've been following the world situation, the conference of non-aligned nations held in Bandung, Indonesia, in April was a bellwether event. Now all the European colonies in Africa are using these countries as models for independence."

"That doesn't sound like an ominous trend."

"It does if the European powers try to suppress these movements. It's now hitting close to home. In May, the French violently suppressed demonstrations in Cameroon. It's literally next door to us, and we're learning that some of the demonstrators have sought refuge here in Guinea. This has the governor all worked up. Now he's looking for any sign of unrest here among our own population."

"Then we need to factor the political situation into all our future planning for our business operations in Africa," Paul responded.

"I definitely agree with that. So, your brief visit of a week is nearly over. You should have all the information you need from me on business operations in Guinea. Tomorrow is Friday, and you're scheduled on the 3:00 p.m. Iberia flight 962 out of Bata on the mainland."

"Yes, will you fly me over in the Beech?"

"No, unfortunately I just found out the left engine has a bad cylinder. You'll have to take the 9:00 a.m. flight 203 over to Bata."

"Isn't that on the old DeHaviland biplane?"

"Yes, unfortunately. That quaint beast is still in service, but it's nearly the end of the line for both the Dragon and the trimotor JU-52 that Iberia also uses here. They're relics from the thirties, but in a few months they'll finally be replaced by Douglas DC-3s for service between the island and the mainland."

"Father, you should be proud of that. You had a major influence in upgrading air service here, as well as from here to Spain."

"Yes, and I'm thankful for that. For our final night, let's go into Santa Isabel and start with some drinks at Bar Polo and then dinner at Bar Africa. Sometimes there are interesting expats dining there. Then maybe we'll end up at the casino," Karl concluded as he downed the rest of his sherry.

"All right, Father. I know I can count on you as the tour guide."

68

New York City.
November 1955

* * *

"Yes, what is it, June?" Paul replied to his secretary on the intercom.

"Your 3:00 p.m. appointment, Mr. Castillo, is here."

"Please show him in." Paul rose and left his desk to greet his guest as Sergio Castillo was ushered into his office suite.

"*Mucho gusto, Señor Castillo.*"

"*El gusto es mio, Señor Hoffman.*"

The two men shook hands.

"Please sit down." Paul motioned his guest to the sofa. "May I offer you a glass of sherry?"

"Yes, thank you, a drier sherry, such as a fino or a manzanilla, if you have it."

"I'll pour you our best fino."

Paul poured and served the sherry and sat in the chair facing the sofa. "*Salud!*" He raised his glass.

Castillo returned the salute and got down to business.

"Thank you for meeting me. I've been looking forward to this ever since I started enjoying your estate wines from Spain. The Reserva and Gran Reserva tempranillos from the '47 and '48 vintages in Rioja were superb. I understand the '52 vintage is good also, but the Reserva and Gran Reserva are not yet released. I hope that when I meet the wine maker, I can congratulate him."

"You will want to congratulate 'her,' Señor Castillo. My cousin Anita Ortega oversees our wine and sherry bodegas in Spain. She is the wine maker in Rioja."

"Then I will want to meet her. Please call me Sergio, by the way."

"All right, and you may call me Paul. I see you've done your homework, and so have I. You have a very successful export-import business in Caracas that covers the Americas and elsewhere. How may I help you today?"

"I will be direct. I would like to have the rights to import your wine in South America, Central America, and Mexico. I know that the market in South America is dominated by producers in Argentina and Chile. I believe the Ortega wines can hold up well there, but you currently have poor market penetration. In return, I can offer you access to Venezuelan crude oil at discount prices. I know that petroleum imports and their affordability are an important issue in Spain. Furthermore, I would like to explore cooperative strategies on cocoa and coffee exports and imports worldwide."

Paul looked at his guest and smiled. *He certainly is bold.*

"That's a rather stunning set of proposals. I'm very interested in the 'wine for oil' idea, but aren't we competitors in the cocoa and coffee business both in production and export-import?"

"Perhaps, but you will soon be hitting production limits for cocoa in Spanish Guinea. In order to take advantage of rising prices, you will need to cooperate with other producers. You have a powerful standing in the cocoa world because of the quality of your product. If you could produce such a quality product elsewhere, and market it as such, then a cooperative arrangement could benefit both of us."

"You have been very direct, Sergio, as you promised. We clearly need to get our staffs and attorneys working on this, after you and I flesh these ideas out a little more. Perhaps you are available tonight as my guest for dinner? We could go to Delmonico's, since they serve our wines through a special arrangement."

"Yes, I know. That's where I first savored them."

"Great. Where are you staying while in New York?"

"I'm at the Algonquin."

"I'll come by with my limousine and pick you up, say, at 7:00 p.m.?"

"That will be fine."

"Over dinner we can discuss your desire to meet the wine maker sometime."

"That would be fine also."

69

Alabos, Spain.
June 1956

* * *

Paul was stunned by his father's announcement. He could see from the expressions on the faces of the other family members that they were also. The regular annual business meeting had started routinely, and everybody had good news to report. All of the family enterprises were making huge amounts of money. Ernesto Ortega chaired the meeting and received the wine business report from his daughter, Anita Ortega, the Spanish real estate report from his son, Alfonso Ortega, the export-import and shipping reports from his nephew, Paul, and the report on Spanish Guinea operations from Karl.

Karl dropped the bombshell after giving his report. He handed a single page document to each of them and described what it meant.

"Would you please repeat that, Karl?" Ernesto said in astonishment.

"Put simply, a multinational conglomerate of cocoa processing and chocolate companies has made a multimillion-dollar offering for our cocoa plantations and land in Fernando Poo."

Paul noted the strained look on Ernesto's face as he tried to digest the high-seven-figure amount shown on the document.

"Father, this is incredible," Alfonso replied. He shook his head. "That amount of money would allow us to develop real estate independently of other investors and provide Anita with funding to modernize wine making in our bodegas."

"You can't be serious, Alfonso! That's the legacy my father left to us. It is not for sale at any price!" Ernesto replied indignantly.

"In my view, this offer is only their first gambit. It is a feeler to see if they can get the plantations cheap. I believe that if we don't accept, they will come back later with a much higher price," Karl said.

"You think the land and cocoa production are that valuable?" Anita asked.

"Yes, in fact, I believe that eventually the offer could be double or triple, or go even higher," Karl said. He looked at the stunned expressions of

Ernesto, Alfonso, and Anita, finally fixing his gaze on Paul as if to say: *How will you weigh in on this?*

"We should get back to them and start negotiating, so that—" Alberto was cut off.

"We will do no such thing because—" Ernesto's reply was also cut off.

"Wait, everybody. There is no need to argue over this. We can have it both ways."

Everyone looked at Paul expectantly.

"We don't have to do anything now, as my father has suggested. We should be thinking about a lot of factors that will affect future cocoa prices and the value of our holdings in Guinea. The independence movement is gaining traction in Africa. This year Sudan, Morocco, and Tunisia became independent. The movement is starting to spread to sub-Saharan Africa already. We need to keep our options open," Paul concluded.

"So you are saying this is a matter of timing?" Anita asked.

Paul could not ignore the furtive admiring glance that accompanied her question. "Yes..." He hesitated, distracted by Anita's glance and what it conveyed.

"Yes, we need to be flexible as this situation develops. It's good that the issue is raised now, so that in future meetings we can approach the issue analytically."

Paul hadn't meant to insult his uncle with that remark, but he observed the cold stare he got from Ernesto, as if to suggest that Paul thought that Ernesto's emotions were controlling him. *It's time to change subjects.*

"I suggest that the business meeting is nearly over. Remember, we have a guest arriving soon for dinner. I've explained who Sergio Castillo is and especially his interest in our wines. Let's see if we can get to know him better, since he has some interesting ideas on economic cooperation between his interests and our own."

* * *

Anita was enchanted with their visitor.

Paul had introduced Sergio to the family, and before dinner the mysterious visitor was able to break the ice. He talked casually about business matters yet spoke eloquently about wine—especially Anita's wine.

As they finished dinner, Sergio continued his praise for the culinary efforts and wine pairing. "I must say that the suckling pig was paired beautifully with the '52 Reserva. It was an astounding match."

"Thank you, Sergio. You are the first outsider to drink this wine before it is released," Anita replied proudly.

"I would like to talk a little more about your winemaking techniques that produced such a splendid vintage."

"Perhaps we could adjourn for a while and let Anita answer Sergio's many questions," Paul suddenly offered.

Anita turned to Paul. He nodded to her approvingly. She understood. "Sergio, let's go have our conversation on the portico, while the rest of the family completes some of the earlier business we discussed."

Anita led him to the west-facing portico overlooking both the surrounding hills and the Ebro River valley. It was 10:30 p.m. on this day before the solstice, and the western sky still showed a trace of crimson. It created soft shadows on the surrounding landscape, which was still readily visible in the warm, clear night air. Anita lit a couple of large candles in holders on the portico's post support beams.

They both quietly admired the view for a while. Finally, she turned to him. "You are an unusual man, Sergio, with your knowledge of wine. What is it that makes my wine so special?"

He pondered that for a moment and turned to her. "I would say it is many things. The subtle flavors coupled with the boldness of the tannin. It conveys a wine with passion, made by someone who is passionate about life and its possibilities."

She looked at him and smiled. "Karl and his late wife, Pilar—that's Ernesto's sister and my cousin Paul's parents—courted on this patio almost exactly forty years ago. For them the world of 1916 presented unlimited possibilities."

"I may suggest, my dear Anita, that the world of 1956 also must present unlimited opportunities for someone as beautiful and accomplished as you are."

"You are very flattering. It is rare to find someone who is not only knowledgeable and refined about such matters, but also bold in how he expresses his emotions."

"I know what I like, and I know the kind of people I would like to be associated with…more closely."

Anita looked into his eyes and saw passion there…and something else that she couldn't quite describe but was also intense. "You've come a long way to meet me and my family. I hope the trip was worth it for you."

"It most certainly was. It was an honor to meet you finally, after several years of enjoying the outlet of your passion. I hope we will be meeting again much sooner—and often."

"Don't your business interests keep you occupied in the Americas?"

"I have senior managers who take care of the mundane day-to-day activities. The exciting part of managing a business empire comes early, while you are struggling. I am past that now. I can spend my time as I want to, anywhere I want to—and with whom I want to spend it."

Anita was overwhelmed with emotion and excitement in Sergio's presence. This had not happened since a beautiful moonlit night in Taos, New Mexico, six years ago. She closed her eyes to try to erase that searing moment.

She opened her eyes. Sergio was still there. *This is now, not then. I mustn't be afraid of where this will lead.*

70

Madrid, Spain.
July 1956

* * *

Alberto sat expectantly as Admiral Luis Carrero shuffled through some documents on his desk, finally finding the one he wanted. Alberto had been summoned to Carrero's office following the change of command ceremony on the destroyer *Audaz*. He had actually been relieved as the acting commander of a destroyer flotilla several months earlier to work on a special project for Carrero. The ceremony was a formality to signify that Alberto was again on shore duty, much to his chagrin.

Carrero shook his head as he finished reading the document. He finally looked up without welcoming his subordinate, holding the document up. "This is such a tragedy, Alberto. This is the summary of the events in Morocco over the last few months. *El Caudillo* is severely depressed by the loss of the protectorate due to Moroccan independence. He and I are now determined that there will be no further surrender of our African territories."

He shook his head again, placed the document in a pile, and looked up. "It's not only that. I thought that, with the pact with the Americans in 1953 and our admission to the United Nations in December 1955, our standing in the world community would be enhanced. But now the UN is demanding that we provide intimate information on our African territories and their populations. Can you imagine? They are demanding to know what our plans are for self-determination in these territories. That is inconceivable. We are determined to resist this."

Carerro paused and sighed deeply, finally turning to his key aide. "I'm sorry for all that. Thank you for coming by, Alberto. Did the ceremony go all right?"

"Yes, sir. The new flotilla commander was eager to assume command."

"The flotilla command is a billet for a captain, rather than a commander such as yourself, but I'm glad I was able to engineer the two-year assignment for you in an acting capacity. The naval personnel staff wasn't pleased, but everyone agrees you did a superb job, and it will enhance your career. We must now attend to other matters. What is the current status of your new assignment?"

"I have worked closely with the naval element of the American military assistance group here in Madrid. Thanks to the Americans, our air force now finally has jet fighters, and our army has modern tanks. Now it is the navy's turn. The Americans will be transferring five Fletcher-class destroyers to us. The first two, the USS *Capps* and the USS *David W. Taylor*, will be ready by next May. We will rename them *Lepanto* and *Almirante Ferrandiz*. The other three will follow in about three years."

"Excellent. They will improve our capabilities."

"Yes, although they were built during World War Two, they are sturdy, and they will have a limited antisubmarine modernization. They will do until we are able to start building our own naval vessels again."

"Yes, and at some point we might like to explore the possibility that the Americans will transfer larger ships to us. Perhaps you can investigate this when you are in Washington, Alberto."

"Excuse me, sir?"

"You can expect to travel there in a few months on a fact-finding mission for me, perhaps after the American elections. We need to find out how far the Americans are willing to go to help us with our military modernization. Also, did you receive your invitation to the reception at the American embassy tonight?"

"Yes, sir, I did."

"I want you to meet the new American naval attaché and also speak with the outgoing officer. See if they might assist you with your trip to America. Your stated purpose for the trip will be to work on the destroyer transfers."

"Very well, sir. I'll take that on."

"Incidentally, you might have the pleasure of meeting Ambassador Lodge's beautiful and intelligent daughter, Beatrice. Take a look at this cover."

Carrero reached across his desk and handed to Alberto a copy of the July 9 issue of the American *Life* magazine.

Alberto gazed at the cover for a long moment and then looked up at Carerro. "You're right, sir. She is absolutely stunning. I think she looks like the

American movie actress Grace Kelly—or more correctly now, the princess of Monaco." Alberto recalled Kelly's April marriage to Prince Rainier.

"Very good, Alberto, your diplomatic skills and knowledge of society will carry you far." Carrero then lost the smile that he briefly exhibited. "There is one more item that I must raise, and it's a little delicate."

"Yes, sir?"

"How old are you, Alberto?"

"I am forty-one, sir."

Carerro sighed. Alberto noted that and had an uneasy feeling, as the admiral continued. "I know you haven't exactly been a monk, Alberto, but I must be blunt. Being married is essential to your future advancement. Even with your extraordinary skills, I cannot guarantee your further rise if you remain single. Please understand this is not personal, but Spain is a conservative Catholic country. I hope you will take this advice in the spirit in which it was intended."

"Of course, sir. Thank you." Alberto could not suppress his frown.

"Cheer up, Alberto. The young American debutante will undoubtedly attract a crowd of eligible señoritas, as well as men, at tonight's event."

"Yes, sir, I'm sure she will."

"I'll look forward to seeing you tonight at the reception."

"Yes, sir," Alberto responded and then promptly excused himself.

* * *

Alberto stood alone at the side of the reception hall, in full-dress uniform with champagne glass in hand. The evening's mission had been a success so far. His conversation with the two American naval officers, and an introduction to their visiting chief of naval operations, Admiral Arleigh Burke, had resulted in a firm invitation to America in a few months. He had never been to America before, and he was now glad that he had worked to perfect his English over the last five years.

Alberto caught a quick glimpse of Beatrice Lodge as she was surrounded by male and female admirers. *I wonder who the lucky man is who will win her heart.*

"She is quite beautiful, isn't she?"

The soft female voice surprised Alberto. He turned to see a beautiful, petite woman with medium-length raven hair and deep blue eyes. She was in a conservative, but attractive, full-length gown that fit her perfectly.

Alberto was momentarily speechless.

"I'm sorry, Commander. I didn't mean to sneak up unannounced."

Alberto finally smiled uneasily and recovered his manners. "Allow me to apologize. Yes, the ambassador's daughter is beautiful, and so are many other women here tonight." He looked directly at the woman with warmth and a more genuine smile.

"I'm Lucia Aznar Sedeño."

"I'm Commander Alberto Ortega Lopez. I'm pleased to meet your acquaintance."

"Are you the Spanish naval liaison with the American staff in the embassy, Commander?"

"In a way, I am. I have a special assignment now after returning from sea duty. It will soon take me to America for a short period."

"I see. How long have you been in the navy?"

"Since 1934, so I am definitely a career officer. What about you, Señorita Aznar? What brings you to the embassy tonight?"

"I was invited because my boss is an editor at *Hola.*"

"I see. So you are a journalist?"

"Actually, I am an administrative assistant. I only recently returned to Spain, and I'm trying to become established. My parents were killed by the Republicans at the Battle of the Ebro in 1938. I managed to hide. Even though I was only fourteen, I was lucky to avoid an orphanage. I had many relatives in South America, and I went there in 1939. I had relatives in Chile, Uruguay, Peru, and Venezuela, so I moved around a lot. I moved back to Europe in 1950 to work in France for a while. Then I went back to South America, and finally I came back here. It's good to be home."

"That's an astonishing story. You must have had trouble adapting to all those moves," Alberto said.

"Actually, I became used to it. The only problem is, I was never able to form many relationships, and I'm still unmarried." She paused. "Surely you and your wife must be looking forward to traveling to America soon."

"It will just be me. I too am single."

"I can't believe that, Commander! Surely someone as handsome as you would have found a wife by now."

"I suppose I will blame it on all the sea duty," he replied sheepishly.

Alberto and Lucia continued their discussion as the evening wore on. Alberto was almost oblivious to the remaining activities at the reception. Fortunately, he had accomplished all of his business and related glad-handing earlier, and he was free to concentrate on this enchanting woman who had suddenly appeared in his life.

71.

New York City.
November 1956

* * *

Paul and Jack took their barstools at the Minetta Tavern on MacDougal Street in the West Village. "You and I have become so used to our world travels that it's a miracle we were able to finally meet again," Paul said.

"Yeah, it's getting to be a rare event for us. I guess that makes it even sweeter."

Paul looked around the bar, taking in the classic tin ceiling, checkerboard-tile floor, mirrored bar, and finely crafted woodwork. "Each time I come home, I can't wait to see Liz and the children and then visit our favorite haunts in the Village. What about you? Do you look forward to getting back?"

"Sure, but I guess I'm always charged up now. In three years in the agency, I've been to Europe, the Middle East, Central America, and Southeast Asia. It gets in your blood, or in my case I guess it never left. Ever since Spain in '42, I've been hooked on it, and I finally realize it's my calling."

Paul was surprised by Jack's frankness but knew better than to press him for details. Still, there was more than enough world news to feed the fire.

"Now that Ike's been reelected, I suppose the second-guessing and hand-wringing on Suez and Hungary will start."

"What do you mean?" Jack replied.

"Well, we left the Hungarian freedom fighters in the lurch after the Voice of America sort of implied we'd help them eject the Russians. It seems to me that—"

"Jesus, Paul, what's that supposed to mean? You weren't there and what I saw—" Jack stopped in midsentence, catching himself. The two men became silent. Paul didn't want to provoke his friend. *Maybe switching to a new continent might help.*

"The Suez mess sure created a problem for Eisenhower. It looks like Britain, France, and Israel stepped out of bounds with their invasion."

"So they should let the Egyptians get away with their nationalization of the Suez Canal and put a critical waterway at risk?"

"Well, after all, Jack, the land does belong to Egypt, and they're trying to break the leftover colonial yoke. Maybe we should support them on the Aswan Dam idea, too. If we miss the boat on this opportunity and side with the former colonial powers, we'll probably drive Egypt into the Soviet orbit."

"I guess I just don't want to talk it about it, Paul."

Paul watched as his friend, unable to engage in the political discussion for fear of revealing his recent activities, turned away. *Once more I'll try to change the subject.* "We have had some interesting developments in the extended family."

"Oh, so what's going on?" Jack perked up and turned back to Paul.

"I introduced Anita to a business acquaintance from Venezuela, and they hit it off right away. It looks like it's getting serious in a hurry."

"No kidding? That's good news for her. She's a beauty."

Paul let that one drop. "The other news is that the same thing is happening to her brother, Alberto. He met a beautiful señorita at an embassy reception in Madrid several months ago."

"No shit? Why, that old dog! It's about time for him, too. So are wedding bells in the future?"

"I guess only time will tell."

Paul noted that Jack had only partially relaxed. He felt sad for his best friend and for their formerly easygoing relationship. *Can the tension from his job be that severe? What kinds of clandestine activities had Jack been involved in?* Paul hoped this did not signify a permanent change in their friendship.

72

Madrid, Spain.
November 1957

* * *

Alberto was walking toward Carrero's office following an urgent summons from his boss. Something was brewing, and Alberto suspected it involved the emerging crisis in Ifni in Spanish West Africa. This little Spanish colonial territory was surrounded by the newly independent state of Morocco and separated from the larger land mass of Spanish Sahara. There were reports of an indigenous uprising sponsored by the Moroccan government. Alberto wanted to get up-to-date on that fast. He had only returned from the United States in June, after successfully getting the two American destroyers commissioned in the Spanish navy.

He smiled as he thought about the recent momentous event in his life—and the other event in the Ortega family. Alberto had married Lucia Aznar in August, and this had followed Anita's marriage to Sergio Castillo in June. Alberto was still trying to get used to married life. He had a premonition, however, that the weeks of marital bliss and several weeks of official leave were about to be interrupted.

He finally approached the Dirreccion de Marruecos y Plazas y Provincias Africanas at 5 Paseo de la Castellana. He corrected himself—the office was now known as Direccion de Plazas y Provincias Africanas, after the loss of the Spanish Morocco protectorate the previous year. If Carrero wanted to meet here, then surely it must be about the Ifni crisis.

Within minutes, Alberto was ushered into Admiral Carerro's office. He approached his desk and came to attention. "You wanted to see me, sir?"

Carerro looked up, put a document that he was reviewing aside, and welcomed Alberto. "Please take a seat and relax. I have a number of things to cover."

Alberto sat down. *This must be big. He will probably work into the main subject slowly.*

"I hope you enjoyed your leave, Alberto, and I'm glad to see you here today. There is a lot going on in Spain and the world. Domestically we seem to have been sidetracked by recent student demonstrations, but at least this recent cabinet shuffle may restore some order. As you probably know, we have a new foreign minister. I hope Castiella and I will hit it off, but I already detect that we have different ideas about our African territories. On a more positive note, we are making progress laying the groundwork for economic reform, and I want to commend you and your cousin Paul Hoffman for the key role you both played."

"Thank you, sir. I'm sure Paul will be happy to hear that."

"I should get to other urgent matters. First, effective immediately, you are being promoted to captain."

Alberto was stunned. He hadn't expected that. "Thank you for your confidence in me, sir."

"You have earned it, Alberto, and you're going to keep earning it. I'm giving you command of the cruiser *Canarias.*"

Now Alberto was really stunned. This was the assignment of his dreams—command of the largest ship in the Spanish navy and its flagship.

"Now the bad news. I'm afraid your honeymoon will be a short one, both for your new bride and your new command. You will proceed to Cadiz immediately to assume command of *Canarias.* The current captain is sailing from El Ferrol as we speak, and you will meet the ship at Cadiz. He reports the ship as battle ready, which is good since you will sail immediately to Ifni to provide support to our forces there. You will get details from the navy ministry. Do you have any questions for me?"

"No, sir. Thank you again."

Carerro rose and walked around to Alberto. As they shook hands, Carerro said, "Good luck, Alberto, and good shooting. It's likely to come to that."

73.

Off the coast of Ifni,
Spanish West Africa,
December 1957

* * *

Alberto grabbed his seat on the bridge of the *Canarias* as the ship shuddered from another salvo from its four eight-inch double-gun turrets.

Within seconds the gunnery officer reported the results of the salvo. "Sir, the spotter aircraft reports direct hits on the formation of insurgents. The survivors are dispersing and running from the battlefield. The combination of our shell fire and the bomber attacks has crippled them."

"Very well, cease firing and secure from action stations," Alberto said.

"Aye, sir," the officer replied and then barked his orders to the fire-control station.

Just then, Alberto looked up at the formation of CASA 2.111 bombers flying west, back to their base in the Canary Islands. At the tail end of the formation several minutes later was a single Hispano HA-1112-MIL piston-engine fighter plane. *That must be the plane that spotted our gunfire.* Alberto then noted a formation of trimotor CASA 352 transports headed eastbound, probably to drop paratroopers into the combat zone or deliver supplies to the airstrip at Sidi Ifni.

Alberto could only shake his head. These were obsolete German designs from before World War II that were built in Spain under license. Fortunately, the insurgents did not have either aircraft or an effective antiaircraft capability. Alberto was puzzled, because the Americans went to great length to pressure Spain not to use its more modern jet aircraft that America had recently supplied. Was America trying to send a message about the advisability of conducting this counterinsurgency operation?

Indeed, Alberto was feeling very much like Don Quixote right now. *Perhaps this is a fool's errand and this obsolete cruiser is my Rocinante.* He mulled that over. *No, maybe I'm Rocinante.* "*Que era antes y primero de todos los rocines del mundo*"—*The first and foremost of all the hacks in the world.*

Alberto sighed. *The insurgents will return after dark. Perhaps Cervantes was right. We're just tilting at windmills.*

Alabos, Spain.
December 1958

* * *

Karl had again stunned the family with his announcement at the beginning of their periodic business meeting.

"Is this real? Is this offer real?" Ernesto asked as he looked at the eight-figure offer—three times the amount of the previous offer.

"It is very real, I can assure you. You must realize that cocoa prices have nearly doubled since 1954, and this has created rapid speculation in the value of our plantations. As with all speculation, this bubble could burst at any time, and I believe we are nearly at a peak," Karl replied. Paul noticed a worrisome frown on his father's face.

"Then we must sell immediately, or else we risk—" Alfonso exclaimed excitedly.

"We must do no such thing! As I said two years ago—" Ernesto interrupted.

As before, Paul cut them off. "Listen, please! I'm sure there is more to the story. Father, can you elaborate? What is troubling you?"

"Yes, Karl, please tell us," Anita said.

"It is such a tragedy, I can hardly describe it. We had an activist for political independence for Guinea. His name was Acacio Mane Ela. The governor had him murdered in September, and the civil guard threw his body into the ocean. He had just been to confession, and the priest betrayed him."

"This can't be true!" Ernesto gasped. Anita put her hand to her mouth in shock. Alfonso merely shook his head and looked down at the floor.

"I can assure you, it is true. I have reliable contacts among the people, the colonial guard, the civil guard, and even in the BPS."

"What does it mean, Father?" Paul said quietly.

"It means we should consider accepting the offer. I need a few more weeks to sort this out, and then I will recommend our final strategy for replying to this offer."

The others merely nodded in silent concurrence.

Santa Isabel, Spanish Guinea,
January 1959

* * *

"Governor, you must change your policies with respect to development of the native population. Africa is now on the verge of massive political change. We must prepare for it, not only to ensure that the population is ready for independence, but also to ensure Spain's interests are protected afterword," Karl asserted.

"How dare you speak to me like that? I could have you—"

"You could have me arrested or killed and thrown into the sea perhaps?" Karl's boldness and his risky attack caught the governor off guard.

"You hide under Admiral Carrero's protection!"

"I'm not trying to hide at all. Governor, the good admiral and people like me are trying to change the economic balance for Spain. I believe that even Franco understands this. We must now take the next steps to ensure an orderly transition of power from our colonial administration to eventual independence."

"That will never happen in our lifetimes."

"It won't? Take a look around you. In 1957, the British gave independence to Ghana, their richest colony. Last year, French Guinea became the independent nation of Guinea, spurning French efforts to join the impending French African Union, which will make many more countries independent, probably next year."

"Both the admiral and I agree with your economic policies, Karl, but you will find us both holding the line on independence. We have selected some reliable figures in the native population to provide a token African presence."

"The individuals you have selected are stooges who follow your commands. They are not the ones you should have selected."

"The only relevant issue, Karl, is that I alone have the power to do just that. This I told you ten years ago. It seems that you have yet to accept that reality."

Karl sank back in his chair. He realized that it was futile to argue with this authoritative bureaucrat. He realized what he must do next.

76.

Alabos, Spain.
February 1959

* * *

"This offer is truly amazing. I can't believe they upped the ante again," Ernesto exclaimed as he looked at the figures on the offer.

"My renegotiation proposal caught them by surprise. I believe they felt pressured to accept my counteroffer," Karl replied confidently.

Even Alfonso was quiet, obviously dumbfounded by the extravagant offer from the consortium of cocoa companies.

"So this means that all of our holdings in Fernando Po are included?" Anita asked.

"Yes, everything except the hacienda and our office in Santa Isabel."

"What about our lands in Rio Muni?" Alfonso asked.

"No, they don't care about the mainland properties, since they constitute only ten percent of our cocoa production." Karl paused. "This means that I will be able to continue working with our *emancipados* and other laborers to help them advance economically. They also agreed to give me a ten-year contract to manage operations in Fernando Poo for them, with a guaranteed fee and share of the profits."

"Does this mean that if we go ahead with this, you have no intention of retiring from these activities and moving to Spain or New York?" Paul inquired.

"That's correct. I have lived there since 1935, and those people are as much my family as all of you are," Karl responded, sweeping his hand around the table at Paul, Ernesto, Alfonso, and Anita.

The room became silent for a minute, and then Karl continued.

"In fact, I don't want to jeopardize or risk the financial interests of any of you. Therefore, I propose to buy out all of your interests in the Rio Muni plantations from my proceeds."

"Father, why won't you come and join us in New York, or even here, to be closer to your grandchildren and—"

Karl shook his head and cut Paul off. "No. I've decided this already and you must respect my decision. So how will you all vote on this? We have five days to respond to their offer."

"We must accept this time," Alfonso agreed and then turned to Ernesto. "Father, won't you agree this time? I believe we need to emphasize our real estate and tourism strategy, the fine wine that Anita produces, and the export and import operations that Paul oversees."

"This sounds so momentous. How do you feel about this, Paul?" Anita asked.

"I believe my father and Alfonso are right. This is a pivotal point in both history and our family's future. The colonial era is over, whether Spain accepts it or not. The future of the world's economy and our business will be driven by a shrunken world created by the jet airplane, cheap fuel, and consumers with leisure time."

"Then, do we have a consensus to move forward?" Karl asked, looking first at Alfonso.

"Yes, I agree."

"Yes, we must," Anita replied in response to Karl's nod to her.

Karl then turned to Paul.

"Yes, Father, I'm in favor of it, but I wish you would plan to spend more time with us in New York," Paul replied with some frustration.

Finally, Karl turned to Ernesto, his brother-in-law, whom he had known for sixty years.

They were all silent in deference to the family patriarchs.

"Yes, it is the only logical move for our future," he finally replied, sighing deeply and lowering his head.

77.

Tirana, Albania.
April 1959

* * *

Yuri Sergeivich Kozlov, relieved of not having to assume his alias of Sergio Castillo, walked slowly across the main square of Albania's capital and largest city to meet his boss, Vladimir Morozov of the KGB. There was not a car or individual anywhere around, except a solitary traffic cop in the middle of the square to direct the nonexistent traffic.

"It is good to see you after eleven years, Yuri." Morozov offered his hand.

"I am happy also to see you, Comrade Morozov," Yuri replied with a handshake.

"How was your journey here?"

"It was routine, if somewhat roundabout. I traveled to Stockholm using my other alias as a Chilean businessman. I then took the Czech airline, CSA, to Prague and then Budapest and finally here. I am sure I traveled here undetected. I hope your journey was also pleasant."

"Yes, but it was even more roundabout. My key role in counterintelligence is such that I didn't want to be recognized by any Western agent or even by our more attuned allies, so I wanted to avoid Prague. I flew from Moscow via Kiev and Odessa to Bucharest, which is a backwater of espionage. I picked up CSA there and flew to Budapest and then here, as you did."

"So we are secure here in this square?"

"Yes, the Albanian secret police, the *Sigurimi*, are extremely efficient, and there is no threat from outside detection or surveillance."

Morozov paused as the two men stopped walking. He then continued. "Yet we are meeting here out in the open next to the statue of Comrade Stalin."

"Yes, it's a little ironic, isn't it? Stalin is out of favor now at home, but Comrade Hoxha maintains the tightest of police states here, such that even Stalin would blanch," Yuri replied.

240

The two men stopped to briefly look up at the statue. "Accordingly, to prevent our conversation from being monitored, we meet here," Morozov said.

"I understand that Hoxha views Comrade Khrushchev as a revisionist or worse."

"That's true, Yuri. I believe our days in Albania are numbered. Hoxha is aghast at our policy of 'peaceful coexistence,' and so are many in the party and military at home. Unless the Americans reciprocate in some way, tensions may escalate. You may not be aware, Yuri, but the Americans are using an advanced spy plane that has made many flights across the Soviet Union."

"Why don't we shoot it down?"

"It flies too high, but our missiles are improving, and we may soon be able to bring one down. That could change the equation and escalate tensions."

The two men again looked up at Stalin's statue.

Kozlov finally decided it was time to find out why he was summoned. "Comrade Morozov, I know you didn't bring me here to admire Tirana or see Stalin's statue."

"Of course not, so let me get to particulars. First of all, I will congratulate you on your stunning success in setting up a very effective espionage network in Latin America. You also took a chance in merging the activities of Agents X and Y, but it was indeed fortuitous that you did so."

"Thank you, Comrade Morozov. I have also activated and redirected Agent Z in Europe, so we may continue to pursue Operation Valhalla. This has been my only frustration. Despite progress in monitoring the Hoffman, Ortega, and Kurtz families, I seem to be no closer to uncovering this scheme. Under the auspices of my marriage to Anita Ortega, I have been able to gain intimate access to the family, and I've made three trips to Spanish Guinea. However, I still have not uncovered any clues as to the whereabouts of the Valhalla cargo."

"That's all right, Yuri. You must continue to pursue this mystery, but I am ordering a major redirection of your activity."

"I am eager to learn about this, Comrade Morozov."

"You will first transfer the information and direction of your Latin American network to our emerging Cuban comrades. They are in a better position to encourage indigenous revolutionary movements in the Americas, they will have more credibility than us, and it will be less threatening and harder to deal with for the United States."

"I see. What will my new venue be?"

"Africa is the new frontier for confrontation with the West. We are on the cusp of a historic shift in the balance of power there as the colonial powers withdraw. We already have a foothold on the continent. Sekou Toure leads the former colony of French Guinea, now independent as the Republic of Guinea. He is supporting socialist revolutionary ideas and has secretly agreed to provide us with a secure base of operations from which to build a network and conduct revolutionary activities throughout the continent."

"Will I move there?"

"Yes, and you will drop any pretense of maintaining your status as a Venezuelan businessman and go underground."

"This means I will leave the orbit of the Ortega family."

"That's correct. You will also engage Cuban support in this theatre. They will provide you with surrogates and operatives to carry out required operations throughout Africa, including continuing the Valhalla investigation, which is still a priority for us. In fact, our continued mining of captured German archives has verified our earlier conclusion: it is essential for us to discover the Valhalla cargo because of the advances in biological warfare that we are now certain that it contains."

"Very well, I can begin preparations immediately."

"How long will it take you to fold up operations in Latin America, Yuri?"

"Not long. I have kept the considerable profits of my successful businesses in liquid assets. I can transfer these assets back to Moscow through Switzerland."

"No, keep them to finance your new operations. That way I won't have to explain them, and you can self-finance your activities."

"All right, I understand that."

"I have another step you must take, Yuri."

"Yes?"

"I assume you know of Comrade Che Guevara?"

"Of course, Comrade Morozov. He is a key figure in the Cuban Revolution and its worldwide outreach."

"In a couple of months, he will be making a highly public worldwide trip that will include Morocco. I am arranging for him to make a clandestine visit to Guinea from there. You will work with him to transfer the Latin American network and obtain surrogates for your African operations."

"I will look forward to that, Comrade Morozov."

"Fine. Is there anything else you will need as support?"

"Yes, Comrade Morozov. I believe I need an operative within the Western community in Africa, perhaps someone from the Portuguese colonies, or better yet, South Africa."

"I believe I have an answer for that one. We are courting a new South African contact, courtesy of our operatives in the British MI-6 intelligence service." Morozov was looking to conclude the meeting. "We will have to engineer your disappearance so it looks like an accident. I have some ideas, and we can talk about them in the morning before we depart."

"It shouldn't be hard, Comrade Morozov. My cover as Sergio Castillo caused me to travel extensively."

"No, it won't be hard, but it also means that your marriage to Anita Ortega will be over."

"That's all right, Comrade Morozov. She means nothing to me."

78

Nzerekore, People's Revolutionary Republic of Guinea, Africa.
June 1959

* * *

Yuri Kozlov watched as Che Guevara entered the small building at an isolated part of the Nzerekore Airport in this remote area of the Republic of Guinea.

Yuri stood, and the two men stared at each other for several seconds. Yuri slowly approached his guest and extended his hand. They shook hands and then embraced. "Welcome, Comrade Guevara. This is a great honor for me."

"I also am honored, although mystified at the location you have chosen for us to meet. I can only assume that Comrades Castro and Khrushchev must have their reasons."

"I don't believe our two leaders are sure yet of the other's intentions. For now this will just be an initiative between the KGB and your emerging equivalent. More important, I hope it will result in an informal agreement between you and me."

"So I assume that this meeting has some urgency, Kozlov."

"Yes, this is urgent, and the only way to keep our meeting secret was to spirit you away from Morocco for a couple of days. I apologize for this location, but we couldn't guarantee secrecy in the capital, Conakry. Even though Nzerekore is the second-largest city in the country, it is off the beaten path for Westerners, and it will be my base in the future." Yuri pointed to the two chairs and plain table in the center of the austere room. "Please have a seat."

Yuri knew he would have to make his case strongly. He noted that Guevara exactly matched his popular image in dress and appearance, complete with beret, beard, and fatigues. *But what motivates the man underneath? Will he cooperate?*

"I will be blunt, Comrade. You and I have it in our power to encourage powerful socialist revolution and liberation movements here in Africa, as well as back in Latin America."

"Comrade Kozlov, your reputation precedes you. I know all about your network in Latin America, and I respect what you have accomplished. More important, I know that you are half Venezuelan and have powerful revolutionary roots there."

It looks like I already have credibility and enjoy his confidence. "I'm flattered, Comrade. I do believe, however, that it is time to turn my network over to you and your other comrades. You will have more credibility with indigenous peoples than a Soviet presence will."

"You are very perceptive, Kozlov. What then will you do next?"

"My mission is to lay the groundwork for liberation and socialist revolution here in Africa. For that, I will need your help also."

Kozlov watched as Guevara pondered that for a moment before replying.

"That goal means that you must aggressively pursue armed struggle. The revolution is not an apple that falls when it is ripe. You have to make it fall."

"I agree. That means that we must pick the targets that are ripest for the fall. I certainly believe the Belgian Congo falls into that category. They had massive riots there in January, to demonstrate for independence. Their Belgian colonial masters are starting to crack by conceding that independence will be granted sooner rather than later. Furthermore, there is a politician with revolutionary zeal named Patrice Lumumba who can lead them to independence. I met him last December at a conference of native African leaders in Accra, Ghana. He is no doctrinaire Marxist, contrary to Western fears, but he still supports a practical socialist revolution that is opposed to both colonialism and the neocolonialism and exploitation by Western multinational corporations."

Kozlov could see the shock of his analysis registering visibly on Guevara's face. *This could be the turning point.*

"You amaze me, Kozlov. It's almost like you were reading my mind. I will definitely cooperate with you on this venture. What do you propose?"

"I can provide resources. We can become active in the Congo, but there are two things I need from you. First, I ask that you assign a leader to oversee operations from Africa, since I know you must be in many places. He should be intelligent, multilingual, a risk taker, and he should be black, in order to have credibility. Second, although the Congo is our initial focus, we should not ignore other opportunities. I believe that Spanish Guinea could provide you a base of operations, since Cuba has a consulate in Santa Isabel, and the West will not suspect that it is a focus for us."

"All right, Kozlov," Guevara said. "I can see that you have thought this through carefully. Let's discuss a few more details before I must return to Morocco, including why you are interested in such a remote Spanish backwater."

79.

Havana, Cuba,
September 1959

* * *

Yuri Kozlov was extremely pleased. Jorge Sanchez met all the criteria that he wanted in a chief operative for Africa. He was descended from American slaves, who in turn were descended from the Fang tribe in Cameroon. The American Civil War hadn't improved their lot much, and these ex-slaves left the harsh post-Reconstruction American South for Cuba in 1886, when slavery was abolished there. They joined a community of other blacks with a Fang heritage. Eventually their descendants prospered, even in the face of racist challenges in Cuba. Sanchez's parents created a business that took them throughout the Americas. They came to loathe the corrupt Batista regime that had ruled Cuba from 1952 until overthrown the previous January by the Cuban revolution.

Sanchez was a frontline fighter in that revolution. He was intelligent, well educated, and well-spoken. He was multilingual, speaking Spanish, English, French, Portuguese, and most important, Fang. In many ways, he shared Yuri's background, attitudes, and comprehensive world view. Like Yuri, he subscribed to socialist principles, yet he was no knee-jerk ideologue and looked at the world in a practical way.

Yuri and Jorge had already bonded on a personal level after several days of detailed planning and were having their final meeting before Yuri departed Cuba.

"I will look forward to seeing you in the Guinea Republic in a few months, Jorge."

"Likewise. I think we have a viable plan. What are your immediate plans?"

"I will return to Caracas to wrap up my front activities. Following that I will travel briefly to Spain to create an alibi there for my eventual disappearance."

"I wish you luck with that," Jorge replied.

"There is just one more thing, Jorge, that I must tell you. I've concluded that you must know this. There is important information about a wartime

German operation that may be hidden in Spanish Guinea. That is one reason why your clandestine activity there will be so crucial to us."

Realizing that he was taking a chance, Yuri nevertheless proceeded to inform Jorge Sanchez about Operation Valhalla.

80.

Washington, D.C.
September 1959

* * *

"I have to hand it to you, Jack. You've done a fabulous job in the last six years. Iran, Guatemala, and Southeast Asia have all been going our way."

"Sure, Allen, I just wish we were more successful in Hungary."

"Don't worry about that, it was beyond your control."

"I sure hope I don't have to stay here in headquarters for long. I feel my place is out where the action is. Also, I find our dingy surroundings here depressing."

Allen Dulles nodded in reply as both men looked out the tiny window of Dulles's office on E Street in Northwest Washington.

"That will be fixed soon, Jack. We'll lay the cornerstone for our new headquarters in Langley in just a few weeks." Dulles beamed proudly as he lit his pipe and took a few puffs before continuing. "As for your next caper, I'm keeping my eyes open, but for now I want you to look into something else for me, and it falls under old business."

"What old business?" Jack replied curiously.

"It relates to Operation Valhalla. Have you ever heard of Dr. Eric Traub?"

"I vaguely remember him. Wasn't he one of the Nazis we scooped up under Operation Paperclip?"

"Yes. His specialty was infectious disease. He claims he specialized in animal diseases, and we've more or less verified that he didn't work directly for the Nazi biological warfare program, although he was on the periphery of it."

"So he doesn't know anything about Valhalla?"

"As it turns out, he does. He knew that it existed. He decided to query us as to whether we knew about it."

"Why did he decide to reveal that, Allen?"

"It seems he's leery of our friend Gehlen. Now that Gehlen leads West German intelligence, the BND, Traub thought we should prod Gehlen to reveal what he knows. We did just that, and it turns out that Gehlen was mighty

249

uncomfortable about it. We presented what we had and confronted him. He came clean about it, although he claims not to know anything more than we know."

"Do you believe him?"

"I don't know, Jack. That's why I want you to put Valhalla back on your radar, without necessarily beginning any active field research to learn more, at least at this time," Dulles said. "Please give me your twenty-five-word summation of where we are with it now."

"Well, we know that Valhalla was designed to transfer information out of Germany that related to their advanced weapons and other technology. We know that the cargo left Germany in a Type 21 U-boat in April 1945 and that it probably wasn't sunk. We also are pretty sure it didn't go to the Americas or Asia."

"So what's your hunch?" Dulles asked, in between puffs on his pipe.

Jack hesitated but finally offered his guess. "I've always thought it must have gone somewhere in Africa, probably to the Portuguese colonies or South Africa."

Dulles sat there for a moment, processing that before answering. "If we ever have to make this a priority again, that's where we will start looking."

"Why would it become a priority again?" Jack asked.

"We're reaching a nuclear stalemate with the Soviet Union, contrary to what we're telling the press about a bomber and missile gap. You've worked with Bissell on the U-2 program, so you know that our overflights have revealed that Russia is behind us on nukes. That's why we think they've accelerated research on biological weapons."

"So do you think they're pursuing Valhalla?"

"We've known they are aware of it ever since you and Paul Hoffman had your little Czech caper back in '48. It could be they're actively pursuing Valhalla."

"Do they have any extra motivation for that?"

"Yes, they do. If Traub is being honest with us, Jack, Valhalla contains information on horrific biological weapons."

Jack nodded; his boss puffed heavily on his pipe.

81

Alabos, Spain.
October 1959

* * *

Paul stared out the window as he contemplated the news. The staff informed him that he had missed Sergio Castillo by a day. Paul had hoped to discuss some business issues with him, but he was told that he had departed with little notice.

"Hello, Paul. I hadn't expected you for a couple more days."

Paul turned to see Anita enter the room.

"I'm sorry to surprise you, Anita, but I had a break in my business in Madrid. Since I had the flexibility of traveling in the Bonanza, I decided to fly here for a day to try to catch Sergio. They said you were in Haro at our main bodega."

"I also finished my business early." She approached Paul, turned to look out the window, sighed heavily, and then turned back to Paul.

"I'm afraid you're too late to see Sergio. He again departed on short notice. He had some urgent business in Angola relating to his oil activities."

"When is he due to return?"

"Who knows? He rarely coordinates his activities with me, and lately he seems distracted by something."

"I'm sorry...I didn't know," Paul replied awkwardly.

Anita walked slowly away from Paul to the other side of the room. Suddenly, she turned and retraced her steps back to her cousin. "Paul, I must talk to you about this. There is nobody else I can confide in."

"Of course, Anita, what can I do?" Paul was caught off guard.

"Sergio began acting strangely about six months ago. He has hardly been around much since then. I knew we would be separated often because of his business activity, even though he talked of liquidating it all so we could be together."

"I can understand the strain this must cause," Paul said, trying to be sympathetic.

"The real change hurts even more."

"I don't understand."

"It's been many months since he has...touched me." She looked away.

"I don't know how to respond, Anita."

"He was here for three solid weeks until he left yesterday, yet in all that time he never—he never even...approached me."

This time she put her arms around him and began sobbing. He embraced her and pulled her closer to console her.

She quickly regained control and pulled away. "There is something else, Paul. I have an understanding with some civil guards at the Logroño Airport that goes back to when I first flew there. They look after the plane and report on anything unusual. It seems that Sergio was surreptitiously inspecting our warehouse at the airport. The staff here also has told me that Sergio was unusually curious about what is stored in our bodegas and other buildings here in Alabos."

That set off a light bulb for Paul. "That's interesting. My father told me that Sergio had the same curious behavior during the three visits he made to Guinea."

"What does it mean, Paul?"

"I don't know. I really don't know."

They stared silently at each other for several moments.

"Do you have to return to Madrid?" she asked.

"Yes, I must. I'm involved in the upcoming visit by President Eisenhower in December, and there is an important planning meeting late tomorrow. But I'll return in three days for the anniversary celebration," Paul replied, referring to Ernesto and Anna's forty-fifth wedding anniversary.

"You'll just miss them in Madrid. They're visiting Alfonso and his family. The five of them plan to return here by car, and they're starting the drive tomorrow to arrive the next day. I already have little Francisca here with us, since she and Beatriz wanted to visit."

Paul only nodded. He was still thinking about Sergio.

82

Madrid, Spain.
October 1959

* * *

Paul finally returned to his room in the Hotel Ritz after his long morning meeting. He arrived at the hotel early in the afternoon and was too tired to even go to lunch. His business in Madrid was finished for the moment, and he was looking forward to returning to Alabos the next day. The meeting he attended took place at a secret location, since the government wanted to keep planning arrangements under wraps for the upcoming visit of the US president.

As Paul sat wearily on the bed, the phone rang. He picked up the receiver. "Yes, what is it?"

"Sir, I have an urgent call for you from Captain Ortega on the cruiser *Canarias.*"

"What, from the cruiser? Well, put it through!"

In a few seconds Paul could hear a strange mixture of warbling and hissing and finally a voice.

"Paul, can you hear me? It's Alberto." His cousin's voice emerged from the hissing, but his voice sounded like it was coming from the end of a long tunnel.

"Yes, I can hear you. Where are you, Alberto?"

"Listen carefully, Paul, because I may lose this link at any moment. I am at sea west of the Canary Islands, and I'm calling on a precarious radio telephone link. We've been trying to locate you all day."

Paul was silent. *What's this all about?*

"Do you hear me, Paul?"

"Yes, I hear you. I'm sorry, but I was at a place all day where I couldn't be reached."

"That doesn't matter. Now listen. This will be as hard for you as it is for me." The warbling got louder but then faded as Alberto continued. "There has been a terrible tragedy. My father, mother, brother, his wife, Francisca, and his son, Pablo, are dead. They were killed late last night in an automobile accident on the way to Alabos."

Paul was stunned and speechless. He stood and grabbed the phone tighter, as if clenching it harder could rescind what he just heard.

"What are you saying? How can this be true?"

"I'm sorry Paul, but … it's true."

Paul was again silent, trying to understand how such a horrible event could occur.

"Can you hear me, Paul? Please respond."

"Yes, I hear you. Go ahead, please."

"Listen carefully. I've been authorized to return to port, but even at maximum speed I won't arrive for three days. Anita, Beatriz, and Alfonso's little Francisca are alone in Alabos. You must go to them immediately. Do you hear me?"

"Of course, Alberto. I'll leave now. I have my plane. I can be there in a few hours. Do you know what happened?"

The hissing grew louder. Alberto's response was muffled but understandable. "All I can tell you is that it was an accident. I don't have the details. I will be there in four—" Alberto was cut off.

Paul clicked the phone several times to raise the hotel operator.

"I'm sorry, sir, but we lost the link." Paul hung up the phone.

He quickly formulated a plan. He tried calling Anita, but he couldn't get through to Alabos. He placed a call to Sergio's office in Caracas, and the staff promised to try to reach him in Africa. He placed a call to New York and delivered the devastating news to Liz. She called back shortly afterward to report that it would be three days before she could get a flight to Spain. Next he cabled his father in Guinea. Finally, he called the Cuatro Vientos Airport and ordered the Bonanza readied for the flight back north. It was only about an hour's flight to Logroño and then another hour and a half by road. He could be in Alabos by 7:00 p.m., he figured.

He couldn't imagine what Anita must be going through.

83.

Alabos, Spain.
October 1959

* * *

Paul walked all through the hacienda looking for Anita and the children. There was nobody there, not even the servants, so he went to the separate guest house where he usually stayed. As he walked in with his bag, he saw her. She had lit a candle and was staring out the window. She heard him enter and turned. They looked at each other for several seconds. Anita walked slowly over to him, the anguish and loneliness written on her face.

She stopped in front of him only inches away and whispered, "The servants have taken the children to our house in Haro. I haven't told the children yet. I told the servants that I wanted to be alone tonight, so I could face the world tomorrow. I asked them not to return with the children until noon. By then I can face them." She paused and then continued, gently touching his left arm. "I've been waiting for you. I knew you would come to me right away. I just wish…"

She broke down then, unable to contain the pent-up emotion and utter despair. She reached around to bring him closer, and he embraced her tightly as they gently wept together.

The long moments passed, each absorbed in their individual mourning. Finally, she pulled back and again whispered. "You are the only person in this world who understands me. You have always been there for me. Tonight, of all the nights that I have ever lived, or ever will live, I need you to be here for me. I can no longer deny my…feelings."

She gently and carefully raised both hands to caress his face, and then she slowly and respectfully reached lower to unfasten the buttons on his shirt. She looked back into his eyes, asking for his love.

Paul froze momentarily, but slowly and naturally responded to her. They did not speak. She took his hand and led him into the master bedroom.

Their movements, their kissing, their impassioned actions could not be contained. They made love, tentatively at first, and then with bursts of uncontained passion. It was not to be a single act of passion but an unending night of love without boundaries, until hours later their passion was quenched, and they collapsed into each other's arms in exhaustion.

* * *

When Paul woke, it was about 9:00 a.m. He quickly showered, shaved, and dressed. When he finished, he went to the door just as it opened. Anita appeared. They smiled lovingly at each other. Paul was shocked at his own reaction. *Perhaps the guilt will appear later.*

"Did you get any sleep?" she asked.

"Yes, a little. Did you?"

"Only for a couple of hours; I was thinking about poor little Francisca." She gazed at him. "You must be there when I tell her, Paul. I need your help to be strong."

"Of course, we'll do it together. Can you tell me what happened?"

"It was senseless, really. They were driving at dusk. As they rounded a bend they were hit head on by a truck. The driver must have fallen asleep. He had been driving all the previous day and night."

Paul embraced her. She started to cry, but then caught herself.

"I've made the preliminary funeral arrangements. This will be so hard for all of us. I'm going to need you, Paul, to step into Alfonso's shoes. I don't really have an understanding of his business arrangements, only that they are in a delicate stage right now."

"Don't worry, Anita, I will handle that. Liz won't be here for a couple of days, probably the same day that Alberto arrives. My father might take a couple more days because of airline schedules. I cabled Sergio's office in Caracas. They will try to reach him in Africa, but..." Paul's voice trailed off, as Anita nodded her understanding.

84

Madrid, Spain.
November, 1959

* * *

The unspeakable tragedy in the Ortega family was compounded by the news about Sergio. He responded by cable that he had learned of the accident and was leaving Luanda, Angola, in a chartered aircraft to return to Spain. The aircraft would take him to Accra, Ghana, where he would pick up an airline flight. He cabled again from Sao Tome where the charter aircraft refueled. The charter aircraft never made it to Ghana.

Paul was in Madrid to meet with Alberto. His cousin was detached temporarily from the *Canarias* to conduct the investigation of the missing aircraft because of the navy's role in the search and the family connection. He had finished the investigation and report and had asked Paul to meet him at the lobby bar at the Palace Hotel.

The two men sat somberly at their table as their drinks were delivered. Alberto pulled a folder out of his briefcase and laid it on the table.

"So can you summarize what you found, Alberto?"

"Yes, and it is remarkably straightforward." He opened the folder and began reading the key points and findings. "The aircraft was over the Gulf of Guinea, about midpoint between Sao Tome and Accra. They radioed that they were on fire and declared an emergency. That was their final radio contact, and the DC-3 never arrived in Accra. We initiated a search from Fernando Poo using the naval corvette *Descubierta* and the frigate *Pizarro*. We were assisted by British ships and aircraft from Ghana and Nigeria. It was *Pizarro* that found the floating wreckage."

"What did they find?" Paul asked.

"They recovered part of the aircraft fuselage with the registration markings that verified it was the aircraft that Sergio had chartered. They also found floating luggage with his personal effects. They recovered three bodies. They had been mutilated pretty badly by sharks, but they were positively identified as passengers on the aircraft."

"What about Sergio?"

"His body was not recovered. The water at the site is about three thousand meters in depth, so we will be unable to recover anything else. Nevertheless, the luggage and other evidence was enough to declare that he and the others perished in the crash."

Paul merely nodded his acknowledgement. Yes, it all seemed so straight-forward...or did it? Paul racked his brain trying to get his mind around this, but something he couldn't put his finger on bothered him.

85.

Alabos, Spain.
December 1959

* * *

Paul had worked hard to stabilize the family enterprises after the tragedy in October and had successfully finalized the enormous real estate deal that Alfonso had negotiated on Spain's southern coast. The family was set to reap the enormous profits that would come with increased tourism and economic activity.

Paul had also been influential in helping Spain's overall economy begin to prosper. The battle between the new technocrats and the old guard of *autarky* advocates was over, and the technocrats like Paul had won.

Politically, Spain's isolation was ending as a result of Cold War necessity. The visit by President Eisenhower in a few days would be a capstone of that transition.

Paul had returned to Alabos to brief Anita on the real estate activities he had negotiated. He was reasonably upbeat and anxious to get back to New York to see Liz and the children.

What Paul could not reconcile was what had happened between him and Anita in October. He knew it wasn't just a reaction to their mutual grief, yet he tried not to dwell on its deeper meaning.

Anita knocked and then entered the room in the guest quarters. As Paul turned to greet her he noticed the restrained look.

She approached him slowly. "Hello, Paul."

They embraced briefly.

"How have you been, Anita?"

She hesitated before answering. "I am...fine. Thank you."

"I can brief you on how I've concluded Alfonso's business arrangements, if you'd like," he offered.

She looked deeply into his eyes, and he noticed that she tensed up, as if to get her courage together.

"Is there something wrong, Anita?"

"No, it is not wrong, but it is something I must tell you now."

Paul's mood changed instantly. He sensed something important was about to be said about their relationship.

"What is it?"

"I'm pregnant," she replied simply, with restrained emotion.

He was thunderstruck. "I see. How far along are you?"

"The doctor said about six or seven weeks."

Paul nodded. *Yes, of course.* "Did he say that everything is all right, that the child is all right?"

"Yes, of course." She smiled briefly.

"Is there anything I can do for you? I mean—"

"Please, Paul. There is no reason for concern. I am fine, and it will all work out."

"How will we explain and cope with—"

"There is no need to explain anything to anyone. Sergio left the day before you arrived at the end of his three-week visit. No one will know that you are—"

"That I am the father?" He finished her thought.

"Yes, you are...the father. I am very at peace with that reality, and I hope that you will be, too."

"I am already."

They embraced each other.

86

Madrid. Spain.
December 1959

* * *

Paul looked out the window of his room at the Palace Hotel. It had been an eventful week. He'd had a prominent place in the receiving line that greeted President Eisenhower the previous day. His father was there, as were Alberto, his wife Lucia, and Anita.

Paul realized that this was a momentous moment in history, and it capped a decade of effort on his part to reconcile Spain and America. He realized he should be happy and satisfied with the result. Yet even now he detected storm clouds that went beyond the bilateral relationship between the two countries.

The Cold War was at a critical juncture. Would tensions ease or would a new round of conflict begin?

The situation in Africa was ready to explode. The colonial era was coming to an end as a result of the pending independence of numerous countries that would happen the following year. How would that play out in Spanish Guinea?

Spain was poised to begin a period of strong economic growth. The Hoffman and Ortega families were positioned to benefit from this, even as their wealth had recently increased enormously from the eight-figure sale of their properties in Guinea. Yet this astute move now seemed hollow, following the family tragedy that had occurred.

Paul also could not escape the nightmares that still plagued him from the past. He could not find his missing brother, Hans. The legacy of Operation Valhalla still hung over Paul and his family like a curse.

Above and beyond all of this was the deep soul-searching that Paul had done regarding his relationship with Anita. How could he reconcile what happened? How could he face Liz? Was it possible to love two women at once? His family had survived tragedy in the past, but now he was facing a more personal challenge. *How will I deal with this?*

He realized that, as the fifties closed, his world in the next decade would be far different.

Part 3

* * *

Connections

1960–1968

"To those new states whom we welcome to the ranks of the free, we pledge our word that one form of colonial control shall not have passed away merely to be replaced by a far more iron tyranny. We shall not always expect to find them supporting our view. But we shall always hope to find them strongly supporting their own freedom—and to remember that, in the past, those who foolishly sought power by riding the back of the tiger ended up inside."

—Excerpt from President John F. Kennedy's inaugural address, January 20, 1961

New York City.
May 1960

＊ ＊ ＊

"Well, it's a whole new ball game now, Paul. Khrushchev is holding up that U-2 wreckage and that damn pilot as if they were trophies."

"I suppose they are, Jack, but when and where is the other shoe going to drop?"

"I don't know. It could be Berlin, Cuba, or some other flash point where the Russians will try to get even at our expense."

Before replying, Paul raised his hand to the bartender at the White Horse Tavern, indicating that another round was in order.

"I guess Ike is miffed that his last chance at a summit was ruined. How's the morale at your place?"

"It depends on who you are. Bissell may or may not survive this. Everybody wishes that Powers had taken his 'sleeping pill' rather than submit to capture," Jack replied.

"This doesn't affect you, does it?"

"No, all this stuff was orchestrated above my pay grade. Someday it might be different. Most people give me a wide berth, thinking I'm under Allen's protection."

"Well, if you don't mind me asking, isn't that sort of true?"

Jack took a long draw from the beer that was just placed in front of him, sighed, and turned back to Paul. "Yeah, I guess so. In fact, I better make that part of the calculus from now on. This is an election year, so who knows if Allen will be around this time next year."

"Have you noticed the pace of newly independent countries in Africa this year?"

"Sort of. How many have happened so far?"

"It's just been Cameroon and Togo so far, with maybe fourteen more this year."

"What about Spanish Guinea, Paul?"

"Not anytime soon. Madrid is taking a hard line, just like the Portuguese."

Near Niefang, Spanish Guinea,
June 1960

* * *

Karl was surprised again by his brother's unannounced arrival. This time, how-ever, there was less agonizing, as Walter took little time to accumulate another large portion of the material stored in the cave on their Rio Muni plantation. The day after his arrival, he was ready to depart. The two men stood watch-ing uneasily as Wekesa and his grandson Felipe walked up to announce that the single truck was loaded. They then discreetly walked away, while Karl and Walter said their good-byes.

"Well, I'll be gone and no longer a nuisance to you, Karl."

"That's not the issue, Walter, and you know that. The war has been over fifteen years now. Why can't you surface? Kirsten would be so ecstatic to see her father. You would be so proud of her. She is only twenty-eight, yet she has won awards for the '53 and '59 Rieslings that she produced."

"I will always be proud of her, Karl, even if she were not a famous wine maker. You just don't realize how volatile the situation remains with Operation Valhalla. The people protecting us have shown us the extent of the threat against us should we surface now."

"What about Hans?"

"As I told you last night, Karl, we don't stay in touch anymore, although that is not my choice. He chose to create a new life for himself and remain anonymous. You must come to accept that."

"I will never…accept the loss of my son."

"I'm sorry that it must be this way, Karl."

With that, his brother turned and walked slowly to the truck that would carry the cargo away. He got in it and drove off.

Karl could only wonder—*Will this be the last time I see him? Will I never see my oldest son again?*

Alabos, Spain.
July 1960

***

Paul watched the scene as the family gathered on the west portico of the hacienda. It included his wife, Liz, their twin children, Robert and Pilar, Anita's daughter, Beatriz, from her first marriage, and Francisca, whose parents and only brother had been killed in the auto accident the previous year. Kirsten had also traveled from Germany for the event.

It also included Anita and her newborn daughter, Isabel. Paul grimly considered that thought, but then he forced it from his mind.

It was a bittersweet reunion because of the lingering effects from last year's tragedy. Nevertheless, Anita had insisted that the reunion take place.

In a significant and culturally controversial change, and with Alberto's help and influence, Anita had legally changed her name to drop the family names from her two marriages. She would now legally be known as Anita Ortega de Alabos. Her two daughters would simply be known as Beatriz and Isabel Ortega.

Alberto had also ceded to Anita his rights to lead the estate as a surviving male family member.

This year, as in 1959, Paul had his family in Spain for the entire summer. It gave his children the chance to perfect their Spanish and appreciate their cultural heritage. Meanwhile, Liz, Anita, and Kirsten had bonded even more closely.

Paul's father was due to arrive the next day in Madrid, and Paul would fly the Bonanza there to pick him up.

The vast increase in the family's wealth had now enabled Paul to consider upgrading the aircraft they possessed. Paul planned to replace the Bonanza in Spain with a twin-engine Beech Baron. Of greater significance, he planned to replace the obsolete B-23 Dragon converted bomber in America with a new four-jet-engine Lockheed Jetstar that would become available late in 1961.

This would give them enormous travel flexibility and speed for travel within the United States, as well as to the other continents.

Yes, Paul thought, *the world is shrinking rapidly. Would this be a good thing or a bad thing?*

That thought was interrupted as Liz and Anita joined to hold up a smiling infant Isabel for the others to admire.

Paul turned away.

90.

Nzerekore, People's Revolutionary Republic Of Guinea.
August 1960

* * *

Yuri Kozlov and Jorge Sanchez had just sat down at a table on which was spread a map of Africa. Yuri's plan was to reach a consensus with Jorge on their strategy and plans for revolution on the continent.

"I'm glad you finally arrived here, Jorge. I hope your journey was easy."

"It was, and I'm sure it was without as much adventure as yours entailed."

"Yes, it was quite a convoluted exercise. We faked the DC-3 crash in the Gulf of Guinea. A Soviet submarine left some convincing wreckage in the water for the searchers to discover. Meanwhile, we continued our flight in the real DC-3 by overflying Ghana and Ivory Coast to land here. So for all practical purposes, Sergio Castillo is dead. I have another alias as a Chilean businessman that I can use when I need to travel, but for now I plan to spend a lot of time here planning, organizing, and leading our activity."

"I understand," Sanchez replied simply.

"That brings us to our respective roles here in Africa. For me the first priority is counterintelligence. The Americans, especially their CIA, are already heavily involved in the continent, especially in the Congo. As soon as the Belgians left two months ago, the CIA started backing reactionary leaders such as Joseph Mobutu rather than the elected government of Patrice Lumumba. I need to focus on CIA plans and activities. My secondary role is to support socialist revolutionary activity."

Kozlov then stood and bent over the map of Africa before continuing. He pointed to various locations as he spoke. "For you, Jorge, I propose that the roles are reversed. Your main mission, as I understand it, is to encourage and support revolutionary activity throughout sub-Saharan Africa in key countries." Kozlov pointed at the map as he continued. "For example, the Congo is a key priority for us, and the airlift that we are currently conducting there is designed to maintain Lumumba in power. However, we must not ignore opportunities in Angola, Mozambique, even South Africa." Kozlov swept his hand over South Africa and looked at Sanchez for his reaction.

His comrade quickly nodded in agreement. "It seems we have a fine working partnership, Yuri. I essentially agree with all that you have proposed. My only question relates to our priorities in Spanish Guinea. I understand the importance of this Valhalla operation that you previously briefed me on. I have concluded that it would be best for me to engage there in a clandestine manner. I have a solid alias as a Cameroon worker who lived in France for ten years, so my return to Cameroon will not be suspicious. From there I will easily be able to infiltrate across the border with Spanish Guinea and stay within the confines of the Fang tribal territory. I can establish clandestine contact with the Cuban consulate in Santa Isabel when I need to."

"You have summarized the situation well, Jorge. I approve of your strategy for infiltrating Spanish Guinea. Remember that I have resources that can help you travel and also provide aid to local liberation movements."

"I appreciate that. Travel for me will be easy to any location in the French African Union. That means I can easily get to Congo Brazzaville and then cross the river to the former Belgian Congo. From there I can infiltrate into adjacent Portuguese Angola."

"Is that your first priority for infiltration?" Kozlov inquired as he looked back to Angola on the map.

"Yes. We already have intelligence that a local revolt is simmering just below the surface, and it could break out in a few months. My job is to encourage that activity."

"That's an excellent approach. We should maintain our clandestine communication and continue to coordinate our activities."

"When will I need to plan to enter Spanish Guinea?" Sanchez asked.

"That's a little way off in the future. I'll let you know."

91

Washington, D.C.
September 1960

* * *

Paul hurried to Allen Dulles's residence at 2723 Q Street in Georgetown. Jack had told him that Allen wanted to meet them there to discuss an important matter that would be off the record. Paul thought that sounded ominous. He rang the bell and was promptly admitted to the house. Dulles showed him to his study, where Jack was already waiting. Allen did not offer them drinks and got right to his purpose as they sat on the couch, facing him.

"I asked you two here so I can give you a heads-up on something without it being too official."

Paul looked at Jack, whose facial expression indicated that he didn't have a clue what Allen meant and then turned back to Dulles as he continued.

"Paul, I'm sorry to report that the FBI arrested your nanny, Margarita, about one hour ago, and she is being detained for espionage."

The silence was overpowering.

"Can you please explain that?" Paul finally answered with a question.

"The FBI has been tailing her for months. They were on the trail of an espionage ring in New York and discovered Margarita's involvement by accident. Her role in the ring they were investigating was only peripheral, but along the way they discovered she was supplying information on your activities, Paul, and leaving the information at a drop."

Paul was stunned. He wasn't sure how to reply.

"How can this be? She has been so faithful to us over the years. What information could she have been passing and to whom?"

"At first we thought it might involve your activities with the Franco government. That's still likely, but we now think it may also involve Operation Valhalla," Dulles responded.

"I thought we were finally rid of the Nazi element and now—"

"It wasn't the Nazis, Paul. It was the Soviets," Dulles interrupted.

"So it's true. The Soviets are on to Valhalla now for sure," Jack said.

"I'm sorry I didn't get it right away. Of course the Soviets must be involved. It looks like they've put a higher priority on discovering Valhalla than we have," Paul said.

"Yes, but that will change now, you can be sure," Dulles said.

"How does that affect me?" Jack said.

"I'm not sure yet, but you'll certainly hear as soon as the folks above our pay grade decide what to do."

Paul immediately realized that the only person above Dulles's pay grade was the president. He then thought of something else. "What will happen to Margarita?"

"At this point, I don't know. The FBI, despite their usual reticence, agreed to keep me informed."

"I suppose they'll 'beat it out of her,' just like they did to Helga back in '51," Paul concluded somberly.

"That's probably not true, Paul. The FBI has changed a little since the McCarthy days."

"That old bastard Hoover sure hasn't," Jack said.

Dulles scowled at him. "That's it for now. I'll update you as soon as I get my marching orders."

92.

Washington, DC.
November 1960

***

The summons for Paul and Jack came from Dulles on short notice again. This time they went to his regular E Street office.

"It's good to see you boys again so soon. Take a seat."

Paul noticed that Dulles, unsmiling, was puffing hard on his pipe. Paul figured that was to be expected given the election results. Kennedy had beaten Nixon.

"I need both of you for a special project, and we need to act fast," Dulles said. "By way of background, the crisis in the Congo is out of control, with four different governments vying for power. We're up to our eyeballs along with the Soviets. Our station chief there has his hands full, and we need to support him on the periphery in surrounding countries. We need to provide electronic monitoring, counterintelligence, logistics support, and occasional special operations. That's why I asked you both to come here."

Paul looked at Jack, who could only return his confused nod. Paul decided to ask for a clarification.

"If you don't mind me asking, since I'm a Spanish citizen, why am I involved in this conversation in CIA headquarters?"

"Paul, we need Spain's support, because we've determined that Spanish Guinea would be an ideal place to base the support operations I just mentioned. We need you to convince Admiral Luis Carerro to allow us to use Spanish Guinea. Therefore you have a need-to-know regarding this operation."

"Where do I fit in?" Jack interjected.

"I want you to set up the operation, Jack, and to lead it. My technical types tell me that Fernando Poo and its ten-thousand-foot peak are ideal for an HF/DF station to help monitor activity in the Congo. You're familiar with HF/DF, I assume."

272

"Sure, we used high-frequency direction finding to locate U-boats during the war. But we need to have two or more stations in order to triangulate on the signals to pinpoint them."

"We are working with the French. They have a station in Fort Lamy in Chad. We're also cut a deal with Portugal to set up monitoring stations at Sao Tome and in the Cabinda enclave in Angola. The current HF/DF technology is more precise than the old stuff from World War Two, and with those four stations we can do a good job of monitoring most of the Congo."

"I'm really not a good tech weenie, Allen," Jack said.

"Don't worry. I'm giving you one of our best eggheads to run the electronic stuff. You'll also have a specialist to run your air operations and logistics. That way you can concentrate on the stuff you like best such as counter-intelligence and special ops."

"It sounds good to me, boss."

"All right, we need to move fast. We want to have all this done and also get some things resolved in the Congo before Kennedy is inaugurated," Dulles said.

"Are you talking about Lumumba in the Congo?" Jack inquired.

"Yes, that requires resolution," Dulles responded.

Paul wondered what the term "resolution" meant, but he decided not to comment.

"When can you two leave for Spain?"

"I can go right after Thanksgiving," Paul responded.

"Same here. I just need to finish the stuff for the Cuban project," Jack added.

Paul saw Dulles give Jack a cold stare. Maybe Jack wasn't supposed to mention the Cuban project, whatever it was.

Paul decided he would change the subject. "Will you stay on during the Kennedy administration, Allen?"

Dulles was silent for a moment. "I don't know, Paul. It depends on... events."

93.

Madrid, Spain.
December 1960

* * *

Paul, Alberto, and Luis Carrero were briefed by Jack on the proposed activities in Spanish Guinea. Paul watched as Admiral Carerro silently processed what he'd just heard. Paul thought they had won him over, but he couldn't be sure.

Carerro finally nodded as he reached his decision. "I clearly see the benefit to Spain that comes from being able to monitor Soviet revolutionary agitation and other activities in Africa. We must support that activity. For other. . .special operations, Señor Kurtz, I will insist that you coordinate your activities with us. I am designating Captain Ortega as my liaison for military and the special operations that you propose conducting while using Guinea as a base. For political and other issues, I request that you initiate them through Paul Hoffman," the admiral concluded and gestured toward Paul.

Paul was surprised by this vote of confidence from Carerro.

Jack immediately responded. "Thank you, Admiral Carerro. We'll ensure that such coordination takes place."

"There is one more thing," Carrero added. "Spain's partnership with America is solid, but it must be a two-way street. I know you will understand this, and I hope you will convey the following message back to your superiors and the other agencies in your government: We will be seeking additional military assistance to modernize our armed forces. Perhaps in the spirit of our partnership, America will see fit to fulfill this request."

"I'll see that the message is conveyed, Admiral," Jack responded.

Paul suppressed a smile. Carrero clearly knew how to negotiate and was playing his initial hand early. The initial Pact of Madrid term was for ten years and would come up for renewal in 1963. Spain would obviously seek more favorable terms for the renewal of the agreement.

A lot could happen in the next three years to influence that outcome.

94

Greenwich Village, New York City.
January 24, 1961

* * *

"So have you been following events in Africa, Paul?" Jack posed his question as he and Paul were downing their last beer at the bar at Minetta Tavern.

"Yeah, it looks like the trouble in Angola is escalating and might end up as a full-blown revolt."

"Yep, and my guess is that it's orchestrated by the Soviets."

"Isn't that what your new facilities in Spanish Guinea are supposed to detect?"

"That's right. Remember, I have to return there next month, and you've signed on to go with me. We're also supposed to rendezvous with Alberto."

"He may end up there in his cruiser. My father cabled and said there were demonstrations there by independence activists."

"We need to keep a lid on that, Paul. Our new facilities and base of operations are crucial. Spanish Guinea is now the only piece of territory in that part of Africa where the colonial power still holds sway."

"I hear you." Paul paused. "Hey, let's go next door and see what's happening at Café Wha'."

"If you insist. I'm not big on that folk-music stuff."

The two men got up and left the Minetta and crossed the street to Café Wha. A couple was emerging from the club, so Paul decided to ask what was happening. The woman had long raven hair and the man had a goatee and long disheveled hair.

"Say, who's playing tonight?"

"Hey, man, it's some dude named Bob Dylan," the man said.

"He's supposedly from Minnesota, and it's his first night in New York," the woman added, smiling as she eyed Paul and Jack.

"Is he playing folk music?" Jack inquired.

The man with the goatee stared at Jack, frowned, and turned to Paul. "Hey, man, who's your square friend? He looks a little uptight."

"What's that mean?" Jack replied.

"Forget it, Jack," Paul said.

The man with the goatee turned to his companion. "Let's go to my pad and have some tea. These two aren't with-it at all."

"See you later." The woman smiled at both Paul and Jack as the couple left.

"They don't look like tea drinkers to me," Jack observed.

Paul smiled at Jack and shook his head. "You don't drink their tea, Jack, you smoke it."

"Oh, I guess I understand now," Jack replied after a long pause.

"They're classic beats," Paul observed.

"Is that like that guy who wrote...what's the book?"

"Jack Kerouac. It was *On the Road*."

"I wonder what he's like."

"You should have asked him. He was sitting right next to you at Minetta's."

"No shit! Maybe you should have introduced us."

"Maybe we can chat with him some other time. I guess the culture and times are changing on us, Jack."

"We're both getting too old for this crap."

"Speak for yourself. I'm still in my thirties, at least for six more months."

"I wish I could say the same," Jack grumbled.

"Say, Jack, with all that electronic gear that you have now on Fernando Poo, is there any chance we can eavesdrop on whether the Soviets are aware that the Valhalla trail leads to Africa?"

"You can bet on it. Allen wants me to keep that on the radar, so to speak. More important, we'll be in a better position there to do a little exploring ourselves."

Paul nodded, but he had an uneasy feeling about where the trail might lead. "I'm going in to see what Mr. Dylan is singing about," he finally announced.

"Suit yourself, Paul. I'm heading home."

As Paul entered the club, he thought about his increasing involvement with CIA activities in Spanish Guinea. *Am I doing the right thing? I've tried to be an honest broker and go-between, but maybe I've crossed the line. Will helping America in Africa really help Spain? What about the native peoples there? How will they be affected?*

As Paul later listened to the music, he began to doubt the course of action America was following, but he couldn't resolve how that affected him.

95

Santa Isabel. Spanish Guinea.
February 1961

* * *

"The revolt in Angola seems to be spreading. The Portuguese have their hands full now," Jack said.

"Yes, but they seem ready to maintain their African empire by force of arms if necessary," Alberto replied.

"Will Spain do the same?" Paul responded.

"I think the evidence of that is right here in the harbor." Alberto swept his hand toward the cruiser *Canarias*, which he commanded and which was anchored in Santa Isabel harbor.

The three men sat outside under an umbrella at La Rosaleda, a popular harborside watering hole on Avenida General Mola. They had just returned from a meeting with the governor regarding the clandestine CIA activities that were now fully underway in Spanish Guinea. Earlier, Paul and Alberto had met with Paul's father to "grease the skids" and obtain his acquiescence with these activities, since his property would be used for some of the electronic gear needed for the surveillance activities. Paul thought the meeting had not gone well, since Karl Hoffman was convinced that the colony would be sucked into the Cold War battlefield to the detriment of the local population. Paul knew that his father might be right.

Two men approached the table. To Paul's astonishment he recognized one of them. *I hope that Alexandre Santos will be discreet.*

"Welcome both of you. Sit down and I'll introduce you," Jack said enthusiastically. He rose to shake their hands as he continued in Spanish, the common language of all the attendees that day. They were at an isolated table, and there were no other patrons present in the middle of the late afternoon siesta. Nevertheless, Jack was careful to visually sweep the area to ensure they were not being observed.

"This gentleman is Henri Fortier." Jack pointed to the tall thin man with wavy black hair and Gallic features. "He works for the French SDECE and is my equivalent. His main base is Fort Lamy in Chad, but he also has a base in Oyem, Gabon."

Fortier acknowledged Jack's introduction with a quick nod and a smile.

"This other gentleman is Alexandre Santos." He was shorter than Fortier, but equally thin, with a mustache. As Jack continued, Paul noticed that Santos was grayer than when they last met.

"Alexandre works for the Portuguese PIDE and is based in Angola, but he now has responsibility for Sao Tome as well." Jack paused as he noticed the final attendee arrive for the meeting.

"Finally, I'll introduce Mike Henry. He works for me and is in charge of air operations here. Mike, you should sit next to Paul. You're both pilots." Jack then completed all the introductions. Henry was handsome and of medium build, with distinctive blue eyes. He appeared relaxed without being cavalier.

"I thought we should get together here in casual surroundings and get to know one another, since we'll all be working together. Needless to say, there's a lot going on in Africa right now. The announcement of Lumumba's death a few days ago has set off a firestorm in the Congo. Kennedy has warned Moscow about interfering there, so this conflict already has Cold War overtones," Jack said.

"The Soviets already have a base in the Republic of Guinea. Unfortunately, earlier this month we almost shot down a Russian IL-18 that was carrying Khrushchev on a goodwill visit from Morocco to the Republic of Guinea when it strayed into Algerian airspace," Fortier added.

"I see where earlier this week the UN passed Resolution 161 to use force in the Congo to restore order," Alberto said.

Jack nodded his head. "Getting back to the Soviet presence in the Republic of Guinea, our new monitoring capability has helped us pinpoint the location from which they are actually directing their operations. Thanks to the intercepts and DF recorded from Fort Lamy and Cabinda"—Jack turned to acknowledge Fortier and Santos respectively—"as well as here, we were able to triangulate on their locations. All of their key messages to their operatives in the Congo originated from Nzerekore in the Republic of Guinea. We hadn't intended for our plan to include monitoring transmissions from that direction, but the geometry is still pretty good for an accurate DF fix."

"I suppose we should discuss air operations and logistics," Santos suggested.

"That's a good idea, Alexandre. Please fill us in on that, Mike," Jack replied.

"We're all set up to support transient aircraft at the Santa Isabel airport. Heck, I might as well give out green stamps for each fill-up." Henry noticed the perplexed look he got from most of those present and returned to a serious tone. "Right now, for example, I have a Portuguese Air Force DC-6A freighter refueling before heading on to Luanda with a load of ammunition. They can't carry much payload on a nonstop to Luanda from Portugal, but they can carry a full payload if they stop here to refuel. There's also a French Air Force Noratlas on its way from Timbuktu in Mali to Brazzaville. I'm also running a couple of DC-4s between the Azores, the Canaries, the Congo and Angola, and they always stop here. They carry civil markings and are part of a Spanish 'airline' that we set up with Alberto's help."

Alberto nodded his acknowledgement.

"What about special operations, Mike?" Jack asked.

"I'm also running a pair of DC-3s and a Curtiss C-46 Commando out of here for special missions to the Congo and…elsewhere. Along those lines, I've established a forward airstrip at Medouneu on the Spanish Guinea and Gabon border. The town is in Gabon, but the airstrip is just over the border in Spanish Guinea. It's only thirty-five hundred feet, but it's got good approaches, so it can take a loaded DC-3 or C-46…barely. I've got fuel in barrels there and a support team, and it reduces the distance to the Congo more than two hundred nautical miles."

"That's great. Thanks, Mike. I know you just arrived from Vietnam where you were an adviser to their air force. You did a good job on setting up here on short notice."

Paul noticed Henri Fortier shaking his head. Jack must have noticed also. "Is there a problem, Henri?"

"*Oui*, but it's not relevant to our discussion."

"That's not a problem. What's your comment?" Jack asked.

"I wish you Americans the best, but I hope you don't get sucked into Vietnam. It's a quagmire, and there's no way to win in that terrain, given the enemy you face and the local politics."

"Thanks for the advice, Henri. Maybe our experience will be...different here in Africa," Jack responded delicately.

"Maybe we should all pause to consider what our role is in Africa," Paul interjected, as all eyes turned to him. *Boy, I asked for it this time.*

"What's your take, Paul?" Jack said, accompanied by a quizzical look.

"I'm just playing devil's advocate now. In a way, we're all facing a new world here. The Western powers are portrayed as the bad guys by the Western press and the Soviets, and they're attacking our colonial and 'neocolonial' policies."

"So what is your point, Paul?" Alberto inquired.

"I'm just thinking that we should have some kind of 'civic action' programs, better health care and education, and other assistance that would smooth the path to self-government. Maybe it should be like what France has done with the French African Union." Paul noted Fortier nodding in agreement.

"I don't know, Paul. Portugal has made our African territories part of the mother country. We don't visualize independence in our lifetimes. For example, I consider Angola my home, rather than Portugal," Santos said.

"That is also Spain's policy, Paul, as you know. Both Guinea and the Sahara are now considered Spanish provinces rather than colonies," Alberto said.

"I understand. I'm just trying to play devil's advocate," Paul repeated.

"You sound like your father, Paul. In any case, we can't solve the geopolitical problems," Jack said. "I think the 'business' part of this meeting is over. Let's order some more drinks."

96

Madrid, Spain,
March 1961

* * *

"Your mission to Spanish Guinea must have been successful, Alberto. The unrest has been quelled, at least for the moment," Admiral Luis Carerro said.

"Yes, sir, that part of it was."

"What about the other elements of your mission there?"

"Paul Hoffman and I had successful meetings with Jack Kurtz and our French and Portuguese allies in the counterintelligence arena. I summarized that in my report."

"Yes, your report answered the questions I had." Carerro gazed at Alberto. "What about the other element of your mission regarding Valhalla?"

"I met with Karl Hoffman and inspected the cave where the materials are stored. They are still secure."

"That's good. I hope with the passage of time their importance will diminish to the point where we need not worry about them anymore."

"Yes, sir," Alberto replied simply.

"Alberto, I must now ask for your loyalty again. I am relieving you of command of *Canarias* and sending you to Washington as the naval attaché. Your experience and contacts are needed as we approach the ten-year renewal period for the agreements we made with the Americans in 1953. In addition, I want you to lay the groundwork for increased defense assistance from America. Our modernization program must continue, and we need more American equipment and support."

"Yes, sir," Alberto again replied.

"I know that you will miss sea duty and the *Canarias*, but I need you for this assignment, Alberto. Besides, you and Lucia will find Washington and America an exciting place to be right now with the Kennedy administration installed."

"Yes, I'm sure we will, sir."

97.

Luanda, Angola.
April 1961

* * *

"I appreciate the support that you have provided us, Jack. It's been helpful to us to reduce the number of border incursions from the Congo. It's a long border to patrol, and having accurate intelligence has allowed our forces to slow down the rate of infiltration," Santos concluded.

"I'm glad we could help, Alexandre. It's a two-way street for us. We need to reduce the Congo rebels' ability to use Angola as a sanctuary. The several days I just spent in the field have been really helpful in working with my agents in Angola," Jack Kurtz replied.

"That's good. I'll look forward to continued cooperation," Santos said. "There is one other matter I should mention, as a result of our meeting two months ago in Santa Isabel."

"Yes, what is it?" Jack replied curiously.

"I know you are close to Paul Hoffman. You should know that we already knew each other. He came here about nine years ago, looking for his missing brother. Evidently he thought he might be here in Angola."

"Did you give him any information?"

"I did not know where his brother was, so I was unable to help him," Santos answered truthfully. "I assume there is more to the story."

"Yes, there is. I'm afraid it's a long story, and it's beyond the scope of our working relationship, Alexandre."

"Yes, of course. Since you have been in the bush, perhaps you have not heard about the invasion of Cuba by exiles from the Castro regime."

"What happened? Tell me what you heard!" Jack exclaimed excitedly.

"They landed at a place called the Bay of Pigs. The invasion failed, and all of the exiles were killed or captured."

"Oh shit!" Jack blurted out. *Now Allen is a goner for sure.*

98.

Off the mouth of the Cunene River, Portuguese Angola.
October 1961

* * *

The South African navy survey ship *Natal* was anchored about two kilometers off the mouth of the Cunene River, which represented the border between Angola and Southwest Africa. The ship and its crew were charting the Skeleton Coast of Southwest Africa and were investigating a report of a sunken vessel at the place where *Natal* was currently anchored. The report had been filed by some fisherman who frequented the area.

As the *Natal*'s recently assigned executive officer, Lieutenant Dieter Gerhardt was overseeing the diving team that was exploring the alleged wreck. He had recently been attached to Britain's Royal Navy and was now on a rotation for sea duty.

He thought that this particular event was a wild-goose chase. The diver had been down for a while at a depth of only about 120 feet, where the bottom was at this location.

Suddenly, the petty officer manning the communications with the diver made a report to the bridge. "Sir, the diver is finished with the investigation and is on his way up."

"Very well, let's get him up and get on with it," Gerhardt replied.

Gerhardt found the surveying activity tedious. Since they had charted and reached the territorial limits of Southwest Africa, Gerhardt was hoping that the *Natal* would be able to put in to Walvis Bay for a few days of shore leave and relaxation.

Within a half hour the diver had been retrieved. He came up and was hoisted on the aft deck with a box containing something retrieved from the bottom.

Gerhardt turned the bridge over to the new watch officer and hurried down to the aft deck to see what was recovered. He had a big surprise when he addressed the diver. "Well, what did you find?"

"It's a submarine, sir, a German U-boat. I was able to access the bridge through a large side hatch, and I found these."

The diver handed Dieter some acetate-protected charts. As he looked at them, his eyes nearly bulged out his sockets. He immediately called the bridge. "Summon the captain immediately and ask him to come to the fantail!"

99

Washington, D.C.
November 1961

* * *

Jack was stunned. He couldn't believe what he just heard. "Boss, you're going to have to say that again slowly."

Allen Dulles took two final puffs from his pipe and placed it in the ashtray before shaking his head and replying. "I know this is difficult, Jack. The FBI kept following up on the Soviet spy ring that Paul's nanny, Margarita, was involved in. The trail eventually led to Sharon McKenzie, and they had the proof they needed that she was a Soviet agent."

"How...how could she have been involved?"

"They eventually were able to trace back to her recruitment in 1939, when she was a freshman at Barnard and active in Communist cells. She apparently was tasked to work with Margarita in 1950. That's why the two of them arrived on the scene together at the abortive kidnapping of Paul's children in Central Park in April 1951." Dulles nodded to Paul as he finished.

"Whom did she report to?" Jack said after a long pause.

"Neither we nor the FBI have an answer for that yet. There was apparently a controller involved here in the States," Dulles said. "But we do have an important clue that Sharon provided."

"Have you picked her up then? Does she have an explanation?" Jack asked hopefully as he leaned in his chair toward Dulles.

"I'm sorry, Jack, but she's gone. Either she or one of her accomplices must have got wind of the FBI dragnet. Sharon had a passport, so she just got on a plane and fled."

"Where did she go?"

Paul could see the agony on Jack's face.

"She shook her FBI tail and took an Air France flight to Paris. By the time the FBI caught on and alerted the French, she had flown on. She knew she didn't have time to arrange an escape to the East, so she just bought a ticket to Conakry, Guinea, in Africa. That pretty much confirms her involvement with the Soviets."

Jack sank back in his chair as Dulles continued. "Both the CIA and the FBI are following up. Sharon may have fled to her main controller, who is now in Guinea. But we have a few clues that Sharon was also meeting another KGB contact from Washington who traveled regularly to New York. She slipped up a little and left a couple of notes in a diary that she left behind."

"What was in the diary?" Jack asked.

"For example, there was an entry on one day that said 'meet Z in Central Park' and another that said 'meet Z at Grand Central on DC train,' so we think that refers to a KGB controller from Washington, maybe an official with a cover from the Soviet embassy. All of this has occurred in the last six months."

Jack only nodded his reply.

"How does this affect Jack working with us?" Paul asked.

"As far as I'm concerned, Jack is in the clear, since no classified information that we know of was revealed to Sharon. Look, I'm out as the Director in a few days. Kennedy was kind enough to keep me on until we can dedicate the new headquarters in Langley. I've squared it with McCone, the incoming director, so you're going to survive this, Jack. He knows your record, so you can continue to progress here. Bissell also liked you, but I'm afraid that after the U-2 and the Bay of Pigs, he'll be gone a few months after me."

Jack nodded as his facial expression turned from shock to determination.

Paul decided to jump in. "Come on, Jack. Let's head over to Georgetown. Allen must have a lot on his plate right now."

"Sure, yeah, you're right, Paul."

The three men rose. Dulles came around to shake their hands.

"Good luck, Jack."

Jack didn't reply, but he smiled weakly as he shook Dulles's hand.

Paul picked up the slack. "Good luck, Allen, in your next incarnation. Thanks for allowing us to help the cause." He and Dulles looked somberly at each other.

100

Santa Isabel, Spanish Guinea,
September 1962

* * *

"It seems that you were right all along, Karl. The dissidents here in Spanish Guinea plan to put their case before the United Nations later this year. You'll also be happy to know that I'm being replaced after thirteen years in this post. The new governor will have a mandate to initiate some kind of self-rule here."

"Thank you for informing me, Governor. I wish you luck in your next appointment," Karl Hoffman replied in a noncommittal tone. Paul Hoffman knew that his father was not surprised by the news, since it had already reached him through unofficial channels.

"You were also right regarding the timing of your sale of the cocoa plantations. The price of cocoa has plummeted in the last three years."

"Yes, but that's to be expected for such a commodity," Paul interjected.

The governor did not comment, but Paul could see from the icy return stare that the governor regarded both father and son with contempt, as they represented the new world commercial order and were attuned to the emerging end of colonialism.

As Karl rose, Paul did also, since the meeting was clearly ended. They did not shake the governor's hand and quickly exited the palace. They started walking the one block down Calle de 19 de Septiembre to have a drink at Bar Los Polos.

"There was certainly tension in the air between you and the governor, Father. I thought you might be more magnanimous toward him, since he has clearly been replaced because of his policies."

"How can I be magnanimous? The man was a butcher. He ordered the murder of two dissidents in 1958 and 1959, and he has poisoned relations with the people. This will be hard to overcome, and it's compounded by his selection of slavish and incompetent stooges to serve as figureheads in the local government. We should have been educating and nurturing those who seek full independence, so that we can live peacefully when that moment arrives."

"Alberto tells me that Admiral Carrero and Foreign Minister Castiella are politically at odds over the decolonization issue. Carrero is trying to hold the line, but Castiella believes that we cannot fight the international community over self-determination."

"Well, you know Castiella is right on that, Paul. Yet I predict it will be several more years before this is resolved. It's also complicated by your friend Jack Kurtz and his CIA team here in Guinea. I can see this creating a Cold War confrontation. You may not know it, but the Cuban consulate is a front for Soviet agents and their agenda. This is clearly a response to the CIA provocation."

"It may be more complicated than that, Father."

"So it might, yet this mindless competition between the superpowers may end up destabilizing us here, not to mention throughout Africa."

Paul knew that his father might be right. As the two men turned and walked into Bar Los Polos, Paul wondered if there was some way he could serve to mediate the competing ideologies, at least within Spain.

"So let's have a manzanilla or two, and then tomorrow we can get in the Beech and head back to the Rio Muni plantation," Karl suggested as they sat down at a table.

"I'm sorry, Father, but I need to get back to New York first thing in the morning." Paul was shocked that his father had forgotten.

"Ah yes, I did forget. So you will get in your new expensive Lockheed Jetstar and whisk back across the ocean."

"Yes, with stops at Villa Cisneros and the Azores. It's already becoming an essential part of managing our worldwide operations. It's the only way I can oversee our commitments in North America, Europe, and Africa. The world is shrinking."

"Yes, Paul, it is. I just wonder if it's for the better, or not."

Washington, DC.
October 1962

* * *

The three men sat somberly in the Town and Country Bar of the Mayflower Hotel. They had just watched President Kennedy's televised address announcing the naval quarantine of Cuba to force the removal of Soviet missiles. If it came to a nuclear confrontation, they all realized they were at ground zero. *At least it justifies ordering a third round of drinks*, Paul thought, as he raised his hand to the bartender and turned to face his friend. "I suppose you can't talk about it, Jack, but this must be causing all hell to break loose in the agency."

"That's an understatement. I can at least acknowledge that."

"Perhaps my meeting at the Pentagon next week will bear fruit on getting increased military assistance. Spain also hopes it will expedite the renewal of our defense pact, since the ten-year term expires next year," Alberto commented.

"That's almost a certainty, Alberto. We also need to maintain our facilities and operations in Spanish Guinea," Jack replied.

"That's promising," Alberto said simply.

"Has Lucia been enjoying Washington?" Paul asked.

"I think she finally is. When we first got here, she spent most of her time in New York. She said the shopping was far superior. It didn't hurt that you and Liz were so hospitable, Paul," Alberto responded.

"She can stay with us anytime, and you should find time in your schedule to join us, Alberto."

"I will certainly make the effort."

Paul thought that Lucia was extraordinarily independent for someone who had never been to America. She did not hesitate to circulate on her own when she was in New York.

Stellenbosch, South Africa,
November 1962

* * *

Yuri Kozlov sat quietly at the outdoor table at the winery just outside town. He had to remind himself that his alias during this trip was Esteban Gonzalez, a Chilean wine merchant. As he relaxed, he took an occasional sip of the chardonnay that he had purchased.

"Excuse me, but I was wondering what you thought of the chardonnay?"

Yuri looked up to see a smiling man of medium build and fair complexion.

"I think it's dry and appealing, but with just a little too much oak," Yuri replied.

"Yes, I prefer a crisper chardonnay," the man responded.

Yuri looked around casually yet thoroughly before answering. "Please sit down, Gerhardt," he finally said.

His new agent had successfully identified himself using the agreed code words.

"Will you be visiting me regularly?" Dieter Gerhardt inquired.

"I don't know. It depends on the urgency. What do you have today?"

"I thought I would ask you about this map of the vineyards."

"Excuse me?"

Gerhardt laid three pages on the table in front of Kozlov. "This is the map of the wineries around Stellenbosch, and I'd like to recommend two in particular."

Kozlov looked at the first page and noted that it was an overview map of the local wineries and other attractions. He looked back at Gerhardt with a questioning expression.

"Now if you'll look at this second map, I can show you a better winery to visit."

Kozlov looked at the second document and noted that it was a map in German. It showed the entire Atlantic Ocean and traced two routes, one from

Denmark to Spanish Guinea and the other from Spanish Guinea to the coastal border between Angola and Southwest Africa.

"You mentioned another winery map?" Kozlov said as he looked at Gerhardt.

"Yes, and this one is the most desirable of all."

Gerhardt revealed the third page. It was a map of Rio Muni, the mainland portion of Spanish Guinea, and it traced a route from the coast to a point east of the town of Niefang. That point was labeled HOFFMAN PLANTAGE LAGERPLATZ. Kozlov's command of German was rudimentary, but he knew this meant "Hoffman plantation storage site."

"Where did you get this?"

"It's a copy of a map that was retrieved from U-3696, a scuttled Type 21 U-boat resting in twenty fathoms of water about two kilometers off the mouth of the Cunene River at the Angola-Southwest Africa border. The original maps were well preserved under a layer of plastic. They were sent to Pretoria for examination, but copies were made and filed at the navy intelligence office where I now work at the Simons Town naval base. I made these copies from them. They are yours now."

"Are you sure you were not detected?"

"Absolutely. I took my time and arranged this meeting through the system that I was given for contacting you, including this winery venue."

"Very well, I will be in touch if I need additional assistance. Contact me if you find any information that elaborates on these maps," Kozlov commanded.

"I will."

"Whom did the original maps go to?"

"They were sent to Hendrik van den Bergh, who is in intelligence and counterintelligence at the national level in the government."

Yuri nodded in reply. *Would he be competing with the South Africans for the Valhalla secrets?*

Madrid, Spain.
November 1963

* * *

"I assume you heard the news about President Kennedy," Carrero asked.

"Yes, sir, it's shocking. I sense this will be a true crisis of identity for many Americans," Alberto replied as he shook his head.

"That's true. But for us, life must go on. You have done a good job on the extension of the base agreement, Alberto. Since it was renewed in September, my little running argument with Foreign Minister Castiella has died down a little. He wanted us to bargain harder with the Americans, but I'm not sure that would have helped us."

"That's correct, sir. The Americans have now completed their B-52 bomber production, and the older B-47 is being phased out, so the three American air bases in Spain have less value. Also the American Minuteman ICBM and Polaris submarine missiles are a more effective and lower-cost nuclear deterrent."

"Where are we on naval assistance from America?" Carrero inquired.

"I've finalized the arrangements for the transfer of two transport vessels, the USS *Noble* and the USS *Achernar*. They will be transferred late next year and renamed *Aragon* and *Castilla*. I also pursued the possibility of an aircraft carrier. The American *Essex* class has been modernized, and the Americans will not part with any of them. They still have a handful of small escort or 'jeep' carriers, but these are not practical. I'm therefore focusing on the light, Independence-class aircraft carriers. The Americans have three left in their mothball fleet out of the original nine," Alberto summarized.

"Will one of these ships work for us?" Carrero responded.

"Yes, sir, they have great range and can operate helicopters easily for either antisubmarine or amphibious transport. Such a ship would greatly expand our strategic reach."

"I knew you would be thorough, Alberto. When you return to Washington, please follow up on this plan with the new Johnson administration."

New York City.
July 1964

* * *

Paul, Jack, and Alberto were enjoying the scene in Greenwich Village on this sultry summer evening and so far had visited the White Horse Tavern and Minetta's. The plan was to have dinner at Delmonico's, where they would be joined by Liz, Lucia, and Anita. Anita had just arrived in New York with daughters Beatriz, Francisca, and Isabel.

"So are you and Lucia enjoying New York?" Jack asked.

"Oh yes. Lucia always enjoys it here, especially visiting Paul and Liz." Alberto replied.

"This year is a little different. Just for a change we're having the summer vacation in America rather than Spain," Paul said.

"I'm still wondering why Anita selected the schools the girls are attending," Alberto said.

"Anita wanted Beatriz and Francisca to come to school in America. Liz and I sent Pilar to the Northfield School in Northfield, Massachusetts, and she loved it. She started in 1961 and will be a senior this year. Based on her recommendation to Anita, Beatriz and Francisca started in 1962, since they're a year younger. They love it, too."

"Why didn't Anita consider schools in Spain?" Alberto wondered.

"She said that boys have excellent education options in Spain, but girls don't yet. I'm afraid that Anita has firm opinions on educational opportunities for girls," Paul responded.

"Yes, I guess that's the result of a family emerging mostly with women." Alberto sighed before continuing. "Yet that's not completely true. How is Robert doing?"

"He's following in my footsteps and will be a senior at Choate this coming year," Paul replied.

"He's also following the old man and his grandfather as an aviator. He already has his pilot license," Jack interjected.

"So perhaps he will join the air force?" Alberto asked.

"I don't know," Paul responded thoughtfully.

105.

Alabos, Spain,
July 1965

* * *

"I'd like to propose a toast to *Contraalmirante* Alberto Ortega," Paul said as he raised his glass. He was joined by Anita, Lucia, Liz, his father, Karl, and his son, Robert.

Alberto was promoted to rear admiral at the completion of his tour as naval attaché in Washington. He was then reassigned as the head of naval intelligence and counterintelligence.

"Thank you for your toast. It's a great honor for me and a culmination of thirty-one years in the *armada*," Alberto replied with sincerity. He was not given to focusing on himself, so he turned to praise Paul's son.

"I understand you have been accepted at Columbia University, Robert. What will you study?"

"I'll major in business with a minor in history, just as my father did."

"Where will your sister go?"

"Pilar has decided to go to Middlebury College in Vermont."

"Both Beatriz and Francisca will expect a full report at the end of her freshman year. They may follow in her footsteps next year, just as they did at the Northfield School," Anita announced.

"You still think they will get a better education in America?" Alberto asked with just a hint of sarcasm.

"Yes, they will, at least at this time. Maybe in the future, Spain will be more encouraging to its young women," Anita replied firmly.

Anita decided to change subjects. "What's the situation in Guinea, Karl?"

"As you know, it's now called Equatorial Guinea, rather than Spanish Guinea. It's fully self-governing except for defense and foreign affairs. All the factions are lining up to support independence as soon as possible. I'd guess it will be about three more years."

Paul knew that his father had left a lot unsaid.

Madrid, Spain,
February 1966

* * *

"This is proving to be a real crisis for us, and I just hope it doesn't become a public relations disaster," Admiral Luis Carrero said.

"We're working feverishly with the Americans to contain the public outcry as well as to locate the last hydrogen bomb," Admiral Alberto Ortega responded.

The two naval officials were discussing the crisis resulting from the catastrophic collision of an American B-52 bomber and a KC-135 tanker over the remote small Spanish village of Palomares on the south coast of Spain in January. The bomber had been carrying three hydrogen bombs, and only two had been recovered so far. Fortunately, no nuclear explosions had occurred.

"Yesterday, I had to listen to Castiella rant about the downside of our alliance with America. He says we became a Cold War ally with America only to see them drop nuclear bombs on us rather than on the Russians."

"It was an accident, sir, and the Americans are moving swiftly to clean up the mess in Palomares and recover the last bomb."

"That's true, but this incident could affect the status of the American's basing agreement with us when it comes up for renewal in 1968," Carrero said. "Alberto, I want you to go to Washington and push hard on the Americans for that aircraft carrier. Maybe we can take advantage of this situation to at least get them to accelerate the tacit agreement we have with them on the former USS *Cabot*."

"I can do that, sir. It will also allow me to pave the way for the transfer of additional naval vessels including submarines."

"All right; let's proceed with that plan. We need to continue military and naval modernization. It's essential for us."

"I'll make travel plans right away, sir."

Nzerekore, People's Revolutionary Republic of Guinea.
July 1966

* * *

"Are you sure you have looked in every conceivable place on their plantation?" Yuri Kozlov asked emphatically.

"Yes, and I've made sure that my inquiries and curiosity didn't attract suspicion," Jorge Sanchez replied.

"I still believe that the map that I got from Gerhardt was accurate. Yet in more than three years of sporadic searching, you have turned up nothing," Kozlov responded.

"Perhaps the materials have been moved to another place in Equatorial Guinea or taken out of the country. Perhaps the Americans have located them."

"Do you think that's possible?" Kozlov asked, turning to Sharon McKenzie.

"No, I don't. At least until I escaped from America in November 1961, I could not detect from Jack Kurtz that they knew about their location. Although the Americans knew about Valhalla, they were not privy to where the materials were taken."

"You're sure about that?" Sanchez asked.

"Yes, I am. After twelve years of living with Jack I can assure you that a little 'pillow talk' goes a long way in surfacing facts subtly," Sharon asserted.

"I'm sure you were persuasive with your subtle charms," Sanchez sneered.

"That's enough. This is getting us nowhere. Jorge, when you return to Equatorial Guinea, you must maintain the search. In addition, we must ensure that we are positioned with the new regime when it comes to power. Do you have a plan in place to approach key individuals?" Kozlov inquired.

"Yes, I do. I believe that Francisco Macias Nguema will succeed in his bid for power. He was a civil servant and is currently the deputy prime minister in the transition government. He is ruthless, but he will do our bidding as long as we loyally support his rise to power. Yet, I am uncomfortable with him. Before Comrade Guevara left last November, after his year in Africa, he observed that most Africans lack revolutionary fervor and require more education before they can appreciate the benefits of socialist revolution. I believe that Macias fits this mold. He doesn't really care about ideology and seems more motivated by the need to have revenge against the Spanish."

"That doesn't matter, Jorge. What matters is that he does our bidding."

"If that's our credo, then we are no better than the imperialists with their neocolonial policies and local puppet leaders."

"You may be correct, Jorge, but we will still make him the centerpiece of our strategy. When independence comes, we can lift the veil on this and confront the Hoffman family directly, and with whatever it takes to find the Valhalla cargo."

$\mathcal{B}ata, \mathcal{E}quatorial \mathcal{G}uinea.$
$\mathcal{J}une\ 1967$

* * *

Karl watched as Iberia Airlines flight 963 taxied in on schedule at 12:20 p.m. on this Thursday after its flight from Madrid, with a brief stop at Santa Isabel. The Douglas DC-6 had replaced the Lockheed Super Constellation used previously on this route, but both propeller aircraft were an anachronism in the jet age. Within a few minutes Karl greeted his son, and they embraced.

"Welcome, Paul, it's good to see you. Where is your Lockheed Jet Star?"

"It's in a heavy maintenance cycle and being prepared for sale. In another six months or so we expect to take delivery of a new aircraft model, a Gulfstream II. It has better range for our worldwide travel needs. Meanwhile, I'm reduced to flying in another old propeller airliner. I understand that this may be one of the last runs here before Iberia switches totally to jet-powered DC-8s."

"Yes, I've heard that, but I've also heard that they may keep another propeller plane on this run, probably a DC-7."

"So Guinea remains an aeronautical backwater." Paul shook his head.

"That's all right, my son. It is still an improvement on the old days. Let's go get your bags and head over to Bar Gloria on the beach for a drink before we drive to the plantation. We have a lot to discuss."

"All right, father. Lead the way."

The two men walked to Karl's car and he resumed the conversation as he began driving.

"The other reason that I'm happy you are here is so we can discuss what you can do in Madrid to help Guinea's transition to independence."

"What do you suggest I do, father?"

"They are planning to convene a constitutional convention in Madrid in October to develop a governing framework for this country. It might be our only chance to get it right, but I'm not optimistic that the Franco regime can create an empowering democratic framework."

"Have any credible indigenous leaders emerged that can pave the way for the transition?"

"There are three front-runners. Two of them favor an effective constitutional approach, but the third is Francisco Macias Nguema, and he is a very dangerous man. He has masqueraded as a loyal stooge of the colonial government, but he actually hates Spain and Spaniards. He is a Fang from the sect that is centered in Mongomo in eastern Rio Muni."

"What specifically do you suggest that I do?" Paul persisted.

"You have great influence with Admiral Carrero, who is still calling the shots here. He is at loggerheads with Foreign Minister Castiella. You could bridge the gap between them at the constitutional convention. It's important for us to achieve effective independence with a credible leader and a solid constitutional framework."

"I see your point. When I return to Madrid, I will collaborate with Alberto on this. We can come up with some kind of plan to intervene."

"Thank you, Paul. It will ease my mind to know you are trying."

"For Liz and me, it would ease our minds if you could see your way to retire and come to New York, or at least Madrid. You'll be seventy-five soon."

"I think you know the answer to that." Karl smiled. "I do miss my grandchildren. Are they doing well?"

"Yes, they will be juniors this year. Robert is in a reserve officer training program, and when he graduates in 1969, he plans to go on and fly for the air force for his required active duty."

"I hope he does well, but I regret that he will probably get sucked into that unwinnable war in Vietnam. I know you may object, but it's my view that America is playing a neocolonial role in what is truly an indigenous uprising rather than a Cold War battlefield. We have also seen enough of that here in Africa. I'm glad that Spain has decided to peacefully relinquish its remaining colonial holdings. The Portuguese are getting increasingly bogged down in Angola, Mozambique, and Portuguese Guinea. They cannot possibly prevail."

"Rob is very much like you and me, Father. He's his own man, but he also has a sense of duty. You served in World War One. In World War Two, I tried to enlist, but—"

"You served in your own way, Paul, and your efforts helped keep Spain out of that tragic war. It took your mother, Ernst, and—"

"It may have taken Hans from us, too, Father, but I will continue to look for a way to find him."

"I believe that he ultimately realized, unlike my brother Walter, that the moral price we pay for war is high, and it ultimately creates a burden that we find hard to accept. I only hope that Robert is able to sort through these choices before he creates a moral dilemma for himself."

"I think you can be assured that he will." Paul decided to change subjects. "We have another aviator in the family besides Robert. Beatriz is now a pilot, and Anita is encouraging her to finish her college education and remain in America for a while if she desires."

"Is that a good thing?" Karl responded.

"In a way, she is following the family tradition, as you and I have. She is a loyal Spaniard, yet she also views herself as a citizen of the world. I'd like to say that this doesn't create divided loyalties and instead serves to broaden our perspectives. Pilar, Beatriz, and Francisca are part of a new generation of women who refuse to be constrained by old conventions. Liz and Anita support their quest, and so do I. We believe that they should get an international perspective and one day help to change societal norms in Spain."

"I can't argue with that. But you might want to consider that even American women still conform to societal norms. You see it constantly in the marketing of products in the American magazines. It's the happy-housewife-and-consumer image."

"That's true, Father, but the new generation of American women are trying to change that rigid image, and I suppose that makes them mavericks."

"Well, you and I have always been mavericks, so I suppose it's only natural that the women in the family should also be...different."

109.

Madrid. Spain.
November 1967

* * *

Paul sat across from Antonio de Ortiz at their table in the lobby bar of the Palace Hotel and quietly observed the thirty-two-year-old diplomat. They had just met, and Paul was impressed with Antonio's eagerness to embrace the issues involved in the impending independence of one of Spain's remaining African colonies. Antonio was well educated, handsome, youthful, and eager, yet he was savvy enough to realize the competing interests that were involved in this issue. The constitutional conference for Equatorial Guinea had started several days ago, and it was clear that Paul and Antonio were key figures in its potential success.

Paul reminded himself that Antonio worked for Foreign Minister Castiella and needed some slack in dealing with the issues. In a meeting yesterday with Admirals Ortega and Carrero, Paul was given the challenging assignment of brokering a deal between the decolonization strategy favored by Castiella and the continued colonial arrangement favored by Luis Carrero. Naturally, the indigenous representatives from Equatorial Guinea had their own ideas about independence and governance.

"Tell me, Antonio, what are Spain's continuing economic interests in Guinea?" Paul asked, as the waiter brought their glasses of manzanilla.

"An interministerial commission that met from April to June concluded that all of our economic interests are defensible within an independent Equatorial Guinea. We should therefore seek a constitutional framework that provides them with a maximum of political and economic self-determination. Did you read my notes on this?"

"Yes, and I believe that your approach is astute and could be the basis for bringing the competing interests together. Those favoring self-determination, both here and in Guinea, should be able to agree with those here in Spain who favor a continued neocolonial approach," Paul responded.

"Did you also look at my suggestions for the constitutional framework?"

"Yes, I did, and I'm impressed with what you are suggesting. Your proposals are actually quite bold and depart somewhat from the government approach that currently holds sway here in Madrid." Paul hoped that his candid assessment of the country's leadership was not misinterpreted.

"Perhaps we must take certain. . .liberties, in order to achieve the end state we all desire in Guinea," Antonio responded with a wry smile.

Paul knew why he liked Antonio so much. They thought exactly alike.

"If we can get all parties to agree with this constitutional framework, that's a major step forward. The other ingredient we need is good leadership in the new government in Guinea. What are your thoughts on this, Antonio?"

The wry smile evaporated as Antonio shook his head. "I'm afraid the situation on that front is not as promising. Unfortunately, the leaders that the colonial government has groomed for this role are not up to the challenge. They do not have the education, experience, and belief in representative government."

"My father and I certainly agree with that assessment. We are particularly worried about Macias Nguema. We think that his repressed hatred of Spaniards will come back to haunt us when power is transferred. The tension is barely disguised now. His behavior could be unpredictable when we withdraw."

"Then we shall need to give this conference our best effort, to at least ensure that a constitutional framework is in place and functioning before independence." Antonio raised his glass. "Here's to our success in providing Guinea with a constitution."

"Here's to our success and Guinea's future," Paul responded.

110.

Mongomo, Equatorial Guinea,
April 1968

* * *

Yuri Kozlov watched the brief introductory exchange in the Fang language between Jorge Sanchez and Francisco Macias Nguema. Kozlov couldn't help noting the fire in Macias Nguema's eyes, as if they were expressing a hatred seething within.

Kozlov determined that he must be at this meeting that Sanchez had arranged at Macias's austere shack in the center of town. Kozlov had clandestinely slipped across the nearby border with Gabon and joined Sanchez for the meeting. It was critical to engage Macias in an operating alliance, whatever his true motivations.

Kozlov decided to be direct and shifted the conversation to Spanish. "Señor Macias, we truly want to support you as your regime comes to power. We and our Cuban comrades can provide financial aid, arms, and advisers. We can also help you in the international arena to resist continued occupation by Spain and inroads from other countries."

"What is it you want in return?" Macias answered slowly and suspiciously.

"We hope that you will host us here so that we may use your country as a base to prevent a colonial or neocolonial resurgence. We also wish to have access to records and materials that the Spaniards may leave behind. We have reason to believe that they may be hiding certain items here in Guinea."

Macias looked directly at Kozlov, as if he were evaluating his sincerity or true motives. His suspicion gave way slowly to acquiescence. "I do not trust the Spanish to truly give us independence. They treat us condescendingly, and they will soon pay the price for their arrogance. We do not wish to become vassals of another foreign power."

"We have no such intentions, I can assure you," Kozlov replied.

"You spoke of secrets that the Spanish might be hiding. Who among them do you suspect of such treachery?"

303

Kozlov looked at Sanchez, who nodded and then answered Macias. "We have reason to believe that Karl Hoffman may have such secrets in his custody. I understand that he has been very benevolent to your people, but we—"

"Do not mistake Hoffman's supposed benevolence for something we value. He seeks to make us like them, by instilling in our people notions of European life and values. In his own way he attempts to dominate us like the worst of the Spanish oppressors. He will pay the price for his oppression when we come to power."

Sanchez looked back to Kozlov. It was clear to Kozlov that Sanchez was equally taken aback by Macias's barely repressed anger and potential savagery. Yet Kozlov knew that Macias was overwhelmingly established within the Fang community and was likely to assume power upon independence. He decided he must agree. "Very well, I can assure you that once independence is achieved and we have located and obtained any secrets that the Spanish may have hidden, we will not object to any actions you may take against your former colonial oppressors. We will also provide the support that I spoke of a few minutes ago."

Macias nodded enthusiastically. He then stood and walked quietly around the room. He returned to the table and spoke slowly and deliberately. "It will be chaotic here when the Spanish leave and I assume power. I will only rarely be found in Santa Isabel. This town is my true home and that of my people."

"Don't worry. We will be able to find you when the time comes," Kozlov replied.

Madrid, Spain.
July 1968

* * *

"I hope all of our good work on the constitution will make a difference, Antonio," Paul said. He and Antonio de Ortiz sat at an outside table at Cerveceria Alemana in the Plaza de Santa Ana on this hot evening. The bar was famous as one of Ernest Hemingway's many watering holes, but it was also one of several on the plaza.

Paul was on his second glass of fino. Antonio was still nursing his first glass.

"I hope so too, Paul. Getting it approved last month was a coup, but now it has to pass muster in next month's referendum in Guinea."

"How do you think that will go?"

"The problem as I see it is that Macias Nguema has now clearly staked out a position against the draft constitution. The two opposition politicians, whom the government in Madrid is supporting, may split the vote when the elections are held. If that happens, then Macias will be the front-runner."

"What will happen if he wins the election and the constitution still gets adopted?"

"That's a good question. Macias is very anti-Spanish. He could be very unpredictable. Right now he is stirring things up against us."

"My father says that the Soviets and the Cubans are there already. Of course, the CIA is also working there. I'm concerned that the CIA effort is more focused on electronic monitoring of neighboring countries and supporting operations elsewhere, rather than trying to counter the Soviets and Cubans within Equatorial Guinea. I'm also concerned that the colonial government hasn't done enough to prepare the local population for any meaningful administrative activity. They'll still be heavily dependent on Spanish administrators."

"Macias will use that against us."

"Yes, Antonio, it sounds like a recipe for chaos."

Over Northern Gabon.
October 7, 1968

* * *

Paul looked out at the endless jungle panorama below them as the smooth drone of the Beech 18's Pratt and Whitney engines continued. He had arrived early for the independence ceremonies scheduled for October 12. His father asked him to come on this trip to recruit more workers for the cocoa and coffee plantations. The supply of workers from Nigeria had dried up because of the civil war created when part of that country attempted to secede as the independent country of Biafra. Unfortunately, the Franco regime had tacitly intervened in that war by allowing the island of Fernando Poo to be used as a staging area for aircraft flying to and from Biafra.

They were now flying west to return from Ouesso in the Congo Brazzaville, as that former French colony was called to distinguish it from the former Belgian Congo, now called Congo Leopoldville. They had taken off almost two hours ago on the 450-mile trip and had only another 140 miles to go to Bata, where they would refuel before flying to Santa Isabel on Fernando Poo.

They had departed early in the morning after staying overnight on the unsuccessful search for more plantation labor. They were accompanied by Felipe Mukasa Ondo, their plantation business manager. Felipe was also a pilot, but on this leg sat in the Beech's passenger cabin.

Paul was amazed at the stunning view of Equatorial Africa from the cockpit, as he had been on each preceding trip. He was also watching the billowing cumulous clouds that were already forming at 9:00 a.m. The inevitable afternoon thunderstorms might be starting early.

It was difficult to talk in the Beech because of the noise level, so both men wore earphones and were mainly silent during the flight. Paul was currently fiddling with the automatic direction finder trying to identify the radio beacon at the Oyem, Gabon, airport, somewhere off to the southwest. All he heard on the assigned frequency was static.

Paul had flown the Beech on the outbound trip, and his father was now in the left seat at the controls. Paul admired his father's still sharp reflexes and aeronautical astuteness. Both men agreed that the popular image of pilots as daredevils was flawed, and that flying was essentially an exercise in risk management.

They were about to test that premise.

Felipe urgently shook Paul's shoulder as he came up and alerted them. "There's a lot of oil coming out of the right engine! I saw it happen just as I looked out. Something must have given way inside the engine!"

Paul looked quickly out the right window at the streaming oil now covering the engine nacelle. He looked back to the right engine oil pressure gauge, catching it just as it began to fluctuate.

"We've got to feather it right away!" he shouted to Karl.

Paul reached over and pulled the right throttle all the way back to idle. He then reached up and pushed the right engine feather button overhead. Finally, he brought the right mixture control back to idle cut-off. He quickly looked out again at the right engine.

"We're all right. It feathered all right." The propeller was stopped.

While all this was happening, Karl maintained smooth control by compensating for the loss of one engine. He retrimmed the aircraft. He then secured the right engine by cutting off the fuel and the magneto ignition switch.

"That's good. Even if we had lost all the engine oil, there was enough left in the standpipe to feather it," Karl noted.

"I wonder what happened," Felipe said.

Paul looked at his father and then posed the key question.

"Should we try for Bata or divert, probably for Oyem?"

He could see his father thinking carefully before answering. "I don't know. The left engine's due for overhaul and we have another 140 miles to go over jungle. We have a clearance to land in Gabon. Let's head for Oyem."

Paul nodded and then quickly gave his father the estimated course.

"Steer about 225 degrees. I figure it's only about twenty miles, and the airport's about four miles south of the town."

Karl nodded as he turned to the new course and maintained altitude. Yet, he couldn't stay high for long. The cloud bases looked to be about twenty-five hundred feet above the ground and were starting to close in.

Paul read his father's mind as he consulted the chart and then looked back up. "The Oyem Airport is at 2158 feet elevation."

He then pointed to his father the aeronautical chart notation for the terrain to the south and east of the airport: MAXIMUM ELEVATION FIGURES ARE BELIEVED NOT TO EXCEED 4600 FEET. It was an all too common notation on African charts.

Paul knew the risks they faced. If they waited to descend, the clouds could become a complete undercast below them. To descend through the clouds would risk hitting high terrain. On the other hand, if they descended below the clouds there might be insufficient room between the cloud base and the terrain and they would again risk hitting a mountain or other high ground. Karl must have read his son's thought process.

"We have to go lower so we can see the airport. As long as we stay visual, we'll be all right," Karl stated as he gently pushed forward on the wheel to begin descending.

"I agree. I'll keep trying on the direction finder," Paul replied.

As the noise level had now dropped with one engine out and the reduced speed, Paul was rewarded in his earphones with the faint identifier for the Oyem radio beacon on 353 kilocycles, or rather kilohertz, as he reminded himself of the new radio frequency term. He looked at the needle on the instrument panel swing twenty degrees or so left and right of center. The airport must be dead ahead. Karl soon confirmed that.

"I can see the town."

The single engine landing was anticlimactic, as they soon rolled to a stop on the Oyem airport ramp. They were promptly greeted by French Foreign Legionnaires. Paul opened the side window and looked out as a man approached. He was wearing khakis rather than a uniform, although he carried a sidearm. Paul instantly recognized him. "Hello, Henri. It's nice to see you here," Paul offered with a smile.

"*Oui*, but I see that this is not a social call," Henri Fortier answered as he looked up at the oilcovered engine.

Their risk management process had paid off.

* * *

The mechanic delivered his assessment following the engine inspection. "You were lucky to have shut it down in time. There's no internal damage but the oil collector ring and several other components failed from corrosion. You might be interested to know that the same corrosion exists on the other engine."

Paul, Karl, Felipe, and Henri exchanged glances. Karl finally responded. "Can you fix them both?"

"Of course, if I have the parts. Be prepared, because that will take months." Karl let out an audible but resigned sigh before replying. "I will have to deal with it later. Right now we need to get a ride to Mongomo in Equatorial Guinea. We can telex my workers, and they can meet us there with a car."

"I will provide you with a ride, Karl, but it will not be to Mongomo. It is too dangerous there, because it is Macias Nguema's hometown. I will instead take you to Ebebiyin, where there is also a good road to Niefang and then Bata," Fortier replied.

"Has the situation deteriorated that badly?" Paul asked.

"I'm afraid so."

"I'm tempted to blame this on the Europeans in general and the Russians, Cubans, and Americans for making it worse. Sadly, it is Spain itself that is responsible for the enormous tragedy that could soon befall us," Karl said glumly.

"You are not alone, Karl. It is the fate of Africa." Fortier shrugged.

Paul could only wonder. *Must that be Africa's fate?*

Ebebiyin, Gabon-Equatorial Guinea border.
October 8, 1968

***

As Paul, Karl, and Felipe stood waiting just inside the Equatorial Guinea border, Paul noticed it right away. There was fear in the eyes of the black territorial guard soldiers as they were stared at by what looked to be some kind of militia. The militia members did not appear to be armed yet. Paul watched as his father approached the white officer leading the territorial guard unit, who was standing next to them. "What's bothering your men, Captain?" Karl asked quietly.

"It's Macias Nguema. They know he is the instigator of the militias. They're afraid of what will happen when he assumes power."

"Is it the same throughout the territorial guard?"

"Yes. We have control of Bata, Santa Isabel, and their two airports. There are a few small regular Spanish army and civil guard units to assist us in these places, but they may be withdrawn upon independence."

"What about the constitution? It guarantees the rule of law," Paul offered.

The Spanish officer merely looked at him and shook his head.

"It may be worse on Fernando Poo. The Bubi tribe predominates there, rather than the Fang. Macias is a Fang. He is also very centered on his own sect and clan in Mongomo. None of this is encouraging," Felipe said.

"The first few months will tell whether or not the rule of law will prevail," Karl said.

"We can see what it looks like when we arrive in Santa Isabel," Paul said.

In reality, Paul didn't believe the new constitution offered any protection. The future stability of the new country would rest in the hands of one man: Francisco Macias Nguema.

Santa Isabel, Equatorial Guinea,
October 12, 1968

* * *

Paul watched as the Spanish flag was lowered, and the flag of the new country of Equatorial Guinea was raised. He thought that it was significant that Spain had only sent the information and tourist minister, Manuel Fraga Iribarne, to represent the former mother country in this ceremony. Paul had actually worked closely with Fraga over the last several years to help revitalize the Spanish tourist industry, with positive results for the Ortega-Hoffman commercial real estate empire in southern Spain.

"This is the end of an era, Paul," Karl Hoffman said softly as he watched the Spanish flag come down.

"Father, you sound uncharacteristically nostalgic."

"Yes, I'll admit it. When your grandfather Ortega came here fifty-five years ago he had a vision that we have since realized, but now I see that it is in serious jeopardy."

"The family has certainly benefited from those years," Paul replied.

"It has financially, Paul, but what of the people who remain here who depended on us? What will become of them?"

"I assume that they will continue to prosper, with your help. I know now that you will not leave here."

"I wish my continued presence was enough to ensure that, but much damage has been created by our own political negligence and our acquiescence in making this a focal point for American and Soviet competition."

Before Paul could respond, Jack Kurtz walked over. "Hello, Paul, hello, Karl." He smiled.

"Hello, Jack, I see you made it here for the ceremony," Paul replied.

Karl merely frowned, held back on a comment, turned, and walked away.

"Was it something I said?"

"Don't worry, Jack, it's not personal. My father is having a hard time with this."

"I understand. I know his feelings are pretty intense about how this developed."

"Is your operation here going to remain in place after today?"

"Yes, for as long as we possibly can. The functions we're doing here are still essential. It looks like Spanish troops will still be here, at least in the two major cities and their airports. All of our key facilities are on a secured site at the Santa Isabel airport, which is still a key logistics and refueling stop. In fact, I'll only return to Washington briefly before coming back here."

"Are you sure you want to do that? It could get pretty ugly."

"Paul, it's ugly in Washington and America now. The two assassinations, the riots, student demonstrations, Johnson's withdrawal from the presidential race, and Vietnam are all creating a nasty mix. It looks like 1968 will be a year to forget. Yeah, in balance I'll look forward to coming back here. What about you? Are you hopping back in your new Gulfstream? How's that working out?"

"It's an incredible airplane. I'll head back to Spain nonstop for some business and then back to New York nonstop. It provides unimaginable flexibility."

"Yeah, it must be nice."

The two men fell silent. Paul decided he would share a premonition that had troubled him. "Jack, it really could get ugly here. I'm concerned about how it all might happen."

"Well, don't worry. We'll find a way to deal with it."

Paul could not dismiss those concerns so easily. He had had several nightmares recently, including one that he hadn't had in more than twenty years.

Last night his nightmare was about playing with his two brothers in the cave.

Part 4

* * *

Darkness

1969–1975

"He cried in a whisper at some image, at some vision—he cried out twice, a cry that was no more than a breath: 'The horror! The horror!'"

Marlow describing Kurtz's dying words on a steamer on an African river. Excerpt from *Heart of Darkness*, Joseph Conrad, 1902

115.

Madrid, Spain.
March 1969

* * *

"Please summarize the plans you have made, Alberto," Admiral Luis Carrero said quietly as he looked at the map of Equatorial Guinea on the table before him.

"Based on your direction, sir, I have already begun executing Operation Ecuador. It calls for the evacuation of the seven thousand European residents of Equatorial Guinea to avert a possible bloodbath caused by the disintegration of the civil government there. We've begun an airlift, but the number of aircraft we can send is restricted by technical issues and the resistance of the Macias government. At best, we'll be able to evacuate half of the refugees."

"So what are your naval plans?" Carrero inquired.

"I've issued sailing orders to the main body of the task force, and it sailed five days ago. At a speed of twelve knots, it will reach Equatorial Guinea in seven days. It consists of the transports *Aragon* and *Castilla*, the oiler *Teide*, and three destroyers. Tomorrow, I fly to Cadiz and will sail in *Canarias* as the task-force commander. At twenty-five knots, I will reach Guinea at the same time as the other ships, and I will be in command of the entire task force. I will rendezvous with the aircraft carrier *Dedalo* south of the Canary Islands, so I will have air support."

"What is the aircraft deployment from the *Dedalo*?" Carrero asked.

"It will carry fourteen Sea King helicopters. Their antisubmarine gear is being removed and will be left in the Canaries. The helicopters will be converted to the transport configuration."

"Alberto, it is important that the carrier be kept out of the news as much as possible. I don't want to advertise that it is there and have certain parties speculating on what its helicopters might be doing besides evacuating refugees. In addition, the ship has a scheduled change of command ceremony scheduled for April 7, when Captain Diaz will relieve Captain Javier. I do not want to change that date and create further speculation on the carrier's role in

314

this operation. Therefore you must wrap up the secret part of this operation and transfer the Valhalla cargo that you retrieve to the *Canarias* where it will be under your personal supervision."

"Yes, sir. The carrier will steam a minimum of forty miles offshore, so it won't be visible. We will minimize the impact of air operations."

"Your humanitarian mission is of course paramount, but the secret element of your mission is equally critical."

"Yes, sir. I'll use the helicopters to retrieve the entire Valhalla cargo from the cave on the Hoffman plantation east of Niefang, Rio Muni, on the mainland."

"I wish we had taken that step before independence, Alberto, but who could have foreseen that Macias would be so unstable and unpredictable?"

Alberto did not respond to that remark. It was clear to him that Macias's instability was known in advance to anyone who cared to look. "Sir, I believe we need to be prepared for any eventuality and a hostile response when we arrive there."

"I agree, Alberto. That's why I am assigning you the entire Unidad Operaciones Especiales force, the UOE, to this operation. The entire 150-man force is being flown to the Canaries as we speak. They will then be flown to the *Dedalo*."

Alberto was surprised but grateful. The UOE was a new and elite force, and this would be their first deployment. "Thank you, sir. I hope that their capabilities won't be needed."

"So do I, but I'm afraid that it is all too likely that it might come to that. To the extent you can, try to keep any combat operations away from the refugee evacuation efforts in the cities, ports, and airports. We can't afford to draw attention from the world press or from foreign espionage services, including the CIA. We face a difficult situation with Valhalla, but I'm afraid we can't go back and do it differently. We must keep our involvement in Valhalla secret. That means that when you retrieve the cargo, Alberto, you must take it to a secret storage location. I don't know how to say this delicately, but I don't want to know how and where this occurs, if you understand my meaning."

"I understand the concept of plausible deniability, sir. We can't take this material to the Americans, thereby admitting our collaboration with the Nazi regime on Valhalla, nor can we destroy the material without knowing what it contains or who may have accessed it."

"Well said, Alberto. I wish you luck in this operation."

As Alberto left Carrero's office he wondered what difficulties he would encounter and where he would take the Valhalla materials that he retrieved. He also wondered what challenges would be posed by Karl Hoffman—and other parties.

116

New York City.
March 1969

* * *

Paul reread the newspaper account of the situation in Equatorial Guinea. He chastised himself for not acting sooner and hoped that it was not too late. Hopefully his son, Rob, would arrive soon with the status of their Gulfstream jet.

As if on cue, the door to their penthouse opened, as Robert arrived from his journey to Teterboro Airport in nearby New Jersey.

"I've been waiting for you. I hope you have good news, Rob."

"It's not the best, but bear with me," his son responded. He walked up to the liquor cabinet and poured himself a glass of fino sherry. His father had already drained about a third of the bottle.

"How are the flight clearances coming?" Paul replied, as his son joined him at the bay window overlooking Central Park.

"Not so good. All of the former French colonies are taking their sweet time approving our landing clearances, although they at least gave us overflight approvals. Our chief pilot said it could take another week of cables back and forth, so—"

"We don't have that much time," Paul interrupted.

"I know, so I went ahead and used your connection through the Spanish air ministry and Carrero's office. We have a clearance to land at Villa Cisneros in Spanish Sahara, so that will at least get us over the pond. I also took the liberty of cabling your friend Santos in Luanda, Angola. He came right back with a clearance to land at Sao Tome. That's as close as I can get us for now."

"What about Santa Isabel or Bata?" Paul inquired.

"They're out of the question. It's considered a war zone now, and the Spanish government said no under any circumstances."

Paul thought about that for a moment. He ran the options through his mind, but none of it would make sense unless he could find out more about the situation. "All right, we have a plan. What are the clearance arrangements and logistics?"

"It's a little less than three thousand nautical miles from Teterboro to Villa Cisneros, and we'll do that nonstop. I've already arranged to take on a full load of fuel there. Then it's a little more than nineteen hundred miles to Sao Tome. The total flying time in the Gulfstream will be about eleven hours."

"Did you set it up?"

"Yes; we'll be ready to depart tomorrow at 0600. With the time change and fuel stop we can be in Sao Tome at about midnight their time."

Paul looked at his son with a puzzled look. "What do you mean 'we'?"

"I mean I'm going with you."

"No, you're not."

"Look, Dad, you don't have a choice. We only have the chief pilot available, because the other two pilots are on vacation, since we weren't planning to fly the plane in the next two weeks. It will take them at least two days to get back here. I'm a copilot qualified in the Gulfstream, so we have the required two crew members."

"You're supposed to be in your last semester at Columbia. What are you going to do about that?"

"I've already got enough credits to graduate. The only mandatory class I've got is an ROTC course, and I can fake that out for a couple of weeks. Remember, ROTC was driven off the Columbia campus, so we have to keep a low profile. I already called the detachment commander and squared it with him."

Paul looked at his son and could not come up with any reason to say no. "All right, but your mother is going to be appalled."

"I already am appalled."

Both men turned quickly, surprised as Liz Hoffman announced her presence.

"I suppose you heard all of that," Karl said.

"Yes, and I don't approve, but under the circumstances, I know it's futile for me to object."

"Mom, there won't be any danger. Spanish troops are in charge there. We just need to get Grandfather out of harm's way."

Liz merely smiled weakly, resignation on her face.

117.

Off the Rio Muni coast, 0800,
March 25, 1969

* * *

"What's the current situation?" Admiral Alberto Ortega addressed the captain of the *Canarias* as he stared through his binoculars at the Rio Muni coastline before turning to his subordinate.

"Sir, we are anchored here for now with our guns trained on the shore in a manner that can be observed by anyone looking seaward. The transport *Aragon* has begun loading refugees from lighters from shore, and one destroyer is also standing by."

"Very well, I think we've made our point with our main battery. I want to transfer to *Dedalo* as soon as possible."

"Yes, sir, a helicopter is on its way and can lift you from the fantail with a winch. I'm afraid it won't be very dignified," the captain apologized. The *Canarias* didn't have a place on deck large enough for a Sea King to land.

"That's all right. It will be exciting," Alberto replied weakly.

"May I ask your intentions, sir? I thought you would continue to fly your flag on *Canarias*," the captain replied hopefully.

"I will continue to do so, but I need to determine the readiness of the UOE force on *Dedalo* for a special mission," Alberto replied curtly.

"Yes, sir," the captain replied, chastised for his inquisitiveness.

* * *

"How soon can the mission launch?" Alberto inquired after arriving on *Dedalo*.

"We'll be ready at 1030 and it's a one hour flight," the UOE commander replied.

"Fine; you should know that I will accompany you."

"Excuse me, sir? I must object. We are likely to be landing in a firefight, and I cannot guarantee your safety."

319

"Your objection is noted," Alberto replied sternly. "I will change out of these dress whites, if that is your objection, and carry an appropriate weapon, but I am going. Is that clear?"

"Yes, sir."

"Right. So please brief me again on your landing plan."

118

Near Niefang. Equatorial Guinea. 0930.
March 25, 1969

* * *

Karl was stunned. *Can this possibly be?* Yet there before him stood his firstborn son, Hans. Karl barely recognized him as he got out of the Land Rover and slowly walked over. Karl did not even bother to greet his brother, Walter, who also got out of the Rover and followed Hans. Karl's paralysis finally ended as he ran to Hans and embraced him and wept for joy.

"I can't believe it's actually you, Hans! Why didn't you let me know you were coming?"

"Father, I'm sorry, but this trip was organized at the last minute," he responded, suppressing a sob and finally pulling away from his father's embrace.

Karl looked at Hans and then at Walter. He finally turned back to Hans. "Of course, I'm ecstatic to see you, but you did pick the worst possible moment. Guinea is in turmoil, and Spain is evacuating all European nationals."

"I know. That's why we're here. We want you to leave with us."

"Why are you here, Walter?" He turned to his brother as his expression changed.

"You know that I'm here to retrieve the last of the Valhalla materials from the cave. It is no longer safe here, and in the future we might not be able to reach this place."

"You're right about that. In fact, I'm surprised you were able to drive here without being stopped by some of the unorganized militias that answer only to Macias."

"It was not a problem, Karl. I didn't even have to bribe anyone. It was as if they were expecting us and had orders to let us pass."

Karl immediately had an uneasy feeling about that, but it wasn't his first priority. "I don't care how you got here or that you are here to retrieve the rest of those cursed materials, Walter. I only care that I finally have Hans back!" He turned to Hans. "Come inside, my son, so we can talk."

Hans did not have time to reply, as both Wekesa and his grandson, Felipe, drove up in another Rover, jumped out excitedly, and ran over to Karl.

Wekesa described what was happening. "There is a large group of militia in Niefang. They are agitated, and I believe they are headed here!"

Karl thought quickly. They might be coming for him—or for Walter and Hans. He couldn't be sure, but he knew they should prepare for the worst.

"Wekesa, we'd better arm ourselves!"

119

Bata Airport, Equatorial Guinea, 0945,
March 25, 1969

* * *

Jack's chief pilot, Mike Henry, approached him after returning from the airport operations center. "What did you find out, Mike?" Jack Kurtz asked excitedly.

"We might want to get out to the Hoffman plantation right away. I learned that the local militias were excited about two white men who arrived from South Africa on a ship and were headed to the plantation. The militias were ordered to let them pass."

"Shit, I bet that's Karl's brother and maybe his son. All those pieces we've been playing with in the last few months are finally coming together, and the chickens are coming home to roost. That undercover contact I have in South Africa may have paid off. I think it might involve Operation Valhalla. Somebody must have authorized letting the two white men pass. The only question is who is pulling the strings behind the scene."

"It could be KGB or Cubans."

"Yeah, but we can't sit around and wait to see."

"We can be there in about twenty-five minutes in the Helio," Henry replied, referring to the ex-US military Helio U-10 Courier aircraft that was assigned to them. The Helio only needed a couple hundred feet of runway to operate.

"All right, we'll do it, but here's the deal. You're only going to drop me off and then get your ass back to Santa Isabel."

"No way, boss; the landing zone could be hot, and you'll need me."

"Listen, Mike, and don't argue. You're my deputy here, and your first responsibility is to get all that equipment on Fernando Poo secured, knocked down, and transported out of there. The C-123 that arrived at Santa Isabel is for just that purpose, and you need to be there. We may only have a couple of days. I'll be fine. If I can't get out to the coast, I can get over to Oyem in

Gabon, where Henri Fortier is currently holed up and pretty much doing what we're doing. After the C-123 departs, you're to follow it in the U-10 over to Sao Tome, where our other station is still secure. Santos knows you're coming."

"Jesus, boss, I can't just leave."

"Oh yes, you can! You know the score. The company insists we do it this way."

Mike Henry bit his lip, unable to argue with that CIA missive.

120

Near Niefang, Equatorial Guinea,
March 25, 1969

* * *

Yuri Kozlov stared through his binoculars from his hidden position. He was in a stand of trees, next to the access road from Niefang on the north side of the east-west airstrip on the Hoffman plantation, east of Niefang. He could clearly see the hacienda, aircraft hangar, and some of the outbuildings about three hundred meters away on the south side of the airstrip. As he finished his assessment, he turned to his chief operative, Jorge Sanchez, who had pulled up in a Jeep and walked and crawled over to join Kozlov.

"What's the situation, Jorge?"

"I have thirty men here on this side, and another twenty are quietly approaching from the south side of those buildings that you are viewing. Per our direction, the national guard and militias let the two white men pass when they arrived in Bata. They asked about renting trucks. We told them we would deliver two trucks wherever they wanted, and they told us to bring them here. They are South African and are almost certainly Walter and Hans Hoffman. They have only been here an hour or so. One of my men observed the shorter one, probably Walter, as he walked off to the east along the south side of the airstrip. My man then lost sight of him."

"What about that plane that landed here about fifteen minutes ago?"

"I believe that aircraft is used by the CIA. It dropped off a single white man before taking off. I'm certain it was Jack Kurtz, who is the lead CIA operative here."

"So it seems that everything is happening at once as the chaos deepens here, Jorge. We must seize this opportunity to uncover the Valhalla secrets."

"Shall we move now to take the place?"

"In a few minutes, but first I want to see who comes out of the hacienda, where they all seem to have gathered."

* * *

"You must be reasonable, Karl. Why have your brother and son arrived here? Does it have anything to do with Valhalla?" Jack looked toward Hans, who stood there silently.

"You may be Paul's friend, Jack, but you and your brethren disgust me. This country has enough problems without interference from the CIA, KGB, and their operatives. Why don't you return to Santa Isabel while you still can?"

At that moment Wekesa arrived to give his report. "I've sent Felipe to the village of Ngon to the east of here near our plantations. He will return in an hour or so with additional men and arms."

Karl nodded. He had dismissed the domestic help and other staff the previous day, telling them to return to their villages, where they would be safer.

"So, we only have a handful of pistols and one rifle. You can find more ammunition and several rifles in the storage building."

Karl paused as he sized up their bleak situation and then turned to his son. "Will you go out and retrieve those, Hans? It's the second building behind the hacienda."

As Hans nodded, Jack intervened. "I'll help him. It's probably too much to carry."

Karl scowled at Jack but finally nodded his approval. He turned to Wekesa, but waited until Jack closed the door behind him before speaking. "Let's go out on the airstrip and see if we can spot Walter. He probably went to the cave."

"Yes, and I'm sure when he returns, he will want help loading the cargo into some kind of vehicle," Wekesa replied.

* * *

"All right, we're ready. Here come Karl Hoffman and his friend. Call your men on the south side and tell them to begin. Remind them that they must take all the white men alive," Kozlov commanded.

Sanchez nodded and spoke briefly in both Fang and Spanish into the walkie-talkie. When he finished, Kozlov gave the signal to the rest of their men. Within seconds, they started the Jeep and two large trucks and drove the brief distance on the access road, around the trees, and onto the airstrip.

They headed directly for Karl and Wekesa, who were standing in the middle of the airstrip looking east.

* * *

"Is that Felipe and our men?" Karl knew almost as soon as he said it that it wasn't.

"Shall we run toward the house?"

"We'd never make it, Wekesa. We need to stand our ground here and buy time for Hans, Jack, and your grandson. Don't draw your pistol."

Wekesa nodded as the Jeep came to a halt five meters away. Both men watched as a white man and a black man leaped out of the Jeep, pistols drawn, followed by a couple of dozen militiamen from the two trucks. The militiamen were carrying AK-47 automatic rifles and lesser weapons. They quickly formed a circle around Karl and Wekesa.

Karl watched as the white man and his aide approached. He was stunned as he recognized Sergio Castillo, who supposedly had died ten years ago.

"Hello, Karl. It's been a long time."

"You—you were supposed to have...died in a plane crash!"

"You're right, Karl. Sergio Castillo did die ten years ago. I am someone else, you see. Such details are unimportant now. What really matters is cleaning up some other old business. For example, perhaps you can share with me where the cargo is stored that your brother and son brought here twenty-four years ago."

"I don't know what you're talking about."

"Don't be ridiculous, Karl. You, your brother, or your son will eventually provide me with that answer. So why don't we save some time?"

All of the militiamen were intently watching the conversation and did not notice as Walter approached the group from the east end of the airstrip. He must have naturally assumed that these were the two trucks he was told would be delivered to the plantation. Yet, he must have sensed some danger, because he drew his Walther P-38 pistol.

"What's going on here?" Walter shouted.

One of the militiamen turned abruptly, startled by Walter's approach. "It is the other white man!" he shouted in alarm as he raised his AK-47.

Instinctively, and without delay, Walter aimed and pulled the trigger on his P-38.

As the man fell, the others shouted. Two opened fire on Walter. He died instantly.

Wekesa ran toward Walter without thinking. Two men fired AK-47s at him. Wekesa also died instantly.

Instinctively, Karl had unholstered his own P-38 and fired reflexively at one of the militiamen who had raised his AK-47 toward Wekesa. He got off one shot, which struck one militiaman in the left temple. He died before he hit the ground.

Other militiamen quickly recovered from the surprise and raised their weapons.

Kozlov and Sanchez were now screaming at the top of their lungs in both Spanish and Fang. "Stop the shooting now!"

All the men obeyed, except one, whose friend Walter had shot. He fired a quickly aimed single shot with his AK-47 at Karl.

The round struck Karl in the stomach, and he lost consciousness as he fell to the ground.

Without hesitation, Kozlov walked over to the militiaman, raised his pistol, aimed it at the man's head, and fired. He fell backward and died.

Sanchez immediately shouted in Fang. "The next who fires will answer personally to Macias, who will drink his blood!"

The group of militiamen immediately became silent as their fear of their country's president and his reputation registered with them.

A militiaman leading the other squad came running from behind the hacienda, approached Sanchez, and reported. "We have two more white men that we captured. They are a South African and an American. The South African was slightly wounded in the struggle."

Kozlov cursed as Sanchez berated the militiaman. Kozlov interrupted him. "We don't have time for that. Tell him to take them both to Mongomo now. They must keep both white men alive at all costs, or they will pay for their incompetence."

Sanchez repeated the instructions in Fang and dismissed the militiaman leader. Sanchez and Kozlov returned to where Karl had fallen. He was being attended by a militiaman medic. He was semiconscious and groaning in pain. Kozlov looked at Karl and shook his head, finally turning to Sanchez.

"He probably won't make it. We should go to Mongomo right away and ensure that Kurtz and Hoffman's son are kept alive. Tell your men to search the premises before we leave."

Sanchez barked his orders and then jumped in the Jeep with Kozlov, who started the vehicle and began driving back to the access road north of the airstrip. Pulling off the airstrip and under the canopy of trees, Kozlov stopped and looked back. The militiamen were firing their guns in the air in some sort of disorganized celebration.

"Let them have their rape and plunder. We only want to find out where the cargo was moved to," Kozlov said cynically.

"What's that noise?" Sanchez asked.

Both men became silent. The faint deep rhythmic beating sound increased slowly in volume as the two men looked at each other.

"Those are helicopters. Let's get under cover over there quick," Kozlov urged.

The two men had barely reached a thicket where they could safely observe when the first Sea King swept overhead followed by three more. As the helicopters flew over the airstrip, the militiamen did just the wrong thing by firing their small arms at the rotorcraft. The response was instantaneous.

The first four Sea Kings were each equipped with two .50-caliber Browning machine guns and immediately returned fire in a continuous circle around the forty or so militiamen milling around on the airstrip, where there was no cover. Within seconds more than twenty of the militiamen fell to the deadly fire, and the rest panicked and scattered in every direction, followed by the helicopter gunships. Only about ten made it to the jungle underbrush, and several of them were wounded.

Eight more Sea Kings then appeared. Two landed just east of the aircraft hangar near the south perimeter of the airstrip, near the entrance to the cave. The other six split into a semicircle, landed, and disgorged sixty UOE members in full battle gear. They promptly began to secure the airstrip perimeter and follow the militiamen who had escaped.

Kozlov watched the entire battle scene in fascination. "There is a reason why these helicopters are here, Jorge. It obviously involves more than just a rescue operation."

"Yes, it must. We can safely observe from here. Our vehicle is well concealed. What are those helicopters?"

"They are American-built Sea Kings, and they are flown by the Spanish navy. My guess is that they are under the personal supervision of Admiral Alberto Ortega."

* * *

"We have secured the perimeter, sir. The few remaining militiamen have fled," the UOE leader reported, saluting as Admiral Ortega exited the Sea King.

"That's good. Take a few men and search the hacienda. Get the loading team to work right away in the cave. You can find the entrance about fifty meters east of the hangar, as indicated on your map. Have your medic follow me. I see there is a white man moving over there," Alberto noticed the man trying to get up.

Alberto and the UOE medic rushed over to the man, who staggered a few paces and then fell again. As he and the medic rushed over to him, Alberto was dismayed to see it was Karl. The medic began attending Karl's wounds as Alberto spoke quietly.

"Please be still, Karl. My medic will fix you, and we'll fly you to a hospital."

"It's...too late...for...that." Karl struggled for air.

Alberto looked at his medic, who shook his head. Alberto turned back to Karl. "We are taking all of the Valhalla materials away from here, Karl."

"That's good. It has been...a curse on...this country." Karl grimaced in pain.

Alberto was interrupted as a UOE officer came up to him, followed by a black man whom Alberto recognized as one of Karl's key staff. Alberto rose to meet the officer.

"This man says he's an employee of the plantation, Admiral. He brought a number of armed men with him to repel the militia."

"I'm afraid it's too late for that," Alberto replied.

Felipe had quickly gone over to see where his grandfather, Wekesa, had fallen and died and then came back over to kneel beside Karl.

"Where is...Hans?" Karl struggled as he recognized Felipe.

"They took him away, Karl," Felipe said after a brief pause. He reached around Karl and held him slightly upright.

"Alberto…it was Sergio. He led…the attack. He's…alive and…" Karl turned to Alberto, but could not finish as the pain deepened. He struggled to breathe.

Alberto did not want to question Karl's assertion about his sister's supposedly late husband and did not reply.

Karl looked at Alberto, then at Felipe, and finally back to Alberto.

"Tell Hans and Paul…that…I love…them," Karl said slowly and then collapsed into Felipe's arms, slowly letting out one final breath.

The medic checked for a pulse. He turned to Alberto and shook his head.

Alberto stood, looked around at the carnage around them, at the surrounding jungle, at the hacienda, and back to Karl. After a long silence, Felipe finally spoke.

"We will bury Karl, his brother, and my grandfather, Admiral. We will also tend to the others." Felipe swept his hand around toward the other bodies.

"Did you see who was leading the militia?" Alberto asked Felipe.

"No, I left to get additional men and arms before they arrived."

They were interrupted as the commander of the UOE force approached Alberto. "We have finished loading the materials, sir. There was only enough to fill one helicopter."

"Did you thoroughly search the cave? Were there any white men among the attackers that we killed?"

"Yes, sir, we did a thorough search. There were no whites among the dead attackers."

Alberto reflected on this for a moment. He racked his brain trying to remember the details of the plane crash ten years ago that supposedly killed Sergio Castillo, or whoever he may have really been.

"Did you search the rest of the premises?"

"Yes, sir, we found no one else and no other items of interest, but there is a single-engine aircraft in the hangar." The UOE officer pointed to the hanger where the Spartan Executive aircraft that Karl had acquired in 1940 was stored.

"Pull the aircraft out of the hangar and destroy it."

Alberto looked around him again. He would have to think about the pieces to this puzzle later. He and his team needed to depart before more militia arrived, and he needed to fly the cargo he acquired from the cave to the safety of his cruiser *Canarias*, which he had ordered to sail to Santa Isabel harbor and anchor.

* * *

"I should have checked for that all along. That cave made an ideal storage site," Sanchez cursed.

"You could not have known. The cave was totally hidden," Kozlov replied, as he observed the UOE force finish shuttling between the cave entrance and the Sea King. It had taken a while for him to realize what was happening, since the cave entrance was hidden by vegetation from their vantage point. Finally, he realized what the portable generator and lights signified.

"Where will they take the materials?"

"My guess is they will go to Spain itself, since they no longer securely control any other territory other than Spanish Sahara," Kozlov replied.

"That will present us with challenges."

"Yes, Jorge, it will. That's my job to unravel, while you continue the struggle here."

"You cannot return to Spain."

"That's probably true, but I have another option."

Villa Cisneros, Spanish Sahara, 1900,
March 25, 1969

* * *

"Did you find out anything?" Rob Hoffman asked as his father approached him in the airport operations office.

"The news is pretty sparse. The evacuation is fully underway and might only last a couple more days. According to the reports I could get, there hasn't been any violence that affects the evacuation."

"Well, I haven't had any further luck getting landing clearances for any of the former French colonies. They're all paranoid about coup plots and the like. I guess they don't trust people arriving in private aircraft," Rob responded.

"I managed one feat. That DC-8 you see over across the ramp was chartered to bring a few Spanish military medical personnel to Santa Isabel and return to Spain with refugees. It now has clearance to land in Guinea, and it leaves in one hour. Between my letter from Carrero and the circumstances of our being here with the Gulfstream, I managed to talk my way onto the flight, since it's only half full," Paul said.

"That's great, so there's room for me, too."

"I'm sorry, Rob, but I was barely able to get myself on board. Besides, I need you for the crew on the Gulfstream, and you need to launch for Sao Tome first thing in the morning. Our landing clearance there expires at midnight tomorrow."

"Dad, I don't like you going in there alone."

"Don't worry. The airports are secured by Spanish military personnel and civil guards. I need you and the Gulfstream nearby when the time comes."

"We aren't ever going to get landing clearance for Equatorial Guinea."

"I know. So sit tight in Sao Tome, and keep working on clearances for Cameroon and Gabon. I might need you in Yaounde, Cameroon, or Oyem or Libreville in Gabon."

"You've got a plan," Rob replied, smiling.

"Yes, but I'll have to see what's happening on the ground first."

Santa Isabel Airport, Equatorial Guinea. 0600.
March 27, 1969

* * *

Paul walked carefully across the airport ramp toward the hangar where the CIA kept its aircraft. Since he was already inside the secured perimeter, there were no guards to challenge him on the ramp, although that could change as he approached the hangar.

The previous day Paul had kept a low profile as he sniffed around the airport, looking for information about his father as well as for a means to get to Rio Muni. He sensed that there was no official way to do that, so he decided on a reasonable alternative. He would "borrow" the CIA's light aircraft that they kept here for local transportation.

Paul quietly approached the hangar in the early predawn. He saw with relief that the door was open. The Helio U-10 Courier sat there invitingly. Paul walked over to the aircraft, opened the cockpit door, and placed his duffel bag on the rear seat.

Now if only I can get this thing running and taxi out quietly, I can...

"Looking to take a little scenic flight, Paul?"

Paul turned with a start to see Mike Henry.

"Oh, hi, Mike. I was just checking out your neat little plane. It must be able to get in and out of short fields real well," Paul responded lamely.

"Yeah, sure it does. Look, I know what you're trying to do, and it's too dangerous."

"I suppose. Where's Jack?"

"He's not available."

"He's in Rio Muni, isn't he?"

"Yeah, maybe he is, but it was against my advice."

"You need to fly me over there," Paul said firmly.

"Not a chance. As I said, it's too dangerous, and I have my marching orders."

"What are those?"

"You see that C-123 across the ramp, Paul? Last night we finished loading it with the remaining sensitive gear we had here, and the crew will fly it over to Sao Tome about an hour from now. I will follow in this U-10 that you came to steal."

"I was only going to borrow it."

"Of course. Well, the answer is still no."

"That's fine, Mike, but if you don't take me, I will find a boat or some other way to get there. I don't care. I have to get to my father. So if you'll excuse me, I'll head downtown to the harbor and find my way." Paul turned to grab his duffel bag.

"Wait a minute. You're serious, aren't you?"

"Of course. Put yourself in my shoes."

Henry was silent for a moment. *Obviously thinking of a way out*, Paul thought.

"All right, here's the deal. Follow me over to the chart board over there." Henry pointed to the desk at the side of the hangar.

Henry quickly did some quick measurements on the L-3D tactical pilotage chart that covered Equatorial Guinea, Sao Tome, and parts of Cameroon and Gabon.

"It's about 238 nautical miles direct to Sao Tome, and 392 if I detour by way of your Rio Muni plantation. Heck, that's only a little over an hour extra, and I've got enough range to do that. But the deal is just like with Jack. I come to a stop. You jump out. Then I'm on my way. Will that work for you?"

"Of course it will. I'm ready when you are."

"I assume you're carrying a piece with you."

"It's in my bag."

The two men walked back over to the U-10, and Paul retrieved his Beretta M1935.

"That's a cute little gun." Henry smiled.

"I've already killed one man with it who tried to kidnap my children."

Henry nodded grimly before replying. "I'm sure you did. You'll need something with more stopping power here."

Henry walked back over to a storage cabinet near the chart table and returned with a standard Colt M1911 pistol with a custom silencer.

"This has more stopping power than the Beretta. The silencer may also come in handy. Come around back of the hangar, and I'll give you the quickie course. We'll take off as soon as the C-123 departs."

* * *

"Admiral, we'll be ready to weigh anchor and depart in about an hour," the captain of the *Canarias* announced to Alberto as they stood on the port outside wing of the cruiser's bridge and watched the activity on shore.

"Thank you, Captain. Has all the special cargo been loaded and secured?"

"Yes, sir, the UOE commander and I personally supervised it. The UOE will maintain a round-the-clock guard of the materials while they're on the ship."

Alberto already knew that, having observed the activity from the bridge as the Valhalla materials were loaded off the Sea King helicopter and back onto the cruiser two days ago. Nevertheless, he felt obligated to confirm their presence on the cruiser. "What about the activities ashore? Is everything being wrapped up?"

"Yes, sir, the remaining members of our forces and the few remaining refugees were escorted to the transport *Castilla*. It weighed anchor and departed an hour ago, as you observed."

"That's good. So it's just us, then."

"There is one other thing, sir. Late yesterday, the UOE team went to the airport to ensure that all refugees were accounted for. They discovered one man who would not return to the harbor with them. He was carrying a letter from Admiral Carrero that authorized him to be in Guinea and remain, so the team did not view it within their authority to detain him."

"Who was it? What was his name?" Alberto immediately replied, although he knew what the answer would be.

"It was Paul Hoffman, sir. He said he was looking for a way to get to Rio Muni."

Alberto's heart sank. He wished he had anticipated that move by his cousin.

337

At that moment the two men looked up as they heard and then observed the U-10 aircraft over the city as it flew southeast.

"We don't have a clearance on that aircraft, sir."

"That's all right. I believe I know where it's headed." *Good luck to you, my cousin.*

124

Near Niefang, Equatorial Guinea,
March 27, 1969

* * *

Paul jumped out of the U-10 as it came to a stop. As soon as he was clear, Mike Henry applied power, and the airplane was off the ground in less than two hundred feet. Paul watched as the plane banked toward the southwest and headed toward Sao Tome. He then ran toward the hacienda. Before he reached it, Felipe came out of the building.

"What are you doing here, Paul? They've already evacuated all the Europeans."

"Where is my father?" Felipe did not answer. Paul instantly knew. The two men were briefly silent.

"I'm sorry, Paul. He and my grandfather were killed by the militias," Felipe finally answered.

Paul closed his eyes, suppressing a tear.

"I'm sorry about your grandfather. What happened?" Paul answered when he finally composed himself.

"The militia came here looking for Karl and your uncle."

"My uncle—what was Walter doing here?"

"He came for the...for the Valhalla materials," Felipe answered, obviously struggling with whether to tell Paul the complete truth.

Paul nodded. *Now it all made sense.*

"Where were the materials stored?"

"They have been hidden in the cave on the airstrip ever since the war."

Paul nodded again. *Of course, that's why I have been having nightmares for all these years.* Paul reflected briefly on this before returning to the present. "Did the militias take the materials?"

"No, Admiral Ortega arrived with many helicopters and commandos, and they killed most of the insurgents. They then took the materials out of the cave, loaded them in the helicopters, and flew away."

That was logical. I will deal with that when I return to Spain. "Where is Jack Kurtz?"

Felipe hesitated. Paul could see he was struggling with something.

"Where is he, Felipe?"

"He was here. He was asking about the Valhalla materials when the insurgents arrived. They captured him and took him to Mongomo with—"

"Yes, they took him with whom else, Felipe?"

"They took him with…with your brother, Hans."

"Hans was here? Is it true?"

"Yes, he came with your uncle. He was here to take your father away, rather than to help Walter with the Valhalla materials."

"We have to get to Mongomo right away. I suppose the roads are guarded and…" Paul's voice trailed off as he looked to Felipe for guidance.

"It will be impossible on the roads, of course. Both the main road to the south through Evinayong and the road to the north through Anisoc will be guarded by militia and national guard. You would be arrested immediately."

"Then there must be another way to get there," Paul answered, realizing that the smoking wreckage of the Spartan that he saw outside on the airstrip ruled out that element of his earlier plan.

"There is one way, Paul. It will be dangerous, and it will take several days, but we can get there if we follow the River Mbini upstream. You might know it as the Rio Benito. It goes through the territory of my family's clan, and there is no militia there. We will be on foot most of the time, but—"

"I don't care about the difficulty! How do we proceed?"

"Come over to the wall map in the study," Felipe answered.

The two men entered and walked through the hacienda to the study, where there was a wall map of Equatorial Guinea.

"We can take the Rover east to the Mbini, where it runs south to north, and follow it south to the bend. It then runs east to west, and we will follow it on foot upstream to the east. It is impassable for the Rover, but there is an ancient trail we can follow to Mongomo. We will have assistance from my clan at a couple of points, but the trail is mostly isolated."

"When do we leave?"

"We can leave right away." Felipe paused and then asked, "Would you like to visit your father's grave first?"

Paul nodded as he bowed his head. Felipe led them out and to the south of the hacienda to a place with a view west toward the sea. As they walked over, Paul could look west and see the Rio Mbini in the distance.

Paul walked over to the graves marked by three crosses and fresh flowers. His father's was in the middle, with Walter's grave on one side, and Wekesa's on the other.

"My grandfather and your father were like brothers," Felipe said quietly as the two men stood there.

Yes, they were, Paul thought, *even more so than Karl's real brother, Walter.* Paul stood there silently as he thought of all that had happened over a half century. *Would all that my father strived for now be in vain?*

Paul shook his head, not wanting to answer that question.

125

On the Mbini River, Equatorial Guinea.

March 28, 1969

* * *

Paul struggled with the heat and humidity. Although he was born and raised in Equatorial Guinea and considered himself in excellent physical condition, it had been forty years since he had moved away, and the relentless tropical environment took its toll. He watched as Felipe maintained a steady but measured pace ahead of him, obviously accounting for Paul's reintroduction to the tropical environment.

The previous day they had got as far as a village near the bend in the river, where they had to leave the Rover. Today they had made good progress since morning yet could only have progressed a few kilometers east because of the river's meandering.

It was now about noon, but Paul was struck by the darkness that seemed to surround them even at midday. The tall jungle canopy of vegetation in some places reached across to both shores of the river, completely shutting out the sun. The feeling of confinement was nearly overpowering, as the jungle sought to imprison them and impede their progress.

Paul and Felipe said little to each other as they maintained their steady pace. Paul watched as his partner pressed forward, occasionally using a machete to hack through thick vegetation. Felipe said little, but Paul knew he was completely aware of the world events that had created their current situation. As an emancipado whom Karl Hoffman had sponsored and overseen, Felipe had spent time in Spain that most Equatoguineans could only dream of. Felipe was educated in Madrid at Complutense University and was better educated than most Spaniards, yet he chose to return here.

Felipe had his own family to worry about, but he willingly was risking his life to help Paul reach his brother Hans and best friend, Jack Kurtz.

What does Felipe see right now? What is he feeling? I wonder if Felipe sees the future of this place—or whether he feels the darkness.

* * *

It was late afternoon. They had stopped for a break, and both men sat there quietly as they contemplated what might happen in the next few days. Paul had shared his plan with Felipe, but neither man could predict what obstacles they would face when they reached Mongomo.

Paul thought about the current situation in Equatorial Guinea. What had been a relatively prosperous country for Africa was now in chaos and economic collapse after the Spanish withdrawal. Paul pondered that for a moment.

The colonial period was virtually over. With the independence of Equatorial Guinea, Spain's only remaining territory was the desolate Spanish Sahara. Spain had ceded Ifni to Morocco in January. The Portuguese still held out, but their days were clearly numbered as they fought bloody colonial wars in their three continental territories in Africa.

What of the legacy the European colonial powers were leaving behind? Economic misery and continued neocolonial exploitation, unstable governments, and surrogate Cold War battlefields seemed to be Europe's, the Soviet Union's, and America's gift to Africa. Perhaps Felipe had an opinion on this.

"Would you mind if I asked you a question, Felipe?"

"Of course not; ask me anything," Felipe responded with a surprised look.

"In balance, has the presence of Spain here for all those years had a positive effect on the people and culture of your country?"

Paul could see that Felipe was taken aback. "I would...I would have to reply in two parts. For my own clan, your father was a gift to us. He gave of himself and his treasure to care for us. He provided health care, education, and steady, rewarding employment. In my own case, I could not fathom how I would otherwise have a position of such responsibility were it not for him."

"You mentioned your answer had two parts."

"Yes, I did. I think I know you well enough to be honest. Spain was like the other colonial powers, no better and no worse. I have seen what the French have done in Cameroon and Gabon, what the Belgians have done in the Congo, and what the Portuguese have done in Angola. I must be frank in saying that the rule of all these powers was brutal and without regard for the real welfare of the colonized peoples."

"I see. What about the education, eradication of disease, and other benefits that colonialism brought?"

"Those benefits were only incidental to the colonial powers' goals of exploitation. In the process, they destroyed tribal cultures, upset economic and environmental balances, and left us with a legacy of barbaric leaders who are just as bad, if not worse. This is not just the fault of the European powers. America, the Soviet Union, and China continue to follow exploitive practices," Felipe added.

"What about multinational companies?" Paul knew the answer, even as he asked.

"With the exception of your company, which I know follows fair trade practices, these companies are as bad or worse than the countries I mentioned."

Paul pondered that for several moments before he finally replied. "Thank you for your candor, Felipe."

Felipe nodded and smiled. "Perhaps we should get moving, Paul."

The two men picked up their small packs and again began their trek.

As they started down the trail again, Paul reflected on Felipe's wisdom. *Is that all that Western civilization can deliver, just the. . .darkness of colonialism and neocolonialism?*

Hours later, the two men stopped to create a camp at the end of their first full day. The jungle night rapidly encroached on the structure and obstacles that Felipe had created to encircle the site. These precautions and the open fire would keep animals away. They later sat quietly by the fire, eating from the meager provisions they had brought.

Both Paul and Felipe had similar personalities, more reflective and contemplative than open. Accordingly, they were each lost in thought.

Paul wondered what the future actually held for them. His immediate concern was finding and rescuing his brother and Kurtz, yet some things were no closer to resolution. What about Felipe and his family? What would these events mean to Paul's own family? What about the enigma of Valhalla that still hung over their heads?

All of these events were partly clouded over by a more existential question. *Is the darkness of the human soul our most dominant motive, or is there something better that we can achieve?*

126

Near Mongomo, Equatorial Guinea,
March 31, 1969

***

Paul had been waiting for nearly three hours for Felipe to return. It was the fourth day since they had abandoned the Rover and begun their trek up the river, and they were near Mongomo. Paul was exhausted but clearly anticipating what Felipe's scouting trip would reveal. Felipe knew people in the town, and he went there to size the situation up before he and Paul entered the town to face likely danger.

As if to answer his thoughts, Paul heard a noise from the brush near where he was waiting. He went to grab the pistol from his bag, but before he could, Felipe emerged from the brush and ran over to Paul.

"We are in luck. Your brother and Kurtz are there. The militia members guarding them are expecting their leaders to arrive in a couple of hours. Security is pretty loose right now, but will probably tighten up before they arrive."

"What leaders are we talking about?"

"It wasn't clear. It could be Macias, but there are foreigners involved also. Someone mentioned Cubans and Russians."

"All right, so we have to move fast," Paul said urgently.

"Your brother and Kurtz are being held in a small building on the outskirts of the town. There is only a single guard in the building. The others in the militia security team are several buildings away. They are mostly drunk, getting drunker, and playing loud music, so we have the element of surprise."

"What's your plan, Felipe?"

"They have three Jeeps. One is parked near the building where your brother is held, and the other two are near where the other militia members are. While you take the guard by surprise, I will disable the other two Jeeps and the radios in them. Two of my relatives will cut the two phone lines leaving town. We will then get in the remaining Jeep, and the four of us will escape toward the border with Gabon, which is only about two kilometers away. We will have to go another kilometer or so from there to reach the border station where your French friend might intercede."

"Great. We'll try to link up with Henri Fortier or his men there, or else head for Oyem, where he is stationed. My father's Twin Beech is there at the airport and supposedly ready to go."

"Good luck to us," Felipe said as the two men shook hands.

* * *

Paul approached the building with great care. He had already drawn the Colt and attached the silencer. He knew he must be ready.

As he rounded the corner of the building, he saw that the door was open. He approached it quietly. He could hear the loud music and drunken shouting several buildings away, and he hoped that Felipe and his relatives were successful in their tasks.

He reached the door. He took an extra breath and raised the pistol. *This is it.*

He walked swiftly through the door and into the dimly lit room. He saw Jack. His friend looked up with a surprised look. Paul looked quickly to the other side of the room.

The guard looked up in alarm and reached for his AK-47.

There was a muffled crack as a round from the silenced Colt found its mark. It hit the guard in the chest before he could even fully grab the AK-47. The impact from the .45-caliber round pushed the man backward into his chair. He fell against the wall.

Paul quickly walked over to fire again at point blank range, but saw that it wasn't necessary.

"Man, I'm glad to see you! Come over here and cut the cord on my hands. That guard has a knife in his belt," Jack exclaimed.

Paul quickly retrieved the knife, noticing the huge pool of blood on the floor next to the guard. He frowned and walked over to his friend and quickly cut the cord holding Jack's arms behind his back.

He saw another man lying on a stretcher on the floor. He walked over slowly. Paul was shocked. His fifty-two-year-old brother looked twenty years older. He was delirious and did not recognize Paul.

"He's in a bad way, Paul. His wound wasn't treated correctly, and he's gone downhill since yesterday. He must have a bad infection," Jack said gingerly, as he placed his hand on Paul's arm.

Paul had no time to respond as Felipe burst into the shack. "We need to go right now! My friends said the leaders are coming in from Bata, and they're only a few kilometers away."

Jack ran over to grab the dead guard's AK-47.

"Get him in the jeep outside quick, while I cover us," Jack said to Paul and Felipe, pointing to Hans's stretcher. Jack quickly exited the shack.

Within a couple of minutes they secured Hans and his stretcher to the Jeep. Felipe jumped in the driver's seat. Paul steadied the stretcher, and Jack sat in the back, AK-47 at the ready.

The Jeep lurched forward and tore down the dirt track toward the south of town. They weaved through the streets and came to town's boundary, heading for the stand of trees covering a bend in the road. They almost made it.

Screaming militiamen came pouring out of a building. They raised their rifles, but in their drunken stupor could not quite beat Jack to the trigger.

Set on automatic, Jack's burst of fire cut down three men. The rest dropped their rifles, panicked, and scattered.

Just as the Jeep rounded the corner, a militiaman appeared from around a building. He was not drunk, but as he started to raise his AK-47 Paul fire three rounds from his Colt. The second round found the mark. The left side of the man's head exploded.

They finally rounded the bend and lost sight of the town. They careened down the road for several minutes, as Paul held firmly to his brother's stretcher. Finally Felipe stopped the Jeep.

"We have to get out here. The border station is around the next bend. We need to take the stretcher and walk the rest of the way."

They removed the stretcher. Paul and Felipe carried Hans. Jack walked ahead of them with the AK-47, following Felipe's directions.

In about ten minutes they emerged in a clearing. Jack saw it first.

"There are soldiers at the border!"

"Yes, we're on the Gabonese side," Felipe responded.

"Oh shit, here comes trouble," Jack announced as they all saw a large mob of militiamen approaching the crossing from the Equatorial Guinean side.

One of them saw Jack and pointed. Within seconds they were all screaming at the Gabonese border guards.

"They're demanding that the border guards return us to their custody!" Felipe said.

"We need to get away." Paul saw that it would be difficult to do so, as the head of the border detachment and two other guards approached them with their weapons drawn.

"Paul, Felipe, I hope we have something up our sleeve for this."

They were rewarded almost immediately, as two truckloads of French Foreign Legionnaires arrived, deployed from their vehicles, and drew their weapons. Henri Fortier jumped out of the cab of the lead vehicle and walked over to them.

Jack laughed with relief. "Wow, I love it when the cavalry arrives in the nick of time! Henri, old boy, you're a sight for my tired, sore eyes!"

"Let me handle this, Jack," Fortier replied.

"I need a medic for my brother," Paul said.

Fortier motioned for the medic and then immediately became embroiled in an argument with the Gabonese commander. They screamed at each other in French.

Paul helped the medic and another legionnaire as they carefully took Hans and the stretcher over to one of their trucks. Hans was starting to come out of his delirium as the French medic continued to treat him.

Paul heard more screaming and arguing as the militiamen shouted from the other side of the border.

Finally, Fortier and Jack joined Paul and Felipe near the truck. "Gentlemen, we should get out of here immediately, since you've apparently worn out your welcome," Fortier suggested.

"I guess you worked some magic with the border guards," Jack said.

"Only because I had the legionnaires with me; the Gabonese resent us."

"Henri, my brother needs medical attention," Paul interrupted.

"Yes, of course. We'll be at the Oyem Airport in just a few minutes. It's only about twenty-five kilometers."

As they pulled away, Paul looked back at the mob of militiamen at the border crossing. A white man had emerged in front of the crowd. Paul had to squint to clearly see the man and was shocked by the man's appearance.

He looked like Anita's deceased husband, Sergio Castillo. How could that be?

Oyem, Gabon,
April 1, 1969

* * *

Paul sat with his brother all night as he came in and out of delirium and the effects of medication.

Paul took a quick nap, woke, and returned to his brother's side as the sun was rising. The medic and Henri Fortier were there. As Paul approached, Fortier came over to him.

"Paul, I'm sorry to say that your brother has a bad infection that has spread to his bloodstream. We can do nothing for him. He is awake now, and he asked for you."

Paul nodded and gingerly approached his brother's bed in the makeshift hospital tent. He sat in the chair next to the bed. He looked at Hans, who was awake, yet obviously struggling.

"Hello, Hans. I'm so glad I finally found you," Paul said softly in Spanish.

"Ah, my brother; I am so glad to see you. I'm so...so...sorry that I—"

Paul took his brother's hand to comfort him. "There is no need to be sorry, Hans. All that happened before means nothing. What matters is that we are finally united."

"I just...wish that it could have been...different for us."

"It happened for reasons that no longer matter. I just want you to recover so that we can take you home," Paul replied as he looked first at Hans and then the medic.

The medic shook his head somberly.

Hans clenched Paul's hand.

Paul looked up at the medic, who quickly came to his side.

"Paul...please promise me...that..." Hans was now struggling for air.

"Yes, go on, Hans," Paul gently urged.

"Promise that you will look...forward...not...backward..."

"Of course, Hans. I promise that I will do just that."

Hans smiled weakly and closed his eyes. His hand went limp.

Paul looked at the medic, but he knew. There was no pulse.

Oyem. Gabon.
April 2, 1969

* * *

Paul stood quietly beside Hans's grave. They buried him in a small cemetery at a mission, just outside Oyem, near the airport. As Paul looked at the simple cross, his thoughts were a kaleidoscope of nearly fifty years of memories. He finally turned to face Jack, Felipe, and Henri Fortier. They had been standing quietly and respectfully several paces behind Paul.

"I guess that closes an era for our family," Paul said simply.

The nearly quarter-century search for his missing brother was over.

"I'm sorry to press you, Paul, but there are two Noratlas aircraft waiting to take the rest of our men and equipment to Fort Lamy in Chad. When we leave, you will not be safe here."

"Is my father's Twin Beech ready?"

"Yes, it is. Our mechanics repaired it, and one of my pilots took the liberty of test flying it. All is in order. We also filled it with fuel before we destroyed the remaining supply in drums. Where will you go? You're surrounded by hostile countries."

"We'll go to Sao Tome. It's only about three hundred nautical miles, less than two hours."

"Santos is expecting us," Jack added, smiling.

"So that's it, then." Fortier motioned them to his waiting truck.

* * *

"It's ready to fly. Let's get aboard, Jack and Felipe."

"I'm not going with you," Felipe answered firmly.

"What do you mean? It's too dangerous for you to return," Jack answered.

"You can come with me to Spain," Paul added, after a brief hesitation.

"My wife, family, clan, and country are here. I must stay."

350

"That's ridiculous. You will be in danger as well as—" Paul replied, but was cut off by Felipe.

"Put yourself in my place, Paul. You would stay to protect your family."

"I can find a way to get you all out and—" Paul insisted but was again cut off.

"It is no use, Paul. You will not change my mind."

129

Portuguese Sao Tome.
April 3, 1969

* * *

Paul and Jack had been sitting at a table in the hotel for a half hour, nursing their beers silently. In fact, they had hardly spoken since landing at Sao Tome late the previous morning. Paul felt the tension was thicker than the tropical air around them.

Jack finally raised the issue, as Paul knew he would. "You know, it was a strange experience when we were captured. I heard a lot of helicopters in the background. The guards were screaming about an attack by Spanish commandos. I guessed that it was your cousin Alberto, since he was the only one in the area with that kind of airpower. I don't suppose you know why he conducted the attack, do you?"

"It seems obvious to me. He came to rescue my father," Paul replied curtly.

"That makes some sense, but why did he have such a large force? It seems he would have trouble justifying that for one white settler, even if he's an uncle."

"So what's your point, Jack?"

"I'm guessing he was there for something else."

"What might that be?"

"C'mon, Paul, I'm no idiot. We both know that Spanish Guinea was an intermediate destination for that U-boat that Hans and Walter were driving. Your father must have been privy to what they were doing and was a willing or unwilling participant in hiding the cargo."

"What are you saying?"

"I'm saying that Alberto was there to pick up the Valhalla cargo."

"That's kind of speculation, isn't it? I think it's far more likely that the cargo ended up in South Africa."

Before Jack could reply, Alexandre Santos entered the bar and walked over to their table. "So, I see that you two are having a little afternoon refreshment after your miraculous arrival. Where is your son, Paul?"

"He's at the airport preparing the Gulfstream for departure and getting our clearances. We plan to depart for Spain in the morning."

"How long will it take you?"

"It's about five and a half hours nonstop."

"That is truly an amazing capability," Santos said in awe.

"Yep, that's what three million dollars buys you," Jack added.

Paul looked at his friend in surprise. He had never heard Jack express envy.

"Why don't you come back with us, Jack?" Paul said.

"Thanks, Paul, but Alexandre and I have some business back in Luanda."

"I see."

Santos interjected with a smile as he tried to break the icy atmosphere. "By the way, Paul, I wanted to provide you with this bank transfer receipt and other paperwork for your sale of the Beechcraft to us. We will put it to good use in Angola, and it will start by taking Jack and me there in a couple of days." Santos had offered to buy the aircraft from Paul, and Paul accepted instantly. Santos had spent the last couple of hours on the paperwork.

"Thanks, Alexandre. I certainly will have no further use for it." Paul paused and then said, "You'll both have to excuse me now, but I have a lot of cables to reply to before we can leave here. I'll see you both later."

Paul looked at Jack as if to provoke a response. "We'll see you, Paul. Think about what we discussed."

"I will." Paul walked out of the bar. *Why is Jack pressing me on this?*

Paul knew he would have some questions for Alberto Ortega.

* * *

130

Alberto sat in his chair of the admiral's cabin, staring at the four ledger books on the chart table in the middle of the cabin. The cruiser was passing through the strait separating Tenerife and Grand Canary Islands. At its current high cruising speed, it would still be two days before it docked at the Ferrol naval base in Galicia, Spain.

Alberto sighed and got up to look at the books one more time. As he approached the table, he realized that they documented the sinister cargo carried by the U-boat. Unfortunately, not all of the cargo had remained in the cave in Rio Muni during the twenty-four years since it was deposited there.

He skimmed through two of the ledgers. They represented two distinct categories of the Valhalla materials. One was an inventory of the industrial and medical secrets, and the other contained an inventory of the nuclear weapons research of the Third Reich.

The notations made by hand in German on the first pages of each ledger told the story. In the industrial ledger, the notation said, "Delivered to Cape Town, December 1950," while the entry in the nuclear weapons research ledger stated, "Delivered to Cape Town, June 1960."

The remaining two ledgers most disturbed Alberto. They were duplicates of each other and contained an inventory of the biological warfare secrets of Nazi Germany. It was this category of Valhalla materials that was stored below deck in *Canarias*. It included a number of containers, including one sealed canister marked for special handling and precautions.

Alberto realized that there were probably duplicate ledgers for both the industrial and nuclear weapons categories of cargo. He assumed they were also delivered to Cape Town, South Africa. *Since both copies of the biological weapons category ledgers are here, I can presume that this category of materials is intact.*

Alberto was concerned about maintaining a tight lid of secrecy on this mission. *But where will I store these materials?*

131.

Alabos, Spain.
April 1969

* * *

Anita Ortega was not happy with her brother. "Would you please tell me what this is all about, Alberto? Who are those serious-looking men by the truck, and what is in the truck? I'm also mystified why you told me to send the household staff and Isabel to Haro for the afternoon."

"I'm sorry for the surprise, Anita, but this is of great importance. Those men are my most trusted associates from various elements in the navy. The materials in the truck are of national importance and must be hidden. I need your help for this. Where can we safely store these materials in a hidden place on our properties?"

"I would think that it's more important for you to tell me what happened in Guinea. Was Paul involved? What about his father? You must tell me because—"

"Listen to me, Anita. Karl is dead." Alberto paused to let that sink in. "Paul went there to bring him out, but Karl was already dead. I'm afraid that Paul is still missing. I'm doing everything in my power to find out his status. For now, you must concentrate on my request. Where can I safely hide and store these materials?"

Anita thought quickly and came up with an answer. "There is a large storage area in an old grain mill just north of Alabos. It belongs to another bodega, but they recently offered to lease it to us because they aren't currently using it. Access to it can be secured, and it's out of the way."

"That's perfect. We'll use that. It's perfect that it's not on our property in case someone comes here looking for the materials. But before we take the materials there, Anita, I must insist that nobody else must ever know about this."

"What about Paul? Doesn't he know that—?"

"I mean especially Paul. He was shielded from the knowledge of these materials by his father and me for a reason. It's especially important to keep it from him because of his American connection to Jack Kurtz, who works for the CIA."

Anita nodded her head in agreement, but did not speak. *How can I possibly keep this from him?*

132

Madrid. Spain.
April 1969

* * *

"I don't care why you've withheld this information from me for all these years, Alberto. That's not relevant anymore. Jack Kurtz knows that you took those materials from the cave, and he will be on your doorstep sooner or later about it."

"Please understand, Paul, that the circumstances were far different in 1944 than they are now. It is too late to let the genie out of the bottle on Valhalla. We must—"

"The horses left the barn a long time ago. The Soviets know about this, and we can presume that others do also. I've already killed four men to protect myself and my family from this curse. You need to tell me what you've done with these materials."

Alberto did not answer. He went to his desk in his private secure office in the navy ministry. He sat down, looked at his cousin, and finally replied. "I will be blunt, Paul. This matter is now a state secret, and you do not have a need to know any more than you already do. Furthermore, I must insist that you guarantee that you will not disclose what you know to anyone else. That includes your friend—and CIA operative—Jack Kurtz."

Paul controlled his response. *Of course Alberto is right. But I must set the tone.* "I understand what you've told me, Alberto, but please believe me when I tell you that I have disclosed nothing to Jack Kurtz. Yet he will persist until he understands what happened in the last month. More important, other, more sinister forces will pursue the secrets of Valhalla. I hope you're prepared to deal with that."

"That is my responsibility, Paul, and I will fulfill it. In a way, I guess this goes all the way back to 1943 with us. We both respected the boundaries and agreed not to dig too deep. I hope that will govern us now also."

"Perhaps that is possible, Alberto. Yet I suspect that this time there are events beyond our control that will shape our destiny."

133.

The next day. Alabos. Spain.
April 1969

* * *

Paul walked in unannounced. She was standing at the bay window looking westward. She turned as she heard him enter. For a frozen moment they looked into each other's eyes from across the room. Anita finally rushed over to him.

"Oh Paul, I knew you were still alive!" She wrapped her arms around him and put her head on his shoulder as she suppressed a sob.

Paul returned her embrace, and for a long time they held each other tightly. They finally loosened their embrace and faced each other.

"When did you find out?" Paul whispered.

"Alberto called me yesterday right after he learned you landed," she replied softly.

"It's been a nightmare."

"I'm sure it was. I'm so sorry about your father and...Hans."

Paul nodded but couldn't release or take his eyes off Anita. At age fifty, she was just as beautiful and desirable as ever.

I must stop this now. He slowly pulled back from her but took her hand and briefly caressed it before pulling farther back.

"I need to return to New York, but I couldn't leave without coming here first."

"I'm so glad you did. How did you get here?"

"I came in the Bonanza. I told Rob and my chief pilot to return home in the Gulfstream ahead of me. Life goes on, and the jet is needed for some pressing business in the Caribbean and several countries in South America."

Anita had acquired a new twin-engine Beechcraft Baron in 1964 for her regular travels around Spain. She had also replaced the older single-engine Bonanza that year with the newest model and based it in Madrid for Paul to use.

"When are you going back?" she asked.

"Tomorrow. I'll fly the Bonanza back to Madrid and catch an Iberia flight."

"Of course, but tonight let's celebrate your safe return with a special meal. We can try the outstanding Gran Reserva from the fabulous 1964 vintage. It will be released soon. I already gave Alberto a bottle, so he and Lucia can enjoy it before the release."

"Alberto was here?" Paul replied with a surprised look.

The sudden change in Anita's composure was a giveaway.

"What did he bring here?" Paul asked the obvious follow-up question.

He could see her struggling with the question; she was torn between two loyalties.

"It's all right, Anita. I don't want to put you in the middle of all this, but please realize that a wartime Nazi scheme called Operation Valhalla has saddled this family with a burden we didn't ask for. Three Hoffmans have already died because of it. Alberto retrieved the Valhalla materials from a cave in Guinea where they had been hidden since the war." He looked at her. "Did Alberto bring those materials here, Anita?"

He again saw here struggle as she balanced competing loyalties. "Yes, yes, he did. He came here in a truck with several military members who were not wearing their uniforms."

"Where did they put them?"

"They are in the cellar of the old mill on the hillside that we leased from one of our neighbors. The materials are secure there." She finished blurting it out and closed her eyes.

"You must show them to me."

"All right, I'll take you there," she replied with a sigh as she opened her eyes.

It only took a few minutes to drive to the mill about two kilometers away. Anita led Paul into the building and to the secure room, where she unlocked a massive lock and separate padlock. They walked in carrying two flashlights.

Paul took his time and looked carefully at all the sealed containers before coming to a larger well-sealed canister. It had skull-and-crossbones symbols on the side with a faded label that said in German. "WARNING: Biological Hazard requiring special handling upon unsealing. Refer to notations in inventory document."

"Is the document that it refers to in the cellar?" Paul asked after reading the label.

"No, but Alberto was referring to some kind of document as he stored each of the containers. Perhaps that was the inventory."

Paul nodded.

"What does it mean? What is in the canister?" she asked.

"I don't know, but it is probably associated with Nazi research on biological pathogens that could be turned into weapons."

Anita gasped. "Oh, what have we done, Paul? This canister could have deadly contents!"

"Perhaps that's true, but it's sealed, and that's the important thing."

"Why didn't Alberto turn it over to the Americans?"

"It's probably too late for that. Hiding it all these years and then revealing it raises uneasy questions about Spain's wartime collaboration with the Nazis on Valhalla. It's critical for Spain to continue its alliance with America."

"But you insinuated that other powers are looking for this also. Your father, brother, and uncle may have died because of it. Won't they come here looking for it?"

Paul pondered that for a moment before answering. "I don't know. It's unlikely they would have any idea it's here, only that it was taken somewhere in Spain and hidden in a secure government facility. Spain is still not America, and it's difficult for any foreign agents to operate here freely because of police and civil guard surveillance," Paul said without convincing himself.

"What will happen next?"

"For now, nothing; only time will tell how we deal with this ongoing curse."

134

Conakry, Guinea,
June 1969

* * *

"What have you decided to do about the Valhalla operation?" Jorge Sanchez inquired of his partner.

"I'm not sure yet. Whatever actions I take will have to be slow and deliberate. Admiral Ortega will obviously have secured the materials under maximum security in a country where a foreigner would be watched. It's not as easy to operate as in America and elsewhere in the West, despite the liberalizations under the Franco regime," Yuri Kozlov said.

"That's all quite true. Meanwhile, there are other urgent matters here in Africa."

"You're correct, Jorge. We need to continue the struggle. What is the situation, what are your intentions, and how can I support you?"

The two men had decided to meet here to map out future activities in Africa. For the last year, the events in Equatorial Guinea had occupied their attention. Without the imperative of Operation Valhalla, it was time to return to the remaining armed struggles in other countries.

"The situation in the Congo is somewhat stalemated, but the Portuguese colonies are ripe for the fall. The Portuguese are their own worst enemies. Their brutality is driving support to us."

"So how would you assess the situation in Portuguese Guinea, Angola, and Mozambique?" Kozlov asked.

"We are supporting the PAIGC in Portuguese Guinea and FRELIMO in Mozambique. They are slowly but relentlessly gaining the upper hand over the Portuguese, who only control the cities and not the countryside in those two places. It's more challenging in Angola, where we support the MPLA. However, the opposing movements FNLA and UNITA have support from the Americans, the South Africans, and the Chinese. We need to increase our level of effort to counter recent assistance from the CIA to these two groups."

"Then I will make that happen, but you should be on site and leading our assistance to MPLA," Kozlov asserted.

"I was going to suggest that, as well as more direct assistance from Cuba."

"Yes, Jorge, that is a good idea. An increased Cuban presence will have great credibility. The Soviet Union will continue to supply and bankroll your efforts."

"What will you do, Yuri?"

"I will spend most of my time supporting you, as soon as I can reactivate Agent Z in Europe to find a way to penetrate the Spanish veil around Valhalla," Kozlov said.

"Won't that be risky, considering Agent Z's position?"

"Yes, but I know of no other way to accomplish it. It may take a while to place Z in the right position, but I'm confident of our ultimate success."

135

New York City.
September 1969

* * *

"Here's a toast to Rob," Paul proclaimed as he raised his glass of manzanilla sherry to toast his son, who was about to leave for air-force pilot training.

"Yes, and please promise us you won't take any chances," Liz added.

"Really, Mom and Dad, you should realize we're not under your protection anymore," Pilar, Rob's sister, said.

"That's all right, Pilar. I accept everybody's best wishes." Rob raised his glass in acknowledgment.

As they all downed their sherry before dinner, Paul looked at his twin twenty-two-year-old children and marveled at how different they were. Rob looked very much as his father looked at that age, tall and slim with sandy hair, and he was following a pretty conventional path for a male college graduate in 1969 in the middle of the Vietnam War.

Pilar, on the other hand, was following a different path. She elected to stay in Vermont, where she had graduated from Middlebury College. She wanted to live an "alternative" lifestyle with some friends on a farm. Neither Paul nor Liz could dissuade her, and they finally decided to bow to her decision.

As Paul looked at his daughter he was struck by the similarity of her features to those of her late namesake grandmother. She was also tall and slim, with beautiful facial features and long sandy hair. Paul found it hard to grasp that his mother had died thirty years ago this month, on the first day of another war. He tried to erase the thought that his son could end up in Vietnam after his pilot training.

Washington, DC,
March 1970

* * *

Jack stared at his boss, CIA Director Richard Helms, as he waited expectantly for him to finish reviewing a document. Jack was a favorite of Helms, and the relationship went back to OSS days. Jack couldn't help but notice how different Helms was from Allen Dulles, who had died the previous year. Dulles was casual and liked to look at their business as a big game, while Helms was more somber and all business.

Helms finally looked up from his document and greeted his protégé. "Welcome back from Africa, Jack. I've read your report. You don't sound very optimistic about the situation in Angola."

"We're facing some formidable support that the MPLA is getting from the Soviets and Cubans. The Portuguese are facing opposition at home from draftees who don't want to fight in some colonial war, to maintain an empire they have no interest in. It sort of sounds like—"

"Like Vietnam, I suppose you're trying to say," Helms interrupted.

"Well, yeah, boss. That's what I'm trying to say."

"As it turns out, I'm going to throw you in that briar patch next."

"What's going on in Vietnam that requires my skills?"

"Actually, the problem is in Cambodia."

"Yeah, I've been following that in the dispatches."

"Then you'll understand, Jack, why I need you undercover for a while in Cambodia, as well as Vietnam, Laos, and Thailand. Our intelligence and special ops needs coincide with your availability, your previous Southeast Asia experience, and your success in managing the operations in Spanish Guinea, including your Mongomo adventure."

"I was hoping I could follow up on the Operation Valhalla issues. I'm convinced that the Spanish know more about Valhalla then they've let on."

"We'll get to that eventually, Jack, but we don't want to pressure Spain right now. They aren't as important for SAC bases as they used to be, but they are politically crucial. They're our most reliable ally in Europe. They replaced Foreign Minister Castiella last year and the tone of cooperation has shifted. It's not the time to raise Valhalla."

Jack nodded, but did not reply. *I'll bide my time. There will be another opportunity to confront Alberto.*

137.

New York City.
April 1971

* * *

"We've tried to follow your letters, but please tell me what's really going on," Paul inquired of his son, Rob, who had just arrived home on leave.

"I can probably sum it up better now. I graduated from undergraduate pilot training, that's UPT, in September 1970. I did all right and graduated just barely in the top third of my class."

"That's good, but I thought you might have even been higher, given that you were already a pilot."

"Sure, I aced the flying part of UPT and most of the academics, but I guess I'm not their model of 'Mickey Mouse' military tradition stuff. They think my attitude is bad. Not only that, but the academy lifers always get the best deal, and since I'm just an ROTC graduate, I have to feed on the leftovers."

"What's a lifer?" Paul inquired.

"A career person. It mostly applies to enlisted men, but I apply it to officers also. The lifers watch out for each other, and 'citizen soldiers' like me are viewed with suspicion."

"I see. So how did this all play out for you?" Paul was growing more curious now.

"Well, I didn't get to choose my flying assignment. In fact, they've been cutting back and now have a surplus of both pilots and officers. They threatened me with a desk job, so I volunteered for the only aircraft assignment that was open, and that was C-47s."

"That's like an old DC-3. I thought they were all gone in the military."

"They're about to disappear from the SAC inventory, but when I finished the short C-47 course in November, they assigned me to Malmstrom Air Force Base in Montana, where they have a single C-47 on the 'base flight.' That's the unit that does miscellaneous flying missions there to support the Minuteman missile wing, which is the principal activity at that base. Just before I left on leave, they informed us that SAC was ditching all the remaining C-47s. Ours will be gone in June, so I'm up for reassignment."

"After this point, your last letter was a little confusing."

"It's simpler than I let on. They initially paired me with a missile officer on the base to learn what he does, hoping it would 'inspire' me to seek a non-flying job as a missile officer."

"I take it you weren't inspired."

"The guy they paired me with turned out to have as bad an attitude problem as me. He and I have a few things in common. We were both born on July 19, although he's a year younger. He's also named Robert, and he also flies, although his vision wasn't good enough to enter air force pilot training. He and I both rebel at the chickenshit in SAC. Other than that, our backgrounds are different. He's from a middle-class family. Yet he's the only guy in the air force I've been able to make friends with."

"He sounds bitter about being forced to serve."

"Actually, he's not. He believes in universal national service. He says that if enough rich kids got their asses shot off, then there would be fewer wars. He believes that most of the wars we were in were screwed up initially by the professional military, like Pearl Harbor, and are then won by citizen soldiers like him and me."

"That's an interesting philosophy. So what happened next?"

"I raised hell up the chain of command about not getting a flying assignment. So they finally are sending me to OV-10 school next month. I'm pretty excited about that."

"I'm not familiar with that aircraft," Paul replied.

"The OV-10 Bronco is called a LARA, a light armed reconnaissance aircraft. It does special missions in Vietnam, for example."

"So, that's where you'll go when you finish your transition course?"

"That'd be my guess. Heck, I'd do anything to avoid being a missile weenie or a paper pusher."

"Don't let your mother hear that. She won't like the fact that you could be going there. It was traumatic enough for her when you and I had our little African adventure."

"Actually, it was kind of exciting, wasn't it?"

Paul just shook his head.

Alberto Ortega's apartment.
Madrid. Spain.
June 1971

* * *

"I'm worried about you, Alberto. You always seem to be working so hard lately and putting in too many hours in your office," Lucia Ortega said to her husband with a serious tone and anguished expression.

"There is a lot going on now, my dear, and it's something I must do."

"Maybe you should talk about it more with me. Perhaps I can help you relieve the tension you must feel."

"Thank you, Lucia, but I can assure you that I'm handling it just fine."

"I'm still trying to recover from your assignment to Guinea more than two years ago. I couldn't find out when you were going to return or where you would be."

Alberto looked at his wife with curiosity. *She seems rather distressed by this.* "Well, you shouldn't have worried so much. I returned to El Ferrol because of our mission requirements, and then I had some family business to attend to in Alabos. I guess I was distracted by that and neglected to contact you first. I promise that in the future I'll let you know immediately when I return from official travel."

"Thank you, Alberto. Speaking of Alabos, I have something I would like to ask you."

"Yes, of course, what is it?"

"You travel a fair amount in Europe and to America. When I don't accompany you on those trips, I would like to visit Alabos while you are gone."

"Why is that?" Alberto responded with a perplexed look.

"I find the society here in Madrid a little stifling sometimes. I feel more comfortable in the rural and peaceful environment in Rioja. I also enjoy spending time with Anita and her children. I can even watch over young Isabel when Anita travels to her vineyards around Spain."

"Yes, of course, if it's all right with Anita then it's all right with me," he replied, pleased that this might satisfy Lucia's loneliness during his absences.

Pretoria, South Africa.
January 1973

* * *

Hendrik van den Bergh was ushered through the lush gardens surrounding the Liberta—the official residence of the prime minister of South Africa, Balthazar Johannes Vorster. As the security guard escorted him inside, van den Bergh admired the Cape Dutch architectural style of the mansion, built in 1940. He reflected on the information he was about to share with Vorster as he was ushered into the study.

As Vorster entered the room several minutes later, van den Bergh rose.

"Good afternoon, Prime Minister."

"Yes, Hendrik, it is a good afternoon. I'm glad to see you. Please be seated." Vorster motioned Van den Bergh to the two sofas separated by a coffee table. "So I will get right to the point, Hendrik. We have concluded a secret alliance with Israel on nuclear weapons. We have both a uranium supply and some important technology from Operation Valhalla. They have already built nuclear weapons and are seeking to improve them. The Nazi research on the enhanced radiation bomb, the so-called 'neutron bomb,' which we possess, will be highly prized by Israel. In return, they will offer practical information so that we may speedily develop our own nuclear weapons. Meanwhile, I understand that you have surfaced new information that could affect us in these efforts."

"Yes, sir. It appears that the Soviets and Cubans have learned a lot about Valhalla and probably suspect that we possess the secrets from that operation. They are, of course, trying to create an insurrection in Southwest Africa. If the Portuguese are ejected from Angola, the rebel movement and their Soviet and Cuban sponsors will be on our doorstep."

"That is what I'm afraid of, and it is why we must have nuclear weapons. That way we can deter Soviet-sponsored aggression. Tell me, Hendrik, about the other elements of Valhalla that we don't possess."

"As you know, both Walter and Hans Hoffman were killed in Equatorial Guinea after we dispatched Walter to retrieve the remaining portion of the Valhalla materials. Walter claimed that these included key information on biological toxins that could be converted into a weapon."

"Remind me again what happened to those materials."

"We believe that they were removed and taken to Spain."

"How can we confirm that?"

"I have already quietly asked Santos in Luanda, but he claims that the Portuguese PIDE has no reliable information on that. Of course, our contacts in the CIA can't be approached on this subject."

"What about the Mossad, Hendrik? Maybe our new alliance with Israel can be useful to us here."

"It's too soon for that, sir. We need to proceed cautiously with that relationship."

"Yes, of course, I agree. Perhaps we can sweeten the deal with our offer of a place to test nuclear weapons. What progress have you made in that area?"

"I have initiated a long-term scheme for testing called Operation Phenix. We are quietly surveying atmospheric testing possibilities above or near the Prince Edward Islands. They are deep in the Indian Ocean, and a test there would be hard to detect."

"I assume you will keep this planning under tight security."

"Yes, the plan is being developed by a reliable naval officer who was involved in the salvage of the Valhalla U-boat. His name is Dieter Gerhardt."

140

Nakhon Phanom Royal Thai Air Force Base, Thailand.
August 1973

* * *

The US Air Force OV-10, call sign "Nail 21," of the 23rd Tactical Air Support Squadron taxied in and shut down. It had landed with one engine feathered. As the pilot shut down the remaining good engine, Jack Kurtz walked up to the aircraft to greet its pilot.

"Well, if it isn't Uncle Jack. Why am I not surprised to see you here?" Captain Rob Hoffman exclaimed from the opened cockpit as he saw his uncle approach.

"You're back from another successful mission, I see," Kurtz said as he examined the badly damaged airframe and engine of the OV-10.

Rob dismounted. "Yeah, it was a little hot out there today," Rob responded with a weak smile.

"Well, judging from the decorations you've received, it's been pretty hot for a long time for you. Let's see if I can remember." Jack smiled as he put his finger to his forehead. "As I recall you have a Distinguished Flying Cross, a Silver Star, and two Purple Hearts."

"Don't forget the National Defense Service Medal, or as we call it, the 'I have a pulse and served in 1972' medal." Rob laughed.

"Well, at least you're staying out of trouble with your superiors."

Rob's smile disappeared. "What do you mean by that?"

"Hey, don't take offense. I mean that your commanding officer thinks very highly of your flying performance and your courage and is willing to overlook your occasional insolence and temerity in questioning why we're here."

"Look, Jack, it would take a moron not to recognize that we're breaking most of the rules in the book, the neutrality of Laos, and the Paris Peace Accords that claim to have ended the Vietnam War. The B-52 and other bombing may have stopped this month, but I've been flying special operations nearly every day. Your agency is in the thick of it and up to its eyeballs in questionable activity. We're supporting questionable 'allies' in South Vietnam that don't have popular support, and now we're devastating Laos and Cambodia."

"That's what you signed up for, if you don't mind me reminding you."

"Is it, Jack? Is that what we're all about over here?"

"I don't want to get in a pissing contest with you."

"That's fine. I've only got a week more on this tour. My mandatory one year 'in-country' tour ran from February 1972 to February 1973, when we had to leave 'Nam. Then I got extended six months to operate here. I just want to get out of here. In any case, the 23rd is supposed to wrap up operations on the fifteenth of this month."

"So what happens next?"

"I don't know. I'm just FIGMO—you know, 'fuck it and give me my orders' and send me on," Rob said in a disgusted tone.

"Well, your commander said you might get a desk job or a missile officer assignment next as we cut back on flying positions."

"I'll take one of those early-outs like my buddy Bob Wright got back at Malmstrom rather than submit to that. He got out in November '72 after only two years active duty."

"You won't have a choice. You know damn well that the early-out program was only for nonrated officers like your missile officer friend, rather than pilots like yourself."

"So what's your point, Jack?" *What is he getting at?*

"I mean that you have a five-year commitment to serve after completion of your training. You finished training in November 1970, and so you're in until November 1975. I can offer you a better deal."

"I'm listening," Rob replied after a long pause.

"If you sign on as a contract pilot with CIA, you will be reassigned to me. You keep your commission, and you can run the clock out on the CIA payroll."

"So I'd be doing the same thing here."

"It wouldn't be here."

"Well, fuck the suspense. Where do I go?"

"It'll be Africa. The operations will be in Angola, Sao Tome, and some other places, so it's familiar terrain for you. You'd be flying C-47s and other aircraft that you have experience in. There'd be no more military chickenshit, and you'd report directly to me. You'd also be working with Mike Henry again, so you won't have to worry about your loathing of 'lifers.' When your tour ends in November 1975, you pack up and go home or wherever you want."

"When do I need to decide?"

"I need to know by tomorrow. I'm not trying to pressure you, but I need to get over there right away."

"When could you spring me?"

"You can leave with me if you want. I can turn the screws that fast. I'm supposed to be on a KC-135 that leaves Thailand for Nairobi, and then an unmarked DC-4 takes us on to Luanda."

"OK, sign me up."

"That was fast."

"I just want out of here. My conscience is starting to bother me concerning all I've seen...and done."

141

Madrid, Spain.
November 1973

* * *

"Please come in and have a seat, Alberto." Admiral Luis Carrero Blanco greeted his subordinate with a rare smile.

"Thank you, sir." Alberto took the familiar seat opposite Carrero's desk.

"I don't want to hold back the news. I want to congratulate you on your promotion to *Almirante.*"

Alberto was genuinely shocked. He had been promoted to *Contraalmirante*, the equivalent of a US commodore or rear admiral lower half, in 1964 and then to *Vicealmirante*, the US equivalent of rear admiral, in 1970. The new flag rank was equivalent to a three-star US vice admiral. It was a significant rank in the Spanish navy. Alberto could command a major fleet or other command, yet he did not expect to get far from Carrero's orbit.

"Thank you, sir. This is unexpected," he finally responded.

"As always, it is well deserved. For now you can expect to remain detached for special duty, and you will continue to report to me."

"Very well, sir, it is always a privilege to serve under you."

Alberto watched as Carrero shuffled some papers. *There is something troubling him today.*

"There is a lot of turmoil around us, Alberto."

"Yes, sir, the Arab oil embargo after the Yom Kippur War could affect us as well as America."

"That's true, but I was also thinking about the Basque separatists, as well as...*El Caudillo's* health."

"I know he has been ailing, sir. After all, he is now eighty-one."

"That's true." Carrero nodded. "Have you ever had discussions with Juan Carlos?"

"Not really, sir. I have only chatted with el principe de España at several receptions and formal events." Prince Juan Carlos was the designated successor to Franco.

"Then it is time for you to have more serious discussions with him. Since the Law of Succession was passed in 1969, it is clear that his leadership will be crucial after *El Caudillo*. . .passes."

"If I may be so bold, sir, it was my impression that you would succeed Franco."

"Perhaps, Alberto, and perhaps not. The world is changing."

"We have made stunning economic progress in the last decade, and we are slowly becoming part of the European community again," Alberto responded.

"Yes, and our goal must be to formally join that community as well as NATO, and that won't happen until—well, let me set up a meeting with you and the prince. You must get to know each other better."

142

Alabos, Spain.
November 1973

* * *

"You're arriving early to pick up Lucia," Anita announced as she greeted her brother.

"Yes, I thought it would be nice to visit with you for a while."

"She is actually in Haro to do some shopping."

"All right, so we have a little time to chat."

"I've been waiting for just such an opportunity, Alberto." She smiled. "Actually, I wanted to talk about Lucia."

"What do you mean?"

"I find this a little awkward, Alberto, but..."

"Please go on. Is there something wrong?"

"I don't know. During her frequent visits, and especially recently, she seems unusually curious about our operations here. She wants to know about all of our facilities and what they're used for. Sometimes she poses these questions to our staff when I am not around, and she also pokes around our various buildings. She seems to time her visits to arrive early before I've returned from a trip or to leave after I depart on one."

"Does she give a reason for her inquisitiveness?"

"She says she's only curious about how our wine is made."

"Perhaps we should spend more time talking about it with her," Alberto suggested.

"There is one more thing, Alberto. Several times she has appeared confused—or she has contradicted herself—when I asked about her time in other countries."

"It has been a number of years. Perhaps her memory is rusty. It's also possible that she is a little insecure because of her rootless existence during those years between the civil war and her eventual return to Spain," Alberto hypothesized.

"Maybe you could do a little research and help her reestablish that timeline."

"Yes, that's a good idea, Anita. I'll poke around a little myself."

143

Madrid, Spain,
December 20, 1973

* * *

Paul had arrived in Madrid a day early to coordinate some business matters and then pay a courtesy visit to Luis Carrero. Alberto promised to pick Paul up an hour before the noon meeting so they could catch up and allow Paul to be more fully informed before the meeting with Carrero. Paul was looking forward to the meeting, since Carrero had been made prime minister of Spain in June and seemed almost certain to be Franco's successor.

In two days Paul was planning to travel to Alabos for Christmas and New Year's. Liz was scheduled to fly in the next day with their daughter, Pilar, who had only recently completed a two-year stint in the American Peace Corps in Mali, West Africa. Rob was also in Africa, probably somewhere in Angola. Paul was worried about his son but knew he would be looked after by Jack Kurtz.

Paul was initially angry with Jack for recruiting Rob for the CIA assignment, but he had since calmed down. Liz was still livid with her brother, and they had a serious confrontation when Jack and Paul came back to America briefly in November. Liz was preparing a story for a national journal that could expose the CIA role in the overthrow of the Allende government in Chile.

Paul thought about all of this as he sat in the lobby bar of the Palace Hotel and waited patiently for his cousin. He looked at his watch. It was now 11:20 a.m. If Alberto didn't arrive soon, they would be late for the Carrero meeting.

Paul noticed a commotion in the lobby. *What are all those armed soldiers doing here?*

His question was answered almost immediately as Alberto appeared in uniform and with a grief-stricken face. Paul quickly rose from his chair to meet him.

"What's wrong, Alberto? Are you all right?" He noticed the tears on Alberto's face as he struggled to answer.

"No, I am not. I'm sorry to tell you that Admiral Luis Carrero Blanco is dead. He was murdered in a car bombing, probably by Basque separatists."

"I'm so sorry, Alberto. How could this happen?"

"He was returning from morning mass, as he does every day. It was just so...pointless." Alberto struggled to stay composed.

"What will this mean for Spain?"

"I don't know, Paul. There must soon be a transition, of course. But now our hope for an eventual orderly transition of power may be in jeopardy."

"What about the prince, Juan Carlos?"

"He cannot accede to power unless Franco dies or is disabled. I'm scheduled to see him soon. Admiral Carrero arranged it."

"When you do see the prince, Alberto, you should be bold in your support of Spain's future monarch. Just as Admiral Carrero trusted you as a close adviser, he would expect you to perform the same service for the future king."

"Yes, yes, of course. Thank you for that, Paul. I'm sorry you won't get to see him again. He greatly respected you."

"I greatly respected him also, my cousin," Paul responded somberly.

144

New York City.
July 1974

* * *

Anita was visiting as a part of a business trip to promote Ortega wines and sherries in America. Before launching the trip in the company Gulfstream the following day, Paul, Liz, and Anita welcomed the opportunity to exchange information on their children.

"From your letters, Anita, it seems that Beatriz and Francisca are doing very well," Liz remarked as Paul poured them each a glass of Anita's newly released oloroso.

"Yes, and I'm very proud of them. Francisca is already putting her Stanford MBA to work and is taking charge of the family's real estate holdings in Spain. Beatriz has finished her viticulture and enology studies at the University of California, Davis. I feel so inadequate in my education when I listen to her! She has some great ideas about how to improve our wine making."

"I'm excited that Pilar and Beatriz enjoyed some time together in New Mexico," Liz responded.

"Yes, they have enjoyed it. I have some additional news in that area. Pilar raved about Taos." Anita exchanged a furtive glance with Paul. "She said she enjoyed it more than her current home in Vermont. As a result, Beatriz and Pilar decided to go there and Beatriz also fell in love with Taos. However, that isn't all she fell in love with."

"What happened?" Liz responded as both she and Paul looked up in interest.

"She met a man there. He shares our family name. This Ortega, his given name is James, can trace his family roots totally within New Mexico back to a land grant issued to them by the King of Spain in the sixteen hundreds. His family has lived in the Taos area ever since that time."

"Does he then have American Indian bloodlines also?" Paul asked.

"Beatriz says he doesn't think so. He says his lineage goes back to Castile and Aragon. I wish I had brought his photograph that Beatriz sent. With his curly hair, facial features, and light complexion, he reminds me of…of my father." Anita closed her eyes.

"That's wonderful, Anita. Is the relationship serious?" Liz responded.

"I'm afraid it is." She frowned. "The young man is a US Marine officer and helicopter pilot assigned to an aircraft carrier. They met when he was on the beginning of a two-month leave after returning from duty at Subic Bay in the Philippines. He is due to go back next month at the end of his leave. That worries me."

"The Vietnam War is over, at least for America." Paul said.

"Still, our family has had more than enough wartime tragedies," Anita responded.

"I wouldn't be worried, Anita, unless you think this is a poor match," Paul replied.

"Who am I to dictate whom she will love?" She took a breath before saying, "But I have been dominating the conversation. What about how Robert and Pilar are doing?"

"As you noted, Pilar is doing fine and is still searching for her niche. Robert, on the other hand, my brother has…" Liz began to weep.

"Rob is in Africa and can take care of himself. He'll be fine," Paul said.

Anita quickly changed subjects. "I do have a request to both of you about Isabel."

"Yes, how can we help, Anita?" Liz responded, as she recovered.

"As you know, she will be fourteen in a couple of weeks." She gave Paul another furtive glance. "I want her to come to America for her secondary education, perhaps at the Northfield School in Massachusetts like Pilar, Francisca, and Beatriz did. Since neither they nor Pilar will be as available to help, I was hoping you could do that for me."

"There are good schools in Spain, so isn't it time—" Paul began.

"Yes, there are excellent schools and universities in Spain. But I want Isabel to receive the same liberal education as my other daughters. Perhaps when she is ready to attend university in four years, the situation in Spain will be…different." Anita emphasized with obvious reference to the Franco regime.

"Of course, we will be glad to watch over her, Anita," Liz comforted.

"I know someone else who can help. Rob's friend from the air force, Bob Wright, is getting his master's degree at the University of Massachusetts near Northfield. Maybe he can help us also."

145

Madrid, Spain,
July 1974

* * *

Alberto was surprised when he was summoned to a meeting with Juan Carlos. The prince was temporarily assuming Franco's duties while the dictator was recovering from an illness. Alberto was further mystified when he was told that the meeting would be in an unused annex of a little-used government building.

Upon his arrival, Alberto was ushered into an unimposing isolated office in the building. As soon as he entered, Juan Carlos got up from his desk, walked around it, and walked over to greet Alberto.

"Thank you for coming on short notice, Admiral." He smiled and offered his hand.

"Of course, Your Highness; I am at your service." They shook hands.

"Please take a seat, Admiral." The prince pointed to the two facing couches.

As they seated themselves, Alberto was struck by the prince's easygoing nature.

"This is our first opportunity to talk, Admiral, alone. Let me begin by commending your service. Admiral Carrero was always effusive in his praise of you. He told me I could rely on you for advice on a wide range of matters."

"Thank you, sir. I greatly miss Admiral Carrero."

"So do I, but we must continue to face challenges with courage and determination," the prince replied with conviction.

"I agree, sir."

"Then I will begin with a summary of the latest challenges. The so-called Carnation Revolution in Portugal has upset the balance on the Iberian Peninsula. Demonstrations in Portugal have had catalytic effects here in Spain also. We will deal with that during a difficult period of transition...for both countries. Meanwhile, the Portuguese have indicated their intention to grant independence to all of their colonies in Africa, as well as Cape Verde and Sao

Tome in the Atlantic, and Timor in Asia. We have similar unfinished business in our last remaining colony, Spanish Sahara. I would like you to carry out a special mission to speed this along. I am asking you now, because I temporarily have *El Caudillo's* executive powers for a few weeks, and I want to speed the decolonization process in Sahara. Will you be my emissary in this process?"

"Of course I will, sir."

"Excellent, Admiral. I'll see that my aides provide you with the information that you will need for this effort. Before you go, however, I have one further question to ask you."

"How may I assist, sir?"

"You and I both know that Spain will soon undergo a difficult transition. The future of Spain will be a democratic one. Yet these changes can produce turmoil and even violence. When the time comes, I need for the military to support a peaceful transition to democracy. I know you understand these facts."

"Yes, I do, sir." Alberto gulped hard and responded honestly.

"That's good. You have a wide range of influence, not only in the navy but in the other services also. Can I count on you for assistance when the time comes?"

"Of course you can, sir," Alberto responded firmly.

"Thank you, Admiral. Is there any way I can help you?"

"Yes, there is, sir. I may need the support of someone with diplomatic skills. I know such an individual. He currently assigned to the office of the president."

"Who is he, Admiral?"

"His name is Antonio de Ortiz, sir."

"Yes, of course, I know him." The prince paused and smiled. "I'll see that he is assigned to work with you." He got up and offered his hand.

"Thank you again, sir." Alberto immediately rose and took the prince's hand.

146.

Santander, Spain.
April 1975

* * *

Alberto was pensive as he sat on a couch in this remote, Spanish navy former safe house overlooking the Bay of Santander on Spain's north coast. He was waiting for a special guest, and he had picked this location for a reason. Yet his mind wandered from the business at hand, as he mentally reviewed the results of months of intermittent research on Lucia's previous life. A few things didn't make sense. Alberto needed a little help in the right places to resolve those issues. He hadn't had the time to obtain closure on the matter. For example, he had spent far more time on the Spanish Sahara problem than he thought would be necessary.

Above all, as he stared at the two ledgers on the table, he wondered if he was making the right decision. Alberto's thoughts were interrupted when Jack Kurtz entered the room.

Jack looked at Alberto, said nothing, and walked over to stare out the window.

"I've always thought this was a great view, Alberto," he finally said with a smile.

"Then you remember," Alberto replied, as he joined Jack.

"Sure, it was July 1943, and it was when we first met. You had set up the meeting between General Donovan of the OSS and Admiral Wilhelm Canaris of the German Abwehr. Who could forget that?"

"I'm glad you associate this place with momentous events," Alberto replied.

Jack turned to Alberto. His smile changed to a more serious look. "That sounds ominous."

"Actually, it's more about closure, Jack. Events in Spain in the near future could auger a major shift for us."

"I'd say major changes are affecting the world in general. Vietnam is disintegrating, the Portuguese are about to leave Africa after four hundred years, and we're fighting our own domestic intelligence legacy back in the good old USA."

"That's all true, Jack, but what I'm talking about is final closure on a legacy of World War Two."

"What might that be?" Jack asked with curiosity.

"Let's talk about Valhalla."

"What about it?"

"Isn't it time for closure on that?"

"How would we do that?"

"Why don't you look at those two ledger books over there?"

Alberto watched Jack's eyebrows arch. Jack then walked slowly over to the table where the books sat. He looked back at Alberto and back to the ledgers.

Over the next several minutes Alberto watched as Jack pored over the two documents.

"Let me know if you need help with the German," Alberto offered.

"That's all right. I remember the crash course I had in the OSS."

Finally Jack closed both books. "They were at the plantation all those years, along with the items listed?"

"Yes. I suppose you also noted the handwritten remarks on the front pages."

"So I'm to believe that South Africa got all this material in 1950 and 1960?"

"That's correct. Walter Hoffman evidently made common cause with the South Africans after they discovered him in Swakopmund, Southwest Africa, and learned his true identity," Alberto said.

"It all makes sense, in a way. The South Africans built advanced coal gasification plants in the fifties, and this explains how they got the know-how. It might also explain, ah—"

"It might also explain why they're developing nuclear weapons now in collaboration with Israel. That's all right, Jack. We have our own intelligence sources."

"What about anything on biological weapons research?"

"There was nothing for them to take," Alberto responded. *That's true enough, since I removed all those materials—after the fact, of course.*

Jack stared at Alberto with a neutral look before finally looking back at the ledgers. He then looked back up. "Our guys would love to analyze this material. It could provide clues to what the processes were, even without the backup materials."

"Then take them."

Jack looked up in surprise. "Why do you want to give them to me?"

"As I said, we need closure on Valhalla. In a short time, a different Spain will emerge, and we don't want the baggage from this operation hanging over our heads."

"That's pretty bold for a senior admiral in Franco's navy."

"His condition is obvious. I'm sure the CIA has copies of his medical reports."

Jack frowned with a slight look of embarrassment. "So that's it, Alberto, no quid pro quo?"

"Well, actually there is one thing I want in return."

"I thought there might be a price."

"It's not much. I'm going to give you a list of names. I believe it could be one person in South America with multiple aliases. We have expert resources, but yours are much more extensive. I need this person's real identity," Alberto concluded as he handed Jack the list. He looked at it quickly.

"It's a woman?"

"Yes."

"All right, we have a deal. I'll see what I can do."

147.

New York City, America, May 1975

* * *

"I can't believe what a tragedy this is," Liz exclaimed as she suppressed her tears.

"I know, I feel so sorry for Beatriz and Anita," Paul replied somberly.

"You said you were able to get more information on what happened?" Liz asked.

"Yes, I just got off the phone with the contact I have in Washington. He confirmed that James Ortega died during a rescue mission that was part of the evacuation of the US and South Vietnamese armies on the last two days of April."

"I just can't believe it. They married so quickly in August before he had to return to his ship. Beatriz is carrying their first child, due later this month. The child will never know..." Liz broke down and began sobbing.

Paul walked over to comfort her.

"I know that it's sad and tragic—another family member claimed by a distant war." He put his arms around his wife.

"It seems all the more tragic for him to die at the end of the war, supposedly after US involvement had ended." Her sobs were tinged with bitterness.

"In fact, he could have been one of the last who died."

"Is that supposed to be some honor? What of our son? Will he be the last to die in some obscure place defending the Portuguese empire against the Red menace?"

"Rob is capable and cautious, so you don't have to—"

"I don't have to worry about my son? I hope that's not your only thought! You know that my brother is culpable in recruiting him."

"That's not fair, Liz. Jack was only doing his duty and—"

"He was doing his duty? What about Guatemala, Iran, Chile, and who knows where else? Is there no end to this?"

Paul could not answer.

148

Over the North Atlantic Ocean.
November 1, 1975

* * *

Paul sat in the plush executive cabin of his company's Gulfstream II corporate jet as it flew eastward at 460 knots on the thirty-one-hundred-nautical-mile direct flight from Teterboro, New Jersey to Madrid. After six hours and forty-five minutes, he would land at about 9:00 p.m. local time. Paul would not deplane when he arrived. He instead was expecting Alberto and Antonio de Ortiz to board. They would refuel and then immediately depart for Villa Cisneros in Spanish Sahara.

Paul finished his glass of fino as he stared at the headline from this morning's *New York Times*: JUAN CARLOS AND CABINET CONFER ON SAHARA CRISIS. He quickly finished rereading the article and then put the paper back on the writing desk. He got up, went to the liquor cabinet just behind the cockpit, and poured another glass of sherry.

As he returned to his seat, Paul was struck by how close he was to what was likely Spain's last colonial crisis. He had planned to leave for Spain the following Tuesday on business, but Alberto had called and asked him to fly over several days early. Alberto wanted Paul to fly him and Antonio in a nongovernment aircraft to Villa Cisneros for secret negotiations to prevent a war between Morocco and Mauretania on one side and Algeria on the other. Inevitably, Spanish forces garrisoned in the Sahara would be involved.

Paul shook his head over the insanity of this potential war over a mostly desert wasteland. Yet he realized that Juan Carlos was in the driver's seat as Spain's de facto ruler as Franco's health deteriorated. The prince of Spain was determined to shed this last vestige of Spain's nearly five-hundred-year-old colonial empire.

It looked like the Portuguese would beat Spain to the exit gate in Africa. Mozambique, Portuguese Guinea, Cape Verde, and Sao Tome had all achieved independence earlier in 1975. On November 11, Angola would achieve its independence. It was Armistice Day, the anniversary of the day World War I ended, the event that had propelled Paul's father to his African destiny—and his death years later. Paul's son was now in Angola working for the CIA to preserve—what?

Paul could not reconcile the ironies.

Madrid. Spain.
November 20, 1975

* * *

Alberto sat in his office trying to concentrate on the documents he had received by diplomatic pouch several days ago, but he couldn't get his mind off the more current public events dominating his life—and the lives of all Spaniards.

Franco had died early that morning. The official public mourning and impending funeral were the events before the public eyes. Yet Alberto knew that events behind the scenes would determine Spain's future. He had already prepared a secret plan to defend a transition to a democratic government, but he hoped that Juan Carlos would never have to call upon him to implement it.

At least a crisis had been averted in Spanish Sahara. An agreement had been signed on November 15, and Spain would peacefully relinquish power and leave the territory on February 28, 1976. It was anyone's guess what would happen next, but at least Spain could close this chapter in its history and concentrate on a much different future that now beckoned.

Alberto was finally able to bring his mind back to the documents that Jack Kurtz had sent him. Alberto reread them, but he was still confused. The person known as Lucia Aznar Sedeno, Alberto's wife, had in fact lived in several places in South America and France. Yet in each place she had assumed other identities. *Why would she do that?*

In the diplomatic pouch, Jack had also enclosed a letter explaining that he had one more source to check out and would get back to Alberto as soon as he obtained the information.

Alberto also had two more sources that he wanted to check in Spain. One was the church records in the village near Zaragoza where Lucia said she had grown up. The other source was sealed records from the civil war, which included captured documents from the Republican government in power from 1931 to 1936, and against which the Nationalists under Franco had staged the uprising in 1936 that started the civil war.

These records might be difficult to access, especially now.

Alabos, Spain.
December 1975

* * *

Anita returned earlier than planned from meetings with her vineyard managers around Spain. She drove quietly up behind the hacienda. She wanted to prepare for the family members who would be arriving for the weekend, including Paul, who was supposed to arrive later in the day. The house staff had the afternoon off and was in Haro to prepare for a weekend party for many of the family's local workers. For now, Anita would be able to go her study and complete some paperwork without interruption.

Anita got out of the car and walked around to the south entrance. She noticed another car, a SEAT 600. It was a very basic car, but nearly eight hundred thousand had been built before production was complete in 1973, and it was a symbol of Spain's burgeoning middle class and the economic revival that began in 1959. The ugly little car had many unflattering nicknames. Anita's favorite was *ombligo*, or "navel"—because everybody had one. It was not typically a car that would be seen in the hacienda driveway in Alabos.

I wonder whose it could be? Perhaps one of the staff bought one.

She quietly entered the hacienda from the private entrance that led directly to her study. That way, if anyone was still here, Anita would not disturb them, and she hoped they would not disturb her. She took off her shoes and walked down the corridor to her office. As she approached, she could see light coming out through the open door. She shook her head. *I must again remind the housekeepers to turn the light off and keep the door closed and locked when I am not here.*

Now she heard low voices as she approached the door. *Are they are cleaning the office now? Why? It's late on a Friday afternoon.*

She rounded the corner and walked into her study. Two people were bent over her desk facing the other direction.

"What are you doing?" she demanded.

They turned in surprise. It was Alberto's wife, Lucia, and a husky male stranger. The man raised his pistol, an ancient Ruby modeled after the American M1911.

Anita started to scream but suppressed it. "What is this? What is going on, Lucia? Tell me!"

Lucia stepped forward, using her left hand to restrain the man, and confronted her sister-in-law. "I don't have time for this, Anita. You will immediately tell us where you have hidden the Valhalla materials, or it will be very difficult for you."

"What are you talking about? I don't know what that is."

Lucia nodded to the man. He approached Anita and without delay swung the palm of his hand swiftly. Anita wasn't ready, and the blow hit her hard on the left side of her face. She fell over backward.

"I told you I don't have time for this. Tell me where it is."

"I told you I don't know!" Anita replied, holding her hand to her face where she was bleeding slightly from the cut caused by the man's sharp ring.

"All right, then, we will apply whatever force is necessary to get you to talk."

Lucia again nodded to the man, who approached Anita as she tried to crawl away. He pointed his pistol at Anita's head.

"Stop!" The booming command caught both Lucia and the man off guard.

The man turned to face the intruder, but he wasn't fast enough.

Paul's M1911 Colt fired only once, hitting the man in the center of his chest. He fell over backward, grabbing a doily on the side table next to him, pulling it and the table lamp to the floor with a loud crash. The man was dead before he hit the floor.

Paul tried swiftly to redirect the pistol toward Lucia, but she fired her Walther PPK before Paul could fully turn his weapon. He had shifted his body slightly. The round missed his torso and hit the arm holding the Colt. Paul dropped the gun and fell toward Anita, catching himself as Anita reached for him.

It was over in seconds.

Lucia walked slowly over to them and stood in front of her dead partner, facing away from the office's door about two meters away. She kicked Paul's pistol off to the side.

"All right. One or both of you know where Alberto hid the Valhalla materials. You must certainly know, Anita, so if you don't tell me, I will kill Paul. I will give you thirty seconds to think about it, and then *I will kill him!*"

She had raised the PPK slightly, as if to provide them a thirty-second respite.

"So what will it be?" She added several seconds later.

"*Put the gun down, Lucia!*" a husky voice said firmly. All three of them turned with a start to look at the door.

It was Alberto. He was pointing a .38-caliber Smith and Wesson at his wife.

The silence was overpowering.

Paul could hear everyone's heavy breathing. He looked at his Colt lying on the floor about four feet away. *That won't work. I'll have to let Alberto resolve this.*

"Put the gun down, Lucia. You know that it's over for you now—and for us."

Paul watched as Lucia, panting and sweating, stared at her husband with a cold and calculating look. *There is no love there.*

As the tension built, Paul tried hard to think of something to help Alberto, but he knew that it was better to sit motionless.

It happened in an instant.

Lucia rapidly swung her arm with the PPK toward Alberto. In the split second it took to turn toward him Alberto fired a single shot from his .38. It hit her in the upper chest.

She dropped the PPK, grabbed her chest with both hands, and looked at Alberto in confusion. He stood there ready to fire again. It wasn't necessary. Lucia toppled to her knees and then fell over sideways, landing only inches away from her dead companion.

Alberto lowered his weapon and walked slowly over to Lucia's body. He knelt gently beside her on one knee. He tried whispering to her, but nothing came out.

How could you do this to me and to my family?

Paul watched as Alberto knelt there for several moments. He couldn't imagine what Alberto was going through, but Paul had an idea of what must have occurred.

"You are wounded, Paul," Anita said with concern as she reached over to gently touch him.

"It's all right, Anita. It just nicked me. You're bleeding more than I am," he replied, as he pulled out a handkerchief and gently wiped the blood from Anita's face. He reached over and grabbed the doily that fell on the floor and wrapped it around his own arm to stop the minor bleeding.

Alberto finally got up, walked over to them, and again knelt.

"I see that you are both all right. I'm so glad I got here in time."

"I am so sorry, Alberto. You must feel—"

"Don't worry about me now; I will deal with it later. You must, however, know the truth about Lucia."

Paul and Anita looked at each other and then back to Alberto.

"She was a Soviet agent and has been for at least thirty-five years."

"What are you saying? How can that be?" Anita replied with a shocked look.

"When you raised questions two years ago about her memory, I thought I could help her if I used my position and sources to retrieve information on her background. I even enlisted Jack Kurtz's help, since the CIA has a network in South America better than our own. It turns out that Lucia used various aliases to spy on South American governments, using the cover of a commercial firm in Caracas, Venezuela. We were able to confirm that she was the same individual."

"What firm was she working for? Was it a KGB front?"

"Yes, it was. The controlling agent in that firm that she worked directly for was Sergio Castillo."

Anita gasped. "It can't be! He died in 1959 when his plane—"

"Listen to me, Anita. He didn't die. He faked that plane crash so that he could go undercover in Africa. He went there to look for the Valhalla secrets, since he was unsuccessful in finding them by penetrating our family."

"He is...he is alive now?" she finally asked.

"Yes, the CIA thinks he has been in Algeria most recently, although his main base was in the former French Guinea. The CIA believes that he and a

Cuban operative are currently masterminding the Angolan civil war that just erupted when the Portuguese departed," Alberto said.

A light bulb finally went off for Paul. "Do you mean that Sharon McKenzie and our nanny, Margarita, were all part of the spy ring?"

"Yes, Paul, I'm afraid so. Sharon was KGB Agent X, Margarita was Agent Y. and Lucia was known as Agent Z. When I was the naval attaché in Washington in 1961, Lucia coordinated with both of them. As you know, Margarita was eventually caught and Sharon escaped to Africa and to Sergio. This was the final piece that Jack provided me. Sergio's real name was Yuri Kozlov. He had a Russian father and a Venezuelan mother. I am sorry to tell you, Anita, but Sharon McKenzie appears to be Sergio's—I mean Yuri's—mistress."

Anita gasped again and put her hand to her mouth.

"So it all fits together. It's a complete betrayal of our family. We were all used—me, Jack, Anita, and now you, Alberto." Paul shook his head in disgust.

"I always admired her story about her family in the civil war. What really happened, Alberto?" Anita asked.

"She always claimed that her parents were murdered by the Republicans at the Battle of the Ebro. I was able to compare both church records and BPS records and determined that the opposite happened. Her parents were actually Republican spies and were caught by the *Falange* and executed. Meanwhile, the Republicans evacuated Lucia, and that is her real given name. They sent her on a boat to Moscow in early 1939, and according to CIA intelligence, she was educated and indoctrinated there and sent to South America in the late forties."

"That's frightening. I imagine that the CIA was surprised when they put it all together."

"Yes, the pieces were all there, but it took my inquiry to Jack for the CIA to put the puzzle together."

"So what do we do now? How will we explain this to our staff and to the police?" Anita asked with concern.

"Don't worry, Anita. We must coolly and rationally construct what happened here," Alberto replied. He then stood and quickly surveyed the room.

"Paul, it's a good thing it was cold out there today. We are both wearing our gloves," Alberto added.

"Yes, I think I understand," Paul answered as he instantly figured it out.

"I don't understand," Anita said quizzically.

Neither man answered as Alberto quickly took action. He took Paul's fallen Colt M1911 and walked over to Lucia. He gently put the pistol in her hand, clamped her fingers tightly on the grip, and then gently placed her arm back on the floor. He then took his own .38-caliber Smith and Wesson and did the same thing with Lucia's accomplice. He then turned to Paul and Anita.

"It was unfortunate that Lucia caught a common burglar in the act of rifling our records, looking for valuables. It's clear that they must have fired simultaneously. Even the position of their bodies should make the investigation straightforward. My pistol was an untraceable weapon, and I assume yours was also, Paul."

"Yes, it was given to me in Africa. Its ownership can't be traced."

"Then it's almost time for me to call the civil guard office in Haro. There is one more matter that must be attended to first."

"What's that?" Anita asked.

"The Valhalla materials must be taken away from here."

"Why did you bring them here to our property?" Paul asked in amazement.

"I had no choice in 1969. Now they must be removed from Spanish soil entirely. We are entering a new era in Spain, and I don't want this curse from the past tainting our opportunity to start afresh. I was asked to meet with the king in a few days, and I don't want to tell Juan Carlos that Valhalla ever existed. So I too must be unaware of what happens to these materials next."

"You need plausible deniability."

"Yes, Paul, I do. That means that you and Anita must get these materials out of Spain as soon as possible. I also want to ensure that no one can trace your involvement to their removal. We must therefore create an alibi that does not place you here at this time, but rather at some other location."

"How will we do that, Alberto?" Anita asked.

Alberto thought for a moment before coming up with the details.

"We must create a trail that shows you were in Jerez at your sherry bodega. I can arrange to show that you flew there in your plane. I must change the airport records there as well as here at the Logroño Airport. It will leave a trail that will place you elsewhere. So you must both leave now...before I call the local authorities."

"I understand, Alberto. Anita and I will remove the materials."

"What will we do? We can't take the materials to America, can we?" Anita asked.

"No, we can't, but I do know a place where we can take them," Paul replied.

"If you don't mind, I don't want to hear the rest of this. In any case, I must now call the police and civil guard. By the time they get here, I must be in a state of grief over finding my dear wife. It shouldn't be too...too hard."

Alberto left the room while he was still in control over his emotions.

Anita and Paul rose and quietly watched Alberto leave the room.

"Paul, you must tell me where we will take the Valhalla materials. They must leave Spain, and they can't go to America. Where will we take them?"

"Don't worry, Anita. I know a place."

Washington. DC.
December 1975

* * *

Jack Kurtz was feeling morose. He had just returned from Angola after being directed to start phasing out CIA operations in the newly independent country. He thought that it would all be over in a couple of months. The termination of CIA activity was the result of both a failure of the CIA-backed forces in Angola and intense US congressional scrutiny of all CIA operations. This was highlighted by the Church committee hearings, named after Senator Frank Church of Idaho, earlier in 1975.

The morale in the CIA was at rock bottom after the so-called Halloween Massacre in early November. President Ford had replaced William Colby by nominating George Bush as the new CIA director. Ford made other changes in his cabinet as well. Colby was an OSS veteran, and Jack knew him well.

Jack wondered about his future. He wasn't quite high enough in the pecking order to take the fall for any of the alleged CIA actions that were under investigation. However, for most of the twenty-two years he had been in the agency, he was under the personal mentorship of the incumbent director. Now he had absolutely no relationship to the incoming director. Jack thought about his twenty-six years of government service and wondered if he would make it to the thirty-year retirement mark in 1979. *Is this what I've been reduced to? Am I just another barnacle counting the days until retirement?*

Jack was repelled by the thought, since his true love was special operations. Now they were being curtailed in favor of the CIA's stated mandate of intelligence gathering.

He looked at his in basket and sighed. *Well, I guess I better be damn good at intelligence gathering; otherwise, four years is going to be a long time.*

At least the intelligence analysis he was assigned to was interesting: the status of South Africa's nuclear weapons program.

Maybe I can also find a way to resurrect agency interest in Operation Valhalla.

Near El Serrat, Principality of Andorra.
December 1975

* * *

Paul and Anita had been lucky three times today. The first time was when Spanish customs only gave the truck a cursory look when it crossed the border between Spain and Andorra. Of course, it helped when Anita learned that the customs officer liked fine wines. She provided him with a case of the Bodega Ortega Tempranillo Reserva 1970.

The second piece of luck occurred only moments later when the truck crossed the border and passed the Andorra customs shack. It was empty, of course, since most Andorrans made a living from smuggling and tended to look the other way when a vehicle entered this obscure little country tucked in the Pyrenees Mountains between Spanish Catalonia and France.

It was a good thing they were lucky both of these times. Beneath the twenty cases of wine was a tarp that concealed the Valhalla canisters they were carrying.

They made a quick stop to drop off the wine at a restaurant in the capital city of Andorra-la-Vella. Paul and Anita's grandfather, Pablo Ortega, had kept the restaurant supplied with Ortega wines beginning in the thirties, and he even managed to deliver wine there during the civil war. In return, the restaurant owner served as caretaker for the Ortega family hunting lodge, which was their next stop.

The lodge was near the village of El Serrat about fifteen kilometers north or roughly halfway across the tiny country. Their third piece of luck was having arrived during a thaw when the road was passable, and they were able to drive right up to the lodge. They immediately got out of the truck to survey the place before unloading.

"This is my first time here," Anita said.

"You must be joking," Paul replied in surprise.

"No, I'm not. Hunting was a male thing. I was never invited." She sighed.

"I remember when Grandfather Ortega brought me here in 1933 when I was only twelve. I didn't return again until the fifties. Your father and brother and I came here twice. They came more often. I don't think any family member has been here since 1958," Paul said.

"What did you hunt?"

"Wild boar was the elusive prize, but it could also be Pyrenean Chamois, a kind of mountain goat. Red deer were introduced in 1955, so they could be hunted also."

"Well, we better go in and check things first," Anita suggested.

"I hope my memory is good. I recall that there is a large secure wine cellar. It stays at a constant temperature. That's where I'm hoping we can store everything and lock it up."

"Maybe there are still some older vintages stored here," Anita said hopefully.

"Let's go look."

Within a few minutes they had unlocked the lodge and made their way to the cellar. Anita soon found her quarry among a handful of stored bottles.

"My God, it's a 1920 Gran Reserva! That's the only legendary vintage of the twentieth century that I've never been able to taste. Our library supply was exhausted before I could partake," she said in surprise.

"I remember that vintage. It was the only one that our two fathers worked on together before we moved to Guinea. They always raved about it."

"Let's drink it tonight," Anita said with a broad smile.

"All right; we can go to back to Andorra-la-Vella and have it with a fine meal at our caretaker's restaurant," Paul replied with almost as much enthusiasm.

"So let's get the other work over with," Anita replied as her smile disappeared.

* * *

"We will now see how it held up over fifty five years."

"The color is great, and so is the bouquet," Paul said after swirling the wine in the glass.

After the hard work of unloading and securing their cargo at the lodge, they were looking forward to the meal that had just been served—and the wine.

"Oh my, it's fabulous!" Anita proclaimed.

"I agree. This could be one of the vintages of the century! It nearly matches your efforts in '47, '55, '64, and '70."

"This century is not over yet, Paul."

They both laughed.

"Of course not; I think the '75 could be fabulous, judging from the barrel tasting you offered me before we came here."

"I now have Beatriz assisting me. She is already a talented wine maker and the '75 vintage is as much hers as mine," Anita said proudly as she tasted the wine again.

"The fourth generation meets its destiny. I'm betting that little four-year-old Beatriz Anita will make her mark as the fifth generation. I also wonder if perhaps...if perhaps Isabel may someday..." Paul's voice trailed off.

Anita put her wine glass down and slowly and gently placed her hand on Paul's.

"She is a very special fifteen-year-old, Paul."

"I wonder what her destiny will be," Paul replied.

"She is also interested in wine making. I want her to finish school first and go on to university. I am now hopeful that she can do so in Spain when she graduates from the Northfield School in 1978."

"That would be wonderful. Our country has such a rich culture, history, and heritage. I always wondered about your decision to send Beatriz and Francisca to America for their schooling," Paul commented.

"Don't you think the schools and universities in America are outstanding?"

"Of course I do, but I don't want them to lose their Spanish heritage."

"They won't, Paul. Just look at yourself. If anyone can be a citizen of the world and still be a loyal Spaniard, it is you."

"Our country is about to undergo a profound change, and I wonder how we will cope with the past."

"I remember your father always saying we must look forward."

"Those were also Hans's...last words to me."

Anita put her hand back on Paul's again. "Then we must look forward."

"I will do that, Anita."

"I just hope that the materials that we brought here today to the lodge don't make a mockery out of what I just said," she said with a worried tone.

"Perhaps it's the one thing from the past that we must continue to be vigilant on."

"Did we do the right thing bringing them here?"

"Yes, this place is obscure, and there is no obvious trail leading someone here."

"Yet, I am worried about about Sergio, or whoever he is. He may persist in his pursuit of these materials," she said.

"He will have a hard time entering Spain. His identity is known."

"What about your friend Jack Kurtz and the CIA? What will they do?"

"Jack and the CIA have their own cross to bear right now. Leave that to me."

They were silent for several minutes and then finished their meal and wine with only an occasional comment. Finally it was over and time to go to their guest house for the night.

Anita finally broke the silence.

"I hope that we will have many more of these evenings together, Paul. You are still my best friend and..."

"It's all right, Anita. We will have many more evenings, and you too must look forward and not be colored by what came before."

Postscript

* * *

Light

1976–1979

The Spanish Nation, wishing to establish justice, liberty and security, and to promote the welfare of all who make part of it, in use of her sovereignty, proclaims its will to
- *guarantee democratic life within the constitution and the laws according to a just economic and social order;*
- *consolidate a state ensuring the rule of law as an expression of the will of the people;*
- *protect all Spaniards and all the peoples of Spain in the exercise of human rights, their cultures and traditions, languages, and institutions.*

-Translated excerpt from the preamble to the Spanish constitution of 1978

153.

Madrid, Spain,
January 1976

* * *

"It looks like we passed the first hurdle. The king has successfully put us on the path to a democratic regime and is wasting no time reaching out to other countries," Alberto said confidently.

"Do you see the changes in the office of the prime minister where you are currently assigned, Antonio?" Paul inquired.

"Yes, we have just signed a new security treaty with the United States, and the king plans to visit the United States in June."

"What about the military and other Franco-era institutions, Alberto?" Paul asked.

"So far they are being held in check, despite unrest in Barcelona and Catalonia."

The three men sat in the lobby bar of the Palace Hotel as they brought each other up-to-date. They paused as the waiter brought them another round of fino.

"Spain has indeed turned a corner. It looks like the transition to democracy will press forward, thanks to the king's vision—and courage," Paul said.

"It was rather unexpected. He is following a balanced path between continuity and change. Let's hope he is able to continue," Alberto replied.

"I believe that the three of us are all in key positions to help this effort," Paul added.

"That's true. Paul has the American link. Antonio is the link to the civil government, and I hopefully can maintain a link with the military," Alberto said.

The waiter delivered the next round of drinks.

"Gentlemen, I propose a toast to the new Spain." Paul raised his glass.

As the three men completed their toast, Paul thought about the prognosis. *I hope that Spain is able to move forward as we hope and that...the Valhalla events will not come back to haunt us.*

154

Washington, D.C.
March 1977

* * *

Paul and Jack were knocking down a few at Nathan's in Georgetown on this busy Friday evening. Paul had traveled down in the company's Cessna Citation I business jet that Paul and his management team had just acquired for shorter domestic trips. They still had the Gulfstream for foreign travel as well as several Beech King Airs for regional travel. It was an easy run into town from National Airport.

As usual, this trendy establishment at the corner of Wisconsin and M attracted a mixed crowd of older establishment sophisticates, out-of-towners on business, and preppy college types. These groups pretty much ignored each other in the mindless pursuit of the opposite sex of their own class. It was also a place for casual business and other discussion.

"I'm glad you called, Paul. It's been a long time since we got together."

"Yeah, I know. The last time was in New York in the Village."

"What's it like there now?" Jack asked.

"Like everything in New York, it's gone to seed. The tourists are all over the Village now, and you wouldn't recognize the White Horse Tavern."

"What about all those beats and...folkies?"

"Jesus, Jack, they are all long gone. The big scene now is called punk, and it centers on a raunchy club called CBGB in the Bowery. The music celebrates the decline of just about everything."

"Oh, so it matches the mood here in Washington."

"Maybe. What's the new director like?" Paul knew better than to ask about actual work that Jack did.

"He's an admiral, so what can I say? He's a straight arrow boy-scout type, just like Bush, and he's matched by the guy in the White House."

"That figures, since Carter appointed him."

The two men laughed as Jack raised his hand to the bartender for two more scotches.

"How's everything with the family?" Jack asked.

"Everything's great, but you should call your sister once in a while."

"I'd be surprised if Liz would talk to me. I'm just the evil spy, according to her muckraking ways."

"The CIA will survive all that's happened, Jack. It has to."

"You think it will? I sure hope so. The Cold War still rages, and Africa still simmers. With South Africa getting close to—" Jack caught himself.

"It's all right, Jack. Let's move on to your social life."

"What social life? All I do is work. I was lucky to be able to walk away just for an evening out with you. They're piling it on."

"So why don't you come up to New York for a weekend and make up with Liz."

"Maybe I'll do that one of these days."

He sure has changed. "What are you going to do when you get your thirty years in?"

"I'll retire without looking back and go fishing."

"I can't imagine you doing that. You'd be bored shitless."

"Well, I'm not going to stay in, and I hate being a lawyer."

I've been thinking about it. Do it now.

"Why don't you come and join our firm, Jack? I need a consigliere whom I can trust, as well as an occasional fixer."

"I don't need charity, Paul."

"It wouldn't be charity. You'd work your ass off, but we might be able to have some fun occasionally."

Jack looked up at Paul with one eye. "I'll give it careful consideration when the time comes," he finally replied.

155.

Turners Falls, Massachusetts,
June 1978

* * *

Paul stood on the ramp of the Turners Falls airport and took in the view of the hills surrounding the airport and this old mill town in the Connecticut River valley. While Anita went to call for the car that would take them to Isabel's graduation ceremony at the nearby Northfield Mount Hermon School, Paul walked slowly across the ramp and parking lot of this sleepy general-aviation airport. They had flown up from Teterboro in Paul's Beech *Baron*, which he used for personal travel.

This place held special memories for Paul. He had learned to fly here in 1937 while taking summer courses at the Mount Hermon school in the nearby town of Gill. Pilar had graduated from the Northfield School in 1965, followed by Anita's daughter Beatriz and adopted daughter, Francisca, in 1966. In 1971, the two schools were merged to become the coeducational Northfield Mount Hermon School. The school was part of an informal group known as the Eight Schools Association, a group of elite American prep schools, including Paul's alma mater, Choate, from which he had graduated in 1939.

He soon reached the grassy area on the south side of the airport and quickly found the stone marker placed there in the thirties by a Civilian Conservation Corps team that had improved the airport. As he returned to the ramp, he marveled at the changes that had occurred in America in the intervening four decades.

His swirl of memories quickly returned to the series of family tragedies that had stalked him during those years—including the most recent one.

Two months ago Liz had succumbed to the cancer that was discovered in late 1977. It quickly took her life, despite heroic medical efforts and a courageous fight. Paul finally reached the airplane, stopped, and closed his eyes as he relived those last days with Liz.

He lost track of time amid the kaleidoscope of their thirty-four years together and was surprised as a hand gently touched his arm. He opened his eyes.

"Are you all right?" Anita asked softly.

"I'm as well as can be expected."

"I know how hard it must be as memories return."

"Thank you, Anita. You have felt similar pain and know how hard it is to relive."

"I guess coming here was a catalyst for your memories."

"Yes, but it was especially hard as I recalled her last day, as I sat in the hospital holding her hand. I was reading to her some very good reviews of her last articles when she stopped me. I haven't told you this yet, but..." He suppressed his tears.

"Go on, please," Anita urged.

"She told me that...that I should embrace Isabel. I looked into her eyes and I could see that...she knew." Paul put his hands to his face as he suppressed his tears.

Anita gently put her arms around him and brought him closer. She held him in silence for several moments before replying. "That may have shocked you, Paul, but it doesn't surprise me. Liz was not only courageous but perceptive. You may call it woman's intuition or some other cliché, but it is real. Years ago, when Isabel was young, Liz made an astute remark to me."

"What did she say?" Paul replied as he composed himself.

"She told me that Isabel had beautiful eyes and that they were like her father's."

"Liz hardly knew Sergio."

"That's right, Paul, and Isabel's eyes are blue like yours and not brown like Sergio's."

Paul was struck by the simple truth but could not keep from asking the obvious. "Did you talk about us and Isabel?"

"I didn't have to. She knew as well as I that you rushed to rescue me from despair on the worst day of my life. She sensed that it was I, and not you, who craved intimacy and love at that fateful moment."

"But how can she forgive me for—"

"There was nothing to forgive, Paul."

"How can a man love two women without—"

"Listen to me. Our love is real, and I have known it for nearly thirty years. I will not suppress it because of our family circumstances. We must all find a way to deal with our true feelings while moving forward. You and I have done so, and we have nothing to be ashamed of."

"You're right, of course. I must think of our beautiful daughter. Isabel has made me so proud, and I know you are also."

"I'm especially happy that Isabel will be attending the University of Murcia this fall. I'm comfortable that women will have equal opportunities in Spain now, including in education. It's important that she maintain links to her Spanish heritage."

"I also want her to be proud of her heritage, Anita. Perhaps one day we should tell her of all the events that took place…as a part of that heritage."

"We must do so carefully, Paul. Right now she believes that her father died in a plane crash in 1959 before she ever met him. When she learns that he was a fraud and is not her father, we will need to comfort her. I suspect that there will be aspects of Sergio that we should not share with her."

"Why not tell her the whole truth?" Paul said.

"That may or may not be a good idea. I don't want the curse of Valhalla to follow another generation."

Paul did not reply.

156

New York City.
June 1979

* * *

"It's an unexpected pleasure seeing both of my children at the same time, especially since it's not a holiday. I was expecting Rob, but I'm glad to see you also, Pilar." Paul smiled as Rob and Pilar arrived together at Paul's rooftop penthouse.

"We're sorry to shock you, Dad, but there's a reason why we're both here at the same time," Rob replied.

"Yes, we want you to hear us out. Believe it or not, Rob and I are here for the same purpose today," Pilar added.

"What might that be?" Paul was definitely curious.

"We want to make you a business proposition," Rob said.

"In fact, we want to propose a new business model for all our enterprises," Pilar said.

"You'll have to explain that," Paul replied with a perplexed look as he finished pouring sherry into their three glasses.

"You've been prodding us to decide whether we want to be involved in the management of the family businesses," Rob began.

"So far I haven't been successful. To be frank, Rob, you've always been uninterested." He then turned to his daughter. "And your alternate views of the world, Pilar, ah, they have—"

"Dad, please, I know you've considered me a hippie in recent years, but we're serious about what you're about to hear."

"All right, you have the floor."

"I'll begin with some research I did. I've consulted some investment advisers outside of your normally conservative circle, and they believe that big changes are about to happen in the world," Rob said.

"Such changes would be?"

"We're talking about the emergence of China, new technologies, new trading patterns, US domestic policies like airline deregulation, and other changes."

"What do these changes portend?"

"They will stimulate a more rapid rise of globalization than even you and Grandfather Hoffman even imagined."

"What are the downsides?"

"There are many of those, but they include overpopulation, high energy prices, environmental degradation, the homogenization of world cultures, and above all, the emergence of the new breed of avaricious multinational corporations bent solely on the bottom line at the expense of poor workers," Pilar said.

"That sounds like an excerpt from the *Communist Manifesto*," Paul remarked.

"Actually, it's not. Pilar and I have been working on an international business strategy that develops sustainable economies around the world, rather than the 'slash and burn' exploitive capitalism and commoditization that's starting to emerge," Rob said.

"Now you have my attention. So what are you proposing?"

"We think we might want to realign our investment portfolio to account for these trends. We might also want to tweak our export-import and shipping interests. It also might be a good idea to shift some of our emphasis to the Asian markets," Rob replied.

"The most unique proposal we have concerns a way to build on the heritage that Mom and Grandfather Hoffman were dedicated to," Pilar said.

"What would you do?"

"I think we should create a foundation that would invest in Third World economies in a way that would make them sustainable rather than extractive. It's an approach I've been nurturing since my Peace Corps experience in Mali. Sometimes it's about simple things like better water, sanitation, education, building local markets for goods and services, and similar things," she continued.

"That's what your grandfather tried to do in Guinea."

"Dad, you're exactly right, and our business benefited by having a prosperous, healthy, and educated community there. A rising tide lifts all boats. That's what the multinationals claim now, but they don't invest in local populations and will move their operations in a heartbeat for populations they can exploit for lower wages," Pilar responded.

"That's even happening here in the states," Paul added.

"You got that right. It creates unemployment and emphasizes consumption over investment," Rob interjected.

"What would we call the foundation that will support these activities?"

"We could name it the Hoffman Ortega Foundation, in honor of the two families. We've already approached Anita, and she supports the idea," Pilar replied.

"Your mother and grandfather would be proud. Both of you need to provide leadership for these shifts."

"Dad, we're ready. I'd like to be CEO of the foundation," Pilar responded.

"I'm ready to earn my keep also," Rob added.

"Then you should be COO on the business side. You both can move up as things develop. I'm beginning to fancy myself in the chairman role anyway, rather than leading daily operations forever. Let's have a toast to this new strategy."

Paul couldn't be more pleased. The new generation would now make its mark, just as Paul had done forty years ago.

157.

Washington, D.C.
September 21, 1979

***

Jack Kurtz was nursing his third scotch on this Friday evening at the end of an exhausting week. He didn't even have the energy to go out for dinner, as he promised himself, and opted instead for a quiet evening at home in his Rosslyn, Virginia apartment. It was nearly 10:00 p.m., and he was already dozing off as he stared at a boring television show. His earlier efforts at reading a novel had produced the same results.

He woke up with a start as the phone rang. He cursed, but then he realized that he was the duty officer and needed to answer it. *This better be important.* He finally picked up the receiver. "This is Jack Kurtz."

"Yes, sir, this is Major Reed at the Air Force Technical Applications Center Alert 747 at Patrick Air Force Base in Florida."

"What can I do for you, Major?"

"Sir, could you please verify your birth date and security code?"

Jack silently cursed and then mumbled the requested information. "This better be good, Major. It's Friday night, and it's been a rough week," he added as he poured another scotch.

"Yes, thank you, sir. Sir, the Vela 6911 has detected a nuclear event in the Indian Ocean west of the Prince Edward Islands."

The officer now had Jack's instant undivided attention. "Have you confirmed it?"

"Yes, sir, we checked both bhangmeters on the satellite, and they're functional and operating normally. The satellite is technically nonoperational, because its EMP sensor is inoperative. However, we have high confidence in the integrity of the bhangmeters and their ability to detect and size a nuclear event. In this case it was a classic double flash of a nuclear explosion estimated at about two or three kilotons," the officer replied.

"Who conducted it? I'm not aware of any intelligence on any pending tests."

415

"That's unknown at this point, sir. That's not our job here."

"Tell me where the Prince Edward Islands are."

"Sir, they're about eleven hundred nautical miles southeast of Cape Town." Now it all made sense to Jack.

"Thank you, Major. I assume you've already transferred the technical data to our operations center in Langley."

"Yes, sir, it's already there, along with our assessment."

Jack hung up and quickly got dressed. He called the operations center and told them to get the alert team into the office.

As he drove up the George Washington Parkway on the quick trip to CIA headquarters in Langley, Jack pondered the ability of the South Africans to conduct a nuclear test. Then he recalled the CIA technical analysis of the Valhalla inventory document and realized that all the information they needed was in the materials that the inventory document listed. They must have still had help from someone—the Israelis were the likely choice. He considered that this might not be the only Valhalla secret that the South Africans had accessed. What about the Valhalla biological warfare research?

Alberto Ortega had indicated that there were no biological warfare secrets in the Valhalla cargo.

Where will this lead? I'm supposed to retire in three months. I can't stand this place any longer. Should I leave or pursue this wherever it leads?

Jack finally pulled into his parking place at Langley. There was work to be done. The director and the president would have questions.

158.

Luso, Angola,
December 27, 1979

* * *

Yuri Kozlov had just finished reading several newspaper accounts of the Soviet invasion of Afghanistan, and he was furious as his comrade Jorge Sanchez entered the sparsely furnished room where they were scheduled to meet in this town in eastern Angola.

"I'm glad you're here, Jorge. I'm wondering what idiot in the Kremlin advised Brezhnev to invade Afghanistan. It's foolhardy. I can't think of a worse place, a worse culture, and a worse time to invade a country that has never been subdued. I'm sure that America would never elect such a moron who would attempt this kind of arrogant move."

"I believe it was a perfect time to do so. The Americans are preoccupied with the Iranian hostage crisis, and it's a good time for the Soviet Union to secure its borders. In fact, it may be a good time to increase pressure and destroy the reactionary movements that have plagued Angola since independence. It may then be possible to invade Southwest Africa and liberate it from the South African apartheid yoke."

Kozlov looked at his younger associate and wondered why he didn't share his optimism on such a strategy. He decided to be blunt.

"Jorge, it would be foolish to attempt such a move before we consolidate our gains here. Do not underestimate the South African apartheid regime. They will soon be a nuclear power, and their conventional forces are more than a match for the indigenous forces in Angola."

"I realize that your intelligence sources are more extensive than mine, Yuri. How can it be possible that South Africa has deployable nuclear weapons?"

"It's possible because they have had access to the Valhalla nuclear research since 1960. They also have been assisted by the Israelis."

"But what evidence exists to show that they can explode a real weapon?"

"They already have, Jorge." Kozlov immediately regretted his indiscretion. The two men were silent for several moments.

"I see. I assume that your source in the South African navy provided this information and it is reliable."

Kozlov nodded.

"We can still prevail against them. In any case, America will not interfere now that the CIA has been discredited," Jorge asserted.

"America will not raise the issue of the South African nuclear test, because Israel is involved. America needs its Zionist ally because of Iran. Our sources in America tell us that Carter is furious with the Israelis for double-crossing him by aiding the South Africans, after he brokered the Camp David Accords in September 1978 to bring peace with Egypt."

"Then America is stymied and will not interfere in Africa."

"You should not underestimate America either, Jorge. Our invasion of Afghanistan and the Iranian hostage crisis have galvanized American public opinion. Carter will be swept out of office next year and the reactionary right will gain the presidency, probably with someone like Ronald Reagan. If that happens, I foresee the beginning of an expensive arms race that they can afford and we can't."

"It's unfortunate, Yuri, that we didn't get access to the biological warfare secrets of Valhalla. Agent Z's death was untimely."

"That can't be helped, but it showed the resiliency of the Hoffman and Ortega families. It's now likely that it will be harder than ever to locate that element of Valhalla. I'm sure they are now well hidden from our view, and the location is known only by Alberto Ortega," Kozlov concluded.

"How do you know that?"

"I have other sources of intelligence within Spain besides the late Agent Z. Although diplomatic relations with Spain were only restored two years ago, we had previously established trading entities. Since 1969 our Black Sea Shipping Company has maintained an office in Madrid. It is actually a front for the KGB. After we learned of Agent Z's demise, they made discreet inquires and determined that neither Anita Ortega nor Paul Hoffman were in Alabos at that time. Alberto Ortega probably traveled there unannounced and discovered his wife's treachery. My guess is he dispatched both Lucia and her accomplice and then made it look like the two had killed each other during an ordinary burglary. He then moved the Valhalla materials to a more secure location."

"Your hypothesis is probably correct, Yuri, but where do we go from here? You lost your entire network that was devoted to the discovery of Valhalla by the penetration of these two families. Agent X is in prison, Agent Y is exposed, and Agent Z is dead. The strategy has failed."

"It hasn't failed, Jorge, but merely been delayed."

"What do you mean?"

"So Agents X, Y, and Z are neutralized. There is another way. To use a trite American phrase, the answer is as simple as A, B, C."

159

Madrid, Spain.
December 29, 1979

* * *

The three men had gathered at their usual spot in the lobby bar of the Palace Hotel and Paul wasted no time as the waiter delivered their drinks.

"Welcome back to Spain, both of you. Needless to say, Antonio and Alberto, I'm anxious to hear of your visit to Equatorial Guinea with the king and queen. I'm especially interested in any information you were able to obtain on Felipe and his family." Paul looked expectantly at both men as he finished.

"Conditions there are horrible, Paul. More than one third of the population was driven into exile or killed during the Macias era. It was impossible for me to get to Rio Muni and investigate, as I originally planned. We were on Fernando Poo, or Bioko, as it is now known, the entire time," Alberto replied.

"The main purpose of our visit was reconciliation between the two countries. The living conditions for our delegation were primitive. Even the king and queen were forced to live in substandard conditions," Antonio de Ortiz added.

"When Obiang overthrew his uncle, Macias, I thought it might open a new era and allow us to gain access to the country," Paul said.

"Some things have changed, Paul, and some things have not. I'm sorry we weren't able to obtain more information," Antonio replied soberly.

"It seems like all the progress that my father made in improving the lives of his workers and their families is now destroyed."

"Yes, Paul, to put it bluntly, they're starting over," Alberto said firmly.

"Will they be any better off under Obiang?" Paul asked.

Alberto and Antonio looked at each other. They did not answer his question. They lowered their heads.

160.

Alabes, Spain.
December 31, 1979

* * *

Paul stared out the large bay window as he looked off to the west. His thoughts were a blur as he tried to reconcile the course of events in the last decade. He was too absorbed in thought to notice Anita's approach.

"I thought I would remind you that the Lopez de Heredia family will be our guests tonight," Anita said quietly.

"Yes, I remember. Will the whole family be here?"

"No, it will only be Pedro, his wife, and his ten-year-old daughter, Maria Jose."

"They are a remarkable family that has maintained a strong tradition of wine making in Rioja for three generations," Paul responded.

"Yes, they were my role models for what I should aspire to."

"So, who in their next generation will lead them into the future, after Pedro? Are the sons ready?"

"I hope this doesn't surprise you, but my intuition tells me that the next generation will have different leadership. I have watched them closely, and for some reason I believe that young Maria Jose will rise to the challenge," Anita said.

"I'm actually not surprised at all. I see you, Beatriz, and now, Isabel, leading the way for us. It is time for women to make their mark on our heritage."

Anita smiled at Paul before responding. "What were you thinking when I came in?" she said, gently touching his arm.

He turned to look at her, smiled, and then turned to gaze out the window. "I'm thinking of many things that I can't resolve. I don't know what happened to Felipe and his family, and I feel powerless because I can't get a visa to travel to Equatorial Guinea."

"Things will improve between the two countries. You'll eventually be able to get a visa. You can go there to find out, perhaps sooner than you think," she assured him.

"I'm almost afraid to find out what happened."

"You can't have it both ways, Paul."

"I know."

"What else?"

"I'm so happy about Rob and Pilar and the way they are taking charge of our operations. It's almost like I'm not needed there anymore, Anita."

"That could be a good thing if you want to embrace it."

"Yes, of course." He smiled. "In a way, I feel more secure here than anywhere. Spain has been the center of my universe, with roots in all directions. The roots to the north and east in Germany are distant and no longer a part of me. The roots to the south in Africa where I was born are disrupted and perhaps severed forever. My roots to the west in America are strong, but it is the next generation that will take us to our destiny in the New World."

"You are very eloquent in expressing yourself, Paul. It seems we share the same ideas about where our true home is."

"I am only concerned about the horrible legacy of Valhalla that has persisted in haunting our family."

"We have hidden that physically and in our memory. We must look forward and not back."

"I want to do that, Anita, but forces outside my control will determine that. As a result of Valhalla, I've killed five men to protect my family from its effects."

"So will you be paranoid, or will you accept what fate has in store for you?"

He looked at her and smiled. "I think you know the answer to that."

"So when will you return to New York?"

"I don't know. I look out this picture window and see one thing. I look out my penthouse in New York and see another. I've lived there forty years now, yet I feel more comfortable here, with you. When I'm there I feel... lonely."

"Then why don't you stay?"

"Maybe I will."

"It's all right to look back occasionally, Paul. Those forty years have been tumultuous. But it is the next year ahead that counts the most. Here, in La Rioja, we count the years by the vintages that are released. The 1975 Gran

Reserva is fabulous and soon to be released. Only I have tasted it, and it would be symbolic if you would join me in enjoying a bottle now. It would be our way of looking forward together, as we take each new vintage, and year, as they come."

"That's a fate that I would treasure, Anita. Lead the way."

They took each other's hand and walked slowly to the wine-tasting room.

Epilogue

As the 1980s began, the world was entering a new era. The Cold War that had dominated East-West relations for more than thirty years was about to enter its final, decisive decade. Its end was symbolized by the destruction of the Berlin Wall in November 1989 and the collapse of the Soviet Union in December 1991.

The Soviet Union collapsed from its own internal failings, but it was hastened as America outspent it on military hardware under the Reagan administration. Unfortunately, America accomplished this by incurring a mountain of public debt that was complemented by a private sector consumption binge fueled by private debt and cheap foreign imports. Many high-wage American jobs began to disappear as multinational corporations exported these jobs to Third World countries—and China—to take advantage of low wages in sweatshoplike conditions. The end result has been the stagnation of the American middle class and the rise of an expanded plutocracy bent on conspicuous consumption and manipulation of financial and stock markets.

The availability of cheap air travel was tempered as petroleum prices fluctuated, but as the world shrank because of the jet airplane, the homogenization and commoditization of world cultures accelerated. It remains to be seen whether the digital age, abundant bandwidth, high oil prices, and global warming will put the nail in air travel's coffin. Airline profits drop even as load factors rise and passengers are subject to cattle-car conditions that would make an air traveler from the fifties aghast.

The Third World did not benefit from these economic changes. Developed countries continued to exploit commodities and cheap labor while destroying or not permitting sustainable economies to exist in these wretched countries. Africa has been devastated by these economic policies, and the pain has been enhanced as developed countries court corrupt dictators in the pursuit of oil and other commodities—such as occurred in Equatorial Guinea. Despite high economic growth rates in some of these countries, hardly any of this reaches the average African citizen. The legacy of surrogate Cold War battles on the continent are also felt to this day.

The world has not become safer since the end of the Cold War. Regional conflicts rage, and terrorism continues to threaten us. The events of September 11, 2001, in America, and other terrorist events around the world, still reverberate. America borrowed trillions to fight in Afghanistan and Iraq without producing a clear victory over its terrorist enemies. Moreover, legislation such as the Patriot Act threatens American freedoms as much as terrorism.

Above all, the threat of bioterrorism still hangs over the planet like a pall. It is entirely conceivable that nuclear or biological warfare secrets and materials, such as those hidden by Operation Valhalla, may become available to terrorist nations and individuals. If that happens, how will the civilized world defend itself?

The Hoffman and Ortega families survived thirty-four years of turmoil between 1945 and 1979 and thrived, despite family tragedies. What will the next thirty-four years bring? Where will the next generation of these two families be in 2013?

Will they continue to flourish as a united family—or will the curse of Valhalla resurrect itself in some way and confront them?

TO BE CONTINUED

Author's Historical Notes and Commentary on Valhalla Revealed

The period 1945–1979 was one of the most turbulent periods in world history and its repercussions affect us to this day. It followed an equally turbulent, and devastating, period 1915–1945 that included two world wars, a civil war in Spain, numerous regional and colonial conflicts, and a devastating economic depression. In this historical novel and its prequel, *Beyond Ultra*, I have attempted to accurately portray those events in the context of settings that are seldom written about, such as neutral countries and African colonies. The following comments elaborate on my literary views and objectives, in the context of key historical issues from the period 1945–1979.

1. *Historical fiction and its role as a genre*

First of all, I pose a general question: What is historical fiction, and what is its role? In my view, the purpose of historical fiction is to inform, while using fictional characters to dramatize what might have transpired "behind the scenes" during real events in actual settings. Most of us know about key leaders and figures of the *Valhalla Revealed* era, such as Eisenhower and Franco, but few people know the importance of their key subordinates, such as Allen Dulles and Luis Carrero Blanco, respectively. More important, who were the "advisers to the advisers" who operated another layer below these key persons? I use fictional characters, such as Paul Hoffman, Jack Kurtz, and Alberto Ortega, to fill the key roles that staff people and operatives play in orchestrating actual historical events and outcomes.

In my view, many of today's novels that label themselves as historical fiction are actually a different genre altogether. For example, most novels that are described as "historical romance" are simply romance novels masquerading as history. Indeed, many historical novel conferences that I attend—and forums and websites that I visit—have little to do with history and its crucial impact on our current affairs. Instead, these conferences and forums often emphasize subgenres such as romance, paranormal, zombies, vampires, steam punk, and other flavor-of-the-day fads that serve audiences craving fantasy rather than reality.

2. *The Cold War*

The superpower conflict between the United States and the Soviet Union lasted from the late 1940s until 1991, when the Soviet Union dissolved. This Cold War carried the risk of becoming global thermonuclear war, yet it never reached this point because of the reality of mutually assured destruction (MAD). The prospect of destroying each other in such a war kept the superpowers from ever approaching such a point, with the possible exception of the Cuban Missile Crisis in 1962. Instead, the superpowers used surrogates to conduct this war in places such as Africa, Asia, and South America. The CIA helped destabilize governments deemed unfriendly to us.

As a missile officer in the Strategic Air Command (SAC) during the seventies, I stood alerts as we waited for Armageddon. With three other officers on any given watch, we had the collective power to launch fifty Minuteman nuclear-armed missiles that had more firepower than all the weapons fired in both world wars. I take some satisfaction in the fact that our ability to do so deterred World War III. Yet America has squandered untold lives and treasure in inconclusive "hot wars" in Korea, Vietnam, Iraq, and Afghanistan. These wars become even more impersonal and indiscriminate with the use of drone aircraft, often operated by the CIA rather than the military.

3. *Spain during the Franco era*

Spain was neutral in World War II and was still economically devastated from the lingering effects of the Spanish Civil War. Spain remained an international pariah for the balance of the forties, as a result of wartime collaboration with Nazi Germany and the international unpopularity of the Franco regime. The Cold War, however, worked in Spain's favor, since the United States needed European bases for the performance-limited SAC bombers of that era. The Pact of Madrid in 1953 sealed that deal, which also included economic aid.

An internal debate in Spain about economic policies was finally resolved, as technocrats who favored economic liberalization and foreign investment gained the upper hand in the late fifties. From 1959 to 1973, Spain experienced unprecedented economic growth, as well as an exposure to outside culture, enabled by tourism.

Following Franco's death in 1975, Spain successfully embraced democracy, as King Juan Carlos became a constitutional monarch, rather than a follow-on dictator. Spain prospered until recently, but like many countries is now experiencing painful economic hardships.

4. *The end of the colonial era*

The end of the colonial era took place during the time frame of this novel (1945–1979). All European powers initially resisted decolonization efforts and demands for self-determination. Later in this period, pressures from the United Nations, nonaligned nations, and local leaders advocating independence increased pressure on the colonial powers. Great Britain managed to exit India without fighting, but other European powers elected initially to maintain their presence by force of arms. Despite this, the Dutch were ejected from Indonesia in 1949, the French from Indochina in 1954 and from Algeria in 1962, and the Portuguese from their Goa colony in India in 1961.

Elsewhere, European military resistance was initially more successful. In the fifties, the British put down the Mau Mau uprising in Kenya as well as the Communist insurgency in Malaya. The Portuguese fought colonial wars in the sixties and seventies to retain their African colonies, and Spain fought the Ifni war in 1957 to retain their West African holdings. In all of these cases, the European powers eventually withdrew, despite the temporary military success.

In Africa, 1960 was a watershed year for decolonization, as France gave wholesale independence to its West African and equatorial African colonies, and Belgium withdrew from their vast Congo colony. Within four years, Britain also withdrew from its African colonies.

Spain held on longer than most countries. Although their protectorate in Morocco was ceded in 1956, they held Spanish Guinea until 1968 and Ifni until 1969. The Spanish finally withdrew from Spanish Sahara in 1976, the year after the Portuguese left Africa.

5. *Globalization, neocolonialism, and environmental degradation*

The exit of the European powers from Africa, Asia, and elsewhere was generally neither graceful nor successful, as far as the indigenous populations were concerned. Most of the European powers failed to educate and train sufficient numbers of local people and otherwise prepare them for self-government. Self-determination continued to be a dream, as dictators assumed powers in most emerging countries, often propped up by the former colonial power, the United States, or the Soviet Union.

These peoples continue to suffer from the aftermath of decolonization. Multinational corporations exploit local resources for export while lining the pockets of dictators and their families. Very little of this wealth reaches the average citizen of such countries. For example, Equatorial Guinea has one of the highest per capita incomes in the world, owing to the discovery of oil there in the nineties. Yet its people remain impoverished, thanks to the corrupt regime of Teodoro Obiang. The once prosperous cocoa plantations that enriched both local farmers and Spanish planters, such as my fictional Karl Hoffman, are mostly gone.

Beside serving as proxy battlefields in the Cold War, many African nations have continued to be involved in bloody tribal or regional conflicts, such as the genocide that occurred in Rwanda in the nineties and the fighting that continues today in Sudan and Somalia. The world is focused on the Arab Spring and its aftermath, while it generally ignores sectarian strife, genocide, and civil war when it occurs in Africa.

6. _Bioterrorism_

The world is legitimately concerned about the proliferation of nuclear weapons and especially their use by rogue nations or terrorists who manage to acquire them. I explore this issue in this novel.

I also explore the theme of potential bioterrorism that might be enabled by the use of lethal pathogens that have been developed by advanced powers, in this case the defunct regime of Nazi Germany. Such weapons may be easier to synthesize than nuclear weapons or dirty radiological bombs. They could be easily spread by the jet airplane and our mobile world culture.

7. _Air travel and cultural homogenization_

Speaking of air travel, throughout this novel I highlight the characters' desires to gain access to more efficient air travel, so that they can conduct business globally, rather than regionally. That air-travel world is finally here, and it's a mixed blessing to us.

Since I am a pilot with nearly ten thousand hours in everything from gliders to jets, that last statement may sound surprising. Most everybody assumes that modern jet air travel has been solely a boon to the human race. My protagonists in this novel suffered through three-week sea voyages to get to other continents in the twenties and early thirties. By 1938, however, they could reach equatorial Africa from Spain in a multistop three-day odyssey.

By the early fifties, this was reduced to one long day, and by the midsixties to only six hours.

Right up into the midsixties, air travel was truly luxurious for those who could afford it. Now, however, unless you can afford first class, air travel has become degrading, tiring, and in many cases unnecessary, as the digital age advances. Increasingly, you simply travel in a cramped aluminum tube from one homogenized place to an equally homogenized place that happens to be in another country. The uniqueness of air travel has rapidly decreased, and getting there is no longer half the fun. For business flyers, the speed of light is now the accepted standard of conducting business abroad, as the Internet and abundant bandwidth take hold.

We must also acknowledge that our mobility carries an environmental price. Many believe that technology, including better fuel efficiency, will come to our rescue and reduce travel's environmental footprint. Others believe that we need to rethink how we live and work, using improved bandwidth for virtual rather than actual travel.

8. _Wine making in modern Spain_

The two fictional families in my novel come from a rich wine-making background. I hope that readers enjoy my frequent references throughout the book to Spanish wine and sherry and realize that Spain has a wine making history dating back to the Romans. I enjoy wine from all regions, but I most enjoy the wine, setting, and culture of La Rioja. The fictional Ortegas and Hoffmans often gather at the fictional village of Alabos, which I have patterned after an actual village in Rioja.

9. _Correlation with actual events and settings_

Most historical figures, events, and settings in _Valhalla Revealed_ are portrayed as accurately as possible, in terms of their "real-world" behavior or occurrence. I have dramatized these events by adding fictional characters and realistic plot and subplot embellishments, but I endeavor to stay faithful to the ebb and flow of real history.

To ensure this level of accuracy, I conducted extensive research. I traveled to Spain in 2011 and 2013 to conduct research for both this novel and a prequel, _Beyond Ultra_. For example, I reviewed Iberia Airlines archives in Madrid to obtain information on airline service, schedules, and other data from the forties and fifties. I also recorded settings in locations in Spain and Portugal that historically served as meeting places for spies and diplomats. I interviewed various individuals who had a role in the events described in the novel. For example, I interviewed Sr. Antonio de Oyarzabal, the Spanish ambassador to the United States from 1996 to 2000. He began his diplomatic career in the sixties, while working on issues involving Spanish Guinea.